COME

NOWHERE

Come From Nowhere

a novel by Ellen Greenfield

Brooklyn, NY

Come From Nowhere is a work of fiction. Names, characters, places and incidents are either the product of the author's imagination, or are used fictitiously. Any resemblance to actual persons, living or dead, events, or locales is entirely coincidental.

2012 3Ring Press Trade Paperback Edition

Printed in the United States
First Edition: April, 2012
10 9 8 7 6 5 4 3 2 1

Library of Congress Control Number: 2012932831
ISBN: 978-0-9793527-6-8
eBook ISBN: 978-0-9793527-7-5

Book and Cover Design: Alex Martin
Cover art: Alex Martin
Original art: Rat by Jamie Greenfield
Pia by Tony Robinson

Adobe Casion Pro
Futura Light | Condensed Light | **Heavy**
BIG CASION

3RingPress
191 St. Marks Avenue
Brooklyn, NY 11238

www.EllenGreenfield.com
www.ComeFromNowhere.com
www.3RingPress.com

For Mark, always
And for my parents, Lois and Bill,
and Mary Dallara

You must be a fool, stranger, or come from nowhere,
telling me to fear the gods or avoid their wrath!

The Odyssey, *Homer*

Chapter One

July 13, 1977

"Mami, tell me the story!"

"Which story?"

"You know which story!"

Althea sighed and brushed her thick black hair off her forehead with one hand. With the other, she ushered her nine-year-old daughter through the subway turnstile, down the platform and onto an empty bench.

"Ay, Celia, *kukla*, not again," she smiled to herself. "You already know that one. You could tell it to me." She unfastened a button at the neck of her blouse and pulled the lapels sharply away from her skin to lure the damp breeze that drifted from the dark subway tunnel. Even for July it was too early for it to be so hot. Not even 7:30. And too early for her to feel so bone weary, as well. Although she'd been up since six, she now had barely enough time to get her daughter uptown to her mother's apartment, and get herself to work back in midtown. She could hardly afford to be late – again. She'd been warned twice. Althea listened hopefully in the direction of the uptown train. Silence. She could not afford to lose this bookkeeping job – their only income and barely enough to cover their rent and living expenses.

There were only three other people on the platform this morning, all women, and none of them looking in her direction. She unfastened one more button. From her purse Althea took a small round box of dusting powder and plumped its fleecy puff against the skin between her breasts. The lemony smell of Jean Naté clouded around her head, momentarily replacing the subway stench.

Her daughter jumped up onto the scarred bench and stood resolutely on top of it, arms and legs splayed wide, one hand clutching a bagel with guava jelly that Althea had made for breakfast and served to her on a plate, but which Celia insisted on saving to eat on the train.

"I am the starfish, Mami! I live in the sea and you are walking past my house with your little speckled goat."

Althea tried to look stern. "Celia, stop playing around and sit down. You're too old to be acting like this. If you're not careful, one day you're going to get hurt."

"Then tell me. Tell me the story. Tell me, tell *me!*" The girl jumped down and began to spin in a slow circle, waving her fingers like fat tentacles. The wide legs of her flimsy, blue-and-white-striped shorts flapped around her bony knees. The pants were too large. But they were Celia's favorites, a gift from her Aunt Eleni back in Greece.

Althea knew her headstrong daughter wouldn't give up. Althea's own mother had cursed her with this – that she should have one just like herself. And here she was. A wild thing – always racing away down the sidewalks of Manhattan, as Althea herself had galloped the cobbled paths of Skiathos. But the streets of New York held many more dangers than the urchin-strewn cliffs of that rocky Mediterranean island. In the end, Althea knew she would have to give in if she wanted Celia to be still. The puny breeze from the tunnel had died away. The hope for a train was a false hope. Althea patted the space beside her on the wooden bench and Celia sat down and turned her face up expectantly. Althea planted a kiss on top of the girl's head. The sweet smell of her daughter's scalp melted the last of her resistance.

"Once, on the pine green island of Skiathos, a little girl laid down the first of the morning footprints in the sand where the sea had slept, tossing and turning through the night," she began. The words, sinuous and familiar even in her adopted English, wove their spell, stilling Celia and binding mother and child just as endless re-telling of ancient myths had bound the Greek people.

"Following behind her, a small goat – as black as the little girl's eyes and with speckles as tan as her skin – laid down the second set of tracks. Each morning they walked, the girl heading across the pink sands to school, and the naughty goat, who had slipped out the gate, sneaking along behind. The girl knew the goat was there, and the goat knew the girl would have to take him home if she turned and saw him. But she didn't turn, and he didn't hurry, and in that way they walked the crescent of beach until she disappeared into the schoolhouse with its red tiled roof, and he settled into the shade of an old olive tree to nibble the sparse, dry grass."

Celia was humming under her breath as her mother spoke. Humming and kicking her legs as she sat on the edge of the bench. A bit of jelly stained the corner of her mouth. Althea looked down the tracks for a sign of their train, but there was none, so she continued on with the story before her unruly daughter leapt up once again. It was a fulltime job, keeping Celia safe from her own untamed impulses.

"The sun, rising higher and higher in the tile blue sky, made the day hot. Inside the schoolhouse, the children's eyes grew heavy, hooded; outside, the little goat beat the bare ground with his hooves, making the dust rise before he bent his spindly legs and lay down to sleep, his head in the last sweet patch of grass. Eventually, the special rhythm of the little girl's feet on the sand woke him and he tottered up to follow her back home. Each time, she turned to greet him, pretending surprise.

"'Why, Tragos, how did you find me here?' she crooned to him, slipping her arms around his bony head in a hug. Then they walked side by side, their six feet lapped by the waves."

As she spoke, Althea ran her fingers through her daughter's hair, marshalling the frothy curls into a pair of high, dark pigtails held with a pair of elastic bands she had pulled from her purse. Her daughter wriggled under the attention, but remained seated.

"One day, the goat stopped and lowered his horned head to the water. When he raised it, his nimble lips held a small pink starfish. Quickly, before the animal could swallow the creature, the little girl grabbed at it, and it came away in her hands – minus one pink leg, which the naughty goat dropped back into the sea to be carried away on the next slip of a wave. The starfish's single red eye, in the almost-center of its body, winked with what the little girl saw was a tear. She stamped her feet at the goat. 'Bad Tragos!' she shouted – and in her fury she threw shells and sharp stones until the goat ran from her. From the satchel on her shoulder, she pulled a cup, which she filled with seawater. Gently, she slid the starfish into the cup, and then she hurried the rest of the way home, careful not to spill. She placed the starfish in a large bowl – the one her mother used for pickling – and filled it with more water drawn from the sea."

"But where was Goat, Mami?" Ceci suddenly asked. "What happened to Tragos?" The question troubled Althea. Celia had never asked it before – she had always been more interested in the survival of the starfish – and Althea did not answer. Where *had* the goat gone after she chased it away in a rage? Her brothers told her that it was surely dead, food for the vultures and gulls that wheeled over the rocky spine of their small island. Her mother said it would probably find its way home eventually. And indeed, the following week, a mottled goat – skinny and ragged – came wandering in from the parched hills behind their house, but it never followed Althea to school again, and she knew that it was not her Tragos. Her father slaughtered it the following Easter.

Sitting on the platform, Althea just sighed. The goat had been her responsibility. In one moment of misplaced fury she had failed it. Her gaze wandered now, unfocused from time or place.

"This is what can happen to you in the world," she said, sadly. Her hands floated up, palms open and helpless.

Celia was off the bench again, sweeping away down the dirty platform, her arms and legs once more splayed like those of a starfish. Althea jumped up after her, her heart racing, and quickly looped one arm around her daughter's shoulders as she tottered at the edge.

"What do you think you're doing?" she asked. Her daughter froze, staring.

"Mami, look! What's that?"

Althea followed Celia's hand, still clutching the last bite of bagel, pointing to the tracks. At first she saw nothing beyond the usual accumulation of damp and crumpled newspapers, fast-food bags and gum wrappers. Then a slight movement caught her eye. From under the third rail, a gray and hairy shadow broke, weaving from side to side between the rails, twitching, stopping and moving on at a jerky, broken pace. It was about the size of her two fists held together.

"It's a rat, Celia," she whispered. "An ugly old subway rat. Look at something else."

"But Mami, it's missing a leg."

Althea looked again. Sure enough, the rat's jerky pattern was caused by the fact that it ran on only three legs, giving the creature a little lurch at the end of each step. Celia was as observant as she was energetic.

"Will it grow back, Mami, like the starfish?"

"No Kukla, it won't."

The other three women waiting nearby – all except the one with her nose in a book – were now shooting uneasy looks at the animal and then around the platform. Their eyes flickered in a brief unity of disgust.

But Celia had already lost interest. Now she turned to stare at a homeless woman, mountainous in layers of soiled clothes, who sat slumped on a bench, a paper cup for begging set on the floor at her feet.

"Mami!" Celia began.

Althea took her daughter by the hand. Would there never be a moment of peace?

"Shh, Celia. Come away," she said, tugging. "Nobody likes to be stared at."

❧

Judith took three small steps backward on the platform and then three forward, toward the tracks.

A-do-nai s'fa-tai tif-tach, u-fi ya-gid t'hi-la-te-cha, she chanted in a bare whisper. Open my mouth, oh Lord, and my lips will proclaim Your praise.

The gusts blew from left to right down the platform. With each one Judith adjusted the scarf she had draped over her hair and steadied the onionskin pages of the battered leather-bound book in her hands. This time, the sour wind from the tunnel stole the page from her moist fingertips just as she was about to turn it herself. From left to right, which would have been a hindrance had it been any other book, but with her prayer book it was a *mechayah*, a blessing.

Boruch (she bent her knees) *atah Adonai* (she straightened again)... "Praised are you, Lord our God..." A few stray hairs blew from the edges of the flowered scarf tied around her head and tickled her nose. Ignoring that, she fastened her concentration more deeply on the blessed words before her.

...*E-lo-hei-nu, Vei-lo-hei a-vo-tei-nu,*
E-lo-hei Av-ra-ham, E-lo-hei Yitz-chak, Vei-lo-hei Ya-a-kov,
Ha-eil Ha-Ga-dol Ha-Gi-bor v'Ha-No-rah Eil Eil-yon...

Her lips and tongue raced each other through the holy invocation. It was not enough just to read these blessed words each morning; one must say them out loud, or as she was, in a fervent whisper. Praised are You, LordourGodandGodofourancestors, GodofAbrahamof IsaacandofJacob, great, mighty, awesome, exalted

God who bestows lovingkindness, Creator of all. You remember the pious deeds of our ancestors and will send a redeemer to their children's childrenbecauseofYourlovingnature. Amen.

"This is what can happen to you in the world," she heard a voice say dreamily. A young woman, not much older than herself, with an indefinable accent – Spanish? Italian? – was talking to a young girl beside her; the woman's bare arms raised, palms open, toward the ceiling. Judith followed the direction of her hands. The paint above their heads was peeling in thick, ragged strips. A greasy stain underneath oozed and sweated like skin. But the woman's half-closed eyes looked neither at the ceiling nor at her little girl.

Judith turned her back against the subway wind, and faced down the length of the concrete platform. Under a partially shredded poster still hawking the March opening of *Star Wars*, a beggar woman struggled to her feet gripping the sides of a shopping cart half-filled with rags and sacks. Judith wished she could have plinked more than one quarter into the dirty paper cup at the rag-wearer's feet. It was a *mitzvah* to give to the poor, but it was one Judith could ill afford now that she had to pay for rent, food, books and tuition out of the small salary she earned at her aunt and uncle's jewelry store. Hashem had showered her with so many blessings – chief among them the love of her family. Judith gave thanks daily for them and for the work that allowed her to pursue her aspirations. She watched as the woman rose laboriously and worked her way onto a bench by the wall. Judith looked away, not wanting to be caught staring. Someday, God willing, I will be a doctor, she thought. Will I be able to touch the bodies of women such as this, unwashed and doughy?

Judith adjusted the scarf, which had slipped down around her neck, so that it covered her hair again. As an unmarried woman, she didn't have to wear the headcovering, but modesty was expected in the shop, and the many *frum* customers would assume that at her age, almost 23, she was married. She wanted no speculations raised. She wanted no *shidachs* made, either – no sweaty, nervous young men paraded by in hopes of making a match. Under the scarf, her hair was damp from the shower and from the beads of sweat that were beginning to make her scalp itch. Judith turned her attention back to morning prayers and anchored her heart more firmly to the words before her.

∾❀∾

Ratus Norwegicus. Back when she was an intern, Johanna had seen more than one case of rat bite and the infection that often followed. The suppurating skin and willful fever that left its young victims fretful and moaning. Pediatrics. Her last rotation. Unless you counted Psych. A quick yawp of laughter broke from her throat. Quite an education, being on the sharp end of all that Thorazine, now wasn't it? How long ago was that? She scratched deeply through the layers of clothes that encased her thick torso, from the shapeless pink sweater on down, and took a furtive glance around the platform. Up and down. Up and down. And then again. Of the four people standing before her, waiting for the train, only one seemed unaware of the loathsome creature prowling the tracks at their feet. And that person was talking to herself, her nose in a book.

Johanna watched through hooded eyes as the women darted nervous looks at the rodent and then blinked away, as if they could tolerate the sight for only seconds at a time. But over and over their eyes were drawn back, keeping track, making sure that it didn't get too close – God forbid it should race up onto the platform and touch one of them. She could practically feel these women's toes curl against their fancy shoes. Again and again, the rat darted in and out from under the tracks, looking for food that the filthy pigs who traveled these subways were only too happy to provide, with their greasy McDonald's bags and sugar-smeared doughnut wrappers. European Brown Rat. Most reviled mammal in the world by these same exalted humans who pissed in the corners of the station late at night when they thought no one would see.

Johanna hunkered down on the bench and pulled on a heavy gray wool coat that she yanked from a shopping cart full of her possessions. Even that didn't stop the trembling. She knew – she was a doctor, goddamit – that she needed Amoxicillin, 500 milligrams, *qid*. Her tongue was thick in her throat. She dug through her pockets and found the mirror half of an old folding comb. Sure enough – her tongue was coated. Probably strep. When she wasn't sweating in this hellhole, she was shivering. Fever and chills, fever and chills. Baked Alaska. Another of her hoarse laughs echoed through the station.

That kid – the first to notice the rat – was now staring at her. The child was skinny in that little girl way. Stick figure arms and legs; her torso, not yet touched by puberty, was lost in her tee shirt, which hung from neck to waist like a sack. She was the little girl with the ratbite fever. She was the little girl with the strap marks on her back. Daddy's little girl. Burns on her thighs. She was six and ten and seven and nine. Makes thirty-two. My age? I was born in the year of the Rat. Exactly. Or maybe not. Johanna's mind rolled and tumbled, then halted like a stubbed toe.

The girl on the platform was staring at Johanna and scratching one ankle with the toe of the bright pink sandal on her other foot. Soon her mother would turn to see what her daughter was looking at. She'd pull the girl closer and whisper. *Don't stare. She's nobody.* Or, *that could be you if you don't listen to your mother. Wash your hands when you get to school. Don't touch the strange dog. Nobody likes to be stared at.*

Nobody – that's me, all right. I'm nobody. Who the fuck are *you*? If I were nobody, I'd like to be stared at, too. I used to be somebody. I used to be somebody. I used to be...who?

She had stopped shivering and begun to sweat. The heat made her feel thick and dozy. Johanna lifted one swollen leg onto the empty bench, and leaned heavily against the straw basket she had propped against the arm for padding. She reached out to lift a pen off the desk and wrote herself a prescription. Take two of these three times a day with water, she mumbled. Don't drink and drive. Call me in the morning. Let Hertz put you in the driver's seat.

She dozed then, with one leg still on the ground until the train rushed shrieking into the station with its hot electric breath. The sound split her eardrums. It rushed into the station and screeched to a halt, then stood there panting with fury before rushing away, taking everyone. Taking the little girl away. She'd never see her again. Gone. Johanna opened her eyes and spat at the receding lights – a big soapy gob of spit. Then she pulled her other leg up to the bench and dropped off into the black and airless pit that passed as sleep.

ॐ

Phnf….phnff….phnf…. Rat's soft gray body twisted out from the silver rail following her nose.

Food, where? Here? Not here? No. Here?

There up there under soot black sky.

Toss it here toss it down dammit here. Nasty baby claws. Pink and flutter. Fuck it all drop it here. Nasty baby fingers nasty gnawing baby teeth.

Climbandbite. Grabthefood? Bite hernastylittlehand.

Phnf…phnf… Mine. Food-is-mine. Foodismine bellyfullbitch. Whereismine?

Food? Greasy paper crumple. Greasy-meaty-sharp-and-meaty.

Bait? Poisoned? *Phnf…phnf…* Good then. Food then. Fucking good. Fuckinggreasygood.

Metal roar. Steelroar wind. *Phnf…phnf…*

Steelbeastwindrush. Windrush?

Over and under overandunder overandunder.

Where to hide? Metalstink. Wheretodragfood?

Phnff…phnff…

ॐ

TAKI 183. Swollen letters, green and black and red. Could that really be *TAKI 183*? Pia's arms prickled with electricity, her breath caught in her throat. And again, *TAKI 183, TAKI 183, TAKI 183* – the individual subway cars flashed by. It was all Pia could do to keep herself from running the length of the platform in an effort not to lose them. Her eyes filled – but maybe that was just in response to the stinging subterranean wind. When the train finally slowed to a halt, it was not TAKI 183 but another tag that marked the car in front of her. She felt let down.

The train that swept into the station brought Pia more than mere relief from the stagnant heat on the platform – it delivered the surging energy of rogue art that made each day's journey uptown a carnival – dizzying and aggressive. PISTOL, TRACY 168, BLADE ONE, CAINE 1, STAY HIGH 149. Graffiti tags raged across car after car. Some turned an entire car-length into a vivid mural. Others just screamed FUCK YOU in violent fuchsia. In the brief pause before the train doors opened, Pia's right hand shot up and traced the broad, angry strokes of a tag that slashed across the car's siding. TEENY 128. A broad swath of green rimmed with orange, purple, black. Her fingers curled around a phantom spray can, forefinger crooked over the nozzle. She dreamed of being part of the crews that blazed their marks by flashlight, moonlight and sometimes even torchlight.

This city, she discovered upon arriving only five weeks ago, was literally awash with graffiti, from the strident and malicious to the subtle and the just plain mundane. Advertising posters sported handlebar mustaches, sure, but also, more often than not, poetry. Along the seedy blocks of Brooklyn's Crown Heights neighborhood, where Pia was living with her father's aunt, there were virtually no blank walls. Steel shuttered storefronts wore Mardi Gras colors and abandoned buildings bore vivid memorials to those who'd died in the neighborhood's angry streets. Out her window onto Prospect Place, she gazed upon a 10-foot portrait of a dark, doe-eyed young man. Eighteen-inch letters proclaimed *Shawan James - Never*

Forgotten 1960-1977. Smaller testimonials ringed the memorial. *Yo, Man you the best - Mel; Solidarity, Peace. T, Wherever you gone, I'm coming - Linda.* Every block had its fallen warriors. No one dared paint over their markers.

Aunt Ida clicked her tongue dismissively when Pia told her how the portrait of Shawan moved her.

"Shoot, those boys ain't nothing but criminals," she sniffed. "They just tearing down the neighborhood with they nasty selves." She slammed down the ashtray she was dusting. "Shawan James broke his mama's heart long before that bullet stopped his," she said, sweeping out of the room. Pia never mentioned it again. The whole city was up in arms against graffiti, she knew. It went hand in hand with crime, filthy streets, drugs, and a palpable mounting rage. Still, she savored new tag sightings like an ornithologist tracking rare birds. She had to admit it: her first glimpse of the infamous TAKI 183 made her cry.

In her most secret feral heart, Pia roamed the city's dark byways armed with spray gun and paint. All the while, the rest of her traversed its streets outfitted demurely in the two-piece, polyester-blend armor of the mild-mannered job seeker she was. With her, she toted the large black portfolio full of the drawings she hoped convince some art director to give her a break. She had three more interviews lined up today. Any of them could be The One. Better be. The clock – and her money – was ticking down.

In the beam of headlights that had preceded the train into the station, Pia watched a rodent dive for cover under the electrified third rail. Rats. The city was crawling with them, her aunt had said, but this was the first one Pia had seen. If it came toward her, she could fend it off with her portfolio. Maybe she could find a seat on the train and sketch it before she lost the details. Pale, matted fur flecked the color of pewter, the texture of a moth-eaten pony jacket she'd once found in the attic of her father's cottage on the lake. Whiplike tail. Delicate pink ears, onyx eyes. Harder, though, to capture its gait – more hop than scurry, really, as it swung itself out of danger at the last possible second.

But when the doors slid open, it became apparent that there

would be no way for Pia to dig through her bag for her notebook and pencils and draw. This was one of the few air-conditioned cars on the train. Despite the early hour, it was elbow-to-elbow and hip-to-hip with bodies. Blue suits, white shirts, arms hairy and smooth – Pia worked her way through the fleshy obstacles until she could grasp a few inches of space on the pole in the middle of the car, and there she staked her claim.

ꙮ

Danielle's closed eyelids twitched impatiently. From the moment she'd changed to the express, at 72nd Street, she had held them shut. She steadied herself with her breath. Air in, air out, air in, eyes closed. This is what it will feel like to move through the world blind, she told herself, gripping the slick silver pole with both hands, swaying in the dark as the train lurched around bends, bouncing lightly on the balls of her feet as the subway bumped and screeched along the downtown track.

Even with her eyes closed, Danielle knew what surrounded her on the train. Crushed and tangled pages of yesterday's *Post* and *Daily News* whispered at her feet, and the burnt smell of coffee – a rusty umber scent in her personal mental conflation of tastes/smells/colors – rose from abandoned paper cups printed with whimsical depictions of the Parthenon. The walls and windows of every car were etched with knives or spray painted with the names of faceless thugs who shared an overwhelming need for recognition. Her nose told her that at least one person had relieved himself in this car.

The announcements from stop to stop were, as usual, an auditory jumble, practically indecipherable, but Danielle counted off the successive stations in her head: 42nd Street - Times Square, 34th - Penn Station, 14th Street, Chambers Street, Park Place and now, finally, they were approaching Fulton Street, her stop. There had been a long delay between 14th and Chambers with no explanation. Now she would have to hurry to get to the fish market. The fans went off, then on again, the lights flickered, and finally the train lurched back into motion. It took real guts to keep her eyes closed during the wait. Like a feral creature, she sent mental feelers out into the space around her to sense whether anyone was coming close. No one was. The people on the train this early in the day were drawn into themselves.

The car in which Danielle rode was sweltering. She could scarcely bear to think what it would be like in another hour or so when the hordes of rush hour travelers and gaping tourists began to heave themselves into already-packed coaches. The train shrieked around the last bend and slowed to a stop. The doors receded along their metal runners and the recognizable smell of the Fulton Street station – yeasty and yellow-green like fermenting fruit – rushed in. She had reached her destination. Danielle took two steps away from the pole before she allowed herself to open her eyes. She stepped gingerly across the palm-wide gap between train and platform –she'd have to remember that when she was forced to navigate in the dark – and onto the concrete.

Chapter Two

B lack, black, black, white, Hispanic, black, Asian, black. Pia, her portfolio wedged between her knees, scanned the long benches on either side of the pole where she stood, and did the math. Five out of eight – roughly sixty percent.

She swiveled slightly to scan the benches further down the car. Black, white, dark, light, Hispanic, Hispanic, black, black. Four out of eight – fifty percent black. Or rather, seventy-five percent, non-white. The ratios were almost exactly the same. They always were.

There were eight-point-something million people living in this city – close to two million of them in Brooklyn alone – and Pia had come up with a census of their geographical distribution based on her own daily commute.

This scanning and counting had become habit over her first weeks of life in New York City. From her stop at Utica Avenue in Brooklyn to wherever she was heading in Manhattan, she took periodic readings of her fellow subway riders. At first she wondered how white people got to work. Did they all live in Manhattan? There were so few of them on the train with her. But after several trips, she had begun to discern the patterns.

This morning, she had taken the A train and changed at Fulton Street for the Number 3 train that would carry her uptown to her first job interview of the day. She smoothed her dark skirt against her long legs and hoped it might walk the fine line between business proper and artistic. At her stop, virtually all the riders were black, mainly from the Islands, and most of them women who had left their own houses and children behind with relatives and come here to earn money cleaning houses or watching the children of others. At the next stop, a few bearded men and wigged women, ultra orthodox Jews, she'd learned, boarded the train. Many of the black women read purposefully from tattered and dog-eared Bibles. They immediately ducked behind well-worn black leather books, their pages dense tracts of indecipherable characters. The Jews, too.

With the acuity of the newly initiated, Pia noted this similarity, but she was sure they didn't notice it themselves, since their eyes rarely wandered and never met. Like those of the pale young woman sitting across from her right now, their lips moved quickly as they speed-read through the battered prayer books. Apparently finished with her prayers, the young woman now kissed the spine of the book hurriedly before tucking it away in her purse. Her long buttoned down sleeves and voluminous skirt made her look older than her unlined face. How could she bear all those clothes in this heat, Pia wondered.

Bible reading wasn't the only thing that both the Jews and the black women had in common. Both tended to cover their hair with scarves – the blacks winding them into artful sculptures, the Jews settling for simple knots at the nape of their necks. Pia's hair, wild and abundant when left to its natural predilections, had been blow-dried into submission for another day of interviews, and twisted into a tight bun for extra measure.

She studied the population on this uptown train. What, she

wondered, did the other riders make of her? At college, boys had often called her *exotic*, with her honeyed skin, deep hazel-green eyes, and hair as thickly textured as a Persian lamb coat. Her girlfriends envied her long limbs and her ease on a dance floor, where she could bust some moves. In high school, her gym teachers encouraged her to try out for the women's track team or play field hockey. And in first grade the other kids whispered about her, after her mom, petite and blonde, came to watch the Christmas pageant.

"Am I adopted?" Pia asked that night in a small, tight voice as her mother kissed her and turned out the light. Her mother flicked the light back on and stared at Pia from the doorway.

"Why would you ask that?" she asked. "You see your Daddy every weekend, and you've seen your baby pictures so often you claim you actually remember *meeting* us in the hospital."

"Theresa and Paula said I was adopted." Pia wished she hadn't said anything; the look on her mother's face was so awful. She sat back down on Pia's bed and, placing her pale, freckled arm against Pia's darker one, said: "I am what people call a white person, and your daddy is what people call a black person. And you are a little of me and a little of him. They call that biracial."

Looking back, the strangest thing about that night was really the next morning. Suddenly, all the people she saw every day – her neighbors, her teachers, the lunchroom ladies, the school bus driver – suddenly every single person she saw had developed a previously unnoticed characteristic. Some were as pale pink as the baby mice in the science corner, and some were brown. Why hadn't she noticed before? And what did it mean? A lot, she was later to discover. Sometimes it meant a lot. It meant, for instance, that her first boyfriend in Junior High, James Eric McDonald, would ask Pia to return his I.D. bracelet after she met his mother. Later, it meant that she would get a full scholarship to Ithaca College, as her father had before her.

But what would it mean here in New York City? In 1977? When civil rights was dredged up mainly as a historical reference to the Sixties, and the kids on her aunt's block called each other *nigger* and *boy* like it was a badge of honor. New York City – the original melting pot, Pia had been taught in third grade – seemed more like a rag dangling over an open flame than any kind of pot at all. Unless it was the kind you could smoke, the smell of which wafted into her bedroom window every night along with the car exhaust fumes and the polyrhythm of dueling boom boxes. In her aunt's neighborhood, most of the black boys were lining the corners of the steaming streets, most of their mamas were cleaning houses or offices, and most of the white people were someplace else entirely.

In college, Pia had ping-ponged between dating white boys and black boys. Both tended to treat her as some sort of trophy, which she hated. The white boys acted smug and self-righteously daring for dating a black girl. The black boys showed her off like an especially large diamond earring. Her parents had always maintained a strict no-preference policy. But she detected a certain whiff of guilt. When they had met in college and subsequently fallen in love, they were shunned by both sides. It was the early Fifties, and Brown v. Board of Education had yet to be decided. They settled in Ithaca primarily because they thought that their college town would be more accepting (it wasn't) and because it would provide sufficient distance from their disapproving families (it did).

It's a different world today, her mother insisted. *You have the freedom to choose who you date – who you are.*

Pia once asked her mother if she thought "the racial thing" was what eventually drove them to divorce. Her mother said she didn't see it that way, but admitted that it certainly hadn't helped keep them together.

"We were so young," she sighed.

"What attracted you most to Daddy when you first met?" Pia asked, as she and her mother stood, brown elbow to white, peeling onions for soup.

"His voice, his eyes, the way he knew all the stars in the northern hemisphere by name as if they were his cousins – the fact that he made my parents so angry," her mother confessed. "Nothing to base a marriage on." But the look in her eyes said she'd probably do it all again if it were an option.

At first, most of Pia's close friends in college were white. But as she began to get involved in art, and the politics of art, she started to feel more estranged from their pleasures and tastes. She dropped Billy Joel, James Taylor and Elton John for Bob Marley, Rufus and Chaka Kahn, and Gil Scott-Heron and the status-quo-shattering vibe of The Last Poets. Their words – *When the revolution comes / some of us will catch it on TV / with chicken hanging from our mouths* – made her feel fierce and full of her own supremacy – sometimes even afraid of it.

Her paintings, dark canvases raked and scored with luminous colors, reflected her internal struggle. In her sophomore year she stopped torturing her hair straight and began braiding it into elaborate cornrows, swapping a class in Russian literature for one that sampled the works of Toni Morrison, Tony Cade Bambara, Paule Marshall and Audre Lord. She traded one on European art history for the history of underground art. When she started going on about the need for *social engagement* as the *aesthetic and spiritual sister* (she pronounced it *sistah*) *of the Black Power concept*, her bewildered friends complained that she had become incomprehensible.

Pia moved out of the dorm and in with a black artists' collective patterned after MIT's Chocolate City. Late one night, after a dinnertime discussion about the rogue New York City subway artist Demetrius, nicknamed Taki and better known as TAKI 183 for the street where he lived, some of her housemates spray-painted an upraised black fist on the side of a nearby concrete railroad bridge. They climbed ladders, hung from ropes and hid from the few cars that passed by on the highway that ran alongside, signing their tags in huge block or bubble letters filled with stripes or stars. The *bombing*, as they called their foray into guerilla art, started at around 3 AM and ended at dawn. But she only knew this from their reports the next day.

Pia, who had slept peacefully and unknowingly, was deeply disappointed that no one had invited her to take part. They saw her, she knew, as too soft, too sweet, and too pale. A housemate, but not quite a *sistah*. She began to evolve her own tag, to be ready for next time. She was still evolving it to this day, though she hadn't yet tagged anything more perilous than her bedroom wall and the side of her mother's old VW microbus. Her notebook was full of potential tags: *P-I-A* (or sometimes *P-CHIC* or *P-GURL*) in overblown, assertive blues and purples, 3-D fonts, fantastical riffs on curlicues, serifs or illuminations.

"'Scuse me," muttered a voice close beside her head. Pia jumped as the man's newspaper brushed her cheek. "Sorry," he muttered again. Her face was shoved against the Horoscope page. She squinted and focused on Capricorn, her sign: *In finances, business, the going is tricky, hard to judge, no way to get rich quick. In personal expression you're tops. Can catch and hold attention.* Nice, she thought. If I don't starve to death for lack of a paycheck, I'm going to come up with some great tags.

The train reached Times Square, and Pia gripped her oversized portfolio and floated out the doors on the human tide.

Judith brushed some crumbs off the bench with a handkerchief and sat clumsily as the train lurched forward. She turned her attention back to her prayers, but was distracted by the binding waistband of the skirt she was wearing. She'd spent the previous night in the spare room of her friend Malke's apartment in Brooklyn, and she was now uncomfortably aware that the skirt she had borrowed from Malke pinched around her middle. Judith had balked at taking the skirt, but her friend assured her that it would be some time before she would be able to wear it again. That's when she told Judith about the baby – her and Tzvi's first – due in February.

Thinking of Malke as a mother made Judith pause as she finished her prayer, before she kissed the holy book to God and tucked it into her purse. Malke was the least maternal of all the girls Judith had grown up with, always preferring books to dolls, outings to babysitting. A scant six months of marriage had apparently changed all that, though, because Malke's face really did glow as she confided the news of her pregnancy. The room where Judith had slept would soon become the nursery, and would probably serve that purpose – hosting a succession of small occupants, God willing – for the next ten or more years. Judith wished there was some way she could assist at the birth. It was her deepest desire to be able to serve women through both their good health and infirmity. *Baruch Hashem.* If it is God's will.

Judith hadn't intended to spend last night in Brooklyn. She hadn't spent a night there since she'd left her parents' house over two months ago. Just coming up the subway stairs onto the familiar jostle and shove of Eastern Parkway had sent an unsettling jolt of tenderness running through her. This – the snarled traffic, the street hawkers, the jumble of skin tones and accents – was the world of her childhood. She felt drawn by the gravity of its history and also repelled by the limits it had set on her life. But she'd promised her friend Rachel she would come to the wedding, and, predictably, it ran into the wee hours. She was grateful to Malke for the invitation to stay over. And it was kind of Tzvi, actually a second cousin on her father's side, to give her a lift in his car to the Fulton Street station this morning. She would move the button on the skirt's tight waistband when she arrived at work.

As the train continued to bump and wind uptown, Judith hummed the wordless *niggun* to which they had all swayed at the wedding reception and wondered whether Rachel was as happy this morning as she had appeared last night. As happy, or happier, than when they were girls together, now that she was a woman and united with Aaron, her *beshert*, her predestined other half.

When Judith arrived at Rachel's house the previous day, she paused just outside the open bedroom door. The bride-to-be was as polished as a porcelain doll, shell pink over ivory bisque. The facialist and makeup artist she had visited earlier in the day were the best in the neighborhood, and her daylong recitation of the entire Book of Psalms had heightened the roses in her cheeks as it sanctified her for the marriage bed to come.

Rachel's attendants busied themselves brushing and pinning her hair, even as the bride continued to chant the verses under her breath. The women arranged the coiffure to fit under the headpiece and veil that would shield the bride from all eyes until she had circled her groom seven times and professed her vows of loving obedience and the glass had been broken. By tomorrow, Rachel's hair would be cropped short, and she would wear a matron's *sheitl*, as the *helachas* of modesty demanded. The expensive wig now rested on a Styrofoam stand on a table in a corner of the room. The hair was a deep, burnished chestnut, much like Rachel's own, but the wig had none of the rogue curls that were her hallmark. Instead, it fell into a smoothly subdued bob. Judith stood quietly in the doorway, watching the preparations until Malke spotted her and with a shrill cry brought a half-dozen friends rushing across the room, arms thrust in her direction.

"Jehudit! Jehudit darling, you've finally come," Malke squealed and shoved the others aside. She flung her arms around her friend's neck. Judith noticed that Malke's *sheitl* was several shades darker than the girl's own infamously red hair. Judith smiled, remembering the rumors that Tzvi's mother almost refused the match because the girl was a redhead – a well-known sign of trouble. The new color didn't suit Malke's chimerical personality. But then, Judith thought, perhaps that too had changed. In this room full of old friends, Judith and the bride were the only ones whose heads remained uncovered, whose hair shone long and natural as it had throughout their childhood.

Judith knew that her bare head at the wedding would not only set tongues wagging (wagging once again, since her departure from her parents' home and the community had likely set off fireworks of gossip) but might whet the appetites of the matchmakers to arrange a *shiddach* between her and her own intended one, wherever he might be. Unless, of course, she was already too much of an outcast for anyone to consider. But why think about it – she had no desire to be married off. College, medical school, the life of a healer – that was the future she had chosen, her own intended path.

The girls bombarded her with questions, direct and blunt as ever. They wanted to know if she was happy, if she was lonely, if she missed the neighborhood, if she had bought a television, if she still prayed.

"Is it true that you learn in the same classroom with men?" Malke asked her, and the girls looked on with shocked expressions as she admitted that it was so. She spoke as if it was no big deal, but Judith had almost run from the room on her first evening at Hunter College, when she entered to find a dozen male heads turned in her direction. Even now, she habitually took a seat at the back of the auditorium, where she felt more comfortably invisible to her male classmates. As quickly as possible, Judith turned the subject back to the task at hand – preparing the bride-to-be.

The girls dressed and pampered Rachel and shot Judith sly looks as they tossed out the names of some of the young men who were being mentioned by the matchmakers as looking for brides.

"My cousin Avi has been chosen by the Rebbe to open a new Chabad House near London," Malke told her with a wink. "He has a great future and not such a bad looking *ponim*," she giggled. They were trying to tempt her back into the fold; she swallowed her irritation. This was Rachel's day and no time to mar the festivities with talk that, to some in this group, bordered on apostasy. They loved her. They would never understand her. Leave it alone, she thought.

Finally, it was time for Rachel and the bridal party to make their way to the festivities. Having fasted all day to seek Hashem's forgiveness for any past offences, Rachel paled slightly as she rose from her chair. The girls helped her down the stairs of her parents' house and escorted her along Eastern Parkway to *shul*.

The wedding celebration had already begun, even before the arrival of the bride. The guests had gathered in the *shul*, filling the time before the entrance of the new couple with toasts and hors d'ouevres.

Two local Klezmer bands – one in the men's ballroom and one in the women's – played favorites from the *shtetls*, the Jewish villages of Eastern Europe that had found a future in the crowded streets of Brooklyn. The sliding, taunting notes of the clarinets spilled from the open temple windows. It was music she never heard on the streets of her new neighborhood.

As a group, the bride and her attendants entered the temple and made their way to the ballroom where dozens of women – family and friends – were waiting to greet and bless the bride. In another room, the groom was surely busy enjoying his own reception.

Judith hung back from the center of the action and let her eyes drift over the crowd: She began to cough, as if something tickled her throat, covering up the tears that filled her eyes at the sight of her mother and her three sisters. The intensity of her response shook her. So lovely – they moved in a halo of light, the three of them – wrapped in a cloud of goodness and piety. Someone reached around Judith and patted her on the back.

"Raise your arms over your head and say, '*Khus, khus, khus!*'"

It was her cousin Chana, laughing and repeating the advice their *bubbe* had always dispensed when someone began coughing at the dinner table. Judith hugged Chana and let herself be led to her family.

They loved her. She could feel it in every embrace. They loved her and they were trying to understand. But the veiled look of anguish in her mother's eyes said it all. Her family wouldn't reject her for her choices, as most would, but they feared for her and believed she had departed from the truest, holiest path. And who's to say they're not right, Judith thought. *A stubborn and willful girl*, her sixth grade teacher, Mrs. Fenner, had called her. And indeed, she was stubbornly following a course that only she believed she was called to follow. She hoped that her will wasn't leading her into darkness.

"*Hartsenyu.*" Darling. Judith's mother smoothed the sleeves of the pale blue satin sheath Judith wore. The touch was so familiar. So steadying.

"You look lovely, *mein tokhter*," she whispered.

"As do you," Judith managed, touching, in return, the skirt of her mother's dress. "That's new."

Her mother smiled. "Well, every now and then, a woman needs renewal," she said, solemnly. It was, of course, a private joke. She never appeared at a wedding in the same dress twice; she was a master of turning old gowns into new. Judith admired the deep bronze silk of the skirt, which she recognized from a dress her mother had worn to a Bar Mitzvah the year before.

The musicians slowed their tempestuous beat to a sedate amble. It was time for the ceremony to begin. Judith and her three sisters linked arms and walked to the sanctuary. At the end of the long aisle, the *chupah*, the wedding canopy, filtered the sunlight streaming from a large, high window. Small talk hushed as everyone began singing the traditional *Alter Rebbe's Niggun of the Four Stanzas*. Judith found she could barely sing for the lump in her throat.

The groom, along with his own father and Rachel's, approached the bride and her attendants. With visibly trembling hands, Aaron reached up and drew Rachel's veil over her face. Then, separately, they walked forward to the *chupah*, where Aaron's father untied all the knots on Aaron's clothes and shoes. With this, Aaron broke all other bonds in favor of this one with his bride. Rachel's father handed Aaron the white linen *kittel* robe in which he would be wed and, someday, buried.

Now, sitting on the train, Judith realized she had twisted the handkerchief she was holding into a sodden knot. It was impossible for her to recall the company of her mother and sisters like this without deeply mourning the one sister who was no longer with them. Judith sent out a silent *kaddish* for Rebecca, as she had every day for the last four years.

It was only after Rebecca died that Judith decided, beyond all doubt, to become a doctor. Rebecca, the sweetest of her sisters, the eldest – a bride already by the time Judith turned fifteen. More beautiful than any of them in Judith's eyes, and kinder, too. She was Judith's *mashpiach*, her confidante and spiritual advisor. The cancer had already spread from her uterus to her lymph nodes by the time she was diagnosed. Despite a series of useless surgeries, it was only a matter of months until she wasted away and the dark rings wore themselves into the skin around her beautiful almond eyes. On the night before Rebecca passed away, Judith dreamed that they were dancing. And Rebecca spoke to her in Yiddish, as they twirled to the music – *With you as my healer I shall live to rejoice a hundred lifetimes.* She would never be her sister's doctor, but she prayed she would be someone's.

Judith had always excelled in her classes. She found favor with her teachers and with the Rebbe, who granted her special dispensation to attend two years of community college. But when she unveiled her plan to finish her Bachelor's degree and go on to medical school, her family shut her down. She sent the Rebbe – whose *neshumah*, whose soul, was so holy and wise that the thousands in their community worldwide were willing to live by his word alone – a heartfelt letter.

She begged for the opportunity to fulfill her gift. She told him she devoutly believed it was *bashert*, intended, for her to do this. He sent for her and looked deeply into Judith's eyes as she held her breath and willed him to read what was in her heart. Then he told her it was not for her to look upon the bodies of men in such a way. Frantic, she swore to become only a gynecologist, to treat only women. The answer was the same. No. She should remain the wonderful help she had been to her aunt and uncle in their store. And prepare for the day – soon, *im yirtzhe Hashem* – when she would have a family of her own.

Now Judith put the twisted handkerchief into her bag and forced her hands to lie quietly to her lap. To soothe herself, she tried to recall the familiar scent of the Sanctuary – mingled aromas of polished wood, leather and paper, and the oil from the lamp that burned continuously above the Torah. It was a smell of devotion and prayer that filled her with peace, but also with longing. Leaving had brought her freedom to seek a medical education, but also left her alone with the confusing choices of secular life.

Last night, as the service began, the rabbi and the *chazzan* had taken their familiar places on the *bima*. From beneath the *chupah*, the rabbi raised his arms over the heads of the couple, and the *chazzan* began to chant.

Welcome!

He who is the Almighty and Omnipotent, over all;

Blessed over all;

Greatest of all;

Most distinguished of all;

Shall Bless this Choson and Kallah, this man and wife.

"Amen," Judith whispered under her breath. Not for a single moment had her belief in Hashem flagged. Instead, it was her willingness to let her fate rest completely in the hands of a man – even their most beloved Lubavitcher Rebbe – that faltered when everything inside her compelled her in her singular mission. Judith wondered if the Rebbe was present at the wedding, in the company of the men. She peeked at the women on the benches around her for a glimpse of the Rebbetzin, his wife. There was no sign of her. Judith felt a guilty relief.

The Rabbi raised his hands, uniting his audience under his blessing. "The Talmud teaches that Adam and Eve were created on the sixth day of creation as conjoined twins – one complete being. God then separated the two, forming Eve from Adam's side. Thus, man and woman – that is, husband and wife – long to be reunited. Their love stems from this natural tendency to be one. Marriage is the beginning of a new life as a complete soul for both the bride and groom."

Judith had heard this from earliest childhood – that upon birth each body contains merely a portion of one soul and at marriage the two parts are reunited as one, to the great relief of both parties. Neither could be whole without the other. Was she, then, depriving another half-soul (and not just any half-soul but her very own *beshert*) of its opportunity to be whole by her refusal to be wed?

Judith's younger sisters, sitting on her left, poked one another and giggled. Judith turned and hushed them, and as she did, she caught a peek of Mrs. Streiman, who had made the match that brought them here today, giving her a look with pursed lips that plainly expressed her distaste. Apparently, Judith was *not* considered redeemable as far as her matchmaking went. No doubt others in the room shared the woman's disapproval but had kept their own counsel out of respect for her Judith's family and this joyous *simcha*. Judith felt her cheeks burn and she nudged her sister Rivka rudely before looking down at her hands. Perhaps coming to the wedding was a mistake.

Judith glanced sideways at her mother, sitting to her right. She was dabbing at her eyes with a pale blue handkerchief. Miriam was a woman who cried as easily at joy as at sorrow. In this, Judith was not unlike her. She knew if she caught her mother's eye, they would both spill over with tears, so she kept her face averted and struggled in solitude as the service continued.

"Today we bring together this man and this woman – two shards joined to form another vessel in which to contain the divine Light. But their edges are still new and roughly cut. There are places in which they do not yet form the perfect seal, where some Light may be lost in misunderstanding, in thoughtlessness, in angry words. But their *neshumah* – their souls – now coupled in the holiest of bonds, will grow together through the years until the seal is perfect, the Light shining safe within. Soon, *Baruch Hashem*, they will expand their vessel to enfold the next generation and the next."

Of course, Judith thought: It's all about the Light. Our duty always is to seek out the divine Light in this world and become a vessel holy enough to contain it. *B'Hashem*. Could she become such a vessel? Not for a minute had her faith in *Hashem* flagged. But what of His faith in her?

Althea and Celia got off the express train at 96th Street. Rather than wait for the local, so often plagued by delays, Althea decided they would walk the rest of the way up to her mother's building on 104th

Street and Amsterdam.   In a matter of blocks, her blouse was clinging to her torso and her hair hung in damp strands along her brow.
Celia, however, appeared impervious to the heat, skipping alongside
her and humming tunelessly, banging the shopping bag that held her
swimsuit and sandals against her legs. As they passed the bakery at
the corner of Broadway and 102nd Street, the girl lagged behind to
stare into the window. Impatient, Althea called to her.

"Yiayia is waiting," she told her, to no avail. Althea retraced her
steps and when she got to the window, reached down for her daughter's hand and gave it a gentle squeeze. It was still such a sweet little
hand, Althea thought, the skin like chamois, the bones all tucked up
in a plump package that rested perfectly inside her own palm. Althea
loved those little hands – she had loved them best of all the perfect little parts that had made up her infant daughter. She watched
them for hours as the baby Celia nursed or slept, tiny fingers clasp-
ing and relaxing, the whorled knuckles indented into rosy plumpness.
But now the girl was nine, and already Althea could feel the narrow
bones and sinews of the soon-to-be woman emerging. Celia's hand,
as sweaty as her own, slipped from her grip.

"Look, Mami, cookies!" she pointed. "Let's bring Yiayia cookies."

"Yiayia has plenty of cookies," Althea told her. "We're late.
We have to hurry."

Althea looked up in time to see the baker, carrying a tray of
fresh muffins to the window display. Her head spun a little. She was
hungry. When was the last time she had eaten? She had been too
rushed for breakfast and had skipped dinner last night. Her mouth
watered a little at the sight of those muffins, lined up in ranks like soldiers, their plump shoulders touching. The baker slid the tray into the
window and caught her eye, waving her toward the shop with a grin.

"Let's go inside, Mami." This time, Celia tugged Althea's skirt
and pulled her toward the door. Althea saw the baker wink. Then
she saw her own reflection, damp and disarrayed, the buttons pulled
open at her chest. Althea frowned. With one hand she refastened
her buttons and with the other, she grabbed her daughter's hand once

again. This time she held tight as the girl tried to pull away, and she managed to get Celia moving alongside her. She took the bag the girl was carrying, to help hurry her along.

Celia had stopped humming and Althea could feel a sulk coming on. But there was nothing she could do. She had to get Celia to her mother's and be downtown again before nine. Already, Althea had been late to work three times this month and the month wasn't half over. Since the girl's summer vacation began, it had been impossible to get her moving in the mornings. Celia slept in the soundest depths of that blissful sea and surfaced to the waking world reluctantly, and only with the greatest coaxing. At work, Althea's supervisors were entirely unsympathetic.

"This is a business, and you have a job. And that job begins at nine AM. Sharp." That's what Mr. Barnes told her last week when he called her into his office. On his desk, she noticed the photographs of his three identically beefy boys in team uniforms, each grinning with huge gapped teeth – the oldest sporting silver braces – and each holding a gleaming trophy. Could she appeal to him on the basis of their shared parenthood? But no. Surely there was a Mrs. Barnes, and to her fell the job of waking and feeding, dressing and shuttling the children to school and games and lessons. Althea glanced around the desk. There were no photos of this woman, nothing to celebrate her accomplishments.

Didn't anyone understand what a mother's life was like? Even if they did, she thought, they didn't care. They had told her as much. Yes, she had a job. She was lucky to have work; so many didn't. She saw them on the street, angry and idle. And lost. The city was awash in workers without work. That woman on the platform this morning. Filthy. Crazy. How much separated Althea from that woman? How hard would it be to fall? How easy. For six years now, ever since coming to this city, she felt as if she'd been racing the devil. Racing the clock. And for what? For Celia, that's what, Althea reminded herself. For her daughter and her home.

"Mami? Mami?"

Celia was lagging behind again and Althea yanked her forward. "Mami. Ouch!"

Althea looked down. Celia's eyes looked hurt, guarded.

"I'm sorry, *kukla*. I didn't mean to pull so hard. I'll bring you a surprise tonight when I pick you up at Yiayia's. Can you guess what it might be?"

"What time will you come," Celia demanded. "Tell me what time tonight. Tell me the *real* time. You never tell me the real time. You're always late."

Althea felt a stab of guilt edged with anger. Her daughter was right. Late coming and late going. Last night she said she'd pick her up by six and didn't arrive until almost nine. Althea's mother looked at her with narrowed eyes, but said nothing. Last week Althea called and asked her mother to keep Celia overnight. Her mother had to rinse out Celia's clothes for the next day. Celia had cried, saying they were still damp when she dressed in the morning. All spring Althea had been late picking her daughter up from school. But there was no explaining – not to Celia, nor to her own parents – the circumstances of her missing hours.

"Celia, I'll be back in time for supper tonight. You and I will go out for supper together. Would you like that?" She held her breath as she watched the girl's face work through successive flashes of trust, excitement and distrust.

"Just you and me? Pizza?" The girl seemed placated for the moment. Trust, Althea was happy to see, still won out in her daughter. "Will you still bring a surprise?"

They arrived at the door to the tall brick building – one of a dozen identical doors in identical brick buildings in the city housing project – and Althea pressed the buzzer to her mother's apartment. A moment later the latch clicked open and let them into the lobby, which smelled of a hundred different breakfasts. Again, Althea's stomach growled. She rang for the elevator and smoothed Celia's hair, handing her the small plastic shopping bag that contained her swimsuit and an extra change of clothes, *just in case.*

"You be a good girl today. Don't give your yiayia a hard time, yes? And remember to make a sissy before you go in the pool."

Celia made a face. "I'm not a baby," she insisted disdainfully, hauling open the elevator door as it arrived. Two men, dressed in suits, brushed past them, the smell of aftershave slouching behind, lingering sweet and heavy in the elevator cab.

"So, if you're such a big girl, can you go up to Yiayia's all by yourself?" Althea asked hopefully. The minutes she'd save would, just possibly, allow her to be on time this morning.

Celia looked doubtful. Althea knew her daughter didn't like the elevator. For a while last year, Celia had insisted on walking up the seven flights of stairs rather than riding in it. She was so adamant, Althea wondered if something bad had happened that she didn't know about. Every day, it seemed, she read in the papers stories of children lured and molested by strangers, or even by family friends. She was about to give up and get into the elevator when she saw her daughter's expression brighten.

"If you promise that we can have pizza tonight, and that you'll bring cookies from the bakery, I'll go up to Yiayia's by myself. Promise?"

"I promise."

Celia's face took on a determination Althea hadn't seen before. She really was growing up. Althea bent down and enfolded her daughter in a hug. But before she let the door close – she on one side, her daughter on the other – she reached in and pushed the button for the seventh floor.

"Remember, you promised," she heard Celia call in a singsong as the inner door slid shut between them. Althea felt an unexpected tug somewhere deep inside her chest. She pulled quickly at the door handle, determined to join the girl, but it was too late – the elevator had begun to rise, drawing her daughter upward and away.

"*I love you!*" Althea shouted into the blank metal face of the door. She stood for a moment, her arms at her sides, awash in emptiness. Then she retraced her steps back toward the subway at 96th Street, covering the distance in half the time, letting her long arms and legs swing out as she couldn't with Celia by her side. She was dreading the descent underground into the stale, dank air and was relieved when, just as she turned to look, a downtown bus pulled alongside her at the bus stop. Althea made a sudden decision and boarded the bus. At least the air up here was a little fresher and she'd get to see some daylight before locking herself into the windowless little bookkeeping room.

Her hand rummaged inside her purse for coins, which she fed into the metal hopper. There were a couple of empty seats toward the back and Althea wove her way along the aisle, bouncing from one side to the other as the bus lurched through the potholed streets. Not long after she eased herself into a seat however, the bus came to a sudden halt. A man who had been clinging to the bar above her head pivoted and nearly sat down in her lap. He righted himself with a muttered apology and turned to face the other way.

Althea strained to see the road ahead. The bus was surrounded on all sides by taxis, bobbing in the pot-holed road like a sea of metallic yellow dolphins. Waves of heat shimmered off their hoods. Somewhere up ahead a siren was screaming, but that didn't tell her anything. There was always a siren screaming somewhere in this city. Still, the bus didn't move, and anxiety crept slowly up Althea's spine. She looked at her watch. It still read 8:10, which is what it had read when she reached her mother's building. She must have forgotten to wind it this morning. She turned to the woman sitting next to her.

"Do you have the time?" she asked.

The woman looked up from the book she was reading and sighed.

"Not a clue. My watch got ripped right off my wrist last week as I was waiting for this bus. Filthy hoodlums. Zoomed by on their bikes and almost threw me to the ground." She pulled her purse and book into her chest and wrapped her arms around them, as if Althea herself might decide to make a grab for something. "I think it must be getting close to nine, though." She turned her attention back to the book.

Althea took a deep breath to beat back the nervousness. The bus was only at 88th Street. Should she jump off at the next stop and run to the nearest subway station? There was no telling how long it would take to get to the next stop, a mere block away, but as good as a million miles in this traffic. The Number 1 train was a local, and would take at least 20 minutes to get her down to 34th Street, she calculated. Sweat and fear prickled her skin. There was no way around it; she would be late again.

Until she had arrived in America, Althea believed that time flowed as abundantly as water, bloomed as luxuriously as leaves on the fig and olive trees that had dotted her parents' garden. It was the one thing she believed she would always have plenty of. Her teachers called her a dreamer, said she dawdled on line and lingered over her work longer than the other children. It was not that she was "slow," a term she heard the teachers at Celia's school use to describe the children who resisted their best efforts to instill the alphabet or multiplication tables in their sleepy heads. Rather, it took Althea mere moments to grasp information, but it gave her the greatest pleasure to roll the new facts around in her head, stretching and extending them in all directions. In her imagination, she populated whole worlds with number families, and paved the streets of imaginary cities with words and letters. She spun stories of colors and dreamed up histories for countries that existed solely in her mind.

On Skiathos, there was never much money. Electricity had to be rationed, and skirts were lengthened, as Althea grew, with strips of fabric sliced from even older skirts. But time – time never ran short. Time was like light: endless and boundless. Love, she thought, must be like that, too. When she met Celia's father, Althea was certain that their time together would be endless. Thomas was stationed at an Army base on the island, but his family owned a guesthouse in Athens that catered to wealthy European tourists. After his service ended he returned there, promising to come back and marry her. At first, there were daily phone calls and letters, and then, abruptly, these stopped. The infant Celia would never know her father. From this,

Althea learned that love was not everlasting. But she still believed in the generosity of time.

Just before Celia's third birthday Althea, her daughter and her parents moved to America, where Althea's uncle promised they would prosper. From that day, six years ago, when she stepped off the plane, Althea began to learn the hard lesson of time in America. Money could be earned and banked, but the account of time merely went one way. There was never enough and it was always diminishing.

Outside the bus, a battle of horns started up from all sides. Althea wanted to howl along with them. Instead, she made a low humming noise on a long exhaled breath, something that had always calmed her in the past, but this time was ineffective. Instead, the panic that lately had stalked her began to close in. The diesel smell of the bus' exhaust swirled around her head, nauseating. And the woman next to her unwrapped a fast food sandwich that smelled of pickles and mustard. Althea stood abruptly, knocking into the man swinging above her.

"Excuse me, excuse me," she muttered, pushing past him and working her way toward the back door. The bus began to edge forward, inching along the avenue swollen with rush hour traffic. Althea reached out and pulled the cord for the next stop. Even if she had to walk all the way downtown, it would be faster than this.

But as suddenly as the traffic had clogged the road like an aging artery, it cleared. The bus lunged forward, sending Althea into an ungainly pirouette. It eased into the next stop – the one that Althea had rung for – but she hung back and didn't get off. The driver waited – Althea could feel his impatience as the seconds ticked away – before moving forward again, making better time down the suddenly empty avenue. She wove her way back toward her seat, which was now occupied. She looked around for another, but they were all taken.

Althea shifted from foot to foot, and ticked off the decreasing numbers on the street signs as the bus gasped its way downtown. She hardly missed the years when she and Celia shared a cramped apartment with her mother and father. But ever since her parents had gotten a coveted apartment in the uptown housing project, Althea felt as if she was constantly in motion – a sailor negotiating perilous seas. This summer, with Althea's father back in Skiathos selling the last of the family's homes there, was the worst. Without the money to pay a babysitter or to send Celia to camp, she was forced to make the trip uptown and back again twice a day, five days a week. Unlike time, her fatigue was without limit.

✤

With each step Danielle took down the narrow cobbled street, the reek of fish became more potent. The four tall masts of the German sailing barque Peking, only recently installed at Pier 17 in the South Street Seaport, rose against a backdrop of towering chrome and glass buildings in the city's financial center. Danielle loved this part of the city, where two centuries butted heads and elbowed each other for turf – or in this case, docking space. Only three summers earlier, her first working in the kitchen of La Belle Epoque, she had stared into the china blue sky as a lunatic French aerialist, no larger than a peapod thousands of feet in the air, traversed the windblown distance between the roofs of the towers on nothing but a wire. This city inspired the impossible, she believed.

Whenever she had out-of-town guests, Danielle brought them down here to see the old sailing ships and the even older seaport buildings. She promised them that Louie's, an epicurean diamond-in-the-rough with its crumbling brick facade and dusty windows, would serve them the best clam chowder, the freshest mussels, the brawniest ale on tap, and they'd also get the coolest view of the Brooklyn Bridge towering virtually over their heads. But invariably, what guests commented on most was the overwhelming stink of fish – even hours after the market had closed.

The market opened in what, for most people, were the wee hours of the night. By 5 AM, rain or shine, the trucks unloaded their ocean-fresh cargo onto wooden pallets and long benches and purveyors of all things piscine prepared to sell their goods to the insatiable markets and restaurants of the city. The rough and stocky fish mongers hacked and sawed away at thousand-pound tunas and swordfish, gutted and scaled, chopped heads and tails, and flushed sea-salty blood and ice onto the cobblestones at their feet. By the time the wholesalers closed up shop three hours later, there was no way to wash the stench from the cobbles and curbs, no possibility of masking the putrefying musk of the fishy detritus that remained. Danielle's guests held their noses while Danielle enjoyed deep and satisfying breaths of pure pleasure. The smell was as rich and purple as the last moments of a sunset.

She hadn't been down to the Seaport in months, though. Not since early spring, when she had agreed to meet Paul for one last, futile discussion about why their relationship, perfect in his eyes, would have to end. Now she pushed that from her mind, focusing instead on the more gratifying task at hand. Shopping for fish was one of her favorite tasks. She hurried down Fulton Street, hoping that the restaurant's favorite wholesaler would still have some choice offerings. Wednesday was typically slower than other days at the market, so she felt optimistic. Aside from a few joggers, there was almost no one at the Seaport. The shops that lined the pedestrian mall made it look like a modern materialist take on a Wild West ghost town. By lunchtime, however the space would be heaving with equal parts tourists and businessmen.

Danielle reached South Street and rushed across the two empty lanes against the red light. All the traffic was overhead on the highway, anyway, making the metal supports of the FDR Drive hum with their vibrations.

Only about half the fishmongers were still open, and Danielle carefully negotiated the slime and ice underfoot to get to an area that was piled with wooden peck baskets full of fish. All that melting ice made the temperature under the highway perceptibly lower than it had been across the street.

"Hey, pretty lady, how about a couple of forty-pound lobsters for two bucks?" a man called to her. "Ya can't beat that, can ya?" Danielle turned and laughed out loud at the absurdity. The man, his head wrapped in a threadbare towel and his apron slick with guts, nodded his head in approval. "I like a lady who laughs," he called to her. "You ever think about a fish man? Nice fresh catch I am." Danielle hurried on. "You a Pisces?" he called once more, trying to lure her back.

There were several buyers ahead of her when she reached the stand of P. Willard and Sons. While she waited for help, she poked around the baskets, looking for snapper or sea bass. The snapper would have been brought up from Mexico, the sea bass from Chile. Some buyers relied on the brightness of the scales to determine how fresh the fish was. But the eyes were unreliable, as Danielle knew only too well. She bent down to one of the baskets, shut her eyes and sniffed. The smell was fresh and sweet. Not fishy so much as oceanic, that first smell of the sea she remembered from when her grandparents used to take her to the Cape for a week each summer. For miles before she could spot the ocean, Danielle would test the air with deep breaths from the back seat of the aging Plymouth, waiting to catch that first whiff of salt. Pale blue-gray on her tongue. She told them it smelled *pearly*, and that became their pet name for her.

"You buying fish, or shopping for oh da cologne," a voice grated right next to her ear. Danielle jumped and stared. But the face next to hers wasn't menacing in the slightest. It was just Frank, who often delivered fish to the restaurant and sometimes hung around for a cup of coffee and a smoke. Rumor had it that he was the bastard son of P. Willard himself, not one of the Sons of the company's name, but that he stood to inherit the business since the legit heirs had both heaped shame on the family by running off – one to Vegas and the other to an ashram in India.

"These fish have any credentials? They fresh?" she asked him, adopting the rough market syntax.

"Fresh as your rosy cheeks," he told her. "They just come up from Baja last night. I give you a good deal, since it's Wednesday. Three bucks a pound. Just for you. Good, huh? Two boxes, am I right?"

"Three bucks is not bad. Two-fifty is better," she said. "You sure they're fresh? You got papers?"

But Frank was already marking the sides of the cardboard boxes with a black Sharpie marker. "LBE, right? You want 'em delivered in half an hour, am I right?" All the regular buyers had codes. LBE was for La Belle Epoque, one of the oldest continually run restaurants in the financial district. Danielle nodded.

Her task accomplished, Danielle headed back across South Street. She was happy. Contented. Chef would be pleased. She loved her work and she was good at it. Hadn't she already graduated from lowly *commis*, everyone's humble assistant, to vegetable chef, directly in charge of appetizers, veggies, soup and pasta? She was certain it was only a matter of time until she made *entremetier.*

What would she do with the fish if it were up to her? Something simple – stuff them with a reduction of wild mushrooms to meld the ocean with the earth. Or pad the cavities with thinly sliced lemons and then wrap the whole fish in smoky bacon strips. The deeply imagined flavors arrayed themselves like pigments on a palette, rich and colorful.

Suddenly, a grimy panel truck careened out of nowhere and rumbled across the cobblestones just inches from her feet. She hadn't seen it coming, but worse, she hadn't heard it. She hadn't been listening. Danielle froze to the spot as the truck sped by. How could she have been so careless? Had she learned nothing in all these months? She lifted a trembling hand to her throat. Her legs were shaking, as well. Deep breaths, she told herself. Take three deep, full breaths and pay attention. You must learn to pay attention. She could no longer rely on her eyes, especially her peripheral vision. Turning her entire body to check both lanes of traffic, she continued across the street.

Danielle stepped into a bodega that kept fish market hours and ordered a regular coffee. It arrived in a paper cup sporting the Parthenon on its side. "Have a Nice Day," it insisted in elaborate script. Better for it to command, "Stay alert, stay alive," she thought.

Not quite ready to return to the street, she considered a tray of cheese Danish that glistened with sugary frosting, but stopped short of buying one. She knew it would only disappoint. You couldn't heal everything with sugar and caffeine. Finally, she left the shop and walked, with exaggerated care, the half dozen blocks to the restaurant. She let herself in the back entrance. Geoffrey, *chef du partier*, the man in charge when Chef was not around, was already at work in the kitchen, humming tunelessly to himself as he chopped. She nodded and smiled, but didn't try to engage him in conversation. Danielle knew he was not a morning person. Instead, she washed her hands and headed down to the cooler to collect the vegetables she needed to prep.

Tomatoes, onions, bunches of cilantro, heads of garlic – the ingredients for the salsa she was charged with making rolled through the telescopic field of Danielle's vision. Just off to her right but out of sight, Geoffrey's cleaver marked time against a chopping block with a rhythmic thud. His station was only two feet from hers. Not so long ago, the view of his excellent knife work marked the peripheral frame of her cooking world. With his long, beautifully tapered fingers draped over the wide steel blade, his wrist beat out a tempo that produced anything from translucent shavings of potatoes for a gratin, to Las Vegas-perfect dice of chicken or sirloin. These days however, Geoffrey worked unseen – in Danielle's personal darkness, that underworld in which her vision failed – and she relied on memory and hearing to inform perception. Now, she concentrated all her attention on the narrowing circle of light that held the components of her task.

Her eyes burned from the pile of onions she had just finished chopping, and she swiped at the tears with one cuff as she reached for a tomato with her other hand. Despite an urge to work with her eyes shut, Danielle kept her gaze trained on her hands. Last week she had slipped and chopped a thumbnail into the garlic.

She remembered clearly the first time she'd experienced the shrinking of her visual field, although at the time she thought little of it. She had only been out of cooking school a few months, and in her first professional kitchen for only a couple of weeks. A fishing boat had been hired by the restaurant for a company outing. They trawled Long Island Sound, just west of the Robert Moses Causeway, angling for fluke and flounder that rested like piscatorial doormats on the sandy bottom, both eyes migrated mysteriously to one side of their scaly bodies. Those fish trained their vision through murky water at a wavering disk of light.

Up and down, the boat had rolled through the gray-green waves as a warm front barreled in from the south. Up and down, rolling and reaching. Plastic cups of Corona and Heineken tumbled from their resting places as cooks and busboys and the waitstaff reeled in their catch or stood untangling line from their fellow fishermen.

"Bohemian Rhapsody" blared from a pair of speakers outside the captain's wheelhouse. The boat stank like a brewery. Like a cannery, too, and Danielle's stomach began to lurch with each heave of the bow. Her head throbbed. Finally, she gave up and went to sit inside a small cabin where she hoped to ward off the onset of a migraine or an embarrassing attack of mal-de-mer.

She had been sitting there for half an hour before she turned to her right and noticed the man next to her, asleep with his head drooped on his chest. It was no one she knew from the restaurant – most likely a crewmember. His hands rested on his lap, one cradling the other in what might have been repose, were it not for the large fishhook lodged deeply inside the mound of flesh at the base of his thumb. Danielle was fascinated and repelled by the sight. But mainly she was confused. The man was inches away from her on the bench that ringed the tiny room. She should have spotted him immediately, but it was as if he weren't even there until she turned her body to find him squarely in front of her. She told herself it was a form of seasickness or migraine and indeed, she developed a nauseating headache that lasted most of the next three days. She didn't bother seeing a doctor, but grew accustomed to turning her head to look at things dead on.

Since then, her visual realm had been getting smaller and

smaller – a bright orb in an expanding night sky. Grabbing a tomato and beginning to chop, she thought that she might measure it by tomatoes. Her field of vision, as of today, Wednesday, July 13, 1977, 9:40 AM held at six red, ripe tomatoes wide.

As her field of vision contracted, her fascination with certain details of her surroundings expanded. The blind woman on the train last week: Danielle had been spellbound by her hands. Beautiful, pale hands with polished fingernails and a cluster of rings. Why polish? Why decorate with jewelry? For the secret smoothness, for the tactile contrast of stone and gold? Serene, composed, watching and listening hands. Danielle felt free to stare.

Now, she scraped the seedy remains of a tomato into a bowl and started on the next one.

"What did that tomato ever do to you?" Geoffrey asked, laughing.

Danielle realized she was chopping with a vengeance, and pulled back.

"Spit in my eye, apparently," she said, wiping a streak of juice from her cheek.

Geoffrey lowered his voice to a whisper. "So. Did you hear about Kim?"

She had. Kim had been promoted in June to saucier after years in other line positions, but on Monday morning she had been called into the chef de cuisine's office, and with no warning, was let go. Danielle happened to be walking down the block just as this took place, and Kim burst out the restaurant door. At the sight of Danielle, Kim's usually stoic demeanor – you don't spend years in professional kitchens without growing a thick, scorch-proof skin – dissolved, and the two of them repaired to a coffee shop where Kim alternately cursed, wept and kicked the metal base of the Formica table, while Danielle sat witness.

But Danielle didn't admit any of this to Geoffrey. She wanted to hear what he knew – he was friendly with Roderick, one of the owners. Knowledge was power, or something close to it. She looked at him, wide-eyed.

"She's been bounced, and a close friend of Monsieur le Chef will be taking her place," he said, nodding solemnly to Kim's former station. Danielle recalled the lanky Swiss who had been introduced to them as "my close friend." Through the window in the swinging kitchen door she had seen him drinking cup after cup of espresso and huddling with Chef Denis in the front of the house before opening time. So Kim had been kicked out to make room for this handsome friend. It wasn't surprising. There was often little connection between merit and promotion on the line. It made her realize all the more that she needed to earn some recognition and a promotion soon, before anyone realized she was having trouble with her vision.

"That stinks," Danielle said. She motioned with her chin at the pork ribs Geoffrey had been hacking. "*Les Messieurs sont tous des cochons.*"

Geoffrey looked at her with concern.

"Okay, present company excepted."

Chapter Three

I t was 10:15, and the line stretched around the corner and halfway to the end of the block.

"We'll never get in," Celia moaned, clutching at her grandmother's skirt. A hand shot down and briskly slapped hers away.

"You're pulling my skirt off," her grandmother said. "*Me thelete na eimai gymne?*" Do you want your yiayia standing here naked in front of all these people?

Celia said nothing, although she had a brief vision of Yiayia standing with her crinkled skirt around her ankles, her dimpled thighs on view to the world. Celia knew that if her mother were here, she would correct her grandmother for speaking Greek to her. Mami had always been strict about this one thing: We are in America and we will speak only English – *mono Agglica* – she often said, breaking her own rule, which always made Celia laugh. But her mother wasn't here. Celia imagined her mother rushing off the very second the elevators doors closed between them this morning. She said she was going to work. She *said* she'd be back in time for dinner, but Celia wasn't sure she believed her any more. Last Sunday, her mother had lied. She said she was walking to the supermarket to buy a few things they needed for dinner. But when Celia looked out the window, she saw her mother – as small as a Barbie doll from their 5th floor kitchen window – stepping into a cab. Celia settled down in front of a rerun of *All in the Family* with a mostly full box of Mallomars and a can of her mother's Tab. When those were gone, she tossed the evidence down the garbage chute, careful not to let the apartment door lock behind her while she was out in the hall. She wasn't supposed to leave the apartment when no one else was home. When her mother returned, about an hour later, it was with empty arms, no packages.

"What's for dinner?" Celia had demanded as her mother came through the door.

"I'm too tired to cook, *kukla*. Let's order Chinese food," her mother had replied, bustling past her just as if she had an armful of grocery bags. "Go find the menu from Sun Sai Gai," she sighed, and she lay down on the couch. Celia read out the offerings on the menu and her mother phoned in their choices: roast duck, dried string beans with bean curd, shrimp chow fun. When the food arrived, only 15 minutes later, Celia had to shake her mother awake to pay the delivery boy.

That was the third time her mother had briefly disappeared, and Celia was determined to solve the mystery of it. Mysteries were Celia's specialty, ever since her mother bought her three Nancy Drew books for her birthday. What would Nancy do? Review the evidence. There wasn't much, Celia had to admit. For almost the whole time they had lived in New York, her mother had never once left without saying exactly where she would be. Every morning, as she walked Celia to school – extra early so she could get to work by 8:00 and leave by 2:00 – her mother would tell her exactly what she would be doing all day until 3:00, when she'd always, *always* be standing at the fence outside the schoolyard. Some of Celia's girlfriends got to walk home on their own, through the winding Chinatown streets. But her mother insisted that Celia would not be allowed to cross Bowery alone until she was at least eleven. Every day, her mother would be standing by the fence, without fail. But this summer was different. Lots of things were different and most of them Celia didn't much like. Starting with the way her grandmother smacked her hand.

"We should have gotten here earlier," Celia complained now, twisting a little from side to side for emphasis and letting her beach bag bang against her grandmother's legs. The older woman reached down and caught the bag on the second swing.

"You should have more *ypomone*, more patience," her grandmother responded, and without waiting for a reply turned away to talk to a neighbor who had joined them in the crowd.

The line inched forward. Celia could hear the splash of water as someone cannonballed off the diving board. Just around the corner and inside the high brick walls, children were wet and cool and laughing. And here she was, sweating into her Keds. She took another couple of baby steps forward. At some point, the pool guards would turn everyone away. That's what had happened the last time they came. "Pool's full," a man had come down the line, shouting. "Pool's full. Try again later." And they had walked back to the steaming apartment off Amsterdam, where Yiayia drew her a cold bath and Celia tried to pretend it was just as good.

Celia began swinging her body from side to side again, creating a little breeze that dried the sweat on her forehead. The bag in her hands, the one holding her swimsuit and pink flip-flops and that stupid bathing cap that yanked at the tiny hairs around the edge of her scalp, bounced against her legs with each swing. Her grandmother reached down once more and caught Celia's hand in her own large, soft sweaty one, yanking her still. They moved a few steps closer to the promise of cool relief.

The pool man came around the corner. Uh-oh, Celia thought, here it comes. But this time the man said nothing as he walked past the line, just pulled out a bandanna from his back pocket and wiped his red face as he hurried down the block. As he passed by, Celia caught a whiff of chlorine, like a big tease. She groaned and pulled her hand from her grandmother's.

"Patience, patience, little one," Yiayia crooned down at her. "Look, there is the door." And it was true. All the baby steps had brought them so close to the iron gates that Celia could have thrown a pink Spalding through them, if she had one. Which she didn't, since her mother had decided Celia should take piano lessons and now she was stuck inside practicing in the evening instead of playing stickball with the other kids on the block. The piano had been in the apartment when they moved there two years earlier. The last people must have decided it was too much trouble to take with them. Since the weather turned hot, a bunch of the low notes didn't play at all, or the keys worked once and then sank down wearily until the next day. Celia liked banging them loudly on her way out in the morning and then leaving them to their rest. She played mainly on the high notes anyway.

The line moved forward. People disappeared past the gates, and Celia danced a little ahead as Yiayia pulled some money from her purse and traded it for two tickets that would let them in, like at the movies. After the bright sunshine of the street, the passageway to the pool seemed as dark and sweet as a cave. The smell of disinfectant from the showers prickled Celia's nose but she blinked happily and skipped ahead toward the women's locker room. Her grandmother caught up and steered her by the shoulder into an empty bathroom stall, where Celia changed into her swimsuit and they each took a turn peeing, hovering over the toilet, which Yiayia had lined with paper, just in case either of them should accidentally touch down.

While Yiayia changed in one of the curtained dressing rooms, Celia paced impatiently. At the sound of a thump, she turned to see a slice of her grandmother revealed in the gap between the curtain and the tiled doorframe. A thick mound of flesh spilled over an edge of tight elastic as the older woman struggled fiercely to free herself from her girdle. Celia swung her eyes away from the sight, toward the light spilling in from the other end of the room. Silhouetted against the open locker room door, the pool twinkled with a million blinding stars, and here and there the water was churned to foam as kids kicked and dove and windmilled through its delicious cold. Finally, her yiayia emerged covered in tight black elastic with a flounced skirt that twirled around her soft, round hips.

As quickly as she could, Celia helped her grandmother lay out their towels along one step of the concrete bleachers that ringed the pool. She tolerated having the awful bathing cap stretched over her head, her pigtails tucked underneath. Then, free at last, she spun toward the pool and, against all the rules, leaped from the edge into the slick and icy water. The cold made her head spin and she held her nose until she once again broke the surface. Her feet found the sandpapery bottom and she stood, looking around guiltily to see if she'd been caught. No shrill whistle came from the lifeguard sitting high up on his chair and Celia breathed a sigh of relief and wiped the water from her face. The chlorinated water stung her eyes and she rubbed at her face with both palms.

Dipping so that she was submerged to her neck, Celia spun in circles, enjoying the icy stroke of water against skin. She pretended she was one of the Naiads, daughters of Poseideon, presiding over the pool as her sister nymphs presided over their ancient rivers and springs. Then she began to paddle forward, eyes tight shut, lifting her feet from the bottom in brief tests of her buoyancy. Her mother insisted that everyone, everything alive, floats. That would mean that she could, too. Maybe. But for the moment, she trusted more in her ability to stand in the shallow end.

An arm came up from the water next to her and pushed her roughly.

"Marco!" screamed a shrill voice.

Celia, surprised, turned to see her friend Julie.

"Polo!" someone else yelled.

"You're *It!*" Julie shrieked and then leaped away backward into the water.

Celia closed her eyes again, obedient to the rules of the game.

"Marco," she shouted, flailing wildly in the dark in case anyone hovered near enough to touch.

"Polo," came the response from someone close by, just beyond arm's reach.

Celia swung blindly toward the voice, slapping out suddenly with one arm, but failing to meet flesh.

"Marco!" she called again.

"Polo!" came a chorus from all around her.

This time Celia ducked down into the water and kicked off to the left, holding her nose with one hand and swiping the other one ahead of her to try and make contact. Still, she felt nothing and came up to the surface for air.

"Marco!"

"Polo!"

A set of knuckles bopped her on the top of her bathing-capped head, and she grabbed, too late, for the hand.

"Marco!"

"Polo!" came a voice close by, and Celia kicked backward off the rough pool floor fast enough to crash her head and shoulders into a hard, bony chest. Having made contact, she could now open her eyes.

"You're *It*!" she shouted, turning to see who she'd caught. It was Ray, a boy who lived in Yiayia's building. He glared at her and then tugged the strap of her swimsuit hard enough to pull it from her shoulder, leaving a scratch that burned slightly in the pool water.

"Hey!" she screamed, grabbing for the strap and scratching herself further with her own nails in the bargain. She balled her other hand into a fist and struck out hard, catching him on one ear. He glared at her in surprise, and for a minute Celia thought he was going to beat her up for real. But instead he laughed in her face.

"Saw your titties," he leered, and then he swam away, shouting "Marco!" with his eyes shut. The game moved toward the deep end of the pool, where Celia couldn't stand. Julie swam off with the others. Celia hopped on her tippy toes off the pool bottom and took a few clumsy strokes forward, sinking deeper with each one until she came up sputtering, like always. Now she was over her head, her eyes squinched shut against the chlorine. As her outstretched toes touched down, she gasped and water burned down her nose and throat. She began flailing wildly. Suddenly a strong pair of hands grasped her arms and lifted her up and back into the air. She was staring into the face of a tall, bearded man.

"You okay, little fish?" he asked, laughing. He carried her a few feet back in the direction from which she's come. "Maybe you should learn to swim before you head out to sea," he advised, giving her a little push that propelled her even further toward the shallows. When she reached down one foot, it bumped roughly against the coarse concrete bottom of the pool. Celia stood still for a moment, wiping the water from her face, and then wandered back toward the roped off children's section, thick with five-year-olds, trying hard to look as if she didn't care.

Why was her mother wasting her money on piano lessons, when what she needed was someone to teach her to swim, she wondered impatiently. The sun beat down and her skin tickled as it dried in the heat. She sat in the knee-high water, letting the cool wash over her again. The screams of *Marco* and *Polo* came from far away. They had forgotten her already. She had to learn to swim this summer. She'd just die if she didn't. But she couldn't let anyone see her try. If Ray and his friends found out she couldn't swim, they would chase her and throw her into the deep end. Once, a long time ago, she dreamed she was drowning in a pool full of water the green of the walls in the hallways of her building. Pea soup green. Puke green, her friend Katie called it. She woke in terror.

Now she let herself move in a little deeper. Still, her head and chest topped the water where she stood. She held her nose and ducked under. Part of the problem was that she was afraid to let go of her nose when her head was under water. That meant she could only stroke with one arm. Like Mr. Liu, the man who lived in the apartment next door to theirs. He had only one arm. That day, when she was seven, and they moved into the giant building – as big as an entire city block, so big she was afraid she would get lost and never find her way home – Mr. Liu held the elevator door open with his one arm while Celia's mother dragged bag after bag of their clothes to the apartment, down the long hallway. He, like most of the people in their new neighborhood, was Chinese. Celia couldn't help staring at his empty sleeve, pinned back to the shoulder of his white shirt. She didn't understand what he was trying to tell her.

"The wall, the wall," he said, pointing at the sleeve. "Lost in the wall." He shook his head, sadly. Celia had imagined, with horror, the arm lying somewhere, maybe in the space between their two apartments. Later her mother explained that he had lost an arm in the *war*, probably back in China. If Mr. Liu had found his arm, could it have been reattached? She thought of the three-legged rat they had seen this morning. Even a starfish could regrow a leg, why not rats, or people? She looked at her own hands. Her fingers were prune-y with water and she climbed the ladder to dry land.

Celia smoothed her towel out along an empty stretch of the bleachers. She had left Yiayia deep in gossip with one of the neighbors. The neighbor's granddaughter Marissa – younger than Celia by two years – was off at a swim lesson. Whenever Celia begged her for lessons, Yiayia snorted and said it didn't take lessons to learn how to swim. She said it was foolish to spend good money on being taught something that just came naturally. Yiayia said that in Greece everyone swam, even before they walked. The people of Skiathos – their island – were among the most beloved subjects of Poseidon, who gave them their beautiful pink sand beaches as a token of his love along with the ability to swim like creatures of the sea. She told Celia wonderful stories of the Nereids, daughters of the sea, and the Naiads, nymphs who lived in the streams and brooks. If Celia had grown up on Skiathos, Yiayia claimed, she would swim as naturally as she breathed. But Celia was growing up on the island of Manhattan, where the surrounding water was cold and smelled of rotting garbage and little girls like her might live their whole lives without ever being able to swim.

Celia didn't want to hear one word about the swim class when the little girl returned. It was bad enough they would be stuck togeth-er for the rest of the day. To avoid seeing her now, Celia told Yiayia that Julie's family had invited her to sit with them, and she promised to be back in an hour. It wasn't a total lie. They did invite her, all the time. But instead of joining Julie, her mother and her bratty little brother, Celia found a spot high on the concrete bleachers with a good view of the action in the pool and a little more elbowroom than down below, where everyone was jumbled tight. She imagined herself high on a rocky cliff overlooking a pink sand beach. Celia rolled up her tee shirt from bottom to top, placed it carefully at one end like a pillow and then lay down on her belly to bake in the sun.

With her eyes closed she might be anywhere, she thought. Any-place under the sun. Maybe even on Skiathos with Mami and Aunt Eleni and Uncle Marcus, drifting in the midday heat. The splash of pool water might be waves on the sand, the shrieking children, birds in the trees. What kinds of birds lived on the island? There were the high flying falcons, and the greenshanks, with their long skinny legs wading through the water, but those were the only ones she could name. And even these she pictured mainly as the bright, flat images her mother had hung on her bedroom walls, or on the pages of books. Although they had visited once when Celia was six, Skiathos seemed farther and farther away each year – more like once-upon-a-time than a real place – and Aunt Eleni and Uncle Marcus were almost like strangers now when she spoke to them on the phone.

Things change, Mami said. Celia thought about the stories her mother told about their lives when they first came to America. That first year, according to Mami, Celia took one look at the bare brown trees and burst into tears. She said Celia shouted out in her sleep every night for a month as the icy branches clacked against each other and tapped at the bedroom window in the wind. They all lived together then. Mami and Celia in one room, Yiayia and Papa in the next. Celia didn't remember much about it. But even now, every time spring finally arrived it felt like a surprise, like over the winter she had forgotten that trees could be green and whispery. In the new apartment, their windows were higher than the treetops. She enjoyed what Mami called a Bird's Eye View.

The sun was scorching and Celia flipped over onto her back. Through the scrim of her lashes, the sky was a dazzling, wheeling thing, dizzying and sweet. When she closed her eyes, shapes continued to wheel, orange and black. Things change.

Fourteen, fifteen, sixteen, seventeen, eighteen: Pia counted the steps up to each landing, and finally to the acid glare of 42th Street. Finding herself mid-block and facing two-way traffic, she looked left and then right, taking her bearings. North, South, East, West – *which was which?* Pia paused at the edge of the sidewalk, momentarily confused. A woman carrying a huge leather satchel brushed by. A man jostled her elbow. A bicycle messenger swung past just beyond the curb, wafting a sweatsoaked breeze. It's a stink-o town, she thought. To her left, the buildings receded downhill, framed by a bleached sky. To her right, they grew in stature and thickened into an impenetrable glass and concrete mass. That way, then, would be east. She walked to the next corner. Indeed, it was Seventh Avenue and she felt a small stab of triumph. She was determined to learn to navigate the most secret channels of the city's steel heart. In less than a month, she had memorized the stops of both the local and express trains that ferried her between Brooklyn and the maelstrom that was midtown. Back home – the place that *used* to be home, she reminded herself – her father had taught her early to navigate by the sky: by day, the clouds billowed from the North over Cayuga Lake; by night, the Dippers, Big and Little, pointed like a compass rose.

"As long as you can see the sky, you'll never be lost," he'd told her dozens of times, as they plied the waters of the Finger Lakes in his 27-foot cutter, *Despina II*. The little town of Ulysses, where he had lived in a converted boathouse, was divided by the lake from the tiny hamlet of Penelope where she and her mother lived, outside the city of Ithaca. Each weekend of her childhood, she had shuttled between them. When the weather was good, her father met her at the rickety dock between J & B Liquors and the bus station. In the early morning fog, the prevailing northwesterly wind carried the familiar sound of his outboard motor to her ears even before she could clearly make out the man who stood at the helm, dark and solidly rooted to the stained deck. Her father was a tall man with arms like weathered mahogany, so long that they could wrap around her skinny little girl body almost twice when she was a child. In the sailing season, he'd made his living renting his boat and his services as captain to the tourists who crowded the lakeside communities. In winter he'd worked at a small shipyard, outfitting the boats of rich patrons with cabinetry of exotic woods.

When it was stormy, or when winter had chilled Cayuga Lake almost stiff, he let her ride the bus, which he dubbed her ocean liner, and met her as she stepped from its gangplank. Although he had lived in New York City, not far from Brighton Beach in Brooklyn, until he was seventeen, he had been, all his upstate New York life, a sailor without recourse to the salty sea, she thought. Poseidon of a freshwater realm, and she, his daughter, the nymph Despina – *Despina I* to her father – and Pia to the world at large.

And then, just weeks before her fourteenth birthday, he was gone. *Sudden cardiac arrest initiated by arrhythmia* was the official cause of death noted by the autopsy. He was found in his bed – the telephone receiver in his hand – by his best friend, Frank, whose turn it was to carpool them to work. Pia had seen him only days before. All she could remember of their afternoon together was the argument that ended it – her insistence that he not attend the annual Christmas concert at her school, which she insisted was *completely lame.*

"You're breaking my heart, baby," her father moaned. Okay, it was only an expression, but still. Even now, the image persisted of her father waking alone in the dark of night and dialing a number – hers? – in a cry for help. Pia and her mother clung together in their grief, but the tighter they gripped, the more something hard insinuated itself between them. And Pia, sampling the early joys of adolescent rebellion, suddenly found herself turning into the conformist's conformist, minding every rule and getting a sticky rep as a teacher's pet and general suck-up. Throughout that long winter and into the spring, Pia trailed her mother around the house, half-believing this parent, too, would be snatched from her.

Standing on the avenue, Pia checked her watch. She had ten minutes to get to her first interview of the day, at a small ad agency on Seventh Avenue, between 37th and 38th Streets. She pulled the strap of her portfolio higher on her shoulder and set off, walking with the tide of buses and taxis heading downtown. She had three interviews lined up today. Pressed against her side in the heavy vinyl case was a sampling of the drawings and designs she had worked on in college and all last year as she sketched and saved and laid plans for her departure. In the year since she graduated with her BA in Art, aside from a couple of paintings she had done for friends, and some layout work for the local weekly paper, her paying work had mainly consisted of waitressing at Granelli's, serving enormous bowls of overcooked pasta drowning in red sauce that bore a striking resemblance to the Ragu her mother ladled up at home.

Periodically, she made forays into Mr. Granelli's office bearing bold new menu designs or a series of potential newspaper ads for the local papers. The office smelled of cherry tobacco and the walls were hung with the awful floral watercolor paintings done, he once told her, by his mother, when she lived in "the home." Each time Pia confronted him with new ideas, he nodded and smiled and patted her in a mildly patronizing fashion as he led her back to the dining room. The local papers ran with skeleton graphics staffs, and the few design shops in the area offered only unpaid internships and no immediate prospect for getting properly hired. But her designs, and their execution, were good, and she was determined to find work where she could hone her talents.

In a way, it was her father who made it possible for Pia to make the break to the city, although he himself had abandoned Brooklyn to go to college someplace without sodium vapor streetlights and had never looked back. While Pia had never even met her paternal grands – they had moved out of the city shortly after he did, and lived the rest of their lives in a small town in North Carolina – her father's Aunt Ida, his mother's youngest sister, had made the trip upstate when Pia was born and had sent her a birthday check for ten dollars every year since. For her part, Pia had made sure to send Aunt Ida annual Christmas cards, even though she had never laid conscious eyes on the woman. That had to count for something, Pia thought. It took her weeks to look up the number and get up the nerve to make the call.

"I don't expect you to take me in, like an orphan or something," Pia told her over the phone after she explained who she was. "I was hoping, though, you might have some advice where I could find a reasonably cheap place to live."

"You're family, that's all I need to know," she said, to Pia's amazement. "Everyone else is gone – your daddy, my sister and brother. I got a room here will be empty end of May. You want it, it's yours child."

The timing of Pia's move couldn't have been better. Her mother had just announced that she had decided to move in with the man she had been seeing for several years – an oenologist with a part interest in a local winery – and with Pia's departure, she could sell their house and invest the money in the antiques business she had dreamed of starting. Pia packed up the little she owned and rented a U-Haul van for the one-way trip to her new life.

Aunt Ida's house – one in a short row of late 1800s Romanesque brick villas just off Eastern Parkway – had clearly been elegant in its day. Even now, broken as it was into boardinghouse rooms, it was meticulously kept up – the yard mown, the wrought iron fence painted and rust-free – and stood out in a neighborhood notable for its precipitous decline. The other boarders included two hospital orderlies, a car mechanic and a woman who sewed baby blankets for a small local business. Pia's great-aunt, who turned out to be a scant five feet of feisty capability, warned her not to dawdle on the streets between the subway stop and home, not to shop in the bodega at the end of the block, where more drugs than milk were sold, to keep a tight grip on her handbag, and to show a little attitude when she walked. For the first time in her life, Pia felt herself part of an extended black family. And if Aunt Ida thought it was strange to find herself giving a home to her twentythree-year-old half-white niece whom she had only seen in a bassinet through a glass window, she didn't let on.

In New York City, Pia would become the artist she was meant to be. She'd find a way into that heady, thrilling world where people spoke in form and color and distinguished themselves with pen and brush – and spray can. She would, at last, find a way to expose her own true colors.

At first, Pia was almost wild-eyed with a combination of wonder and anxiety. The headlines in the papers didn't help: "Schoolyard Knifing Leaves Two Dead," "Black, Hassidic Rift Widens," "Bus Hijacker Tells Why He Killed," "Stalk Sam Year After First Kill." After a couple of weeks though, she imagined she had begun to look just about as poker-faced and unflappable as everyone else in the neighborhood. In fact, she was sure she did, since the number of street people and panhandlers approaching her dropped off sharply. Some progress, she thought. I now look as unforgiving as everyone else. Secretly, however, she was proud.

Now Pia stood at the corner of 37th Street, without having found the number of the building she was searching for. She turned and retraced her steps, looking more carefully, but still in vain. Had she misread the address in the ad? Could she have written the wrong number in her datebook? She would be late if she didn't find it soon. That was never a good start, she thought. Once again, she turned and walked slowly up to the next corner, eyeing each storefront: a barbershop (*Mike is Back!*); a window full of cheap imported shoes; another lined with doughnuts, their sugary glazes sweating in the heat; a pair of glass revolving doors only ten numbers off from the one she wanted, as if it were purposely mocking her. At 38th she turned once more, which was when she noticed the small awning marking an entrance a few steps in from the corner. Despite its location on the sidestreet, it held an avenue address – why hadn't the guy told her this over the phone? – and she entered to find the agency's name among those listed in removable type behind a glass frame. *KLC Inc.* -- *12th floor.* The lobby was small, grimy, unattended and distinctly un-air-conditioned. She rang for an elevator and watched the elaborate brass pointers creep slowly around a half-moon as both cars ferried other passengers upward. She would definitely be late. And sweaty, to boot. She could positively feel her hair escaping into a wild froth at the nape of her neck, soon to spread into an inky halo defying any effort at sophistication.

"So, how many words a minute do you type?"

Pia had hardly unzipped her portfolio before this question was lobbed at her by the beefy gentleman in the ill-fitting sports jacket who had introduced himself to her only as Gary.

Gary No-Last-Name appeared to be the proprietor and sole employee. At first, when she knocked on the door and he opened it, she was certain she was in the wrong place. The room was barely as wide as her own bedroom, and a single small air conditioner rattled away impotently in the one grit-smeared window. Two desks and a drawing table nearly filled all the available space. The surface of one of the desks was completely covered with stacks of brochures and magazines. Its chair was stacked with more paper. A displaced telephone sat on the floor next to it. The drawing table was likewise occupied, although the piles were considerably lower and, she guessed, would allow her to exhibit her work.

Gary cleared the week's worth of *Daily News* off another chair and pulled it up to the far side of the other desk, gesturing for her to take a seat and then swiping a line of sweat off his upper lip.

"As you can see, we're a small, independent agency," he said, as he shoved a box of doughnuts toward her, and promptly filled the space it had vacated with the folded newspaper ("City Offers PBA Pay, Hours Deal"). A gesture of offering, or an effort to redistribute space, Pia couldn't tell. In fact, the whole arrangement reminded her of nothing more than one of those children's games where individual tiles slid about in a frame that allowed only one to move at a time. If you could slide the tiles in just the right order, you might make sense of the picture they comprised. Pia had been a wiz at those things.

She ignored the question and offered to show him her work.

"Oh, I'm sure it's very good, but we need someone who can *do it all*, as they say."

Sweet, practiced smile pasted on her face, Pia propped the carrying case against the table and, with a slight flourish triggered more by nerves than bravado, she unzipped it as if she hadn't heard a word. Xeroxes of ads she'd created as assignments and on spec fluttered to the floor. As she dove to retrieve them she knocked hands with Gary, who had left his desk and crossed the room with two steps.

"Excuse me," they said in one voice. There isn't room for two in here, Pia thought. We'd even have to talk on top of each other.

As she showed her work, Gary *hmm*-ed and furrowed his brow and looked completely perplexed.

"I majored in art and art history, but took most of my classes in graphic and industrial design," she told him. "I won the statewide Mary McBurney graphic design competition my junior year and designed the yearbooks for both Ithaca College, where I went to school, and Cornell University, just down the road."

His visage settled into a semblance of nodding appreciation. Each time Pia looked up from her portfolio, Gary's face became more florid. Beads of sweat had re-formed along his upper lip and were growing more pronounced each minute. Finally, he mopped at them with a hanky pulled from his back pocket.

"So, how many words a minute do you type?" he asked once again. "And have you ever done any bookkeeping?"

The smile was drying up and puckering off Pia's lips as she zipped the folder and retreated to the stifling elevator cab. She composed herself as the elevator creaked its way downward; she still had two more interviews today and could not afford to lose her cool in this heat.

Less than twenty minutes after she had arrived, Pia was back in the hot and shabby lobby. She leaned against a wall and opened her portfolio, checking that its contents were safely stacked. Despite the firm handshake and promise of a call that hastened her on her way, Pia was certain this job, like the dozen that preceded it, would not be hers. She did not like to admit that she could barely knock off forty words a minute – and that, with errors. She practically flunked typing in eighth grade and hunt-and-pecked her way through college, favoring classes with projects rather than papers. The ad she'd answered was for an assistant graphic designer, for god's sake. Not a Gal Friday.

In the lobby she checked the zipper on the portfolio one last time and then hoisted her burden and made for the door. She had been warned that the market was tough, but believed that talent and energy would find a way. So far, the only thing she had found was that her money was running out faster than she could have ever imagined. Her aunt was generously letting her have the room for free, but could only afford to do that till the end of the month. After that, Pia would have to meet the going rent for a single room – two hundred dollars a month – or move out and let her aunt rent to someone else. If Pia didn't find something soon, it would be back to waiting tables – if she could even pull that down in this city full of desperate job seekers. There wasn't even any *home* back home for her to slink off to – her mother's house had gone to contract last week and there was no room for Pia at the tiny cottage where the new couple now lived.

But what really galled her was the nerve of men to cast every woman into the role of secretary. What if she had applied for a job as an electrician? Or a cabinet maker, or subway conductor? Bricklayer. Pastry chef. Thoracic surgeon. Astrophysicist? Pia feared the results would be the same, and the dread T-word would arise in each interview. Maybe, given the racial climate, she should be grateful that they didn't ask if she did windows. She felt the anger rising up her throat and took a deep breath to ward it off. She couldn't afford to generate any more heat or she'd look like a cross between a stewed prune and Jimi Hendrix for her next interview. She hummed a few bars of Laura Nyro under her breath as she walked out onto the street. *"Well I got a lot of patience baby; that's a lot of patience to lo-o-o-ose."*

"When did you first begin to acknowledge your fears about your vision?"

Danielle flexed one bare foot and then the other as she lay on the classic black leather couch in the classic therapist's office. It had been her ophthalmologist, Dr. Schein's who suggested she see this woman. Danielle hadn't expected the whole Freudian set-up – the couch and all – but she hadn't been in the mood to look elsewhere. She'd been seeing the shrink once a week, even though it wasn't easy to get a break in the middle of her day in the kitchen. She finally resorted to a lie about needing to see an allergist for asthma shots – a specialist whose available hours were limited. Without them she might suffer an attack, she added. A matter of life and breath, she told Chef, with a grimace.

During the first sessions, she just lay there for most of the allotted fifty minutes, hardly saying a word. She wished that the shrink – Karen – would come out and ask her some leading questions, anything to break the silence. Danielle stared at the ceiling. She scratched one stockinged foot with the other. She tried to read the titles of the many books neatly housed in the glassed-front bookcases. Tried to guess what Karen was doing in the deep swivel chair just behind her head. Occasionally, she heard the scratch of pen on paper. Doodling? Judging? What really irritated Danielle was the strategically placed box of tissues on the floor next to the couch. The unspoken imperative that she lose control, fall apart, in front of this total stranger. She might talk, she thought, but she wouldn't cry.

Sometimes, she stealthily kicked the box under the couch with a toe as she lay down. Out of sight, out of mind.

Then one day she stubbed her toe on her way to the couch and let loose with a string of curses that would have sent a sailor straight to hell. By the time she screamed her final "fuck you," she was in tears. In a blur, she felt about for the damned tissues. In no time at all she was weeping through sessions, although still not parting with much information. That was almost three months earlier. Having moved through silence and tears, Danielle was finally ready to broach the subject of her impending blindness. Last week she told Karen about closing her eyes on the train and sometimes, when she thought no one was looking, at work. Karen had asked her if she wanted to harm herself. Did she? She lay quietly and squinted at the books again.

"What are you thinking about?" Karen asked now.

"Nothing. A million things all at once. Meatloaf. I don't know."

"Just tell me the first thing that comes to mind."

Danielle waited in silence, her eyes closed, until a single image coalesced.

It was early fall, not quite three years earlier. Although it was barely seven, the sky outside the diner was almost black. Danielle scooped the last bites of a gyro platter onto her fork with a corner of pita. The waitress – the same one who had served them on their way upstate, still sporting a vaguely heart-shaped stain on her uniform – came by their end of the counter and, over their protests, splashed more coffee into their cups. Paul asked for the check. While they waited, he leaned over and put his head on Danielle's shoulder and sighed.

"I'm wiped," he said. "Do you think you could drive?"

It was a three-hour trip to Paul's Manhattan apartment from the little furnished house in Tannersville they'd rented for the summer and fall. It was a cheap way to escape the city – the area was mainly a ski resort, and landlords were willing to let the shabby houses go for nothing in the summer. Well, nothing compared with places in Fire Island, or the Hamptons, where a half-share in a cottage on the beach could cost a month of Danielle's meager salary.

Outside, a gust of wind blew sheets of water against the long window, making the diner seem to Danielle more like a boat foundering in a storm. She rubbed her eyes. They'd been hiking for two days, and last night she had hardly gotten any sleep in the lumpy bed. She'd had a lingering bleariness all day. It was another two hours back to the city. Still, he had done all the driving, so far.

"Sure." She drank half the tepid coffee in her mug, astounded that something could be so watery and so bitter at the same time. A coppery-colored taste.

By the time they paid the check and left, the rain had slowed to a steady downpour. The country road flew slickly past the windows. It was so incredibly dark. The few houses they passed seemed deserted, or else inhabited by people who were already in their beds. The mountains were sooty shoulders against a black sky.

Each time the rare oncoming car appeared, Danielle found herself momentarily disoriented by multiple reflections of the headlights on the wet road and distorted refractions on the windshield. She forced herself to look obliquely at the right edge of the road for guidance and to hold the wheel steady without over-steering. She hated driving in the rain or the dark, but this was something she didn't want Paul to know, and she had managed to keep from him for the two years they'd been dating.

"Do you know why?" Karen's voice broke in now.

"Why what?"

"Why you didn't want him to know you didn't like driving in the dark."

Danielle realized that while she had been talking, she'd picked a cuticle bloody. She stuck the finger in her mouth and sucked on it, buying herself a moment of silence. She heard Karen swivel her chair.

"No reason. I don't know. He was kind of a jerk about these things. He'd tease me." She pressed around the edges of the torn cuticle. The bleeding had stopped, but the short, sharp pain was centering. "I just don't like people knowing my failings, I guess."

Danielle pursed her lips and thought back to that night.

He was already half asleep, his head resting against the seat-back, his breath steadying to a soft and regular sigh. The windshield wipers smeared the water like grease across the glass with every pass. When was the last time he'd replaced them?

Danielle tuned around the stations, looking for music, but got mostly static. She turned the radio off and instead, began amusing herself by conjuring new recipes she might develop. Meatloaf – that would be good. She began to play with new ideas for meatloaf. What about adding shallots instead of onions? Too subtle. How about curry powder? Too monotonal. Jalapeños? The taste struck her as too intensely purple in nature. Grated extra-sharp cheddar? Hey, that might be interesting. Her tongue anticipated what her brain conceived, a color paired with each flavor, and before she knew it, she had made it to the Thruway.

She jockeyed the hulking Buick Le Sabre through the tollbooth like a thoroughbred into the starting gate, collecting the cardboard ticket from a pair of thick wool gloves, and then looked for the sign for Thruway South. The wind had picked up again and tossed the rain roughly against the window, rocking the car slightly. Danielle steered right, then suddenly left, as she realized her mistake. A truck behind her blasted its air horn and Paul sat up, saying, "Wuzzamatter?"

"Nothing. Go back to sleep. It's just hard to see."

Hard to see. Now, plunging down the road at highway speed, it was harder than ever. She increased the speed of the wipers so that they whipped back and forth manically. The taillights ahead were some help in steering, but they seemed to be getting fainter and fainter. The racing wipers were making her queasy and she slowed them once more. Cars were hurtling past on both her left and right and Danielle realized that she must be driving more slowly than anyone else on the road. Which was strange, since she was generally the person in the left lane leading the pack.

But it was so hard to see. How were all those other drivers managing it? Curves in the road came at her by surprise and Danielle gritted her teeth and tightened her grip on the wheel until her knuckles showed white. Her heart was pounding all the way to her throat; she had to calm down. She'd driven this road a hundred times. There were no surprises on the Thomas E. Dewey Thruway. They designed it that way. Wide shoulders, subtle turnings, long sightlines.

Suddenly Danielle twisted around on the couch to face Karen squarely.

"What time is it?" She couldn't afford to be late getting back to the restaurant. She couldn't afford to do anything there that would call any negative attention to herself.

Karen reached out and touched her shoulder. She had never touched her before. Wasn't this against the Freudian code or something? Danielle tried to cover up her flinch with a cough. "I just can't be late," she said.

"You've got ten minutes left."

The rain had clattered against the roof of the car. Each time they sped under an overpass the sudden absence of noise startled her and made the resuming sound louder and more raucous. The cars ahead of her were slipping away into darkness. Headlights from the northbound side taunted her. The road teased her. Turn left – no, right. The pavement markings had faded. Why didn't they maintain them better?

Meatloaf. Think about meatloaf, she told herself. A sign read ROAD WORK – 1/2 MILE. Danielle's meatloaf turned to gruel in her mouth. A moment later another read Lane Shift with a bunch of wriggly arrows heading off into space. Shift? Where? She sat forward in her seat blinking and squinting her eyes to get a better view. The road narrowed and enormous machines reared up on either side and immediately disappeared. Her glasses were sliding down her nose and Danielle hurriedly snatched at them with one hand and pushed them back up. They seemed dirty. Hadn't she just cleaned them?

Water on the roadway splashed up against the tires and Danielle nudged the wheel in tiny increments, right and left, staring as hard as she could. Now pale new road markings led across the highway's seams and as she tried to follow them, it felt to Danielle that the car had lifted slightly from the pavement and was floating, floating along at whim. She held her breath. Bile filled the back of her throat and she forced it down. She imagined the headlines: Downstate couple killed in Thruway mishap.

"Paul," she finally managed to whisper hoarsely. "Paul, wake up." Her hands ached from their hold on the wheel, but she kept steering. "Paul, I can't see."

He looked up. "Yeah, it's bad out there. If it's really bothering you, pull over under the next overpass." He rubbed his eyes.

He didn't get it. She couldn't pull over. That would require lifting her gaze from the road in front of her, when she could neither look left nor right, not even to check her mirrors. Their lives depended on it.

"You're failing to grasp the situation here," she shouted. "I can't see!"

"Whoa, you're okay. You're only doing about 50."

"I. Can't. See." She blinked quickly at the speedometer. Not *even* 50.

"Then pull over."

"I *can't*." Now she was sniveling. That made it worse. This was hell, wasn't it? The place where she would be forced forever to drive blind, or die.

"Look, we're almost at the tolls," Paul said. "See? There's the lights."

Danielle let herself glance quickly in the direction he pointed.

"It's wide here. You can change lanes. There's no one on your right." He spoke in measured sentences, like talking to a child. Or a crazy person. "Slow way down. Head for those phone booths."

She could see them faintly. The lights weren't much, but they helped. Painstakingly, she maneuvered the car in their direction, and then stopped. Her fingers released their hold on the wheel, and she began to cry in earnest.

Danielle squinted against the glare as she left the building where Karen had her office. Everything flows from left to right.

That's what she told herself as she listened for cars at the corner before stepping off the curb, eyes closed. Two steps and then eyes open. This is *not* a death wish, she told herself. It's preparation. She brought her wrist close to her face and checked her watch. Just 11:20. She had ten minutes to get back to work, start the water to boil for the pasta special, and chop cilantro into the salsa. It was no mean feat to make it up to Union Square for her session and back downtown in the resentfully allotted time – "and not one second more, if you value your job" as Chef so clearly put it.

After that night when the car and the darkness had threatened to merge into a single killing entity, Danielle had found a thousand reasons to avoid seeing a doctor. Too busy, too expensive, too absurd, she was sure it was something that she ate, or didn't eat, or a fever heralding a virus, and indeed, she did come down with a major cold – maybe even the flu – the following week, complete with body aches and a migraine that caused her to walk drunkenly and bounce off the walls in the long corridor leading to the freezers in the basement at work.

"Have you made an eye doctor appointment yet?" Paul asked repeatedly, until she threatened to stop seeing him altogether.

There was no reason to, really. It was the fever, the food, the long hike in the mountains and not enough water. That's it, she thought – she was dehydrated. The food at the diner was salty. Sometimes she found herself standing at her station in the kitchen closing one eye at a time, testing the view. Hasn't that calendar always been too far away to read, she would ask herself. Weren't the numbers on that dial always faint and scratchy? She refused to believe anything less. But she stopped driving at night. Then she stopped driving completely.

Paul called one Friday and asked if she wanted to see *Marathon Man*. She had also stopped going to movies. The theaters were too dark – a person could get hurt just trying to find a seat. How did people do it? And the pictures were rarely in focus.

She started taking a multivitamin she bought at the health food store. And extra vitamin A, E, and selenium, which the young man behind the counter insisted were especially good for the eyes.

She began to pay extra for organic fruits and vegetables. She thought it all might be helping.

Arriving late for work one day – it was February and the trains were snarled by frozen track signals, or at least that's what the garbled announcement seemed to be saying – she began her prep work as quickly as possible. No one else was in the kitchen this early in the morning, so no one would know she'd been twenty minutes late, but she had a ton of work to do and she had promised to cover for Amy, the pastry chef, and start the yeast batter for a sweet *stollen* cake. She stirred a few scoops of yeast and some sugar into a bowl of wrist-temperature milk and set it near the radiator to become foamy. She figured she had about fifteen minutes to let the yeast soften and begin multiplying before she could add the flour and the rest of milk to make the sponge.

In the meantime, she brought up an armful of vegetables from the cooler and mounded piles of them on the counter. She set about peeling and slicing. But as she reached for another handful of carrots to julienne, she felt a freezing and then burning sensation along the entire side of her left hand. First thought: she had been stung by a wasp. Last fall she had been stung by some bees as she jogged in Central Park. The pain, a mild prick followed by a deeply scorching throb, was not so dissimilar. But where would a wasp come from in the dead of winter? She swung her head to look.

There was no wasp of course, but where it might have been, the large utility knife rested, its honed blade facing in toward her on the countertop. Danielle recoiled in a flash and as her hand clenched into a fist, she distinctly felt the skin separate and both sides of the deep slice pull away from where they had once been joined. Blood first oozed, then ran, down her wrist, her forearm, and dripped onto the countertop. There was no pain, and then there was plenty of it and she grabbed her wounded left hand in her right and turned the pinky side toward her mouth. She licked the salty slit. She sucked deeply. She hadn't expected so much blood. It filled her mouth and overwhelmed her with nausea. The blood was red of course, but the taste was a bilious green. She spit and the blood was everywhere. The carrots, the beans, the broccoli, the tomatoes, all were spattered, all were tainted. The countertop looked like a bloody scene of Homeric slaughter. Everything had to be thrown out. Danielle wrapped her hand in a dishcloth to clean up, but by the time she was done, the cloth was saturated with her blood. She threw the soaked rag in the trash and wrapped up in another, which was drenched and dripping blood in minutes. Panicking, she locked the doors, even knowing that the code of the kitchen demanded that she finish her shift, and fled to the emergency room at Downtown Hospital where she had to wait two hours to be seen by a resident. All around her, people napped and moaned, children cried, orderlies swabbed grime from the floors and nurses shuttled back and forth through swinging doors. The cut itself took six stitches to close and she had to explain to a furious Chef, when she finally got back to the kitchen, why his prep was left undone.

She hadn't seen the knife. *She hadn't seen it*, although it was right at hand. He let her off with a warning that the kitchen was no place for carelessness and that he would have his eye on her. No matter how hard Danielle tried to find one, there were no more excuses to hold back the fear. The scar now looked like a small run of toy train tracks, and a drawing pain at the site foretold bad weather.

When she finally screwed up the courage to see Dr. Schein, an ophthalmologist who came highly recommended by her gynecologist – the only doctor Danielle had ever seen regularly – Danielle tried to make light of the incidents that had brought her there. Sitting in the small SoHo office, she explained her symptoms but made jokes about seeing-eye bats and a blind woman walks into a bar – *oof!* But Dr. Schein failed to joke back.

"Is there any history of eye disease in your family?" she asked.

Dr. Schein was the type of woman who looked good in tailored suits and what Danielle thought of as *ladies' shoes*, with demurely pointy toes and neatly tapered heels. She examined Danielle in a dimmed room with sleek sculptural equipment, buffed black and silver. The furniture in the waiting room was Jensen Lewis modern. Dr. Schein apparently had a thing for Lucite cubes, artfully placed. Even the art was hard-edged and crystalline. It gave Danielle a chill.

"Has anyone in your immediate family lost their vision or hearing, or both?" she persisted. She spoke with the faint undertone of an accent Danielle could not place.

Danielle, whose chin rested in the hard notch of a large piece of ocular equipment, tried to shake her head an emphatic no.

"Hold still," said Dr. Schein.

A sudden puff of air on her eyeball made her jump.

"Sorry," said the doctor. "We need to check for glaucoma. We read the pressure off the eyeball with the puff of air."

Glaucoma. She didn't have glaucoma. That was a disease for old people. Surely, there was nothing to worry about there.

Dr. Schein continued to look at her eyes through an assortment of scopes, making notes and small humming sounds. "Look here, what do you see? Now here. Now over here." Often there was nothing to be seen in those places. Sometimes there were lights. "Gather your things and meet me in my office," the doctor said, rising from the rolling stool that she had propelled around the room from desk to scope, scope to desk. Danielle followed her out of the examining room and into another chilly modern setting.

The door to Dr. Schein's office was hung with a beautifully rendered painting of the Egyptian Eye of Horus. Parts of the eye – its black central pupil, surrounding iris and white sclera – were all labeled as if in a medical text. Danielle was about to knock when the doctor opened the door and waved her into a chair.

"Let me tell you about the eye," Dr. Schein had said, briskly, moving a large plastic eyeball into the center of her desk. "The ability to see is practically a miracle, highly dependent on the actions of several structures in and around the eyeball plus the work of the brain. When you look at an object, light rays are reflected from the object to the cornea, which is where the miracle begins."

At that point, Danielle pictured the cow eye she was supposed to have dissected in high school biology. She had gotten as far as Mr. Harris' opening gambit – "Think of the eye as a camera," and his tossing the cow eye into the air – before she had asked to be excused. Although she had already made it through the pith-ed frog, the idea of slicing into this tender orb was more than her stomach could bear.

"Think of the eye as a camera," Dr Schein said, and in her nervousness, it was all Danielle could do not to laugh. "A camera uses a lens and a film to produce an image." She began to break apart the model as she spoke, verbally labeling the parts as she subtracted them from the whole. "In the eye, the lens' job is to make sure the rays come to a sharp focus on the retina. The retina, like the film, then captures the image – which, by the way, is upside down – and converts the light rays to electrical impulses that are transmitted through the optic nerve to the brain to be developed."

Danielle sat weaving and reweaving her fingers in her lap. She crossed her legs, re-crossed them, and then placed both feet firmly on the carpeting, as she began to jiggle her ankle up and down. She tried to imagine where the doctor's accent might be from. Some part of France? The Mideast? Doctor Schein softly continued naming and pointing out individual parts of the orb in front of her.

"The brain processes the data and translates the impulses back into an image that is finally perceived in an upright position. If any one or more of these components is not functioning correctly, the result is a poor picture."

The model eye lay in pieces on the desk. Danielle was beginning to feel ill, just as she had in high school bio. The plastic parts of the eye – retina, sclera, iris, cornea, pupil, lens, conjunctiva, virtreous, choroids, optic nerve, macula, retina again – began to spin like a giant game of chance. Where would the pointer land, she wondered. Could it be that she had a brain tumor? That her macula was deteriorating? Would she need surgery? How did you stitch an eye back together again? Dr. Schein had stopped speaking. Danielle couldn't remember the last thing she'd heard her say. She was drenched in sweat.

"I'm sorry. I'm feeling a little dizzy. Could I have some water please?" she asked. The doctor got up and poured her a glass from a cooler in the corner of the room. She sat down in the chair next to Danielle.

"I wish I had something better to tell you."

Danielle couldn't recall exactly what the woman *had* told her and forced herself to say so. The doctor explained it once again, without hesitation, as though she had done this many times before.

Rod-cone dystrophy (Danielle first heard it as "Rod Cohen" and wondered briefly who he was and what he had done to get a disease named for him.) was a deterioration of the rod cells that presented as night blindness and progressed to the loss of peripheral vision. This would be followed by similar deterioration of the cone cells and along with them, her central vision. Retinitis Pigmentosa.

"RP isn't one disease, really," Dr. Schein continued. "It's a whole group of retinal diseases, almost all genetically transmitted. It can be inherited by at least three different methods. Severity and speed of vision loss vary with each form of inheritance. That's why it would be critical for you to talk to your family about their history. We might be able to predict the progress of your disease more accurately. As it is, I can only give you the common attributes, many of which you've already described."

The night blindness. The tunnel vision that rapidly began to worsen. The tendency to be literally blinded by the light when she walked outside in bright weather. Dr. Schein made it clear that these were all symptoms and could be expected to worsen, although she would not say how quickly. The doctor made it clear that there was "at present" no effective treatment or cure.

That was two years earlier. For a long time, the disease made no progress at all, leaving Danielle free to engage in magical thinking about mistaken diagnoses and spontaneous cures. In the past year, however, things had worsened considerably. Now, she moved her head to view things only inches to her left or right. She rushed home before dark and stayed there most evenings, and not just because of those hideous news reports about the serial killer who'd begun calling himself Son of Sam. She spent increasing amounts of time 'practicing.' When the darkness became final, she would be ready. She would. She ran through her assets. She had the skills, the smarts, the soul of a chef. And she had a plan. The kitchen was already an organized environment, where everything was kept in its place. How hard could it be? The right restaurant would respect her challenges. They would be proud to be part of a great experiment in equal opportunity.

Now, walking west toward the subway, Danielle looked up. Across the street, sitting in the second story window of another gray building on the Square was Andy Warhol, unmistakable, with his shock of pale hair and signature black turtleneck. New York City was a celebrity-spotting wonderland. From here in the street, Danielle felt free to stare. Besides, staring was a luxury she would soon lose. The artist was sitting as still as stone, turned slightly away from the window, maybe reading or just watching the passersby below. After a moment, Danielle turned to check the one-way street for cars. And just before she stepped off the curb, she looked up at the window once more. Warhol continued to sit. Suddenly though, Danielle realized that what she had thought was the man was only a mannequin, an optical illusion from a master of illusion. Laughing at her mistake, she stepped into the street, and narrowly missed being struck by a bicycle.

"What the fuck, lady?" the biker had screamed at her. "Look where you're fuckin' going!" And he sped off, against the flow of traffic.

Two near misses in one day.

Althea slid her shoulder bag to her wrist and walked quickly and smoothly toward her desk at the end of the long carpeted aisle. Anyone looking from the windowed offices on the far side of the cubicle walls might well have assumed she was just returning from the Ladies', she thought. She hoped. In fact, she had to go, desperately, but that would have to wait. So would a cup of coffee. As she neared her desk, she dipped and slid into her chair in one graceful movement and reached for a sharpened pencil from the mug that was crammed full of them. A large, spiral-bound accounting ledger was already on the desk and she opened it and began doodling in a corner, her head down, forehead furrowed. None of the women working at the desks around her looked up or said anything in greeting that would have called attention to her late arrival. She tapped in some random numbers and pumped the metal arm of the adding machine a couple of times in rhythm with her comrades. Then she tore off the narrow strip of white paper that emerged from the top, crumpled it and tossed it into the trash basket at her feet. Althea didn't dare look up at the large clock over the receptionist's desk. She knew she was late – knowing how late would only be a matter of additional distress.

The usual spot at the base of her neck ached. Her thighs were damp and burning where her stockings were twisted taut. She bent toward the columns of numbers on the pale green page, then jumped at the thump of a coffee mug hitting the wooden desktop just to her right. She turned toward the sound in time to see her friend Rita spin off in the opposite direction. Good to have friends. Good to have a job. She took a furtive sip of coffee and began to work in earnest.

On the left side of the desk, a large packet of receipts, on the right, the adding machine. In the center, what Althea thought of as The Big Book of Numbers. The original Big Book of Numbers – a glossy children's book she had bought to help Celia learn to count in English the year they arrived from Skiathos – now sat at home in a pile of other cast-off children's books, waiting to be donated to the community center. Althea's Big Book was full of serious numbers, though, tracking invoices and reimbursements, payments made and payments due – the lifeblood of Palmer and Burch, LLD.

She began to sift through the receipts and record them, but she couldn't keep her mind on the work. Did Celia remember to go the bathroom before she and her grandmother left for the pool, Althea wondered? Did she bring an extra pair of shoes so she wouldn't have to wear those plastic jelly sandals all day? Althea would have to call her mother's house later and check on these things. She added a few more numbers, then stopped to rub her eyes, as if to wipe the worry from her mind. She began to sail the pencil along the smooth desktop surface, like a *caique* plying the waters between the islands. The phone on her desk jangled.

"Bookkeeping, Althea speaking," she pronounced carefully into the mouthpiece.

"Althea? It's Oscar. I need to talk to you."

Althea could feel her cheeks begin to redden. She ducked lower in her chair.

"I'm sorry, Mr. Stanton," she said, in a slyly singsong voice, "I haven't got that information ready yet, perhaps this afternoon."

"Stop it, Althea. This is important." His words were clipped. Irritated. "Did you take care of that business we discussed last week? Did the receipts go through? Have you amended the dates?"

Althea spun the pencil around and around on the surface of the desk, a ship caught in a whirlpool.

"I'm sorry," she repeated.

"Listen to me, Althea. You need to get those receipts back. Just delete them from the books, okay?"

She kept up the charade of formality. "I'm sorry, sir, that won't be possible. Those accounts have already gone through."

"They couldn't have!"

"Well, they did. I'm looking at them right now. You can expect your check – "

"Althea!" I don't want the check. I want it stopped. This is urgent. We're expecting an audit. I need to get those expense sheets back."

Althea caught her breath. An audit. And he wanted the receipts recalled. She sailed the little *caique* between the rocky cliffs of two stacks of papers. Scylla and Charybdis. Danger.

"I'll meet you on the corner at one o'clock."

"I wasn't going to take a lunch break," she whispered into the receiver.

"Althea!" His voice hissed like an asp.

She cringed.

"All right," she sighed hoarsely into the phone. "One o'clock."

She replaced the phone in its cradle and snapped the little ship in two. Her stomach churned. What did Oscar want from her now? Althea wished she had never agreed to any of the small favors he asked, no matter how reasonable he made them sound. She pushed back her chair and rose quietly. Quickly, she walked toward the door, snatching the Ladies' Room key from where it rested in a deep ceramic ashtray on the reception desk. No one looked up as she slipped out into the gray hallway.

The women's bathroom was down the corridor, past the elevators and around a corner. It was shared with other companies on the floor but, oddly, Althea only rarely met another woman there. This time, however, as she turned the corner she noticed someone struggling with the door handle. Approaching the door, she realized that the other woman – neatly dressed and somewhat younger than herself, but clearly in distress – was trying to get in without the key. Uselessly, the girl yanked at the handle and shoved one shoulder against the heavy door. As she struggled, wild strands of hair escaped from the knot at the base of her neck and formed a frothy cloud around her head.

"Damn it," she muttered through clenched teeth. "Fuck and damn!"

Althea cleared her throat to make her presence known.

"You need a key," she said softly.

The girl looked up, startled. She was beautiful, Althea noticed – a small, perfectly symmetrical heart-shaped face with luminous green eyes set against skin as clear and fine as polished wood. Between her knees the girl balanced a large, black leather portfolio.

"I didn't know," the girl said, quickly bending to retrieve the folder. "I don't actually work here. I had an interview upstairs and I didn't realize how badly I needed to use the bathroom until I was halfway down the elevator. I just got off and hoped for the best."

As the girl spoke, Althea unlocked the door and held it open for her to enter.

She walked past Althea into the room while trying in vain to tuck her hair back into the bun with one hand. "The way my day is going, I'm lucky you're not having me arrested for breaking and entering." She disappeared into the nearest stall.

This young woman didn't have a clue about what a bad day really meant; of that, Althea was certain. She looked as clean and well cared for as the young goddess Hestia. She was probably out of college for the summer, looking for a temporary job to pay for the clothes daddy wouldn't buy. Althea examined her own reflection in the murky mirror over a bank of ancient sinks. With one finger, she swiped at the smudges of eye liner that had already migrated under each eye. The dark circles that remained, however, would not yield to her fingertip. They were the result of too many worries and too little sleep. Only yesterday, the mail had brought notice of a rent increase. And Celia's feet were rapidly outgrowing her shoes. She'd certainly need new ones for school. And now this business with Oscar. Althea sighed weakly and stepped into the stall at the far end of the row.

"You don't happen to work in publishing or advertising, do you?"

Was the woman talking to her? Althea's first impulse was to pretend she hadn't heard her. She had more important things to worry about than this girl's job search.

"No, sorry," she responded with what she hoped was finality. She needed to think. Be calm. There was no reason to panic. Oscar just wanted her to go into the books and take back the most recent claims he had made for reimbursement. He must have submitted them in error – maybe he grabbed the wrong receipts from his desk at home and discovered that he'd actually spent much less on car rental, room and entertainment on his last trip to D.C.

Althea hadn't even remembered that trip, or his being out of town last month at all. Still, Oscar pointed out that he asked little of her in return for the help and advice he gave. He said that he wanted to look after her. What, exactly, did he mean by that? In truth, Althea didn't want to know. The price she was paying for the guidance he gave her at the office was too high. The *little* he said he asked of her was more than she should be willing to give. She knew that was true, and she also knew she felt helpless to turn him away. Was it love? Was it fear? Sometimes Althea didn't know the difference any more.

Back at the sinks, Althea pulled some rough paper towels from the dispenser on the wall and folded them into a neat packet. This she ran under the cold water and wrung out before applying it to her temples and the back of her neck.

She continued to stare into the mirror until the cool compress began to have the desired effect. Her heartbeat began to slow and the mottled color began to fade from her cheeks. There. She looked much better. She straightened her skirt and turned to go, dropping the damp towels into an already overflowing basket.

From behind the closed door of the stall on the left Althea heard a muffled groan. She paused just for a moment. Should she ask if the girl was okay? Should she offer assistance? The toilet flushed, and Althea decided no, if the woman needed help, she would have called out. A sniffling whimper broke out, louder than the flush of water from the toilet. Don't get involved, Althea told herself.

Before she could get out of the room, however, the stall door opened and the women emerged. Her face was a mask of tragedy, long streaks of mascara crossing her cheeks from puffy eyes.

Despite her intentions, Althea found herself asking "Are you all right? Is there anything I can do?"

The woman stopped crying and looked at her defiantly.

"I think I should just give up," she said heatedly. "Sometimes that is best, don't you think? Please. Just tell me to give up and go home."

A crazy woman, Althea thought, handing her a tissue from her purse.

The girl blew her nose and Althea handed her another tissue. All over the city people are out of work, she thought. All over town girls are crying in dirty bathrooms. People are living in cardboard boxes next to the Manhattan Bridge. At least I have what matters most. A job. Celia. My self-respect. And I'm not crying to a stranger.

By now, the woman was rinsing her face in the cold water.

"Look, I'm sorry," she said to Althea, patting her cheeks dry. "I don't know what came over me. Maybe I shouldn't have skipped breakfast. Really. I don't need any help." She began to reapply her wrecked makeup.

Feeling dismissed, Althea began once more to leave the room. But she turned one last time and handed the girl the rest of her packet of tissues. It was all she had to give.

Chapter Four

Mud and slime, mud and slime, steel, steel, steel.
Rat's resilient skeleton flexed to slip beneath the
rail and avoid the oncoming train. Scuttle the bend,
another and another. Wedge of darkness;
slice of bedrock. Pockmarked. Rockdark. Belly full and
bumping steel.

Soot and steel: The road home.

Home: Six tiny mouths, a hole carved in the bedrock. Home-
hole, six naked pink bodies shuddering in a ball. Gaping
for teats full. Milkful. Sootcaked. Stretch and fill gray
furself to navigate steelandstink river.

Dangerdangerdangerdanger. Nothing but scream and
steelsteelsteel.

Aeiiiiiii. Rips thin eardrumskin. Rips the river, dark as knife.
Aeiiiiiiiiii, air rushes and fills, rushes and fills. *Aeiiiiiii.*
Aeiiiiiiiiiiiiii. No space left for anything but the howling.

No air but scream, no place but steel.

Collapsemybones thin as a slice. Sharp and sliverthin as steel.

No room, but the black howling swallows it up. Bodyflat into slime and soot. Deathdark electric beast wheezing overhead.

Rancid breath ruffles fur; sour vibrations shake from tail to teats.

Teats rubbed cinderraw, sootcaked, milksour: steelsourmilk.

Steelsourshriek. Hot wind grinding into sootandslime. Time passes, breathless.

Blackened howl rushes *aeiiiiiii* away down river of *aeiiiiii* steel.

Airhush. Darkhush. Pinprick constellations point the way home to feed babies.

On 46th Street, Pia took the newspaper off the top of the pile and handed two dimes to the man inside the booth. She had bought the paper for the classifieds, but couldn't stop herself from peeking inside for more of the continuing saga of the city's infamous killing spree. Just a few days ago, the *Daily News* columnist Jimmy Breslin had accused Mayor Beame of "Making a Porn Show Out of the .44 Case." He quoted the most recent letter sent to him by the murderer: *Sam's a thirsty lad and he won't let me stop killing until he gets his fill of blood.* He called on Beame and the police to step up the action and step down the politics.

People in Pia's Crown Heights neighborhood seemed only mildly caught up in the general alarm (her aunt had sniffed, "Crazy white boy," when Pia brought up the subject) but from what she saw on TV, the rest of the city was gripped with foreboding and the papers kept up a running commentary on the cat-and-mouse game the killer was playing with the police. Reading the stories with absorption, Pia felt part voyeur, part potential victim. She caught herself grabbing covert glances at the people around her.

That pimply boy in the Army surplus tee shirt, the young man clutching a paper bag to his chest and whistling, the pale guy in shirt-sleeves whose forehead was beaded with sweat beneath a shock of thinning blond hair – in the cold light of the headlines they all appeared furtive and guilty. The tee shirt boy caught her glance and grinned wickedly, eyeing her up and down. Pia quickly looked away. She folded the paper under one arm and took off with what she hoped was a confident gait down Fifth Avenue toward the massive steps of the New York Public Library. When she got there, she placed a section of the newspaper on the step, shielding her legs from the hot, gritty stone.

Pia would have preferred a shadier spot, but the park behind the library, which earlier in the week she'd sought out as a shady respite, had quickly revealed itself to be the turf of drug sellers and users. Under-the-breath mutterings of *loosejointsnickelbags* came to her from passing slack-limbed young men as she hurried down the path toward an exit, clutching her purse tight to her side, her portfolio banging against her leg awkwardly with every step. Now, sitting on the broad stairway to the library entrance, book-ended by the colossal stone lions, Pia felt a relative sense of calm.

Relative, at least, to what she had been feeling when she and Rosie left the Odyssey last night. Rosie, who had been her friend since grade school, was visiting the city from Oneonta, upstate, where she had gotten a job teaching high school English. Rosie's brother and his wife lived in an apartment carved into what was once a crumbling mansion out in Bay Ridge, in Brooklyn. Rosie insisted on going to a disco nearby. It was the very same disco in which John Travolta had whirled his way to fame in *Saturday Night Fever*, the last movie they had seen together before Pia left Ithaca. Although Pia generally sneered at the disco scene, she had agreed to make the trek to Bay Ridge, a predominantly Italian neighborhood at the far harbor end of Brooklyn.

The subway ride on the local RR train (Court Street, Hoyt Street, Prospect Avenue, all those ascending numbered stops, Bay Ridge Avenue and finally 86th Street) seemed endless. Pia had no idea that Brooklyn was so large. And Bay Ridge couldn't have been more different from Crown Heights if it had been on another planet. For one thing, there was not a single black face on the train by the time she reached her stop there. And barely a stroke of graffiti on the platform. She longed to ink her name discreetly on a peeling I-beam pillar. The stores along 86th Street were all thriving ventures, huge plate glass windows packed with shoes, clothes, housewares; people – again, white people – bustled in and out toting fat shopping bags late into the evening. The street itself was wide, but had nothing of the tree-lined grace of Eastern Parkway, up the hill from her aunt's house. On the other hand, it had none of its wary tension. People walked the streets without the jittery watchfulness she sensed in her new neighborhood, where they were prepared to duck at the first sound of gunfire or the rhythm of fleeing footsteps.

But the look of smug tranquility was deceptive, she learned. The disco was loud but half-empty, and when she asked the bartender why, he stared at her as if she had just been dropped onto Earth from somewhere north of the Milky Way.

"Son of Sam," he intoned as he slid their beers in front of them.

"You think people are so afraid he's out there lurking in the shadows that they're actually staying home?" Pia asked him.

The bartender – he introduced himself as Frankie – told them it had been that way all summer, ever since Judy Placido and Sal Lupu left another disco – the Elephas, in Queens – only to be shot by the serial killer. Frankie said he had a buddy tending bar there who bragged he'd actually heard the gunshots shortly after the couple left.

"But I think he's fulla shit," Frankie shouted over the music. "Who could hear anything like that in a place like this?" He slid a bowl of peanuts in front of them. "It's bad, bad for business," he told them, as he mopped the countertop. "It's eating into my tips, lemme tell ya. No one wants to hang out after dark. Four attacks already this year, in Brooklyn and Queens, and the police don't have a frickin' clue. Most girls would rather stay home than be out on the streets after dark," he said.

Most *white* girls, Pia thought, but didn't offer out loud. She took a long swallow of bitter lager and observed the scene over the rim of her glass. Reflected light, like the spume off a wave, sprayed rhythmically across the surfaces around them, a heavy bass beat formed concentric rings on the surface of their drinks and, as if taking part in the conversation, the d.j. turned up the volume as he segued from Donna Summer's *Love to Love You Baby* to the Bee Gees *Stayin' Alive*. The men on the dance floor were mainly pallid Travolta wannabes, with their slicked back hair and shirts open to the navel, twisted golden horn amulets dangling from thick chains around their necks. The women were as thin and straight as reeds, gyrating in dresses enhanced by fringe or sequins. Not a *sistah* in the crowd, Pia though, not a plump, round *botty* or picked out 'fro. She felt surprisingly lonely for the darker and more curvaceous throng she moved through in her adopted neighborhood – the earnest young men who hawked political pamphlets in their dashikis at the top of the subway steps and the burnished Caribbean women in their multi-tiered skirts. Where did she belong? And with whom? The *freedom to choose* had begun to feel more like a sentence of isolation than the keys to the city. Lately, Pia felt more and more like a chameleon, donning the meek and mild business guise she hoped would help her gain entry into the business world, while beating down something wilder and more lawless struggling within.

Rosie and Frank were still talking about Son of Sam, the bartender sounding to Pia like one of those camp counselors whose biggest thrill was to spook kids around the campfire with stories of headless zombies and ax murderers.

"Hey," she shouted above the music, "we came to do the Hustle, not to get all freaked out. Let's boogie!"

They left the bartender watching their drinks while they hit the dance floor, where the two of them twirled and bumped until a couple of guys worked their way between them. From song to song, Pia lost sight of Rosie as they both spun, non-stop, from partner to partner. Dance after dance, Pia swung her hips and waved her long arms overhead through the revolving lightshow until her feet ached and the sweat was dripping down her spine. Inside the thrum of the music, she felt whole; her parts blessedly intertwined.

They danced until they were almost too tired to walk a straight line. Rosie's brother's place was only eight blocks away, and Pia walked her home. On the way, Rosie threw an arm around Pia's waist.

"I've missed you for so looooong," she sang, boozily. "I should just move down here and we can find an apartment together. Wouldn't that be great?"

"Don't bother coming unless you have a job," Pia cautioned, suddenly the voice of reason. And experience. A month ago, she wouldn't have listened to such a warning. Now it was too late. Most of her money was gone. She had two, maybe three weeks of funds left, and then she'd be forced to admit defeat. In a brash assertion of independence, she had actually burned her waitress dress from Granelli's the night before she left for the city. Her mother had pursed her lips in disapproval as the flames leaped from the backyard bonfire and Pia cavorted around them. Walking along the dark Brooklyn streets, Pia could already feel the creeping humiliation of having to ask Tony Granelli for a replacement outfit.

She pushed the thought from her mind. When they arrived at the apartment, Rosie's sister-in-law insisted on calling a car service to take Pia back to her aunt's house. Pia was grateful to lie back in the deep seat, even if it did smell of rancid cologne and cigarettes.

The odor had clung to her hair and infiltrated her dreams as she slept last night. In them, she and Rosie fled across rooftops from an assailant she could smell but could not see, the stars spiraling like disco balls. In the morning, Pia needed a shower and two Excedrin to banish the smell, the dreams and her hangover. Now, as she sat on the sun-baked library steps, Pia's skin prickled with goosebumps. In the news articles, the police said they were searching for a guy who was socially uncomfortable. A loner. Pia looked around. That described half the people on the steps with her, half the people she passed every day in the street. A social misfit. That could be me, Pia thought. She considered that scene in the bathroom this morning. Breaking down in front of a stranger. It was so embarrassing. Pia shivered in the sweltering heat and rose from the stone, glancing at her watch. Almost 1:30. She needed to push on. And she needed to eat something before her next interview or her stomach would do most of the talking for her.

∾⊚∾

It had all become clear. Crystal. There was a reason for everything and there was a reason for her. Johanna had only to come up to the surface to find out what it was. It was a sunny day on the surface. Hotter, even, than yesterday, which was record hot, she had read on the discarded pages of a newspaper. She blinked again in the violent light. How long since she had surfaced like this? A week? Two? She didn't want to be up here. This is where death waited, hiding in plain light. Much safer, the world below. But still, she was called and she would serve.

Johanna maneuvered the balky shopping cart forward and back on the sidewalk, until it was pressed firmly against the plate glass window of the McDonald's, where she could keep her eye on it. You couldn't be too careful. People would steal you blind in this city. Twice this summer crazy people had knocked her down and taken her stuff. Now, she kept her important things and her money stuffed down her pants, and carried a sharp stick in her pocket. She had survival skills.

Johanna puffed out her cheeks and blew – once, twice, three times – and waited for a small clot of teenagers to tumble out through the double doors before she went inside. She spotted their deserted table immediately. It was piled high with crumpled wrappers and cardboard clamshell boxes, all printed with the happy golden arches. She sidled over to the spot and sat down heavily, establishing invisibility by making eye contact with no one. Long lines snaked from each of the registers, keeping the counter help occupied. Johanna cut her eyes around the room once and then reached for the closest of the clamshells. She had chosen well. Inside was half a Big Mac, melted cheese and sauce oozing from its edges. Unfortunately, its former owner had really liked his ketchup and the bun was smeared thick with it. No matter, she thought, as she quickly peeled back the bread, snatched up the meat and popped it into her mouth. A coin of pickle remained stuck to some lettuce. She hastily ate that as well and moved on to the next box. Only the bun in that one, but no ketchup. She swallowed it hungrily. The next box held the torn remains of a fish sandwich, and Johanna passed it by. She thought she was allergic to seafood. Or maybe that was her brother. She wasn't sure, but it was better, better, best to err on the side of caution. The last thing she wanted was to end up in a hospital again. The rest of the boxes were empty. Greedy little bastards had eaten every crumb. Under the mound of papers, however, sat a tray laden with French fries. Carefully, she selected those that bore no trace of ketchup and she stacked them up in one of the empty cartons. Johanna ate all the fries that stuck up higher than the edge of the cardboard. Then she closed the lid and slipped the box into her pocket for later.

From the corner of her eye, she spotted a rush of movement. A wash of light and color in a liquid deluge. Shattered glass. Just like last time. A cataract of shards, blinking, winking, slashing through the sunlight. Johanna jumped up with a strangled yelp, attracting stares from the tables around her.

"Look out!" she shrieked. "Look out for the glass!" She spun in place, her arms flying up to protect her face. The great glazed city was coming undone, falling to razor-sharp pieces around her again and again. Everywhere, denial. Only she saw what was coming, saw the anger erupting into flying splinters of glass aimed at the upturned throat of the city, its people. No one could protect them, their soft flesh ready for splitting like the skin of ripe peaches. No one could protect them, but she had been sent to warn them. To give them one last chance to rein in their cruelty to one another. To call back the envoys of their anger. Plunging back, Johanna knocked into another body trying to flee the rain of splintering glass. Glares from behind the counter. She spun toward the window in horror. A heavy hand thumped her shoulder.

"Is there a problem?" said a deep voice from behind her. The man was dressed like a janitor, but with a pair of arches on his chest. "Can I help you?"

Johanna turned. As if to spite her, the huge window had restored itself into a flawless plane. Where she had seen the jagged rifts, there was a whole, unscathed sheet of plate glass, her shopping cart still pressed up clumsily against it. Only a few sparkles remained in the periphery of her vision. The man reached toward her shoulder and then pulled his hand back, as if he had thought better of it.

"Are you planning to order something?" he continued. "Because otherwise, I think you should move on," and he took a wide step out of her path. "You keep scaring people like that, and you'll end up in jail." She swept slowly by him. "You can't just yell 'Fire!' in a public place, you know."

Fire? Johanna thought. Who said anything about fire? She backed out onto the sidewalk, letting the door fall into place with a sly whisper. The world wasn't going to end in fire. It was going to end in icy shards of glass and metal. She had seen it. She had watched as it rained over her head and shoulders, she had witnessed the spinning blade carve through its chosen victim. That's when she moved downtown to get away from the disbelievers, the disrespecters. They would be the first to feel the glass, she thought, spitting on the steaming concrete to make her point. Johanna retrieved her cart and pushed on down the block. Now that the fever had broken, she knew where she had to go. Whom she had to warn first.

At the corner of Broadway and Chambers, Johanna stopped pushing her cart and sniffed the air. A sea of people swarmed and then broke around her, flowing off the curb and into the gutter to avoid contact. She sniffed again. Somewhere, the smell of home: the smell of onions sizzling in butter and her mother's White Shoulders perfume. New carpeting and clean laundry and Brillo pads. She'd find it. She'd sniff her way home. But now, all she smelled was hot-dogs, greasy water and mustard from a nearby cart, and she continued around the corner toward City Hall. There was safety in the park. Grass did not shatter. The benches were benign and tall trees stood sentry against invaders.

Johanna shuffled these days, like an old woman. It was the meds. She hated the drugs. She loved the drugs. The drugs took away the nightmares. The drugs replaced them with a muzzy muffled hell. A wheel of the cart wedged itself into a space on the cracked sidewalk and pitched her to one side, twisting her ankle.

"Fuck shit piss!"

"Lady, watch your mouth." A man growled, passing her.

"Go fuck yourself, cocksucker. Have a nice day," she tossed back. She puffed out her lips and flipped him the bird.

He turned and took a step toward her, forming a fist with his right hand. She winced, and he spun away, laughing.

"Crazy bitch!" he yelled, disappearing into the crowd. His laughter rang on in her head.

Johanna wrestled the cart out of the crack and limped toward the nearest bench. She was almost there when she heard the glass breaking. Cascades, cataracts, catatonics, the song of shattered glass. The rainbow light teased her eye and despite herself, she looked up. Glass confetti flew from the countless windows of the Munici-pal Building, towering overhead. It sparkled around the towers of the Brooklyn Bridge and plunged toward the river. This time she wouldn't warn them. They could all be carried off in a sea of glass.

She dropped heavily to the wooden seat and began to rum-mage through the nylon satchel that hung from her cart. Somewhere in there, underwear, foreswear, fourscore, foreskin, four tiny pills in a dark vial. She swallowed them without water and gagged on the bitterness. Her eyelids grew heavy. Sleep swirled like pudding, thick-ening her thoughts. A vision of home began to take shape. Table set for dinner. Shag carpet.

Home. In the end it was so simple she could do it with her eyes closed. First came the familiar burnt toast smell of the coffee roaster on the corner, which Johanna followed like a yellow brick road to the large double doors, painted moss green now, not black as when they first moved there, but completely familiar, nevertheless. She couldn't hoist the heavy cart up the four stone steps to the doorway, but she was sure that Melrose, the doorman, would watch over it for her.

She had been ten when they moved here, but inside the lobby nothing had changed. A crystal chandelier hung suspended from the ceiling, high-backed chairs and slippery couches ringed the walls. Johanna glanced at the crystals that tinkled overhead, daring them to get up to their old tricks. They winked back innocently. The elevator door opened without her having to press the button: a good sign, Johanna thought. She pushed 12 and was whisked upward, the floor pushing at the soles of her feet as if hastening her return.

And her parents, would they recognize her? How little they had known her. She would tell them everything now. She would save them as their city shattered. They would be so proud. The door to the apartment was unlocked. It slid open at her touch. Inside, all was quiet. The hallway to her bedroom was even longer than she remembered. She began to count her steps. Sixty-seven, sixty-eight, sixty-nine.

A scream. A crash. Angry voices. Her eyes flew open and her heart leapt to the back of her throat. The half-formed vision lurched and disappeared. The smell of urine suffused the air. A policeman stood, towering, over her. Shit-fuck, shit-fuck. Her cheeks puffed away like steam engines.

You can't sleep here, lady. Get the hell outta the park before I drag you off for disturbing the peace."

Johanna hoisted herself to sitting. The cart had been thrown over on its side. Her precious belongings were scattered. She dragged herself to her feet and struggled to right the cart. The cop kicked its silver wires.

"I'll give you three minutes to get this crap outta here 'til I get back around this way. You'd better be gone by then, or I'll book you and you can rot in jail."

Johanna turned away. Soon he, like the rest of them, would be carried off in a sea of glass.

୬◎୧

"I'm going out for a walk, do you need anything?" Judith called through the curtains to her uncle. There was no answer, just the sound of the radio, droning the news softly. "Tati? Did you hear?"

She was about to push through the dusty draperies when he called out to her. "*Nein*, nothing. Jehudit, will you be having lunch with us when you come back?" Tante Zipporah often brought leftovers from the past night's dinner – plenty for them all. Judith suspected her aunt did it to make certain her niece had at least one decent meal in the day.

Judith took a breath. It had seemed so simple when she'd first made her plans. She would meet Michael for lunch. They would talk about their classes. She could get the readings he had copied for her. They would maybe eat something. She'd come back to work. But now it was as if she were betraying her aunt and uncle. Telling a lie. Not a little *bubbe maysah*, like the stories she and her sisters would tell about why their tights were ripped or how their shoes got scuffed. This felt like disloyalty, and Judith felt the shame hot on her neck. Hotter even, than the day, which the radio had just called one of the hottest of this long, sweltering summer.

"I'll have a *nosh* later," she called, hoping the hesitation she could hear in her own voice wouldn't bring him out to see her. She couldn't bear his scrutiny, his sea green eyes turning gray with the discovery of her dishonesty. Here was something she hadn't rejected in leaving home – her family's stringent sense of truth, a *mitzvah*, and their utter belief that from each individual act the spiritual future is wrought – and yet here she was, stretching truth to the breaking point. Since childhood she'd heard stories of the angels and demons that were born from people's thoughts and actions. Judith turned quickly and let herself out, the bulletproof door clicking locked behind her. What new demons were being unleashed by her deception?

The air outside was unbreathable. Along 47th Street, huge delivery trucks, soot-rimed and throbbing out heat, engines idling, exhaust spewing into the concrete and up the legs of passersby. She tossed one end of her scarf loosely over her nose and mouth and dove expertly into the midtown stream of pedestrians: women and girls like her from the diamond merchants' shops – hunched forward, heads covered or wigged, or those from the tall office buildings along the Avenue, tanned shoulders pulled back, smart, bright hairdos, slingback shoes slapping at their heels – and men, some swathed in black woolen dresscoats and felt fedoras or *yarmulkes* pinned to thinning hair, others in seersucker suits, pale and sweet as ice cream cones. Seersucker. It was one of her favorite words: from the Persian. *Shir o shakkar*. Milk and sugar. She tasted the sweetness of it on her tongue. Families in shorts and tee shirts – tourists mainly – clogged the sidewalks, staring upward to marvel over the tops of buildings or into shop windows lined with gold and diamonds. The Hasids in their hats and cloaks slipped around bare-legged Americans, neither seeing nor brushing against them, while the seersucker suits bumped shoulders with them – muttered and stuttered excuse-me-excuse-*me* peppering the air. Judith crossed the street to the north side, the shady side, and disappeared gratefully into the throng.

She checked her watch. Twenty past twelve; she wasn't meeting Michael in the lobby of his office building until one. She hadn't realized how early it was when she left the shop. All morning she had been anxious and clumsy, losing the thread of conversations with customers and almost dropping a pair of diamond earrings. Her aunt kept shooting dark looks from under her black brows. But these, Judith was already expert at deflecting. Three years she had worked in the store under the eagle eye of her Aunt Zipporah, who was like a fierce second mother to Judith and her sisters. Even

Zipporah's blackest looks couldn't hide her affection.

Of Judith's entire family, it was Zipporah she believed could best comprehend the fervent aspiration that had taken Judith from the shelter of their community to the lonely world of the outsider. As a young woman, Zipporah had displayed a prodigious musical talent – even now her rare and deeply private moments on the violin were like a glimpse into a realm of purest beauty. Tante herself never spoke of it, but according to Judith's mother, word of her gift reached beyond the boundaries of the neighborhood and one day the president of the Juilliard School himself came from Manhattan to hear her play. After much begging, Zipporah was permitted to play for him from the next room, but even at that remove the man was profoundly overcome. He pleaded with her parents to allow her to continue her studies in his school. There was, of course, no question of it coming to pass. Judith's mother said she wept for the change that came over Zipporah, whose natural sunshine withdrew behind a cloud. A year later Zipporah was married to Uncle Chaim, older than her by almost ten years, but a kind man, and generous of spirit. They had no children of their own. If Tante was bitter about that or about the loss of her music, she gave no sign.

The light turned red just as Judith reached the corner of Fifth Avenue. Just ahead of her, stepping impatiently off the curb, was a woman, probably not much younger than herself in a pale green and white print dress that clung to her torso but swirled coolly below the waist as it settled around her legs. Judith couldn't take her eyes off the dress, the way it draped and soothed the curves of the body beneath it. The woman looked like an oasis in the desert, and Judith clutched her hands together to stop herself from reaching out to touch the shoulder that looked powdery and cool. A bead of sweat dripped from Judith's leg and trickled down the back of one well-covered knee, as if to mock her. The light turned green and the crowd strained into the street, the woman vanishing like a mist.

Walking alongside the tall windows of Saks, Judith caught sight of her reflection framed by the crowd, her face puffy with sweat, her body straining ahead as if she were pulling a cart. This was not how she wanted to appear, even if Michael was just a friend.   She stood up straight and rolled her shoulders back. Someone trod on her heel from behind and grumbled an apology.   On a sudden impulse, Judith pushed through the store's heavy doors and took refuge in the chilled and perfumed air inside. It was like diving into a pool, that first moment, exhilarating and dizzying. A *michayah*, a blessing, she thought, soaking up the cool, clean scent. Judith moved along the air-conditioned jet stream deeper into the store, hushed and opulent with its displays of leather handbags and summer hats and shawls, icy glass counters beckoning, full of unimaginable luxuries.

Along the aisles of the makeup department, men and women stood poised at each intersection, each proffering a crystal atomizer or scented card.

"Care to try Opium today?   It's the newest fragrance from Yves St. Laurent."

"Can I offer you a free make-over, compliments of Estée Lauder?"

"Free gift with purchase today at the Clinique counter."

Their voices were as sweet and as false as those of sirens, and Judith navigated the tortuous course between them, shaking her head No, and hurrying on. What would *tante* Zipporah say if she came back to work smelling like the *goyim*? She imagined her aunt's beaky nose twitching at the unfamiliar fragrance – nothing like her own personal cooked-carrot essence – as it wound its way from Judith's skin through the still air of the shop. She would say not a word, but her veiled black looks would say it all: Traitor.

Judith had now run the gantlet and found herself at the very back of the space, where two escalators criss-crossed themselves, ferrying customers up and down the rest of the nine-level department store. She fell into a short queue of women waiting their turn to move up. When the escalator reached its first landing, she stepped from their ranks and paused. The other women continued on. Everyone but her seemed intent on a destination. Where am I going, she wondered, looking around at the display of pale summer eveningwear perched like a flock of vain and gauzy birds.

When she was ten, her family had taken a trip to the Jersey Shore, to Belmar, a sleepy little town where they stayed in a boarding house run by a distant cousin of her mother's. On their first day there, Judith's young cousins took her to the beach to eat lunch. They spread a faded chenille bedspread over the pockmarked sand and anchored its corners with their shoes, leaving their socks on for propriety's sake. They rolled the sleeves of their blouses almost to the elbow and spread their skirts around them.

As soon as they unwrapped their sandwiches, a flock of seagulls began to wheel overhead, the boldest of the birds landing only yards away and hopping aggressively toward the girls' blanket. Judith was terrified. She ran crying all the way back to the boardwalk, dropping her sandwich along the way and bringing the gulls racing after her, while her cousins and the birds laughed themselves hoarse at her panic. These headless mannequins in their evening wear seemed threatening in the same hungry way, with their nipped-in waists and flaring hips.

The next escalator beckoned like a hand. *Come up, come up, come up and see...* She yielded to the lure of the moving staircase and arrived at Designer Sportswear. Here, four or five women got off, and Judith followed. The clothes displayed on long racks and anatomically distorted mannequins were as colorful and happy as flags snapping in the wind. She looked around and suddenly spotted a mannequin displaying the same dress that she had seen on the woman crossing the street. She headed straight for it, solemnly and with as much gravity as if she had been lighting Shabbos candles.

"Can I help you?" A saleswoman appeared at her elbow, her words a melody of unctuous concern, the word *help* a fourth higher than the words preceding it, and *you*, a staccato afterthought. "That dress is beautiful. It's a Diane von Furstenberg. Pure silk jersey. It would look lovely on you." Judith couldn't imagine what the woman could be thinking. To her, this dress was a sociological experience, a trip to a foreign country where the natives had long blonde hair and skin like flawless ivory; where bright tissue fabrics rested lightly on their limbs as they glided through their days and nights.

"Thank you, I'm just looking," she waved the salesgirl away. Judith heard her mother's definite tone in her own voice. The unambiguous way she could steer the family the length of Kingston Avenue or the streets of the Lower East Side without falling prey to the shopkeepers' persistent come-ons. The saleswoman drifted away. Judith moved on to a rack of similar dresses that looked more anonymous and therefore familiar. There were many in size 4 and size 6. Fewer size 8 and 10, but Judith began to page through these, moving the hangers one by one, right to left. She bumped hips with a woman working down the rack from the other direction. They exchanged places and moved on along their separate paths. The dresses were made to wrap around the body, fastened only by a tie at the waist. The fabrics were smooth, silky and cool, and most of the skirts were loose and swingy in a way that would make walking a pleasure. But they were, Judith noted with some consternation, all very short. And sleeveless. She thought again of the woman in the green print dress. She plucked one from the rack. It was a swirl of cream against the blue of a September sky, the fabric both crisp and drape-y at once. Judith wanted that cool cloth against her own skin, even for a moment, and with a quick, nervous look to the right and left, lest the saleswoman come and draw more attention to the act, she made off for the dressing rooms.

Despite the chill in the store, a flush rose to Judith's neck and her eyes darted about, furtively. Like a thief in the night, she was on the lookout for witnesses – someone from the Lubavitcher community who might spy her there. Tongues were long: although refraining from gossip was another of Hashem's *mitzvot*, the women (and men too, she might add) of the neighborhood were rarely without a story about someone. God forbid it should be this. There was enough talk already, about her moving out of her parents' house and into Manhattan to go to college against the expressed wishes of the Rebbe.

Judith pushed the dressing room door shut behind her. It

closed with a sturdy click that conveyed a welcome assurance of privacy. She tried not to be flustered by the mirrors on three sides of the tiny room, and stood facing the door. There were no full-length mirrors at home. She and her sisters averted their eyes from each other while dressing, and refrained from making too big a deal of appraising each other's wardrobes. In the shops along Kingston, many dressing rooms were without mirrors as well. In any case, they were unnecessary. Her mother or Aunt Zipporah passed judgment on how outfits looked on the girls, a question not of style, but of *tznius*, the code of modesty.

She stepped out of running shoes and socks, unbuttoned and unzipped, shrugging quickly out of her skirt and blouse, and without looking up, she snatched the dress off its hanger and let it fall over her head. She wrapped the featherweight material around her torso and cinched it with a series of snaps. The waist was a little loose, perhaps she needed a Size 8 after all, but what difference did it make, she wasn't there to buy, just to try, right? Judith stood and settled the dress around her hips. It floated into place, weightlessly. Under it, her legs felt naked. Or like she was out in only her summer nightshift, a dream she had had more than once.

She quickly blinked down at herself, and then turned toward the mirror on her left and looked up. There stood an unfamiliar woman – someone from outside the neighborhood. But no, of course not. She is me, Jehudit Fein, daughter of Shimon and Chana, sister to Rivka, Chaya, and Kayla. And Rebecca – her memory for a blessing. But this mirror Judith, whom she could see from the front and back and sides all at once, was like a stranger to her. A woman with long tapering limbs, pale arms that ended in slightly reddened wrists and hands, bare but for the birthstone ring her aunt had bought her when she was thirteen. She could hardly stop running her eyes up and down those arms with their faint blond fuzz and assertive shoulders like the bottoms of two hard pears. The crooks of her elbows were a holy mystery. She bent and straightened her arms, watching the dark valley between forearm and upper arm develop and fade away. Surely she had seen her own body before. She had carried it with her for twenty-three years. She had admired the scientific miracle of bones and muscles and internal organs. But not like this.

Judith ran her right palm up her left arm, which prickled with energy. She turned slightly, and caught sight of the elbow, sharp and shapely at once, and knew precisely why the Torah ordered it covered, lest it seduce the eyes of men and steal their attention from their prayers, their journey toward godliness. She turned back to the front mirror and gasped as she saw her legs, freed for once from the heavy drag of her skirts. If her arms made her blush, her legs made her positively woozy. Standing on tiptoe to mimic high heels emphasized narrow ankles and shapely, muscled calves, and oh, the marvelous architecture of her knees (which put her elbows to shame) and the promise of long, white thighs.

This is absurd, she thought, although she still could not take her eyes off the mirror Judith. Wrapped from shoulders to waist, the dress created a deep Y that framed her neck and face. The hollow at the base of her throat pulsed slightly – had it always? – and the thin, fine skin descending toward her breasts glistened.

Your two breasts are like two fawns, the twins of a gazelle, she thought, discovering anew the passage she knew well from Solomon's *Song of Songs*.

She pivoted once and then again in the other direction. The dress waltzed and dipped, its hem stroking the skin of her thighs like a fingertip.

How fair are your feet in sandals, O daughter of nobles! The curves of your thighs are like jewels, the handiwork of a craftsman.

This is ridiculous, she told herself firmly, and most definitely not what Solomon had in mind when he wrote those holy lines of the *K'tuvim*. But she didn't remove the dress. She was an insect caught in amber – her mother had a pendant with a chunk of the stuff, and the sight of the tiny insect inside it fascinated and repelled Judith. There was no moving forward and no going back.

But wasn't beauty another of Hashem's many gifts? Even vanity had its holy uses, Judith thought. Enslaved, depressed, exhausted with their labors, the Jewish women of ancient Egypt beautified themselves and marched out to inspire their husbands to fight Pharaoh's tyranny. Judith lifted the price tag dangling from the waist. $175. A *shanda*, to spend so much money on a dress. Even for a famous designer like Diane von Furstenberg whose label was esteemed among the most fashionable women of Kingston Avenue. Where, after all, could she wear it? And yet, Judith knew she was going to buy it.

"*Im yirtzeh Hashem*, with God's will, I'll know what to do with this," she whispered.

She took the dress to a register, where a woman enfolded it in tissue paper and coaxed it delicately into a crisp Saks shopping bag. Judith placed her credit card on the counter and the deed was done. Throughout the transaction, she stared down at her hands resting on the counter, afraid to face fully the world around her. Her watch read 12:50. Now she would have to rush to meet Michael on time. The escalators whispered their stately way toward the ground floor as if they were reluctant to turn her loose. She hurried to the exit, her palms already beginning to sweat.

When she got to Third Avenue, Michael was standing outside the steel and glass tower in a seersucker suit. A stranger. But he grasped her hands as she approached him. She automatically pulled away – such intimacy was disconcerting – and then covered up her discomfort by fiddling with the Saks bag dangling from one wrist. His eyes looked directly into her face. No man in her neighborhood would stare at her as frankly. She could barely return his gaze.

"I looked in the phone book, and there's no place strictly Kosher around here," he said in a rush. "Can you eat in a regular coffee shop?"

He seemed so eager for her to be okay with this. And she was, partly. Although she had been brought up understanding that eating non-kosher does irreparable harm to your *neshama*, your soul, it sometimes happened that she and her friends would risk this, most often for a slice of pizza. She could order a salad or something dairy. She nodded and he grabbed her free hand and took off for the middle of the block.

"It gets so crowded here at lunchtime; we'll have to hurry to get a table," he explained.

Her hand was damp inside his large one. The touch was so foreign, so insistent. Even the hands of her father – the only other man she could recall touching like this – were softer and far less assertive. Should she pull away? But this is the world in which I am choosing to make my home. What to keep – what to let go? Before she could come to a conclusion, they had arrived at their destination.

Inside the Acropolis Coffee Shop, the smell of the street gave way to the rich odor of coffee, grease and malt. It was a small shop, a row of booths lining one mirrored wall, separated by a narrow aisle from a row of stools and a Formica counter, behind which a battery of cooks labored at top speed over a hissing grill. All the booths and stools upfront were taken. A waitress approached them. The nametag over her ample chest read, LAURA.

"Two? Follow me." She turned and led them to a small table pressed up against the back wall. "Sorry. It's all that's left. Unless you want to wait."

"No problem – we'll take it," Michael said, squeezing into the narrow space. Judith hung her bag on one arm of her chair before sliding into it. The waitress deposited their menus and left. Michael opened his and appeared to be studying it with interest. Judith watched his thick brows furrow slightly, as if he were reading Torah. But Michael didn't read Torah, she reminded herself. He was what her Aunt Zipporah would call, a *goyishe* Jew. So well assimilated he could barely be recognized as one of Hashem's chosen people. And yet, it was their community's mission to bring him back into the fold.

That, however, wasn't her personal mission. When he first approached her at registration, she was startled. On Crown Street, the boys walked and talked and learned together, but they stared into the middle distance dumbly in mixed company. Michael, however, asked unapologetically if she knew where the bursar's office was. She was heading there herself, and he fell into step with her. Long before they reached the office, though, they reached the line that stretched from it.

"Ladies first," he said, with a gallant wave of one hand. And she stepped into the line just ahead of him. She rifled through her backpack, trying to dispel the uncomfortable feeling that he was staring at her from behind.

"So, what are you registering for?" he finally asked.

She turned, in relief. As it happened, they were planning to take the same seminar in *Politics and the Media*, and he had accidentally picked up two copies of the reading that would be discussed the first week. He offered to bring her a copy, which led to the lunch invitation. Not a date, she reminded herself. A mere exchange. He looked up from the menu. The waitress arrived and flicked back a page in her pad with the back of her pen.

"Burger platter, medium rare," Michael said.

"I'd like a grilled cheese and tomato sandwich, please," Judith said at the same time.

"And to drink?"

"Coke."

"Iced tea." Again, they spoke in the same instant. Like nervous children, they laughed. The waitress scribbled and disappeared.

Nothing in her experience had prepared her for this. Sitting across from a male stranger and making conversation. It was strange enough that they were classmates, studying together about chemisty and political science the way her father and her cousins Dovid and Jacob sat and learned Talmud, their heads bowed over the great books or tossed back in the throes of argument over some point of Halachal law. She and her sisters also studied Torah, but in the girls' school, where the hours were shorter, and they were off on Sundays while the boys went back to classes after *Shabbat*. Her education on those days consisted of learning the skills a good homemaker, a *balabuster*, would need to take her place at the head of her family some day.

"I've done about half of the reading," Michael was saying now.

"It's really interesting. Maybe you can call me when you've finished it and we can talk about it. As I was reading, I kept thinking about Watergate and the way politics translates to theater in movies like *All the President's Men* and how that changes what comes to be known as history."

There was an awkward silence. Judith hadn't seen the movie. She had only seen one movie in her life, in fact – *Bambi*, when she was eight – and it had terrified her.

"You know, in the community where I grew up, we don't go to movies," she said, more to the salt shaker than the person across from her. "Or watch television. In fact, we – girls, I mean – don't go to college, either. Or move out of our parents' house until we get married. I'm a pariah. Right now I feel like a woman without a country."

She glanced up to see if he looked disappointed. He must know so many girls, and all of them must go to movies and watch TV shows and wear dresses like the one that was secreted inside the bag on her right. But he looked more interested than disenchanted.

"You mean the Orthodox community?"

"I'm Lubavitcher," she said, wondering if that were still true. "I grew up in a Hasidic neighborhood in Brooklyn. Crown Heights."

"You mean you're one of those people who come around on the subways asking if people are Jewish?" he said in amazement. "I can't believe it. I mean," he stumbled on, "there's nothing wrong with it. I mean... I'm sorry, I don't want to sound insulting; I'm just so amazed that someone like you is having lunch with someone like me." His cheeks were flushed. "It's just that I'm more of a revolving door Jew." He laughed, but she didn't get the joke.

"No, no, I'm not insulted," she insisted. "Believe me, I feel a little amazed, as well." Again the awkward silence of strangers, from which they were saved by the arrival of their food.

"Grilled cheese, iced tea, burger, Coke, can I get you anything else?" The waitress whirled off practically before her last words were fully out. Judith turned slightly toward the receding presence.

"Excuse me?" Michael was looking at her attentively.

"What?"

"You were saying something? I didn't catch it."

"No, I...." Oh. It was such a reflex action, such an ingrained response that she hadn't even noticed. Of course. She smiled. "I was saying the *brochah*."

"The what?"

"The prayer before meals. *Baruch atah Adonai, Eloheinu Melech Ha'Olam Hamotzi lechem min haaretz.* Blessed art thou oh Lord our God, King of the universe, who brings forth bread from the earth." She stopped suddenly, a little embarrassed at the thought that he might think that she was trying to proselytize, *one of those people who come around on the subways.* Her cousin Shevy had always been among the most zealous of these. She had done her part, too, mainly in the more secular neighborhoods of Brooklyn.

"You say that every time you eat? Where I come from it's only for Bar Mitzvahs and holidays!" he laughed.

She rolled the edge of the paper napkin on her lap. "I do."

"Do I have to?"

"To what?"

"Say it."

A tiny bit of paper tore away from the napkin she was still worrying. "It's entirely up to you. I'm not here to convert you."

Of course, Judith thought, according to the Rebbe, it was the job of each and every one of them to go out into the world and rally their Jewish brethren to the joyous task of upholding the Laws. How else to hasten the coming of *Moshiach,*? How else to gather up the scattered Light? Across the table, Michael was waiting. She didn't dare look up for fear that he was staring at her like an exhibit of something in a test tube. He would not eat until she did. He was raised to be polite at least.

Judith addressed her food with exaggerated eagerness. She squeezed the wedge of lemon into the tall glass of tea and stirred it with an elongated spoon. Michael painted ketchup on the charred canvas of his burger. Finally, they looked up, each lifting sandwiches to their mouths. Judith hadn't realized how hungry she was. She had only coffee for breakfast this morning, part of her austerity budget. She bit into her sandwich and freshly melted cheese burned the delicate skin of her palate. But she reveled in the richness of melted butter and Kraft American, familiar and comforting, the mild acidity of hot tomato, and a salty crunch of something else; something both familiar and foreign. Something that seemed more recognizable as a smell – dark and smoky like the scent that lingered in her hair after the bonfires she and her cousins had made at the Chabad camp.

She tried to isolate a bit on her tongue. It was sharp; crisp and harder than the burnt edges of toast. First thought – glass. Awful. Second thought – something Judith knew mainly as a word – *treyf* – a strict prohibition. Meat with milk. Smoky, greasy, alien and foul in her mouth. Bacon! The flesh of the pig. Inside her. The filthy flesh of the pig. Her throat filled with bile. She could neither swallow nor spit. Her head filled with shame. In panic, Judith flung her chair back and reeled from the table, pushed down the aisle and out the glass door into the street. She stumbled to the curb, where she braced one hand against the hood of a parked car and gagged until she vomited into the gutter. The aroma of the meat remained, even after all trace of it was gone from her mouth. Again and again she retched, her eyes filled with tears, blind to the people walking by her. And with each spasm she thought, *now God has truly forsaken me.*

Chapter Five

The street stank. It stank of garbage ripening in the exhaust fumes of delivery trucks idling along West 46th Street. With time to spare before her 2:30 interview, Pia took respite from the heat and the smell in the cavernous Sam Flax store just across the street. The towering windows – just now being squeegeed to a level of clarity at odds with the grime around them – displayed vast offerings of the art supplies, fancy pens and chic office accessories for which the store was famous. Back at school, Sam Flax had been akin to Mecca, and anyone who traveled to the city was given lists of supplies to bring back. Beyond the heavy glass doors, the chill was almost dizzying and smelled deliciously of linseed oil, pigment and paper.

Pia wandered the aisles giddily, fingering cool glass bottles of ink, pens and pencils, brushes and airbrushes, glues, erasers, cubes and bricks of clay, tubes of oil- and acrylic-based paints, tin trays of watercolors like tiny, colorful TV dinners. She cupped a porcelain bowl in her hands to soak in the cold, then set it back among a display of palettes and watercolor supplies. At the back of the store she admired an array of hand-laid Japanese papers displayed on huge racks that turned like the pages of a giant's notebook. A salesperson approached, her rubber-soled shoes making soft squishing noises on the linoleum floor.

"Can I help you?" the woman asked. Pia felt the woman's gaze skim over her, taking in, she imagined, the sweat stain that had bloomed in the middle of her chest and the greasy shine she could feel on her face. Pia imagined herself asking for a long list of expensive oils – cadmium red, cobalt blue, alizarin crimson – to silence the judgmental stare, but on a budget of only twelve bucks a day, that wasn't a practical response to her discomfort.

"I'm looking for a notebook," Pia told her, with what she hoped sounded like brisk authority. "Something about six by eight, with blank sketch pages that can handle ink and watercolor. And some Prismacolor markers. Dual point, assorted colors." She immediately regretted asking for the markers. They were good permanent colors, with thick and thin points, but expensive. And she still had some at home. But it was too late. The saleswoman had sailed off across the floor, leaving Pia to follow in her wake. She led Pia to a short rack of notebooks and sketchpads, ranging from the simplest black-and-white mottled grade school Composition notebooks to an array of brilliantly hued European imports. Pia selected a chunky spiral bound book with a rough chocolate brown cover, hoping it was cheap enough to make up for buying the more expensive pens. The woman returned carrying a package of a dozen Prismacolor markers.

"These are on sale. Reduced from $25 to $17.95. It's a good buy. They almost never get marked down. If you use them a lot, you should take two." She pressed them into Pia's hands. "You can pay for them up front," the woman directed coolly, before heading off in the direction of another customer who was rifling through a display of Plexiglas frames. Pia wanted to linger in the store, to find a quiet corner in which she might hunker down and draw. Or eat a sandwich. She was starving. It was already 2:00 and she hadn't eaten since wolfing down a slice of toast and Skippy this morning. She wondered idly if that rat she had seen nosing around the tracks had ventured up onto the platform to grab the piece of bagel the little girl had dropped. Do rodents like peanut butter? Were they as omnivorous as goats? Her father once had a billygoat. One day, the goat chewed through the door to the house and then ate an entire Entenmann's apple pie – cardboard container and all. Pia wondered if the rat would eat the bagel wrapping and all, or tease the sandwich from between the twists of waxed paper. She wondered if buying the markers meant she would have to sacrifice lunch.

She drifted by a display of half-price pre-matted watercolor prints and paused to flip through them, stalling for time before she'd have to pay for her items and return to the sidewalks. The prints were basically insipid greeting card art from another time, like Rockwell magazine covers. Daisy-strewn landscapes and snowcapped peaks; mothers and children at a picnic; boats docked on the shore of lakes ever unruffled by storms. Who would hang this stuff? Dentists, maybe, Pia thought. Or shrinks in an asylum. Keep the inmates calm. In one, a town of candy-colored clapboard houses and a white church with its steeple set off against a blue sky formed the backdrop for a sailboat and a silvered wood dock. Staring into the painting was like being led back to a day she'd rather forget.

Pia's father's boat had chugged up to the dock that long ago day and he tossed her the rope to tie off to one of the rotting pilings, split and blackened and speckled with birdshit. He jumped onto the pier and swept her up in a big bear hug, knocking her Mets cap off her head and practically squeezing all the air out of her as her feet came off the ground.

"Lay off," she'd wheezed, wriggling out of his arms and racing to retrieve the cap before it rolled into the lake. She didn't understand why, from one week to the next, he couldn't remember that she hated being greeted as if she were five years old. She was almost eleven, for Pete's sake. Aside from the cap, which she'd worn only to keep the hair from whipping her face and sticking in her eyes and mouth while they sailed, she was dressed in a manner that clearly bespoke Sunday morning and church. Her mother had gone to services at the Unitarian church on Pointer Street, where all Pia's friends would by now be sharing picnic breakfast on the grass.

Her father was in the same pair of cut-offs he'd worn all summer – she knew they were the same ones because they had a big purplish stain on the butt, where he'd sat in a plate of blueberries she'd left on the bench by the tiller. He stepped back into the boat and offered her a hand to help her in beside him.

"I thought we were going to church. Mom told me you said you were taking me to church with you," Pia said, suspiciously. "You can't go to church dressed like that." She stepped neatly over the bow, and then smoothed her skirt down over the tails of her tucked-in blouse, as if to draw his attention to her own, more proper, attire.

He whooped and swung the tiller hard to catch the breeze and turn them off from shore. It was a spectacular day, the kind of dazzling blue sky that blazed with late summer fury, as if daring fall to quench it, and Pia squinted hard as the little boat swung its prow into the East. She coiled the rope into a tidy snake charmer's pet and poked the first few stray hairs up into her cap.

Her father had trimmed the sails taut and the boat cut sharply into the dark green water, raising a wake that peeled away from the stern in satisfying spirals. Pia watched them twirl off and finally resettle into the ordinary chop of the lake surface. Her father began singing what he always sang, "*Put 'im in the scuppers with a hosepipe on 'im, put 'im in the scuppers with a hosepipe on 'im, put 'im in the scuppers with a hosepipe on 'im early in the mornin',*" in a nasal cowboy twang. When she didn't join in the chorus, he shot her a questioning look.

"So, are we too grown up to sing with our dad?" he asked.

"So, are we going to church, or aren't we?" she countered.

"Darling," he rounded on her, facing her squarely and ignoring for a moment, the fact that the boat had fallen off the wind, "look around you now." He laughed in a way Pia now hungered for, like someone might hunger for the Saturday pancakes of her childhood.

Pia looked, but all she saw was the dark wash of water rimed with a shoreline of trees in their endless shades of green, the true blue sky and a man who, for the moment and from her vantage point, blocked out the sun like a giant.

"You and me, we already are in church," he boomed. "Welcome to the church of the wind on my neck, and God bless us for it!"

She hadn't a clue, at the time, what he meant. Now, of course, it was abundantly clear. Sailing, she realized, had been his devotion and prayer. Her father loved the water like an acolyte loves his deity. And she knew just how disappointed he must have been when she stamped one Mary-Jane-covered foot and demanded to be taken home. What a little shit she had been.

Up at the front of the store, Pia got on the short checkout line and dug through her purse for her wallet. She was spending her entire day's cash on art supplies. The man in front of her had a shopping basket full of snapshot-sized Plexiglas frames. He kept shifting the basket from one hand to the other, although it couldn't have been very heavy. He shifted from one foot to the other, as well, and whistled, tunelessly. The woman ahead of him was buying canvas, stretchers and a whole lot of paint. Acrylics, Pia noted. Pia never really liked those. Too much of a compromise between oils and watercolors, with none of the subtlety of either. The checkout girl – she couldn't have been more than seventeen, Pia thought, with her braces and a sprinkling of pimples mixed with the freckles on her cheeks – wrapped each item in tissue paper and was struggling to fit them into a bag. Pia didn't mind the wait, but the guy ahead of her clearly did. At one point, he turned around and sent what seemed to be a complicit look at Pia – *isn't this just too much to bear?* – who offered up what she hoped was a blandly neutral smile in return, and looked away after only the briefest acknowledgement.

"She couldn't be slower if she tried," he muttered *sotto voce* to no one

Pia smiled again, wanly, and busied herself rearranging the item in her hands to avoid having to make eye contact. That was what Rosie said her friends from Oneonta warned her: *Never make eye contact.*

The man in front of her sighed once again, ran his fingers through thinning, curly hair, and shot a look around the store. Finally, he moved up to the register and dropped his items on the counter.

"That will be $22.75," the girl told him, pulling a length of tissue paper from under the counter.

The man placed his credit card on the table and the girl started to run it through the card machine.

"Don't bother wrapping," he told her. "Just throw 'em in a bag."

"I'm sorry," she said to him, placing the frames carefully into a plastic bag with an uncertain look. "I have to call in your card. It will just take a minute." She picked up a red phone receiver and dialed. Pia continued thinking about her father. Even after all this time she still pictured him out on the lake, pulling at the sheets, making his little boat tack smartly across the wind.

He'd obeyed when she'd asked to be taken home. They docked in Ithaca, and were walking down the block to Carvel hand-in-hand – Pia's short legs working double-time to keep up with her father's long strides – when a woman walking in the opposite direction suddenly bent toward Pia and asked in a complicit whisper, "Do you need help? Should I call the police?" Pia remembered feeling completely confused, as though the woman had asked a question in a foreign language. And then her father yanked her by the hand and pulled her along the sidewalk even faster than her legs could keep up. She stumbled and put a big scratch on the patent leather of her favorite shoes. She was about to complain when she saw the fury on her father's face. It was years before she understood that the woman thought she was being abducted.

"Shit!" spat the man in front of her, slapping his hand on the counter and snapping Pia to attention. The store was plunged into a moment of silence as conversations halted in response to the outburst. "That's not possible. Try it again."

The girl settled the phone receiver back into place gently, as if she was trying to make up for his eruption. Pia gave her a sympathetic look. The girl held the man's card gingerly, between two fingers, as if it were dirty. "Well, I'm sorry, Mr...." she glanced at the card. "Mr. Berkowitz.   I did try it twice. But your credit card has been rejected. You're welcome to pay in cash."

The man spun around and glared at Pia, saying something incomprehensible through clenched teeth. He thrust a hand into his trouser pocket and wrenched out a couple of bills, which he slapped hard on the counter, making both Pia and the girl jump. Before she could even gather them up, he had snatched up the bag of frames, brushed by Pia and flung open the door, letting in a puff of heat like the bellows of hell.

"Wait," the cashier called. "Your change." But he was beyond her voice, on the other side of the glass, swept up by the crowd in the steaming street. The woman held up the bills helplessly.

"Scary," she said. She giggled nervously. The girl had a chain around her neck with the name Annie in fancy gold script. She reached up with her free hand and tugged at the thick gold letters as if to calm herself.

"Must be the heat," Pia told her sympathetically. Annie looked at her blankly. "Makes people a little crazy." She put her own purchases on the countertop.

"He had almost $18 change coming," she said.

Pia was surprised. She'd imagined the girl would be happy to pocket the extra cash. With minimum wage at $2.30, that was probably a good six hours salary for her.

"You know, Annie," Pia said, "you could always donate the money to a good cause."

The girl looked startled at the sound of her name. Then she remembered reached up and fingered her name in gold, and laughed. "How about I just put it toward your purchase?" She worked the keys of the register. "That would mean you owe me, um, $3.78."

"That would definitely be a good cause," Pia laughed. And the girl wrapped up her purchases and pushed them back across the counter.

"Have a nice day," she grinned.

"Yeah, you too."

Pia had a sudden thought. It was nice here in the store. Cool and clean. If nothing else, she'd be selling the materials of her craft rather than greasy burgers and BLTs, and it was frequented by working artists and art directors she could meet.

"Do you happen to know if the store is hiring?" she asked.

"No, sorry. Actually, they just let go of a couple of salespeople. But if you come back before Thanksgiving, they're always putting on more help for the holidays."

Thanksgiving. A lifetime from now.

Pia thanked the girl again and coaxed the bag into her purse. With one last breath of cool air, she passed through the glass doors, rejoining the crowd on the steamy streets.

～◎～

Celia swung easily, hand over hand, across the series of metal rings suspended along the underside of a playground climbing-frame. Behind her, a small boy was grunting and floundering at the same task, stuck between two rings, his skinny arms shaking and threatening to give way. Reaching the end of the rings course, Celia dropped lightly to the rubber mats and ran around to the beginning to do it again. The boy had fallen and was slinking off, looking sheepish. Celia took a series of shallow hops and then a strong jump that brought her knuckles into hard contact with the first ring.

"Balls!" she yelled and sucked hard at her knuckles before making another leap. This time the jump was successful and Celia was off across the rings once more.

"Ooh, what you said," singsonged a younger girl, standing just off to the side. "I'm telling your yiayia."

Marissa was Celia's "fake cousin." Fake because neither of her parents were actually blood relations of Celia's mother. Cousin, because both the girls' grandmothers came from the same tiny town perched on Skiathos' rocky coastline and they ended up as neighbors in the same apartment project in New York City. Marissa was standing off to the side of the ring course, because she was too afraid to leave the ground. Celia flew across the course, laughing at the look of horror on the girl's face.

"Balls, balls, cock, balls..." Celia sang as she ratcheted through the air, just loud enough for her to hear. Marissa was a baby and a pest. It was just Celia's luck that the girl was also spending the day with her grandmother while her parents were at work. Two years older at age nine, Celia was expected to keep an eye on the little nuisance at the playground. She might have refused, but Marissa's yiayia offered to pay her $3 to baby-sit her for the afternoon. She had been at it for over an hour – ever since Marissa came back from the Midday Mackerels swim class – and the thrill of the money was beginning to wear thin. The girl was afraid of everything. She cried at the top of the seesaw until Celia let her down ("and no bumps!") and she balked at the fireman's pole and had to be half carried down to the ground.

For the zillionth time, Celia wished her mother would come home early and rescue her. All summer she had been promising to do that. Every week she said she would take Celia to the Hayden Planetarium, where you could touch a giant meteorite that crashed into the desert and where you could find out what you weighed on Pluto or on the sun. And she promised they could see the sky show, where she would point out the constellations of the gods and goddesses that had shone overhead when she was born on Skiathos. Today, she hadn't promised that, but Celia hoped for a surprise anyway.

"Yiayia!" the little girl wailed. But no one was listening. Celia glanced over at where the women sat on a green painted bench, deep in conversation, each one fanning herself with a folded section of newspaper.

"Forget it," Celia said, grabbing Marissa by the hand and forcing her to a trot. "Let's go to the slides. Let's make a train."

Marissa broke into a jog, reluctant at first, but more enthusiastic as they neared the pair of towering silver slides.

"You'll remember to wait for me at the top, right?" the girl asked, nervously. "We'll make a train and go down together, right?"

Celia didn't bother to answer, but climbed the metal rungs, then sat down to wait at the top until Marissa joined her. Marissa fitted herself in behind, with her feet wrapped around Celia's waist, and the two girls pushed off together and sped down the slick silver ramp, squealing as the hot metal seared their naked legs. As soon as they reached the bottom, they raced back around to the ladder side to do it again. Once more they flew down the glinting steel and hit the ground running. This time, Celia stumbled and Marissa got to the ladder first and started up the steep climb. She was on the second step when Celia grabbed her by the waist and tried to swing her off.

"Let go," she screamed. "You're hurting me."

"I'm first," Celia insisted. "You have to get behind me."

"No I don't. I got here first. You can get behind me." Marissa struggled up to the next step and Celia held on.

"But I'm bigger. Bigger is first." She pulled harder, gripping the elastic waist of the girl's powder blue shorts, but Marissa clung to the rails with a surprising strength and kicked backward into Celia's stomach.

Na pas sto diaolo! Celia screamed. "Go to hell!"

"Yiayiaaaa!" Marissa wailed.

Off in the distance, the two older women turned in the direction of the playground. Celia knew her Yiaia would slap her for cursing, or at the very least she would lose the $3 if Marissa went home crying. She took one hand off Marissa and waved to them, faking a wide grin. She had plans for that money. She thought of the tray of cookies in the bakery window this morning. How many would $3 buy?

"Big baby!" Celia spat under her breath. "Big stupid crybaby, crying to your grandma."

"I am not a baby and let go of me!" the girl sniffled, still hanging on tight to the sides of the steps.

"If you're not a big baby, prove it. Stop screaming like one."

Marissa stopped howling but the two of them continued to struggle in silence over the ladder.

Suddenly Marissa twisted around and said, "I can swim and you can't. And I know something you don't know."

"You don't know anything I don't know. Now get *down*." She snapped the elastic waistband of the Marissa's shorts hard so that the younger girl flinched, losing her hold just enough for Celia to yank her down. Marissa turned in fury.

"I do so know something. I know something about your mother."

Stunned, Celia pulled back just enough that Marissa gained control of the steps once more. This time she scrambled out of her reach and up to the top. Celia's head spun and her cheeks flared up like the glowing electric saints on her grandparents' chest of drawers. She kicked at the ground with the toe of her jellies to gain time while she struggled with her breathing.

Now at the top of the slide, Marissa waited. Celia wanted to run up the ladder and knock her to the ground. Instead, she walked around to the front of the slide and sat down on the hot and smelly rubber that covered the ground in the play area. Looking up into the sky made her eyes tear. Still, she forced herself not to look away.

"If you're so smart, tell me what you think you know," she demanded.

Marissa looked nervous, up there all alone. She blinked in the glare of sunlit metal.

"Come up and slide me down."

"No. Come down yourself if you're so smart."

Celia couldn't see Marissa's eyes, but she bet they were full of tears. Big baby. Big stupid ugly baby. Marissa knew nothing. Nothing at all. Certainly nothing about her mother. She continued to glare up at the girl whose lower lip was now trembling. She could practically see a shriek forming. Almost see the scream about to burst from Marissa's stupid pink mouth.

"Tell me what you know. Big Baby." Her words stole the scream from the girl's lips. Instead, Marissa let out a whimper.

"Come up and slide down with me first."

Celia stood, seemingly undecided.

"Maybe I will and maybe I won't," she declared. "What will you do for me if I do?"

Marissa was quietly scratching at a bite on her arm. She appeared to have forgotten her earlier words. "I'll give you a dollar."

"Nice try. You don't have a dollar."

"I'll give you my necklace." She pulled at the ugly string of painted macaroni noodles tied around her neck. "Come up now and I'll give you my necklace." Celia almost laughed.

"What's the rush? I have all day."

"I have to make," Marissa whimpered.

"Make what?" Celia asked. There was a long pause, in which she watched a pigeon peck at some crusts on the ground.

"Sissy," the girl finally said in a tiny voice.

"What? I can't hear you!"

"I have to make a *sissy!*"

Celia laughed loudly, bending double. "Oh, you have to *pee!* Tell me what you think you know, Miss Pee Pee pants, and I'll take you to the bathroom," Celia bargained.

Marissa looked closer to tears than ever. "My yiayia said..." she began.

"What?"

"My yiayia said...Celia, I really, really have to *go*..." There was a note of fear in her voice. Celia placed her hands on her hips, elbows out, in what she thought of as her mother's *I'm waiting* position. "My yiayia said your mother has a boyfriend," she said in a rush. "Now please, will you take me?"

Celia was struck dumb for the second time. What had she imagined? That her mother was sick. That she had to go to the doctor for shots all the time. And that she might die, like the mother in *The Boxcar Children*, and Celia would be forced to choose between life in a subway car or living with Yiayia forever. She had dreams where men were chasing her down the dark tracks and she woke herself up, screaming. She had even imagined her mother in some kind of terrible trouble. Running away from awful danger and leaving her behind. But a *boyfriend*?

"Why did she say that?" Celia demanded.

"I don't know," sniffed Marissa. "I think because your yiayia said she was acting funny and was always late."

Celia frowned. A boyfriend. Someone more important to her mother than she was? Was he handsome? Did they kiss? If he married her, would he be a wicked stepfather?

"Celia!" The note of panic made her look up. A thin stream was trickling down the ramp, heading right for her. Celia jumped up in horror and ran around to the steps. Almost to the top, she stopped. How would they come down? She certainly wasn't going to slide over Marissa's pee. But if the fireman's pole was any indication, Marissa wasn't going to want to back down the steps. When she got to the top, however, she realized it was already too late. Marissa had hoisted herself over the side of the slide and was dangling by her hands.

"Help!" she whimpered.

Celia launched herself over the edge and both girls went hurtling toward the ground.

In the tiny bathroom at the rear of the store, Judith stood gripping the porcelain edge of the sink, still queasy from lunch. Once she had stopped gagging, she'd raced down the block and away from the coffee shop without looking back to see if Michael had come after her. She had turned the corner and ducked into the first drugstore she saw, where she bought a packet of Wet Naps that she used to scrub her face until it stung, a tube of Colgate and a toothbrush, and a bottle of Schweppes Ginger Ale, which she drank warm to strip the bacon taste from her mouth. It was only marginally successful. With each exhale, the smoky ghost of the pig revisited her mouth, her nose. Then she made her way back to her uncle's shop, where he and her aunt had just finished a lunch of pot roast and potatoes. The aroma nauseated her all over again. She went straight to the bathroom and brushed her teeth. That's when she remembered the Saks bag and her absurd purchase. Shame heaped upon shame. She should never have bought it in the first place. Now it was gone, left behind in the coffee shop. Better this way. Where would she have worn it anyway? She rinsed her face with cool water and felt, in some strange way, relieved of a burden.

"Are you feeling alright, Jehudit?" her aunt asked, solicitously, as Judith brushed past her behind the counter. "You look very pale. Maybe you should lie down a little, *leibling*." And then, in a whisper just beside Judith's ear added, "Are you maybe unwell? Should you go home?"

"I'm fine," Judith answered testily, irritated by the hushed reference to her menstrual cycle, which wasn't due for a week. "It's only the heat."

But her hands trembled slightly, and she tried to keep them out of sight. A shipment of new gold chains had become hopelessly tangled, and although it always fell to her to pick out the knots – she had inherited her father's sharp eyes and his delicate touch – today she worked clumsily. What had Michael thought, when she flew out of the restaurant like that? Did he see her doubled over and retching against those cars? What sense could he have made of her failing to return, and even worse, leaving him with the bill? Her cheeks burned at this thought.

Maybe this idea – finishing college, becoming a doctor – was all a terrible mistake. How could she hope to get along outside the community? Was she following the will of Hashem, or her own stubborn delusion? She fervently believed as she had been taught: that by her thoughts and deeds she could hasten Hashem's return to his people. But was she driving Him away instead? All her life, wisdom and support had come from the people around her. Now, her questions echoed back from the walls, unanswered and mocking. From where she stood, the stately synagogue on Eastern Parkway felt as distant to Judith as the Russian city of Lubavitch, home to the original Rebbe, and although she knew in her head that she had entered into her exile voluntarily, her heart felt as if she had been evicted and left to wander and stumble through a glass and concrete desert of her own making.

To whom could she turn for guidance? According to the *Zohar*, when the ancient Temple was destroyed and the people of Israel expelled to wander the desert, the *Shekhinah* exiled herself from the Holy Land in order to accompany them. Through each of their many exiles, that blessed Sabbath Bride guided Israel and offered them hope. She rose up from the sands before them like luminous columns of smoke. This was the same vision that Rebecca witnessed, the day before she passed away. Lying in her narrow hospital bed, in a room with no windows, Rebecca had cried out that she saw the *Shekinah* – Jewel of the Torah – an angel with broad wings, towering tall as a flame-lit cloud, welcoming her, offering her succor and eternal peace.

The Jews had no idea how many centuries of wandering lay ahead of them. Judith, however, knew she had two more years of college to complete the required pre-med courses and then at least six years of medical school, internship and residency to realize her goal. And after that? Would she be able to return to her family? Would she find a place waiting in the community? Just as Abraham set out on a journey with no known destination, she too would have to trust in the unknown. Abraham's faith in Hashem was unshakeable. Every night Judith bolstered her own conviction (and fought her guilt) with thoughts of Rebecca, whose memory nourished the stubborn seed of aspiration in her heart.

Judith arranged the knotted cluster of chains so that the short untangled ends spread, spider-like, from the clump in the center. She used a long dressmaker's needle with a faux pearl at one end to tease the individual chains loose from the group. Like unraveling an intricate formula in Chemistry or working through the complex meanings of a Talmudic verse, unknotting finely wrought gold chains gave Judith a feeling of completion. Almost always, there was one moment when the task seemed impossible, and then, with patience, determination or perhaps divine intervention, another moment when the impossible suddenly fell effortlessly into place. With one hand, Judith inserted the tip of the needle into a single miniscule link of a fine chain. She lifted the chain carefully to create a loop. With the other hand, she threaded the loose end of a different chain through the opening she had created. Half a dozen golden filaments now lay separated on the countertop and Judith fitted each one into its own velvet box.

It was both generous and bold of her aunt and uncle to let her keep her job after Judith, flouting the word of the Rebbe, left home. Many families would have shunned her. Perhaps it was Tante's own disappointed dreams that softened her heart. For weeks before she revealed her plans, Judith could neither sleep not eat. Her mother clucked over her and felt her forehead for fever several times a day. She pressed Judith's favorite foods on her. Having lost one daughter, she must have been distraught at the pallor of her next eldest, Judith realized. Week after week came and went as Judith worked up the nerve to tell them that she had received an acceptance from Hunter College and found an apartment in Manhattan. Each night, she cried herself into a restless stupor.

Like the mystics of old, Judith looked for signs everywhere – if the egg she was cracking for breakfast had a bloody spot that meant she should abandon her plans; if the water in the kettle boiled before the toast popped up, she should carry on. Finally, there was no choice. She had to accept the space at school and write a check for the apartment, or lose both. Judith chose the moment just after the close of Shabbat to tell them. The blessings had been said over the wine, the fragrant spices and the braided candle, and the Shabbat candles had been extinguished.

Barukh atah Adonai, hamav'dil bein kodesh l'chol.
Blessed are You, Lord, who separates between sacred and secular.

They had returned to the mundane world in which such an announcement could be made. But when she opened her mouth to speak, all that emerged was a choking sob. Was this a sign she should stop? But no; she forced herself to go on. By the time she had gotten the words out, the entire family was in tears. Her mother fled to the bedroom and father to the Sanctuary. The next morning, Judith packed her bags and left, emigrating by subway to her new life.

Judith now reached for a bottle of Windex under the counter and polished the top of the glass case, ridding it of fingerprints and the cloudy ring left behind by someone's coffee cup. There were no customers in the shop, but a group of middle-aged women stood outside staring through the window at a display of sapphire and diamond rings. The rings were paste, put there to attract customers to the real gems inside. But the women stared, rapt, at the false beauty before them.

The grandfather clock had just chimed three when she heard Aunt Zipporah answer the telephone, and then say, "Judith? There is no Judith here. You must have a wrong number." It could only be Michael, Judith thought. No one else would ask for Judith at the shop. All her girlfriends knew her as Jehudit. Only on her college application had she entered her name as Judith, the closest English equivalent, which she had seized upon in a moment of rebellion after the Rebbe – his word unquestionable law – declared, once and for all, that it was impossible for her to pursue her dream of medical school. So it was Judith, not Jehudit Fein who enrolled in classes. And since a name is a powerful thing, who could say whether that was another person, entirely?

What could Michael be thinking now? That she purposely gave him a wrong number? She wished that she had. She was worse than a *schnorrer*, stiffing him for lunch. Did he think her a liar as well? Again, the chains fell from her hands, and her uncle looked up from the velvet display case of diamond engagement rings he was assembling. Every phone call after that made Judith's heart race and steeped her in further humiliation. What had she set into motion with her agreement to meet Michael? Was God so vigilant in his anger that her life would be nothing but bitterness from now on?

She had been determined, from the day Rebecca died, to become a doctor. When her sisters played house, they were all mamas. When they begged her to join their childish game, she donned her mother's white Sabbath blazer, and played the part of the doctor who came to the house and ministered to the ailments of their doll babies. Who else but Hashem could have blessed her with her talents and the passion to use them to relieve suffering?

What Judith hadn't known that day she left her parents' house was that it wasn't just a simple matter of walking out the door. It's almost like you don't just leave once, she thought. You have to re-leave all the time.

ᘯ⊚ᕇ

Johanna huddled in the alley between buildings so close and tall, they shrank the sky into a thin gray slice of memory, which was just the way she wanted it. Eyes tightshut, her breath throbbed loud in her ears. A lover's breath. Good company. A clammy breeze, smelling of the catch of the day from the seaport a block away, snaked like a river just above the cobbled pavement. Something fell with a damp splat onto the stones just to her right and Johanna wriggled a little further to her left. High-heeled footsteps clacked from beyond the alley, voices echoed and someone hawked up a loud cough. All of it as far away as a dream.

"...eleven percent, no less."

"...stupid bastard."

"Can't you just imagine..."

Johanna's body slumped against the bricks. Rat Alley. No one would come for her in here. She could rest.

"...tickets for the game tonight..."

"It's on sale..."

"...money back next payday."

Payday. Play day. May day. *Mayday*! Johanna pressed her palms hard over her eye sockets to push back the memory. Sirens. Flashing lights. Screams. A sudden downpour pelting her shoulders, catching in her hair. Water turned to glass. Mayday. Slayday. Glass had rained down around her head and shoulders like candy from a burst piñata. People had run, shrieking, but Johanna just stood there, her face tilted to the sky. One small piece of glass tore through her cheek and then she, too, began to run with the herd.

Why had she been in midtown that day? May 16. Eight and eight. Four and four and four and four. Two and... Doctor's appointment. Back when she was still keeping them. Johanna now patted her pockets where the remainder of her stash of pills nestled. Dr. Nash was the only one she trusted. His office at 43rd and Madison next door to the Chinese restaurant where she ordered egg drop soup and spare ribs. Slurped eggs. Dropped soup. Splayed ribs.

Here for a reason. That's what had been singing in her brain all morning. We are here for a reason. You are here for a reason. He, she, it, they are here for a reason. She marched along to that beat. She was full of soup and ribs and about to make her way back downtown. And then the rain of glass. Warn them, her voices taunted her. Just try. Warn. Them. And she screamed out the warning. But too late. Like black lightning, the metal propeller sheared through the air and tore through the woman on the corner, the one in a blue pants suit, waiting for the light to turn green. Johanna saw her drop to the ground, skewered. Red.

That could have been you, her voices told her. Now will you listen?

The reporters had crowded around within minutes. Did you hear the helicopter burst apart? Did you see the pieces fly off the roof and slam into the windows? Tell us, they begged, reaching out in supplication with their pens, their pads, their microphones.

The shattered membrane of the building ascended into the sky above her. Her voices hummed threats in her ears. The world, she told the reporters in a steady voice, will end in a sea of shattered glass. There was silence. The questions abruptly ceased. As one body, they turned from her and began to move away. NEW YORK CITY WILL EXPLODE IN A TORRENT OF GLASS, she screamed after them. They left her standing there in the midst of the twinkling ruins.

DISASTER read the headlines in the papers the next day. *Helicopter crash on roof of Pan Am Building kills five; victim on street stabbed by rotor.* But by then the truth was clear to Johanna. The anger of this city was about to reap its bloody reward. Fire. Glass. Death. And it was up to Johanna to warn them – the innocent ones – and lead them to safety. Grunting, she pulled herself up from the sharp cobbles. It was time to get back underground. It could happen again, today.

☙◉❧

"You must be Pia Richter." The hand extended in front of Pia's face was as pendulant as an aspen leaf, the fingernails glossy and pale, one slim digit graced by a ring sporting the largest, brightest star in the firmament. A wash of Charlie perfume arrived in accompaniment. "I'm Christa Welkind." She pronounced it *Velkind.*

Pia struggled forward out of the deep, soft chair where the receptionist had sent her to wait. She had been sitting in the reception area of Metro Advertising for more than 15 minutes. She had crossed and recrossed her legs, smoothing the dark linen of her skirt against her skin, ruffling it, smoothing it again. Other people came and went through the heavy glass doors. Delivery boys carrying envelopes and boom boxes under their arms, businessmen in Armani suits, women with good shoes and bad dye jobs. They came, they sat, they moved on. Only Pia remained. She tried to focus on the issue of *Metro Home* she had picked up from the table by her side – its cover promised a piece on the emerging hip hop art scene – but she found herself beginning to drowse comfortably in the deliciously cool air. Something silky, like a dream, played in the distance. Now, in a rush to grab the proffered hand, she dropped the magazine. It fell at her feet and both women dove to retrieve it – long hair, straight and blonde, curly and black, mingling for a moment in the rush. Pia was faster, and swept up the publication as she rose.

"Yes, I'm Pia," she managed to say.

"I'm sorry you had to wait. I was stuck in a meeting. Follow me."

The woman pivoted on one high-heeled pump and took off down the sky blue hallway. Pia replaced the magazine on the end table, and hurried to catch up.

They wound their way through a labyrinth of gray-carpeted hallways, the sound of voices and typewriters issuing from behind the office doors. Finally, they turned into a large room with serried ranks of drawing tables, each lit by a cherry red Luxor lamp, the entire room presided over by a large bulletin board covered in what looked like blueprints. A profusion of papers, pens, scissors, tape, and personal mementos littered the tables though there was no one in the room, and Pia felt as if she were on a battlefield from which the combatants had recently fled, laying down their arms in haste.

"Oh, everyone's in the Wednesday morning S & E meeting," Christa explained in response to the question Pia hadn't asked. "I'm actually HR, but I thought I'd give you the quick tour. As you see, this is one of two rooms of the art department. Most of the desks here are layout." Pia wondered what S and E, and HR stood for, but nodded knowingly. "The other room is mainly for graphics," Christa continued. "And then there's the photo lab." As she spoke, she continued to walk briskly, leaving Pia little time to look around. But the bright room, with its large windows facing east from Madison all the way to tiny snatches of the East River, was everything she had dreamed of in a workplace. She could see herself installed at one of the tables, her own assortment of postcards, snowballs, and photos keeping pace with those of her coworkers.

Christa was already out the door at the other end of the room, and Pia rushed to catch up. More carpeted hallways, more ringing telephones and bright, intense voices too muffled to discern. Finally they arrived at a door marked Human Resources. Christa held it open for Pia. Ah, *HR*, Pia thought as she slipped past her guide. The room was completely interior to the building, a dropped ceiling housing a bank of lights that shone mutely into the interiors of a warren of cubicles.

"We can talk in here," Christa said, directing Pia into one of the cubicles. Despite the breeze floating from several air ducts, Pia found herself feeling sweaty and simultaneously chilled. She hoped that her interviewer would not notice the goosebumps on her bare arms. Any room without windows made her anxious. She was grateful that she hadn't come looking for work in HR, where she wouldn't see the light of day for hours at a stretch. She sometimes wondered how she survived so many months in the dark of her mother's womb. She knew that her birth surprised everyone with its early onset – at eight months – and rapid progress. "It was like a dam opened, and out you poured," her mother used to tell her. "You looked happy to see the light of day."

"I got a copy of your resume from Helen at the Harding Agency, and it looks quite good, but I was hoping you could tell me a little more about yourself." Christa rolled herself into position behind her desk, which gave Pia the opportunity to dry her damp palms on her skirt as she sat across from her.

She took a deep breath and steadied herself on the slippery plastic seat. Then she launched into the soliloquy she'd been performing all week. "...graduated from Ithaca College with a major in art and minors in design and political science...designed yearbooks... drawing and painting since I'm six... at home last year to work and save up some money...can cook a mean chili con carne...looking for an entry level position with room to grow...hard working..." Christa looked bored. Give me a chance, Pia thought. Give me a desk. Give me a salary. Give me a break. Give me some kind of sign.

Christa picked up a pen and made some notes on Pia's resume. Pia couldn't read what they said.

"Would you like to see some of my work?" she asked.

"Well, I wouldn't be the best judge of that. That would be something you would show to Mark Roth, our director of design." Christa pushed her chair back from the desk, checked her watch and crossed her long legs. Pia thought this seemed to signal something; was she to suppose that the interview had come to an end? But Christa continued, "He'll be out of the meeting in a few minutes. Maybe you could see him then." As if on cue, the phone rang.

"Yes, she's right here in my office. Sure, I'll bring her by," and Christa was already rolling herself back from her desk as she hung up the phone. "You're on," she said to Pia, who wiped her sweaty palms once more as she stood and gathered her things.

Christa walked her through the catacomb of hallways and left her in front of the door marked Art Director, saying that she'd be back. The door was half open and Pia knocked before walking in. Sitting on a high stool in front of a drafting table, Mark Roth looked like an owl on steroids – a pale full-moon face under a pair of bushy salt-and-pepper eyebrows. A pair of thick round black-framed glasses enlarged startlingly blue eyes. It was a face made to be caricatured, Pia thought, her fingers itching for a pen and a private moment. His head was cocked to the left, crushing a phone receiver against his shoulder. He didn't offer to shake her hand, but gestured with his chin toward a pair of Eames-style chairs and a round glass table at one end of his office. His lips mouthed the words, "On hold, damn it." Pia obediently sat down on one of the chairs to wait. She busied herself with opening her portfolio and arranging some of her work on the table. Having done this, she began to examine the framed prints on the walls. Highly stylized Erte costume design gouaches, mainly. Pia wondered if they were originals. She thought about getting up to examine them more closely. The sound of the phone receiver slammed back into its cradle made her jump.

"Sorry. Sorry. I didn't mean to startle you," Mark Roth apologized, hopping down from his stool. "It's the damned electric company. They're threatening to turn off my power for non-payment of a bill, when I've already sent them a copy of the cancelled check. Is it my fault they hire incompetents? The woman on the phone sounded like she just woke up from siesta. It she was any slower, she'd be..." He stopped suddenly, and thrust a meaty hand in front of her by way of greeting.

Pia's skin prickled with displeasure, but she forced her voice to be cordial as she introduced herself, then sat back in her chair and waited for Mark Roth to begin asking questions. This was the real thing – a New York City graphics department – and here was a guy who had the power to make her a part of it. The art director smiled at her encouragingly and Pia began to relax and fanned a tiny glimmer of hope in her chest.

"We have about a dozen decent clients right now," he explained. "Perfume companies, drug companies, a couple of fashion houses, a sneaker manufacturer we feel is going to go bigtime. They're the bill-payers while the guys upstairs work on pitching our services to some even bigger names. But it's our job down here to make the clients happy. To spin their straw into gold, basically. You know what I mean?"

Pia assured him that she did. She began to touch each of the pieces she had arrayed on the table, trying to turn his attention toward them. He seemed more interested in his own train of thought. He clasped his fingers beneath his chin and turned his gaze inward, pondering some thought. She wasn't sure how, or whether, to wake him from this reverie. She tried to regain his attention.

"Um, of course I'm really interested in the job you had advertised," she began, "but I was also hoping that you could take a look at my stuff and maybe give me some advice about where to concentrate my efforts."

Mark Roth looked startled for a moment.

"The job. Right." He gave her work a cursory glance and then stood and began rifling through his pockets. He withdrew a small wad of papers and began unfolding them. "Well, of course,

you're still young and this is really an entry level position." He selected one sheet and stuffed the rest back in his pocket. "We need a
lot of support. Office stuff, mainly." He looked back at her.

Pia heard a warning bell go off in the back of her mind as loud
as the siren for the VFD that towered over the Penelope town square.

"I'm sure that Christa went over all this with you, but just for
the record, how many words a minute do you type?"

The dingy corner luncheonette looked like an oasis. Inside,
the place smelled of griddle grease and malt – comforting in its way,
although the air conditioning seemed to be failing in the face of the
heat coming off the huge grill. The revolving stools that flanked the
counter all sported plastic seat covers in various stages of decompo-
sition. Pia settled onto the one with the fewest rips and fought her
mounting discouragement. The counterman came by and dropped
a menu in front of her, but she waved it away and ordered a Danish
and an iced coffee.

"Excuse me," she said to him on an impulse. "But you
wouldn't, by any chance, need a waitress here, would you?"

He snorted. "You're too late," he told her, taking a swipe at
some dried egg on the counter with a dingy cloth. "We had a sign
out last week and fourteen girls showed up in one day. We hired
already." He turned away and came back a moment later with her
food. "Would have hired you, though," he said with a wink. "Why
don't you try back in a few weeks?"

Pia felt a low, animal growl build from deep in her gut. She
gobbled the Danish in rapid bites, the sugar hitting her blood-
stream like a drug. The more she thought about her morning, the
angrier she became. Finally, in a fury, she took a black marker and
the new notebook from the shopping bag and opened it in front
of her.

The lines accumulated quickly on the page. With each typewriter she tossed onto the heap she muttered a sharp little curse
until the mountain of trashed machines began to assuage her anger.
By the time she sketched the final one, she found herself giggling

demonically. One of these days, she told herself with renewed optimism, art really could emerge triumphant over the apparatus.

Chapter Six

What would she look like when she couldn't see, Danielle wondered.

She clung to the strap, watching her dark reflection waver in the window as the uptown Number 2 train rolled around a bend in the tracks. At 14th Street the train doors had slid open to reveal a blind man and his dog framed almost directly in front of her. Quietly, but with perfect confidence, the man said, "Forward," and the dog stepped neatly inside and steered them both through the crowded car. A woman sitting nearby asked if he wanted a seat and, almost before he could answer, took his free hand to help him pivot to the seat she had vacated, which she tapped with her other hand. Danielle cringed. Would strangers be grasping her hands, touching her, unbidden, out of kindness? Tapping for her attention, as if she were a child? How did he bear it, she wondered. Her mother used to tap her on the shoulder with one forefinger as a silent, face-saving rebuke in public for some perceived infraction. It got to the point where Danielle would wince whenever she sensed her mother reaching an arm in her direction.

The train jolted forward and the man staggered slightly, then regained his footing and sat down with surprising grace. The dog, a small Lab, black and glossy as a seal and wearing a sturdy leather harness, circled once, then settled between the man's feet, scanning the line of passengers across from him with an implacable gaze. Once, the dog sniffed at something on the floor. Immediately, the man twitched the leash and said, "Leave it" in a voice that brooked no nonsense.

Danielle allowed herself to stare into the man's face, at his eyes in particular, which rested far back in their sockets like forgotten things. How would her face change when she no longer used the muscles around her eyes to focus? She shut her eyes and tried to relax her face completely. Even with her eyes closed, however, she could feel the tiny muscles working, exercising their influence on her physiognomy. Over time they would slacken. Her eyes would remain their unusual shade of hazel, but who would look into them? Her lips would still be full and nicely symmetrical, but she'd have to forego the deep rose lipstick she preferred in favor of invisible Chapstick for fear of making herself look more Pagliacci than Princess Grace. Years of ballet class as a child had given her the posture of a dancer, but most of the blind people on the street stooped, or listed slightly to one side like sailboats in a freshening breeze. Was it vanity or identity that made her dread this so? Either way, Danielle feared losing not only her sight, but her recognizable self.

At 34th Street, a family of tourists boarded, blocking her view of the man and his dog. As the parents clung to each other and wrestled with a map, two of the kids began making faces in the blind man's direction. One boy rolled his eyes up into his head and began flailing around with his arms. The girl giggled. Danielle felt her cheeks grow hot with vicarious humiliation. As the train lurched, she was pleased to see a quick look of fear flicker across the boy's face as he flew backward into legs of a stranger, only to be yanked back to the pole by his father.

When much of the crowd exited at 42nd Street, Danielle

looked for the man and his dog, but they were gone. She was surprised, however, to see that yet another blind person – a woman – had been sitting just a few seats away from him, identifiable only by the red-tipped cane that rested against her knee. Like ships passing in the night, these two had never shared any flicker of recognition. A new crowd of passengers squeezed in and the doors closed.

Ever since she had been diagnosed, it seemed that the city swarmed with the blind. They had become the object of her obsessive scrutiny.

At first, Danielle believed she'd have to make an effort to find sightless people to observe. The only blind person she had known growing up was the son of Dr. Henderson, her dentist. The boy was away at a special school most of the year, but spent holidays at home. Sometimes, during school vacations, Dr. Henderson brought him to work, where Danielle had seen him listening to the radio in the doctor's inner office. As he listened, he rocked back and forth, almost violently, in time to the music. But Chip Henderson, Danielle knew, had so many other disabilities that he would spend the rest of his life in a sheltered living situation of some sort. Still, it was the image of Chip, rocking on his father's deep leather desk chair that haunted Danielle when she first received her diagnosis.

Dr. Schein suggested that she seek out better role models. A few weeks later, down the block from Bloomingdale's, on 58th Street, she found the Lighthouse with its resources and counseling facilities for the visually impaired. Instead of going inside, she sat in a coffee shop across the street and watched as a steady stream of blind New Yorkers entered and left the building. There were those with dogs and those with canes, both groups traversing the city in autonomy. But out-populating these by far were those with what Danielle thought of as "handlers," guardians who, for love or money, steered their disabled companions through life. For all she knew, without their attendants these people might be completely helpless. Shut-ins. One woman, about Danielle's age, walked arm-in-arm with a woman who looked to be her mother. The older woman strode with an imperious glare as the younger slumped alongside, petulant and childlike. Watching them, Danielle's hands had trembled and she felt overwhelmingly nauseated. Once blind, she might become a child again, pathetic and powerless.

But then she started seeing blind people everywhere – subways and supermarkets, on escalators and eating in coffee shops. She stared and stared at them in their perambulations around the city. Actually, she stared and stared at everything these days, as if she were storing up a lifetime of impressions. But these people gave her hope. And a plan.

Somewhere down at the other end of the car a woman was shouting. People backing away from the altercation made the crush around Danielle even tighter; they were truly penned in like cattle. Someone nearby stank of Brut and body odor. There was nowhere to move. *Jews*, the woman was shouting now – *I wish I had been born a Jew!* The breath was nearly squeezed out of Danielle by the crush around her. Danielle's own sweat turned sour in her nose.

The woman with the cane got off the train at 72nd Street. Danielle, leaving the express to transfer to the local across the platform, watched as the woman followed the crowd out the doors and a few steps straight ahead before turning right toward the stairs. This must have been a path that she had taken many times, Danielle thought. She wanted to trail her. She had so many questions. She was so afraid of the answers. But the local train pulled in almost immediately, and Danielle was washed aboard in a swell of other riders. She gripped the overhead strap and the train moved on.

"Your cousin Paula asked for you, by the way." It was the precise tone of that *by the way* across the phonelines that tipped Danielle off to that fact that she would bristle at whatever her mother said next.

"She just rented a nice little house near the beach and said there was plenty of room if you felt like moving in. That would be nice, wouldn't it? You two used to be such good friends. More like sisters than cousins."

Whatever had possessed her to call her mother?

The first thing Danielle had done when she got into her su-

perheated two-room apartment was to turn on the ancient air conditioner and the oscillating fans. The AC chattered and growled as
if angry at being disturbed from its rest. With at least the promise
of a cooling breeze, she dropped gratefully onto her bed and put her
feet up, resting on the soft, gypsy-printed pillows piled against the
headboard. Then, in response to an obviously misguided desire for
connection, she dialed her parents' number in California. As soon as
the phone began to ring, she began to hope that no one would pick
it up and she'd reach the answering machine. She started compos-
ing a message in her head. Her parents, ever modern, were the first
people she had known to purchase one of the clunky things. At the
fifth ring, though, her mother answered. And shortly beyond the
preliminaries, the inevitable harangue resumed from the where it had
left off the week before. This time it led to a suggestion she move in
with her cousin.

What was unspoken screamed through the wires. Not for the
first time, Danielle wished she had actual sisters or brothers. Several of each, in fact. Enough so her mother's overbearing attentions
would be stretched thin.

"Darling, as your mother, I insist that you stop being stubborn
and thoughtless and come home. The university hospital has some of
the most prominent physicians in the country on staff, and I've got
Dr. Mattison looking into ophthalmologists for you. We can make an
appointment as soon as you tell us when you'll be home."

Danielle closed her eyes briefly, leaned back into the pillows,
and breathed in deeply through her nose to a slow count of four: H-
two-three-four, O-*two-three-four*, M-*two-three-four*, E-*two-three-four*
– feeling her belly rise to fill out the black sleeveless tee shirt she was
wearing. "Mom, from three thousand miles away, I don't think you're
in any position to insist," she said more calmly than she felt, "and anyway, I already *am* home. That's where I'm calling from. My home."

She noted with some satisfaction the sputter of indignation
that marked her mother's mounting frustration. "You know perfectly
well what I mean. *Home.* Here in Santa Barbara. With us. You need

help. Or you will. Do you have any idea what this is doing to your father and me?" She paused significantly. "Well, do you?"

The trilling upturn in her mother's voice made it clear she was preparing for a full-scale emotional assault. On the tip of Danielle's tongue was "Oh, so it's *you* that this is being done to?" But what she finally managed to say was, "Mom, I have to go. There's someone at the door," before she replaced the phone in its cradle. She lifted it up again. The blessed neutrality of the dial tone.

She found she still had an urge to dial. A need to work off the nerves that had been revving up all afternoon. Ever since Geoffrey had asked her out for a drink and she'd accepted. A terrible mistake. Now she felt an overwhelming need to make contact. With whom? She imagined dialing Paul just for the comfort of his voice. But that was out of the question. She had vowed not to call him again. It always ended in the same argument. It wasn't fair to either of them. She never wanted to be his burden. And her closest friends, Jane and Hannah, were away together on a two-week trip to England and Spain. She wished she had gone, too. But there was no way to get time off from work. She was skating on thin ice as it was, with all the hours she took off.

I will never see the Alhambra, Danielle thought. *Or the Gaudi park in Barcelona. I will never see Piccadilly Circus.* She still imagined the three-ring kind, although she knew better.

"Look to the right before you step off the curb!" she had warned Hannah as she helped her friend into a cab to the airport last week. Hannah was notorious for her oblivious street-crossing technique. It was a wonder she'd made it to twenty-seven without being creamed by a bus in this city, much less over there, where the traffic whizzed by on the wrong side of the road.

I will never get to look right. Listen right just didn't have the same ring to it.

The humidity was oppressive. Danielle turned the fan on her bedroom floor up a notch. The blades whirred at a higher pitch, and the fan swung its head like an angry elephant. *I will never see the*

African veldt, or India, or Kashmir. Not Venice, or even the elephants in the Bronx zoo. The light in her room shifted as clouds covered up the sliver of blue visible from her bedroom window. The man across the airshaft slammed his window shut and turned on his air conditioner, its dark hum adding to the oppressiveness of the day. Again, Danielle closed her eyes. But she opened them wide right away, staring up into the sky as if to memorize its shifting configurations. *But I will see Geoffrey* she thought, grimacing wryly.

She had intended to take a shower and a nap before meeting for their date. Instead, Danielle stamped around the small, bright apartment, yanking down the blackout shades and pressing their edges against the Velcro she had tacked up around each window frame. It was time to practice. She slipped off her sandals and exchanged them for a pair of sneakers that she laced carefully, ending with a double knot. Soon, sandals would be a thing of the past, discarded along with cameras, kaleidoscopes and charts of the constellations. When you couldn't see, sandals were an open invitation to broken toes.

Practicing had been Danielle's own inspiration. She started with just a few minutes a day, doing ordinary things around her apartment without using her sight. When she got up at night to go to the bathroom, she no longer turned on the light. In the morning when she dressed, she navigated from bed to dresser to closet and back to bed again with her eyes closed. She felt her panties to distinguish front from back, her bra to know whether it was inside out. She still chose her clothes with her eyes open, however. No need to show up with the purple blouse over the brown pants a moment sooner than necessary.

After a couple of weeks, she began extending her practice time to the kitchen. She arranged the foods in her refrigerator in a neat and predictable manner. Milk on the right, juice on the left. Butter, eggs, cheese, each in their place. Jams and jellies, maple syrup, and sweet things on the top shelf of the door; mustard, mayonnaise, Tabasco and other savories, on the lower shelf. She memorized the different shapes of similar containers: the grape jelly jar versus the orange marmalade, the ketchup versus the barbecue sauce. Slowly,

carefully, she sliced onions and garlic with both eyes shut – no peeking – using the bent knuckles of her left hand as a guide for the broad
side of the chef's knife in her right.   Her first attempt at a simple
pasta Bolognese took an hour as opposed to her usual 20 minutes,
and required two Band-Aids and a bag of crushed ice – the former
for matching cuts on the first two fingers of her left hand, and the
latter for a burn on her wrist when she accidentally rested it on the
edge of the hot skillet. The chopped onions were thick and coarse.
The sautéed ground meat was lumpy. There was too much pepper
and not enough nutmeg. But over time, she improved. Only rarely
now did she sustain any damage: a sliced fingernail, a singed knuckle
– nothing worse than the thousand little cuts and burns kitchen staff
suffered every day. What she needed to work on was timing.

The blackout shades were her next flash of inspiration. She
found the fabric for them in a hardware store down on the Bowery.
When she brought the dusty roll up to the register the counter man
said, "You a photographer? Building a darkroom?" No, she would
never be a photographer. Danielle cut the fabric to the size of the
window frames and fixed both fabric and frame with Velcro strips
to create a tight, lightproof fit. It worked almost better than she'd
expected. The utter blackness was as different from ordinary night as,
well, night from day.

At first, it terrified her. She could only stand the total absence
of light for a few minutes at a stretch. She made up rules and excuses
for breaking them. She'd practice for twenty minutes – unless the
phone rang. She'd vacuum the entire room – unless something rolled
off a table, or broke.

She tucked her sandals neatly under the edge of the bed where
she wouldn't trip over them. This sort of thing had become habit, as
Dr. Schein promised it would. Danielle had always been methodical anyway; it was an asset in her work. At school they had taught
her that cooking in a restaurant kitchen required choreography as
exquisite and precise as any Balanchine ballet. *I will never see another
ballet.* When she worked, Danielle felt her arms and hands as sensi-

tive extensions of her will. They lifted, turned, peeled, sliced, scraped, whisked, poured and arranged so that courses flowed smoothly from her station and each dish settled onto its plate with near-perfect composition. Could she ever hope to dance with such grace in the dark?

No one at La Belle Epoque knew about her diagnosis. She didn't trust anyone – not even Kim, who'd been her closest pal there – not to tell Roderick, the restaurant's owner, who would surely boot her out. And now with Kim gone, there was no one to whom she was even tempted to unburden herself.

"There's a reason for all that steam," her advisor at school once told her. "The kitchen is a jungle." All the chefs at the top of the hierarchy felt the younger ones breathing down their necks. And Rod wasn't all that crazy about her in any case. She'd keep practicing. There was still a lot to work out. Timing her work with the other stations, for instance, was bound to be a challenge. But she would figure it out. She had to. Could they fire a blind person who could do her job as well as when she was sighted? Nearly as well? What about equal opportunity laws? This was Danielle's only hope. She had to keep this job. The alternative was a room in that "nice little house near the beach" – within tapping distance of her mother's constant oversight.

She'd been to see Dr. Schein last week. The doctor thought she might possibly have a year before she'd be legally blind, maybe more. A year. A long, long time if you were waiting for your sailor boy to come home from the sea – a scant instant if you were saying goodbye to everything you had once seen and taken for granted. It could be a year. And it could be a month. There was no way of knowing exactly.

When she'd first received the diagnosis of retinitis pigmentosa and realized that the symptoms she'd complained of – loss of peripheral vision, poor night vision, extraordinary sensitivity to glare – were only going to get worse until she had no vision left at all, she considered suicide. And it was not without precedent in her family. As her father drove her to the airport after her visit home the previous Christmas, Danielle pressed him for details about the maiden aunt who had become blind as a young woman. Just as they pulled up the drive to Departures, her father admitted that his mother's sister had died, not in an accident, as the family had always maintained, but from an overdose of aspirin and sleeping pills.

"You don't have to mention to your mother that we discussed this," he said, as Danielle reached her head through the driver's side window to kiss him goodbye. That was the way it was in their family. The difficult truth bowed before the convenient silence.

Death before blindness, Danielle had vowed to herself in those early days. What good would she be to herself, or to anyone, blind? Sometimes, she would close her eyes in the middle of walking down a block and lurch into person after person, apologizing as she went. People stared after her, thinking she was drunk or crazy. She went to bed each night praying she would not awaken in the morning. When death didn't materialize easily, she considered the alternatives – pills, knives, even the quick and thrilling dive from a tall building or in front of a train. She bought the pills, sharpened and honed the knives she already owned and leaned from balcony after balcony, hoping toward death but unable to make the decisive move. The tools remained at the ready; the shame hovered and breathed around her shoulders.

Dr. Schein and her therapist, Karen, both insisted she see a counselor regarding adaptive issues. Danielle told them to stop using that verb.

Practicing pushed back the demons. She stopped hanging over balconies and began developing her training regimen. With enough time and effort, she could do this. She really could.

Gripping the overhead strap by one hand, Judith moved to the side as a fleshy black woman struggled upward from the seat in front of her. The motion of the train as it slowed and rocked into the station worked against the woman, and she fell back into the seat, dropping her purse on Judith's toe.

"Sorry, sorry," the woman winced as she bent to retrieve her bag and then began once again to haul herself to her feet. The train came to a jolting halt, the passengers shifting forward and back into place again as one body. Judith gratefully lowered herself into the newly empty seat, glancing around nervously to see if there were any elderly or pregnant women to whom she would have to relinquish her prize. The car was mainly full of men, however, another reason Judith was happy to be seated. Before she left home, she had driven to work with her aunt and uncle. It was hard to get used to being jammed up against strange bodies. Harder still when so many of those bodies were male, and not at all shy about leaning into her with each lurch of the train. As anonymous and inevitable as it was, the multi-sex mash of bodies made her self-conscious and uncomfortable.

Not at all like the press of maternal flesh that characterized each Shabbat in the women's gallery at *shul*. There, as the Rebbe led the men in prayer downstairs in the main sanctuary, hundreds of women crushed into the inadequate space allotted to them, their bodies a clangorous blend of aromas from Shalimar to chicken soup, from cinnamon to sweat to menstrual blood. But to Judith growing up, the mad crush always felt like the warm arms of mother love – *mamalibn*.

She told Tante she rode the bus uptown – yet another lie – rather than bear her look of pained concern. At first, Judith had indeed ridden the bus, but it took so long, lurching its way through the midtown traffic, and left her feeling sick and queasy. One day, she steeled her nerve and descended into the subway for the ride home. Since then she'd traded her misgivings for speed.

There were so many other adjustments as well, to this strange new life. As a former member of the Rebbe's *shluchim* – that army of outreach workers who approached secular Jews and offered them Shabbat candles and a chance to learn more about their spiritual heritage and Jewish identity – she thought she had gained a pretty broad view of the outside world. It was only after she left the community that Judith realized how much there was she didn't know.

"This is an uptown number two train," the conductor muttered through the muzzy speaker system. "Next stop, Seventy-second Street," and the doors began to close, but not before a couple with a toddler in a stroller forced their way into the already crowded car. The closing doors nicked the rear wheels of the baby carriage and bounced back open, allowing the couple an extra moment to slide inside.

"This is an uptown Broadway express," the conductor announced again. "Please step away from the closing doors." The crowd adjusted to accommodate the newcomers, and then most of the riders returned to their single-minded scrutiny of the newspapers they clutched.

When Judith first began riding the train, she was amazed by this rapt attention to the *Times*, the *News* and the *Post* and conjectured that the papers, and the information they imparted, engendered the same devotion that the *Siddur*, the *Midrash* and the *Tanya* did for her community. One morning, she realized that the woman who was sitting next to her mouthing words of what Judith assumed was prayer, was really only puzzling out something called the Jumble. Even now, the discovery made Judith laugh at her own naiveté.

The child in the stroller, a squirming toddler with curly blond hair and a juice-stained bib tucked under her chin, twisted around and thrust her chubby arms into the air, demanding to be picked up. In response, her mother shook the carriage roughly and the girl tumbled back into place with a sharp wail. The man with them turned to glare at the woman and then knelt down to the child. The passengers nearest to him crushed further into themselves, leaving room for his bent knees. The woman standing above him yanked angrily at his collar.

"Stand up, you prick. Stand up like a fucking man for once."

"Leave me the hell alone," the man burst out. "Why don't you just take your goddamned shit and leave?"

Judith blushed at the profanity. She tried hard not to listen now, but even the shriek of the wheels on the tracks couldn't blot out the words.

"My whole life is shit," the woman whined. "One stinking

ball of hell. You don't know. You don't know how it is." Now the man stared intently down at the floor, frowning, as if pondering some weighty issue. Meanwhile, the child in the stroller writhed halfway out of the straps in an effort to get to the floor. Judith fought the urge to straighten and comfort the child as she would her own sister. Seemingly reaching a conclusion, the man bent down to straighten the girl in her seat, ignoring the rant overhead.

"You know what I hope?" the woman continued, glaring into the empty space where he'd been, seemingly unaware of his disappearance from her line of sight. "I hope that in my next life I'm born a Jew. That's right, a Jew!"

The first mention of the word pulled Judith into sharp attention, although she kept her eyes down on her purse. Her cheeks blazed. It was the way the woman said *Jew*. It might as well have been orangutan, or pygmy, or Martian. She wondered if anyone was looking at her and thinking, *Look: there's a Jew.* She didn't dare look up to see, but her heart raced as though she had taken flight.

The woman's monologue grew louder and Judith could sense that everyone in the car had also stopped whatever they were doing to listen. Only the baby continued struggling to get free of the stroller's restraints, oblivious to her mother's diatribe.

"Those people know how to take care of family. Jews aren't like us. They might put *you* out on the street, but they are good to their *own*." There was a pause.

Is this true, Judith asked herself? Certainly the community she grew up in was close-knit and self-protective, but also prickly and easily prone to breaking out in internal squabbles. Not to mention bitter factional fights with other Brooklyn Chasidic communities: Lubavitchers against Satmarers, Satmarers against Bobovers. Once, when she was very young, Judith woke in the night to hear a terrible commotion in the street below her window. In the morning, when she got to school, the older girls were talking about how Avram Aharon was tossed from a car onto Kingston Avenue after being beaten by a gang of Satmarers in Williamsburg, where he had gone to visit a distant cousin. And, of course, there were the cautionary tales of those girls who were mourned by their own families as dead, for marrying outside the faith.

"In my next life, make me a Jew." The woman practically shrieked. "I'd be happy, if only."

Suddenly, she lapsed into a silence so absolute that it startled Judith into looking up. It was as though the woman had been pitched into a state of suspended animation – her eyelids drooped slightly and one hand remained frozen in a wide gesture in front of her face, while the other anchored her to the strap above her head. In a moment, a dozen conversations grew to fill the space she'd vacated, but Judith couldn't look away as the woman swayed suspended from the strap in her ungainly pose. She appeared to have retreated to a place where gravity was nonexistent. Judith's stare kept returning to the woman's free arm and its incomplete gesticulation.

"Heroin, most likely," muttered a voice from her right. Judith blushed. Her staring had not gone unnoticed. "I just feel sorry for that little girl." Judith looked straight down and studied the familiar lines etched in her own knuckles until the train pulled into the station. Then she clutched her purse and fled. On her way out the door, she brushed the woman, whose uplifted arm fell heavily to her side.

Judith half-ran up the stairs and all the way to 76th Street. She felt queasy with fear, as though she were being chased. All her life she had been warned of the rampant anti-Semitism of the world beyond their little community. She had grown up alongside the children of death camp survivors and victims of horrific persecution in their homelands. Here in America, on the streets of Brooklyn, Jews like herself had created a protective haven and solid ground for practicing Hashem's commandments. Her sisters had wept with foreboding as they carried her suitcases to the subway when she moved out. But nothing had prepared Judith for feeling as exposed and alien as she did now.

As she picked her way through the crowd on Broadway, she thought about coming up from the subway onto Eastern Parkway, where everything was familiar, and half the people she passed knew her by name. She imagined the women especially, dressed in their skirts and stockings, carrying home groceries, most of them leading a brood of flushed-faced children across the broad avenue. I want to go home, she cried to herself. But as quickly as the thought formed, it spawned its own rebuttal. I *am* home, she told herself, pushing through the door to the limestone building on 78th Street.

ु৩৩৩

It was one hell of an enormous lizard, that statue on the roof across from where Pia stood on Fifth Avenue and 13th Street. And *angry* from the look of it. A mouth full of scalpel-sharp teeth gaped, and the ridges along its back stood up like a hedge of swords. Its tail alone shot a good six feet into the air, Pia figured, and its red eyes glared daggers at the puny pedestrians passing below, herself included. Although she was hurrying from the 14th Street subway station to what she hoped would be an air-conditioned office building on 12th Street, Pia stopped on the northwest corner, diagonally opposite the beast, the better to contemplate it. It was astonishing, really, how you could be walking down one of the most famously sophisticated streets in the world and suddenly, there was this, this, *iguana*. That's what it was. Or someone's idea of an iguana, anyway. Someone who had never seen a real iguana, clearly. The sign over the door read *Lone Star Café*. Pia wondered whether it was the kind of restaurant the staff of *Women's Wear Daily*, where she had an interview in ten minutes, might gather for lunch.

She crossed the street to get a closer look at the place. A sign on the door advertised Live Country Music. She didn't really like country music, but the menu offered about ten types of burgers, one more alluring than the next. Her stomach growled and she wished she'd known about this place when she had arranged to meet Rosie for a beer tonight before her friend hopped the bus back upstate. Rosie would love that iguana. Their second grade class had had one as a class pet. Rosie fought for the right to be pet monitor and feed it bits of lettuce and mushy bananas. Pia wondered if she could still reach Rosie, after the interview, before her friend left her brother's house. Then she noticed the prices, and realized with a shock that she wouldn't be asking Rosie to meet her there after all, unless Rosie offered to pay for dinner. It was scary how fast money went, down here in the city. If she didn't get work soon, she wouldn't last past Labor Day. The idea made her slump with despair.

Pia checked her watch and doubled her pace. It would be good to have a minute to use the bathroom and cool down. How many times had she already skimmed the sweat off her upper lip? There must be a mustache of grime there by now. She paused at the corner to wait for the light. Fifth Avenue stretched down toward the Washington Square arch. Above it rose the skyline of lower Manhattan, dwarfed by those enormous new twin towers that anchored the very base of the island. You could see them from everywhere, Pia had noticed. Even from Eastern Parkway. And you could probably see the whole world from those windows. She wondered what it would be like to work there, a hundred stories in the air. The inspiration you could take from such a view. A cab blared its horn at a car pulling out of a parking space across the avenue.

"Whaddya blind? Ya dumb fuck!" the driver called. In response, the car blasted its horn at the cab, which burned rubber and squealed down the street. The waves of heat coming off the car hoods made the scene shimmer like a cartoon dream. A man walking beside Pia bumped against her portfolio and glared at her, murderously. She didn't know whether to apologize or tell him to go to hell. It was a wonder people weren't killed right and left, Pia thought. But of course, if you read the headlines in the *Daily News* or the *Post*, you knew they were. She glanced around her. A crowd of strangers. Some would be victims, she thought, and some, suspects.

She reached the next corner and turned left. The address on the paper said 7 East 12th Street, third floor, and she turned into a nondescript building about midway down the block. There was no desk in the black and white linoleum tiled lobby, so she waited for an elevator. All three were headed up, away from her. It was like some sort of conspiracy.

When one finally arrived, a crowd of bone thin women wafted through the doors, all clustered around one tall, middle-aged woman with the tannest and most wrinkled skin Pia had ever seen. Pia knew she was staring, but couldn't help it. This woman's face looked like a brown paper lunch bag that had been crumpled up and then re-smoothed against the edge of a table. The others were raptly intent on her words.

"I called Bill this morning and he said not to tell anyone, but Nina's dress was designed by...." and the emaciated ones swept out the door before Pia could hear who the dress was designed by and why it was such a big secret. If these were the sort of people she'd be working with, Pia thought, there wouldn't be a lot of lunching in burger joints. She stepped into the elevator along with a delivery boy carrying an overblown bouquet of white lilies. Her hand bumped his as they both reached to push the button for the third floor.

"Excuse me," she said, brightly. To which he answered nothing at all, but grinned lasciviously. Pia stepped back and leaned against the wall.

The elevator door rolled open to reveal a huge, loft-like room filled with clusters of beat-up desks, each sporting a typewriter. Pia's first reaction was one of dismay at how shabby the whole place looked. They were *manual* typewriters, for God's sake. How could this be the most influential fashion paper on the planet? She stood awkwardly, waiting for the boy with the flowers to step out, and then she followed him to a desk where a harried-looking woman juggled a pair of telephone receivers.

Althea's arms floated up past her head and came down with her fingertips grazing the smooth wooden headboard. She settled her shoulders more deeply into the pillows as she reached upward with her hips. Oscar pushed into her in silence, and she felt herself resolve into the familiar image of a peach, bobbing gently from only the slimmest tether, tree-ripe, rounded and plump, a sweet, pulpy mass, rosy and golden and furred, juice-dripping, honey-laden, sun-warmed, fragrant. Settling herself tightly around the rhythmic, rolling pit of him, she slid her fruit-heavy bottom left and right, and a peach-flavored hum rose in her throat. Overhead, his broad shoulders blocked out the walls and ceiling, leaving nothing but flesh visible. And in this state of vegetal madness, she found a path to temporary oblivion. Soon enough, she would be remade bone and sinew. But for now she was as luscious and perfect as this fine summer fruit. She relished her own loveliness, whatever Oscar might be thinking. His movement increased its demand. She raised her legs and rested them on his shoulders, knowing it would make him come sooner. He rose up and pressed her more deeply into the complaining mattress. And then, in a rush, she was taken with the intensity of her own need, and swiftly a feral laugh sprang from her into the thick, fruit-scented air.

Afterward, she rolled away from the touch of him. She knew he would leave her soon – he could never bear to linger in bed – and she was eager to wash the imprint of his skin from her own. She felt feverish. The sheets were hot where she had lain. The smell of ripe fruit clung to the walls, to the thick curtains at the window. Althea drowsed. When she woke, the room was dim and a jolt of fear went through her. She had promised to pick up Celia before dinner. Now, once again, she would be late. She flung her legs over the edge of the bed and sat up, only to fall back, awash with dizziness. Every part of her ached. Her head throbbed. Still. She had to get to Celia. Slowly, achingly, she rose from the bed.

Her bones felt weary, pounded soft by the labor of love, heavy with the tumbler of Port that Oscar had given her when they first arrived at his apartment. It had only been the middle of the afternoon then, but there was no longer any reason for her to be at work.

Fired. Almost as soon as she had returned from lunch.

They had warned her, they said. They had given her every opportunity. Now they were letting her go. They were sorry. That's what they said. No, *she* was sorry. But it no longer mattered. A tall uniformed guard had walked her back to her desk and watched as she packed her few personal belongings. A coffee mug. The painted clay hand that Celia had made in kindergarten for Mother's Day. A sample bottle of Charlie perfume. She stuffed these in her purse with the guard looking on. Then he led Althea from the building. She called Oscar from a pay phone on the street.

From the moment she'd stepped into this apartment, she cried: a loud animal lowing and rasping beyond her control, until her eyes were swollen almost shut and could no longer make tears. She could hardly believe it when Oscar stripped off her shirt and took her nipples between his lips. She wasn't sure if he was trying to comfort her, or put an end to her keening. But she was exhausted beyond all sense of volition.

Oscar overwhelmed her. He frightened her. He was a man without laughter. He was a man with intense longing and not a little anger. Often, he would stare into her face, unblinking, until she felt forced to lower her eyes or ask, *What?* a question that went unanswered. Why did she agree to this arrangement?

He had been kind – well, helpful – to her at work. In her earliest days on the job, he whispered a few hints that saved her from embarrassment, maybe even from dismissal. It was her first real job in America. Before that, she had earned money watching a neighbor's child along with Celia. The agency that had sent her for the interview warned her that her bookkeeping skills were not really strong by American standards and the firm had a bad reputation for using up clerical help and spitting them back out. She promised she would work extra hard. They said they would see.

"Don't work alone with Mr. Platt in the filing room – he's a groper," Oscar once warned.

"A grouper?" she'd asked, thinking he meant the fish and wondering what trait this new expression implied. Even after several years, she was confused by certain American idioms. Likewise, her native expressions were often met with blank stares, as when she wondered aloud why someone would "cut his legs short" by doing something that hurt himself in an effort to strike out at his enemy. Cutting off one's nose to spite his face was the American way, she learned. "Groper," Oscar had explained. "He tries to touch beautiful women. Like you." And he had stared at her with intense appraisal, as if making certain he had judged her correctly. His warning was confirmed by the other file clerks.

"Don't ask to leave early unless it's a matter of life and death."

"Bring Mrs. Boniface a muffin when you stop at the deli."

"Make sure you file Ms. Korn's receipts first and that they're in the right place and can be found at a moment's notice. She's a barracuda." Again, a fish. But this time Althea understood.

Of course, it hardly mattered any more. She had been fired, and in a city choked with semi-skilled women like herself, all begging for a chance to work, another job seemed a distant dream. How would she pay next month's rent, and the months to follow? How would she keep her growing daughter in clothes, shoes, food? What if one of them got sick? How easy it would be to lose everything. But Oscar said he would help. Until she got on her feet. He promised. He cared. She had to believe that.

Over the almost two years that she worked in the file room and then the accounting department at Palmer & Burch, he went from coolly supportive to warmly inviting. He began by dropping by the file room with coffee or a pastry on some days; eventually, he invited her for a drink after work. When she told him she had to go straight home to Celia, he nodded understandingly. He asked her to meet him for lunch at the darkly quiet Spanish restaurant on 48th Street.

At first Althea thought she might be in love with him. He was, indeed, a beautiful man. Compact and muscular, dark skin smoother and softer even than her own. She had never known a man with such silky skin. It was the pure skin of a baby. He wore no aftershave, but carried a sharp personal fragrance that Althea connected with the smell of the salt-baked cliffs of the Aegean coastline. That aroma imprinted her each time she left him.

Oscar was generous, giving her gifts on her birthday and fifty dollars on Celia's for a party and presents. The money embarrassed her, although he convinced her it was a gift for Celia – nothing more. He bought her practical things, too. An electric coffeemaker, a crock pot, a telephone answering machine: he liked gadgets. Finally, he declared his intentions to make her his lover. Not his wife. He already had one of those, he said, although they were legally separated and she lived in another state with their son, a ten-year-old violin prodigy. But he knew Althea belonged with him, he said. They could be there for one another. She felt desired; she felt needed.

He began asking favors in return. Small things, really. Could she put through some expenses he had forgotten to submit from a previous business trip? Could she change the dates so that they would get paid without his having to explain why they were late?

They began taking lunch hours at his apartment on 16th Street, just off Seventh Avenue, a sixth floor loft that they reached by means of steep flights of metal stairs or an ancient elevator that sounded as though it were chewing up and digesting the building as it rose. As the elevator passed by other floors, Althea heard the whine of drills and lathes, sewing machines and the hiss of steam, the rhythmic pounding of looms. Like the levels of hell, she thought. The smells of linseed oil and of hot metal crept in through the ductwork. Lying in Oscar's bed, Althea often worried that rats scuttled around in the hallways where the garbage sat in small mountains between pickup days. Despite the expensive modern furniture, silky sanded floors and enormous paintings that graced the freshly painted walls, she knew there were mice in the cabinet under the sink. She heard them chewing and scratching at the worn shelf paper there. She didn't tell him. She didn't want him to set a trap.

A small patch of violet sky peeked through the Venetian blinds. The clock sitting on the nightstand read 10:30 – not possible – hours too early, or too late.

Where had Oscar gone? She felt his absence from the cavernous loft, not just in the silence but in the disappearance of the thrumming energy that he generated. Through the giant windows facing west across Seventh Avenue, the sun hung angry and low in the sky. Long rays issued from beneath steel gray gathering clouds, showering down on the imposing skyline. Althea could practically smell a storm coming.

She found her skirt and stockings crumpled at the foot of the bed and smoothed them on. Her blouse was rumpled under the pillow and would hold its creases long into the evening. Her mother would notice. One shoe turned up just under the foot of the bed, but the other was missing. She combed her hair with her fingers and patted it behind her ears, and then began a more methodical search for the missing shoe.

She should call her mother and tell Celia she was on her way. But where was that shoe? She searched further back under the bed and on the closet floor. Under the couch and in the kitchen. Althea thought for a moment that Oscar might have hidden it to keep her there until his return. But of course that was silly. She was down on her hands and knees checking under the bed when the telephone rang.

Might it be Oscar, she wondered. She rose to her feet and padded across the slightly tilted floor, but by the time she reached the phone the answering machine had already picked up. There was a period of silence and then the voice she recognized immediately as that of Drew Palmer, one of the partners at the firm, began to speak.

"Oscar? Drew here. I walked by your office and your secretary said you'd gone for the day, so I wanted to let you know what happened. HR let the girl go as we discussed, and we've agreed not to press charges, although I can't imagine why you were so insistent about that. According to Marcia, there were no scenes, but we had her escorted from the building, just to be safe. Stop by my office in the morning and we'll talk."

The machine whirred and clicked off. The tape rewound. The apartment returned to silence, except for the hum of the refrigerator and the thudding that Althea heard coming from her own chest.

○◉◠

Phnnnph....phnnph....chitterchitterchitterscrape.

Hide. Scrape.

Rat pulled herself along the cinders. Phnnff....phnnphnnf.

Urine smell. Here and here. Mysmell. Hereandhere.

Pathtohome.

Rockandturn. Phnnnf...Urine smell.

Here and here. Not mine.

Notmine. Male smell, Sexsmell. Gimmegimmegimme

Malestink. Closerstill, louderstill.

Heat is mine. Sexismine. Here is mine. Hereismine.

Male smell. Gimmegimmegimme.

HERE. Here is MINE.

Mine in heat:

Findminemine. MINE.

Fuck and thrust.

Closer closer deeperdeependeepindeep.

One and anotherandanother.

Fuckandthrust. Skitter chitter, bowandthrust.

Phnnff....phnnphnnf. Pathtohome.

Path to babies.

Feed Babies mine.

࿊

Pia walked into an art department humming with activity and redolent of the characteristic perfume of ink and coffee. She propped her portfolio against an empty stool and launched into her pitch. Almost an hour later, she strode back out.

Chapter Seven

At the door to her apartment, Judith reached up with one hand, touched her fingertips to the little *mezuzah* that hung on the right side of the doorpost and then pressed them to her lips in a gesture that echoed millions of Jewish hands over centuries. The narrow wooden box with its decorative carvings held a tiny scroll of parchment inscribed in miniscule writing with two sections of the Torah. Judith touched it both automatically and with complete mindfulness that the words inscribed therein formed a pact between herself and God.

"And you shall inscribe them upon the doorposts of your house and upon your gates," the book of Deuteronomy commanded. In exchange for obedience to this and all His other commandments, Hashem promised his people safe passage through this world. Perhaps, but Judith nevertheless routinely double-locked her apartment door and fastened the brass security chain across the doorframe upon entering. The apartment was steamy and redolent of the kimchi cooked weekly by the Korean family who lived below her. Tendrils of aroma seeped up through the floorboards and around the pipes. She sometimes smelled it on her clothes even after she left for work in the morning. The distinctive odor of long-simmered cabbage reminded Judith of her mother's *holishkes,* each leaf tenderly enfolding a mound of chopped meat and rice.

Judith opened the apartment's few windows and turned on the oscillating fan to encourage a feeble breeze. She slipped out of her shoes and into the slippers left beside the bed. Only the mourning went barefoot. She washed her hands and face, grateful to rinse away the grime of the subway, if not the discomfiting memory of her ride uptown.

"In my next life I want to be a Jew," the woman had insisted. It was the way she said *Jew* that seemed to hang in the atmosphere of the subway car, like a bad smell.

In the kitchen, Judith turned on the small radio she had brought with her from home. It was tuned to WQXR, the classical music station, and a tinny ghost of a Bach fugue fought for its life against the sound of buses, trucks and car horns from Broadway below. She turned up the volume, but left the windows open. At this time of day what she missed most from home – more, even, than her mother's *heimische* cooking and the smell of roses from their garden, more even than the comfort of the nightly readings and discussions – was the sound of her sister Rivka playing piano. There were practice rooms at school and she had passed under their windows aching with homesickness at the sound of students racing through scales or working painstakingly to the steady heartbeat of a metronome. Each evening, with the exception of Shabbat, Rivka's practicing had provided musical accompaniment as her mother and sisters prepared dinner and set the table.

The Bach ended and a long beep signaled 7:00 and the news. At the sink, Judith took a cup and poured water three times over each hand as she recited the blessing. She poured herself a tall glass of iced tea and began to wash vegetables for a salad, careful that not a speck of dirt or insect material remained. She was ravenous. She opened a tin of tuna fish and tossed it with the greens. The only tomato in the refrigerator had turned bruised and lumpy in the bin and she threw it in the trash. She took two slices from the loaf of *challah* her aunt had brought her from the neighborhood bakery yesterday and popped them in the toaster oven, reciting another blessing.

In the background, the news was far from cheering. The police were still hunting for the murderer of several young women in Brooklyn and Queens. Judith glanced across the narrow galley kitchen and the living room beyond, to the door. The chain rested securely across the frame. The locks were turned. She felt only slightly more protected.

Two weeks earlier, the apartment of the man who lived next door to Judith, Mr. Joseph, had been broken into. It was Judith who noticed the door was ajar. Concerned, she called inside to Mr. Joseph, but there was no answer. She entered her own apartment uneasily, but nothing was amiss. Moments later, she heard her neighbor cursing as he arrived home from work to discover his television and stereo were gone. The burglar had apparently climbed in through the open fire escape window and walked out the front door with his booty. Plus, he had had the audacity to stop at the refrigerator for a pint of ice cream along the way. It made Judith furious that her neighbor had left the apartment with such a blatant invitation as a window open to the fire escape. Didn't he know better? What if the thief came back, and this time decided to break into *her* apartment?

When Judith first moved in, she worried that money would be her biggest challenge. Or maybe loneliness and guilt. But lately, these had taken a back seat to plain old fear for her safety. In the neighborhood paper, which seemed to specialize in stories of muggings and break-ins, she read a tip about securing windows a few inches open by using a long nail and a hole through the window frame, a couple of inches up from the sill. When the summer heat wave hit, Judith tried this, but even that narrow opening made her so uneasy that she quickly reverted to locking the windows shut when she left, despite the stuffiness at the end of each day.

Back in Brooklyn, she never worried about these things. People looked out for each other. They knew each other. Well, not the Caribbeans, of course. While they and the Lubavitchers walked the same streets and shared the same subway stop, their two worlds converged only in the form of commerce, a strict polonaise of measured beats and intervals – dollars and goods or services – each side looking away at the end of the dance like shy newlyweds. On the street there were veiled glances of curiosity, sometimes even intimidation, but mainly it seemed to Judith that the world she had grown up in was one of order and safety carved from a history of global menace and repeated attempts at the extermination of her people.

The real world, the one in which she was free to follow her aspirations, was one of everyday peril. Would the trade prove too costly? Judith couldn't afford to think of it. Instead, she sat down at the table with her salad and her chemistry textbook, prepared to study carbon in its many permutations and combinations.

After only a few minutes, the telephone rang, startling Judith. The fork clattered from her hand to the table and then the floor. The phone rang again, and she realized that she must have been dozing, reading in the oppressive heat. She darted into the kitchen to answer it.

"Judith?" The voice on the other end was not immediately familiar, and in another instant was abundantly so.

"Michael?" She stretched the phone cord to its limit and retrieved the fallen utensil from under the table and brought it to the sink.

"Yes. I wasn't even sure I'd find you. I tried you at work. They call you Jehudit? That's so pretty. I explained to the woman who answered that I was a classmate of yours. She said you were gone for the day. She sounded pretty dubious about giving me your number," he laughed, "she asked if I was Jewish. I'm lucky she didn't test me on anything. I hope I didn't get you in trouble, but I was concerned. Are you okay?"

Aunt Zipporah gave out her number? It was hard to believe, but she had no reason to think he was lying. She wondered what her aunt thought of her going by this new name. She hoped Michael hadn't mentioned anything about lunch.

"I, I'm sorry about this afternoon," Judith finally managed.

"You left your shopping bag behind. I have it with me."

"Thank you." She hoped that he hadn't looked inside the bag. Touched the silky fabric that had glided across her skin so seductively. It was all too humiliating. "I mean, I probably shouldn't have bought that dress in the first place," she managed to add.

"I didn't know what happened…and then I figured it out. The bacon. I'm so sorry I took you there. I should have found someplace –"

"No. It's not your fault. I should have been more careful. It's not your responsibility." Judith nervously adjusted the Venetian blinds across the window so that long ribbons of light created lanes in which millions of dust motes spun.

"Still. I'm sorry it happened."

"Me, too." She let her eyes focus on the dust. It was something she had enjoyed all her life, that trick of light that made the air come alive with tiny beings. As a child, she had associated them with the burst clay vessels that failed to hold Hashem's light and the scattered shards that hid remnants of the light to this day. The phenomenon lasted only a few moments before a cloud cut across the path of the sun, dimming the beams and rendering the motes invisible again. She raised the blinds to try and catch the sunset. To the west, bruised-looking clouds were beginning to thicken.

"Well, I wanted you to know I have your package and that hand-out for class. Are you busy? Did I take you away from something?"

"I was just having dinner. And studying chemistry." She laughed nervously. "Actually, I think I was falling asleep over the book. So thank you for waking me."

"Where do you live? Downtown?"

"No, uptown. Broadway and 78th Street."

"I'm still at the office, believe it or not. I was just leaving, actually. I could come by and drop this off if you'd like."

Judith was dismayed. Michael, come here?

"No. You don't have to do that. I can get it another time. Maybe at school. I want to pay you for my lunch, anyway."

"Forget it." He laughed. "I gave them a hard time for giving you the wrong sandwich, and they took it off the bill."

"Oh. That's better then. I felt terrible."

"I live up at 94th Street. It's no big deal for me to drop the bag off on my way home."

Judith said nothing. Was God tempting her? What do You want me to do, she asked. She didn't expect an answer. She guessed that there would be no answers coming in her direction any time soon. She twirled a strand of hair tightly around one finger and tried to think.

"I have a few errands to do and then I'll grab the train," Michael continued. "How about if I just stop by and drop this and then I'll walk home. Now that you told me it's a dress I figure I can't use it anyway, so I might as well give it back. Okay?"

Judith's glance flew wildly about the room. An erratic pulse at the base of her throat felt like a trout flopping helplessly out of water. She scanned the rooftops of the buildings along Broadway, a mounting panic plucking at her heart. The girl who had been Jehudit would never have found herself in such a situation. The girl she had observed in the mirror of that Saks dressing room, however, had a different life entirely. How could she be both of these women, Judith wondered, without splitting apart? Suddenly, the clouds shifted, and beams of golden light fanned out from beneath them. Was this the sign for which she was hoping? Judith took a long breath.

"Okay." There. She had said it. There was nothing further to be done. She gave him her address.

"Good. Tell me what apartment to ring and I'll see you within the hour."

"4B."

"Four B or not four B. That is the question." He laughed. It wasn't funny, but she laughed too, out of nervousness.

Judith hung up the phone and stood staring around the tiny

apartment as if looking for someplace to hide. Such a small and intimate space, she couldn't imagine how she could share it, even briefly, with a male stranger. No matter where she stood, she felt exposed and vulnerable. There was hardly a spot in the apartment that couldn't be seen from virtually every vantage point. She walked into the bedroom and straightened the spread on her bed. In her entire life she had never been alone in an enclosed room with a boy or man who wasn't her near relation. Such a situation was an intimacy limited only to husband and wife. No, it was simply not possible. But what could be done? It would be beyond rude to refuse to answer the buzzer when he arrived. Maybe she should wait downstairs and take the bag from him there. Or call him back and say she would pick it up from him at work tomorrow. But no, she didn't have his number. Judith assessed the apartment once again. The living room held only a loveseat-sized sofa and coffee table. The dining area was barely large enough for the small round table and two ice cream parlor chairs she'd picked up at a thrift shop. Above the couch, a portrait of the Rebbe glared down as if pondering the trouble she had brought upon herself. Sometimes when she looked at his picture all she could see was the fierce light that shone from his eyes. Other times she saw the tender curve of a smile in his lips.

Judith imagined the Rebbe as she'd seen him last, sitting with his head bent and resting in his great hands, grizzled untrimmed beard crushed against his chest and trailing off onto the desk on which his elbows were anchored. Judith wasn't supposed to have been there, that close to a righteous man whispered to be *Moshiach*, the Messiah, for whose return they all prayed. She had come to deliver a Purim basket to his wife, Chaya, a basket piled high with glossy ripe fruit surrounded by chocolates that her mother had carefully prepared, and she was surprised to be told by the young aide, whom she didn't recognize from the neighborhood or the *shul*, to go up to the apartment over the sanctuary. She had expected to leave it in the foyer with   similar baskets sent over by women all up and down the neighborhood, the way she had for years. Like an army of Little Red Riding Hoods, the girls of Crown Heights negotiated the wilds of Eastern Parkway to deliver their bounty to 770 each spring in celebration of the Biblical Queen Esther and her successful campaign to save the Jews.

The staircase was long and tilted rather sharply to the left. She held the banister and steadied the basket in her other arm. The higher she climbed, the more the ancient smell of the sanctuary – yellowed paper, stale sweat, and a more modern tang of polyurethane from the recent floor repairs – gave way to familiar domestic odors – baked potatoes, fried eggs, lemon Pledge.

The doorway to the Rebbe's study was ajar. She wasn't spying. She couldn't help but see. Sound asleep at his desk, the familiar, massive head rested against the palm of his right hand. His mouth hung open and a bead of saliva pooled at the corner of his lips. What struck her immediately was how much older he seemed to have grown, even since the prior Shabbat, when she had pressed forward in the women's gallery to catch sight of him toward the end of his service. It wasn't the gray in his hair, his beard; it was, rather, the absence of those piercing blue eyes that he turned, like lasers, onto those with whom he spoke.

Even among the Lubavitcher Rebbes of history – each of them miracles of piety and bravery – this Rebbe was unique. Rabbi Menachem Mendel Schneerson, the seventh Lubavitcher Rebbe, was the only one to look beyond the Torah and attend secular schools in Berlin and Paris, where he earned a degree in engineering. Maybe that was what persuaded Judith that he would hear her plea to continue her own education in the direction of medicine. She felt that not only could he read the most earnest secrets of her mind and her heart, but that he would have the most profound understanding of what could drive a person to seek outside the usual prescriptions for a life of meaning. In that, she was destined for disappointment. She had been to see him twice, begging for permission to follow the path she believed was her destiny. Twice he told her no.

"You will be a very happy woman when you are married and preparing for Shabbat with your family," he had said, by which he meant that the subject was closed; his word, like Hashem's, immutable.

But in the instant that she watched him there, asleep in his study on the eve of Purim, the little drop of drool glistening on his lips, she suddenly thought, *he's just a man.* She knew then that serving the commandments of her soul was going to mean disobeying the authority that had shaped her world to that moment.

The silence of the hallway was broken by the insistent tapping of a pair of leather-heeled shoes coming down the corridor. When Judith turned from the doorway, there was Chaya Moussia, the Rebbetzin herself, with an expression that was equal parts compassion and expectation. With a minimum of pleasantries and her eyes lowered to hide her embarrassment, Judith delivered the basket and fled.

Now, Judith moved around her apartment, picking up the few stray items she found. Her hairbrush, a blouse that she had rinsed out and hung to dry, a pair of barrettes: objects at once benign and intimate. Her heart felt as slippery as pickled herring. Michael would be here soon. He, she was certain, had shared this particular familiarity many, many times over with women. He would have no clue that for her, this was almost as appalling as eating bacon. One after another, she was toppling the pillars of righteous behavior. Soon, might not the entire temple fall about her? She was put on this earth to help gather the shards of light through goodness, obedience. Instead, was she becoming an instrument of darkness?

A sudden gust of wind from the bedroom window blew grit from the fire escape into the room. As if confirming her fears, clouds billowed up and obscured the last minutes of sunlight. It was the end of the day, but also the beginning of the new day that began every evening at sunset. Judith prepared to recite the prayers that would herald it, thanking God for the day that was passing and asking protection through the night ahead.

༄

Althea's throat was parched and her skin felt tender, as if with fever. Like a fever dream, too, the one-sided conversation she had overheard on the answering machine. In the time it took for the machine to finish its robotic humming and clicking as the tape reset, she came up with half a dozen reasons why what she had heard clearly wasn't what she heard at all. It was not possible that Oscar had done this terrible thing. But her self-deception was as flimsy as ash. It was Oscar who had had her fired. He had used and betrayed her. It was that simple. He was a man who could crush the fragile life she had created for herself and Celia as easily as he would step on a roach. They would be on the streets, desperate. But no – she would kill him first. Her hands clenched around his imagined throat.

Fear and then fury coursed through her, blurring her vision. Althea wove back and forth blindly through the space like a shark. Fury and then fear – she had long suspected that the receipts he asked her to rush through bookkeeping were less than authentic. That the "late" expenses he brought to her for trips (taken when she was almost certain he had been in town) were all phony. The money he had offered to help meet her bills, the little gifts for Celia, what she saw as kindness, was it all meant keep her from exposing his theft – what the movies called "hush money"? Or maybe it was guilt money to make up for the way he had made a fool of her. And what difference did it make? She stubbed one naked toe on the leg of a couch and collapsed in a heap on the cushions. A dozen visions of revenge flooded her mind. A moment later, she sat bolt upright with sickening realization. She had committed a crime. She was a common criminal. Even with no legal education she knew that accepting the money made her part of the crime. If Oscar could so easily have her fired, he could have her arrested. Arrested, imprisoned, and her daughter would be left both fatherless and motherless in this country that touted freedom and opportunity but harbored only treachery. Or even if he didn't turn her into the police – how could he? He would only be incriminating himself, she realized – she would never be able to be able to find another job without references. Which amounted to the same thing.

Celia. She had to get Celia. The light had drained from the room and Althea stumbled as she crossed the uneven floor in her one shoe. Where the hell was her left shoe? Had Oscar hidden it to keep her here? She no longer put anything past him. In a spasm of frustration, Althea took off the right shoe and flung it at the nearest wall and as she did, the rage in that movement yanked her back in time.

It was a part of the story of Goat that she never told, but could not forget. When her own dear *Tragos*, having once been chased away for biting the starfish, tried again to follow her, she didn't merely shout him away. In her anger, she picked up a heavy stone, flung it with all her strength at the hapless creature and caught one of its delicate legs just above the hoof. The goat had not ambled off as she described in her countless recitations to Celia, but limped away in pain, blood spotting the pink sand in his wake. Her mother sent her up the mountain later that day and told her to call his name. She climbed to the crest, but in a mixture of shame and obstinacy, remained silent. If the poor creature did, in fact, die in those hills, it was entirely her fault. And if anything happened to Celia, that too would be her fault and the guilt she'd have to bear.

She had to make herself calm. She had to think rationally. If she couldn't leave before Oscar got back, would it be best to confront him immediately, or to stall for time until she could get away? She forced herself to breathe slowly, four counts in and four out, and tried to think of the deep blue Aegean waves rolling, rolling onto the shore and back again to their father Okeanos. Like Odysseus, trapped in the cave of the Cyclops, Althea focused all of her mental powers on divining a plan for escape. Oh, would that there were some fat sheep nearby under which she might flee this devil's lair. Or that she, like the great Odysseus, might be clever enough to convince her captor that she was No One, and in that guise, she might blind him and leave him howling in her wake.

Althea left the bedroom and padded into the kitchen for a drink of water. With the glass in her hands, she turned to walk back to the bedroom and almost bumped into Oscar, who had entered the room silently behind her. The glass fell from her fingers and smashed on the clay tiles at their feet.

"Oh! How clumsy!" she cried out. Terror, anger, made spots dance before her eyes.

"Did I frighten you?"

"No. Yes. I didn't hear you come in." She had to think clearly. She tried to step past him, but he blocked her path with one thick arm.

He crouched at her ankles and began picking up the larger pieces of glass. "Don't move," he said.

She froze at his tone. A command. A rebuke.

"You'll cut your feet," he continued. "I'll get your shoes." He rose and deposited the shards into a paper shopping bag that had been lying on the countertop. Then he rolled it up and placed it in the garbage can under the sink.

"We seem to have mice," he observed, peering into the cabinet. "I'll have to set some traps." He left the room. It was as she'd feared. He would set his traps and stupid weak little creatures like herself would stumble in to have their heads snapped off, their lives crushed. She hated him. She feared him.

Now he was back in the kitchen with her shoes, which he knelt to slip onto her feet. How had he found that other shoe so quickly?

"You have beautiful toes," he said, fingering one gently.

Althea said nothing, although she could taste bile at the base of her throat. She would have to be smart, cagey. She tried to read his wristwatch, but it was too far away. Finally, she couldn't take the suspense any longer.

"Could you tell me," she asked, with a calm she did not feel, "what time is it?"

He moved his attention from her feet to his own wrist.

"It's only just eight," he said, rising. He stared into her eyes in silence. She looked away. "Why don't we order some dinner?"

Eight? She had promised to meet Celia uptown for dinner at seven. She tried to keep the tremor from her words. "No, I can't. I'm already late." She fought to keep the pitch of her voice from rising into the register of hysteria.

"No, don't go. Please," he said smoothly, stroking her hair and resting his palm on her cheek. His touch was like a brand on her skin. In spite of herself, she winced and pulled away. "Call and say you met a friend who needs to talk. Did you tell them you've lost your job? No? Then say you have to stay late at work. Please. I'll pay for a cab ride home with your little girl. We can order extra dessert and you can take it to her. She'll like that, won't she?"

His pleading was without humility. More like a list of demands, in fact. Again, Althea's heart sped. Oscar came around behind her and wrapped his arms around her. His smell was acrid with sweat and she could feel the heat coming off his body. She caught sight of his watch: it was past 8:30.

"No, really, I promised my daughter I would be home early to have dinner with her. I'm already so late." Now the words were flying from her lips, but already he was walking toward the telephone to order their dinner. The telephone. He would see the light blinking on the answering machine. Althea's limbs turned to stone, immobile, as she watched him from across the room. He reached for the receiver. He began to dial. Then he paused and put down the phone. It was like the slow cliff-fall of a dream. Oscar punched the button on the machine.

He stopped the message halfway through and turned to her, his expression both question and answer.

"So," he said in a voice barely above a whisper.

"Yes," she said, the word like a hiss.

༝◉༝

"I always thought I'd be a great artist when I grew up," Danielle half-shouted through the Happy Hour bedlam. She was still wondering whether agreeing to meet Geoffrey here had been a good idea, but so far she was enjoying herself. "I read a biography of Georgia O'Keefe in fourth grade and decided that that was what I wanted to do – make extraordinary paintings and sculptures and be as famous as all get out." She took another sip of the Margarita at her elbow, the tip of her tongue lingering on a bit of coarse salt and the inside of her cheeks puckering at the sour bitterness of the tequila and citrus. "I bought the whole thing. I even had a hidden piggy bank with money I was saving up to go to France and rent a garret of my own. By high school, I had about $80, mostly in quarters. I think I eventually spent it on a few ounces of Maui Wowie."

She laughed out loud at the ridiculous notions she'd had as a child. Her art basically sucked. Back in California, in a storage loft in the garage, her mother still had a dozen or so paintings from the bohemian high school period. By now, a thin scrim of mildew would have fogged over the clumsy images. They probably looked better that way.

"I wanted to be an astronaut," Geoffrey boomed. "That was the Florida equivalent of wanting to be a fireman."

Danielle wasn't sure what he meant by that, but the noise level in the No Name, a narrow space with whitewashed pressed tin walls and ceiling and a tile floor like her echoey bathroom, made it too exhausting to ask for clarification.

She felt this as an advantage rather than a detriment. Keep the conversation light, Danielle told herself. Have a little fun. Offer up the entertaining persona. Hold the darkness at bay. Fortunately, the place was better lit than most neighborhood bars. The ceiling was hung with old schoolhouse light fixtures that gave off bold, even illumination, and the pale surfaces didn't suck up all the light. She had stumbled on a step down to the ladies room, but who didn't?

Geoffrey drained his beer and signaled to the bartender for another. He had large hands, like a craftsman's, with neatly trimmed nails. And nicely muscled forearms, too, lightly covered with fine, dark hair. She forced herself to stop right there.

"Refill?" he asked her.

This was her second Margarita. She was usually only good for two, at best. After that, she tended to knock over someone's glass. This had been true even *before*.

"I'm fine," she said, lifting her glass in his direction to show him that it was still almost half full.

"So how did you decide to become a chef?" they both asked at almost the same moment, and then laughed.

"You first," he said.

"No, you."

"Basically," he said, "I flunked out of college my second year – apparently physics and astronomy don't mix well with beer and acid. My parents were so pissed that they cut me off financially and told me to go figure out why I didn't want to be a bum. I decided to go on the road for a while – it was, like, 1967, everyone was on the road. I went West first, of course, working my way across as a fry cook in greasy spoons and truck stops. Once, I worked at a logging camp up in Eastern Oregon. I got good at it. Remind me to show you my technique for cracking three eggs at a time without breaking the yolks. Anyone can do two – my claim to fame, at my peak, was that I could do four."

The new beer arrived and Geoffrey stopped to drain the dregs from his other glass before the bartender took it away. Foam sloshed over the top of the full mug and pooled on the bar, a veteran of many decades of hard drinking if the number of cigarette burns and scars carved into its wood were any indication. Geoffrey took the time to mop up the puddle with a napkin he snatched from a pile near the taps.

"Anyway," he continued, "my uncle Marty had a restaurant – just a little dump, really – over in Philly, and eventually I came back East and worked for him. I bought a lot of fancy cookbooks and tried to improve his menu. He ended up firing my ass, but it sent me back to school. And here I am. The man in the toque. Or at least his first lieutenant."

"I thought you worked in Europe for a while," she probed.

"Truth?" He snickered.

"Truth."

"I pulled pints and boiled the eggs for a pub in Ilkley – that's a little town in the north of England – for about six months after I got out of the CIA. There were no jobs in the States and I thought I could build a resume overseas. But it was even worse there."

He must have seen her disappointment.

"But I did *eat* in a lot of great restaurants in France for a few months after that. It was where I spent almost every penny I earned. It was, like, research. I worked my butt off as the *escuelerie*, or more like the garbage boy, once I finally got someone to let me into his kitchen."

He said it so earnestly. Like he wanted her to approve, Danielle thought. All the time he was talking, she noticed that he twirled a little plastic straw compulsively between his fingers. He had plucked it from the bar where she left it after removing it from her drink. He was a tense and edgy guy. Danielle liked tense and edgy guys. And she liked Geoffrey's smile. And his story. Funny what you didn't guess about people.

"But I'm hogging the stage. What about you? What carried you from art to food?"

"Synaesthesia," she said. She told him about how she had always equated color with taste.

"When I was three, my mother says I used to tell her I wanted something blue for dinner," she said. "And she'd make blueberry pie, and I'd throw a tantrum. Because it didn't *taste* blue. You know, like rare steak marinated in garlic and wine tastes blue – well, maybe almost purple," she said. She could see in his face that he got it. She told him that finally she realized she achieved better results with food than with paint.

As a kid, she had begged her mother each Christmas for an Easy-Bake Oven, but instead, found a series of Barbies waiting under the tree. She fashioned Play-Do into roasts and omelets, cookies and fancy braided breads that she fed to the imaginary patrons of her make-believe restaurant. She pleaded at the kitchen counter for permission to make meatloaf (and to sample a pinch of the seasoned raw ground beef).

Her mother was an average cook for her time. Everything she made tasted pretty much the same – of salt, garlic- or onion-powder and a sprinkling of paprika "for color." The color Danielle tasted was a blandly uniform beige. When she was seventeen, she tiptoed full of curiosity and awe into one of the first Indian restaurants to open in Santa Barbara and on first bite, her eyes filled with tears – not from the heat of the spice, but from the exquisite rainbow on her tongue. In college, Danielle – reserved, reticent by nature – had a huge following of friends whom she'd wooed with picnics on the college quad. She lost her virginity in her dorm room freshman year, after seducing the object of her desire with a midnight supper of scallops and mushrooms in white wine sauce cooked on a hotplate, served with fresh-made linguini and a bottle of Chateauneuf du Pape worth an entire month of what she earned working in the library.

She loved to cook. She liked the meditation of chopping, the chemistry of bringing ingredients and heat together to create something delicious. She loved to think in food. Taste in color. Would she lose this, too, when her vision was gone?

Danielle touched the hand that was still twirling the straw.

"Are you always this nervous?"

"Only when it counts," he said.

Cheesy, she thought. Melted Gruyere. Dark amber.

Her glass was empty.

"You know, maybe I will have one more after all," she said as the bartender came by. The bar was, by now, extremely crowded. People were pressing in on all sides. It was almost as bad as the subway. Geoffrey was drumming his fingers on the bar in time to the Marshall Tucker Band. Or was that the Steve Miller Band? Danielle always got them confused. It seemed a lot dimmer than it had earlier. A couple she couldn't see, just to her right, were speaking a language she couldn't name. Hungarian? Flemish? They were angry, arguing. Danielle wanted to turn her head to see their faces, but didn't. Someone behind her leaned heavily on her, reaching for a beer. His cigarette smoke made her eyes tear. Yes, it was definitely darker in here. Were they turning down the lights for mood? She heard the bartender deposit her drink, but had to swivel her head to find it on the bar. More and more lately, it felt as though she watched things through that long black telescope Dr. Schein had described. She took a pull of the icy drink the bar tender had delivered. Her head whirled. Brain freeze.

"Isn't it?" Whatever it was Geoffrey had just been saying, she had missed it entirely.

"Excuse me? It's so loud in here..."

"I was just saying it's way too loud in here, isn't it? Do you want to go?"

"Sure."

"You want to finish your drink first?"

She did not. Already, she had the feeling that her hands and arms were about to break free of her control, and it would only be a matter of time until someone's drink was being mopped up. She and Geoffrey slid off their stools, which were immediately claimed by the smoker and his friend, and worked their way out through the crowd. The tequila sang in her muscles and gave Danielle a fine floaty buzz.

Outside, the heat met them like rising dough – a thick and tangible presence. In contrast to the smoky chill of the bar, not unpleasant, but a perceptible essence that would not be ignored. Danielle let her arms swing a little for the sake of feeling the air glide against her skin. It was almost nine and the sky had turned the color of an old bruise, purple smearing into a kind of yellow ochre green. The metallic taste of calf's liver, she thought. There was a definite smell of heat lightning in the air. It billowed up from the river, two blocks behind them. The shadows were closing around her. She should get home before it got much darker.

"You okay?" Geoffrey asked. "Tequila get to you?"

"Mmm, fine," she said. They had reached the corner of Broadway and 80th, where they had to part for her to go home and him to head to the subway. He stood close enough to her that she could feel the solid warmth of him against her arm. There was that awkward pause.

"Well."

"Yeah."

"Thanks for the drink. It was a good idea. I'm glad you asked."

"So I can ask again?"

"Absolutely."

"Or how about a movie? Have you seen *Annie Hall* yet?"

There it was. The show stopper. Danielle covered up the panic that shook her by adjusting her bag higher up on her arm and kicking away a wadded up piece of paper that had blown against her shoe. It was too short a distance from explaining that she didn't go to movies to spilling her guts about why not. Weakened by alcohol and a mounting curiosity about what it might be like to be enveloped by those muscular arms, Danielle didn't trust herself to say a word.

"Or maybe not," he said, too cheerily. She realized he had taken her silence for rejection. But perhaps it was better that way. Was this how it would be then? Were the only choices to be dependent or to be alone? It isn't fair, she wanted to scream, not for the first time. "I'll see you tomorrow at work," Geoffrey was saying. "Have a good night." He started to move away. She swayed slightly toward the empty place where his body had been.

"Are you sure you're okay?" he asked again.

"I would be happy to go out with you again," she blurted. Her arms flew up into the air as she said it. She was happy there was no glassware in reach. "I just don't do movies much. How about a walk to the Seaport after work some time?"

"Well, sure." He took a step back towards her, and she was filled with a visceral sense of relief as he reoccupied the space by her side. "Or what about a walk right now? I could walk you home, for instance."

Yes. No. He would ask to come upstairs. He would see the blackout shades and ask questions. No. It was impossible. "To tell you the truth," she said, preparing to tell him anything but, "I have some things to do at home tonight. But another night. Soon."

"No problem. Maybe I'll walk down to Citarella to pick up some fish."

The light turned green to cross Broadway, and, still smiling back at Geoffrey, Danielle sailed off the curb on a Margarita breeze. A car screeched and honked its horn. It slammed to a halt less than a yard away from where Danielle had frozen still. She hopped backward to the curb and the cab took off in an irritated roar. Adrenaline and alcohol flooded her mouth with a bilious green taste. Her eyes stung with tears.

"Whoa! You almost bought it!" Geoffrey's voice came from behind her right ear. She swung her head about to face him. Her hands flailed in the space between them. "Maybe you *should* let me walk you home."

Not fair, not fair was the drunken chant that rang through her head, bumping and echoing off the edges of her skull. "Yeah well, okay," she heard herself saying. He linked his left arm through her slightly sweaty right one and they waited for the next light before heading across the wide avenue. "But please don't ask to come up tonight," she insisted. And then as an afterthought: "The place is a mess."

"Uh-huh, that's okay, I understand."

She regained a little aplomb. "No, really," she continued, "I have a heap of unfolded clothes on my couch roughly the size of Mount Rushmore."

They turned onto her block, sidestepping a couple locked in gooey embrace.

"And you have to wash your hair." He pushed one strand behind her ear.

"That, too." He really did have nice hands.

Johanna fled from the sun, that deceptive orb with its too bright threats and its lies. No matter how far she walked, she never got any closer to home. The city was toying with her. Blowing her off course. She puffed out her lips three times. Four. Hastily, she retreated down the concrete stairs where the dark subterranean tunnels welcomed her with, if not safety, at least solitude. Sometimes, the voices found her even here. Screamed their warnings and their threats. But mainly, the filthy demons in her head were no match for the regular arrival and departure of the subway trains, the shriek of steel against steel that scrubbed her brain clean. Johanna stuffed her pockets and the front of her sweater with the Important Stuff from her bags – a chipped blue mug, a formless mass of tattered clothing, some plastic bags full of half-eaten fruit and bread, a telephone receiver, seven sea green marbles, a brown paper bag full of bills and coins, a couple of sections of newspaper – waited until a train siphoned all the people away, and then shrank to the very end of the platform, invisible. She shinnied down a black iron ladder and disappeared into the darkness of the tunnel.

"Shoot you dead. Shoot you in the head. Grind your bones to bake my bread. Snake and thread. Shriek and shred. Make my bed. Gimme head," she shouted down the black tunnel, and waited for the echo to come back: dead, thread, shred, head. Johanna had a stick now, too. That would be useful. No one would dare touch her; she would break their bones to bake her bed. She clutched the thick piece of wood and an armful of Important Stuff and edged her way into the small passage that branched off from the mouth of the tunnel. No one would see her there. After rush hour the nearest token booth was deserted, that entrance closed until morning. The shifty token clerk who often called the police to roust her from the platform was gone. His absence was a gift. The secret entrance to the tunnel was a gift. So was the stick. She was gifted. They'd always said that about her, hadn't they?

She spread the scraps of cloth and paper over an indentation in the dusty floor – she had been here before; so had others. The light from the station filtered down the tracks – enough to see by, not enough to read by. She hadn't been able to read for months, anyway. The letters were too wily and mean.

The fever was worse at night. She was already shivering and

drenched with sweat. Johanna huddled against the sharp rocks and rested. She wished she'd saved some of the Pepsi she'd found earlier – a whole unopened can in the trash. She emptied her pockets and rooted through the pile of stuff she'd brought in with her. There was the apple. It, too, was a gift.

She smelled the animal breath of the train long before she saw its eyes. The beast roared past her and stopped, panting in the station. Then it went on, and Johanna stared down the blood red eyes guarding its flank until it fled from sight down the tracks to the river.

Chapter Eight

Geoffrey honored Danielle's request and did not ask to come upstairs. He left her at the front door of her small lime-stone apartment building, between Broadway and Amsterdam. But before he walked away into the thickening dusk, he reached out once more and held both her hands in his big meaty ones. Double-cut Porterhouse. She returned the pressure of his palms and then succumbed to embarrassment and took her hands back on the pretense of searching for her keys.

She turned away rather than risk letting him see the desire surely written across her face like graffiti on a subway car. She wanted this man. And if she couldn't hide it from herself, she was pretty certain she couldn't hide it from him. Better, then, to get away quickly. Cleanly.

"Wait," he said. Danielle turned back slowly, wondering if her resolve to keep him out was stronger than her desire to pull him in close.

"What?"

"I was thinking of picking up a sea trout or a snapper for dinner and stuffing it with some goat cheese, chives and pimiento. What color would you say that would be?"

Danielle laughed and thought about it a moment. Her tongue ran around the inside of her mouth picking up cues. Dark chocolate was mauve; caramel was crimson; Brussels sprouts were, oddly, French blue. It had been so all her life. Most people she told this too (and there hadn't been many) laughed. Geoffrey was the first to ask her the color of his dinner. It only made it harder to walk away.

"Chartreuse," she said, pushing open the heavy front door.

"I would have guessed that."

Just as she entered the building, the elevator door swung open. A pair of young men – one as hefty as a linebacker, the other short and wiry – dressed in tight slacks and loud print shirts open to the waist stepped out. One carried a large boom box, currently mute. They looked neither familiar nor unusual – just the customary sort of men Danielle passed all the time in her neighborhood. She gave a perfunctory nod. The taller of the two held the elevator door open and swept his hand, gallantly, ushering her through. Although she generally walked the five flights to her apartment, the tequila had made Danielle's legs rubbery and the last thing she wanted was to generate any more sweat. She followed his gesture into the elevator and heard him click his tongue approvingly, before letting the door close. Catcalls, comments, sometimes even groans of feigned pleasure had plagued Danielle since she grew hips and breasts at 12 – ahead of many of her friends. More than once she had entertained revenge fantasies of construction workers and smarmy curbside idlers swept off into oblivion by a wind whipped up through her fury. But now she wondered, when the mirror was no more to her than another glassy surface, would the whistles and clicks let her know she looked good, even if she couldn't see for herself?

Once in the apartment, her door locked and chained, Danielle went from room to room drawing the shades. Darkness fell into place.

The distance from her bed to the door of her bedroom was

ten steps. The path from the door of the bedroom to the bathroom was a right turn and four more steps. Then up a half step and two short paces to the toilet, where she made a brief stop, one more to the sink to wash her hands, two to the ancient footed tub/shower (stay slightly to the right to avoid stubbing a toe), and three more paces to the window, which faced out onto an air shaft and was so soot-coated on the outside it needed no shade to block the light. She opened the window two fingers' width to let the dampness out. Danielle negotiated each step with greater than normal care. She had left her shoes tucked under the foot of her bed and hadn't changed into her sneakers. Barefoot was risky. She had already broken her right pinky toe catching it on the edge of a doorway, and she didn't relish the thought of doing it again, although she figured it was probably inevitable.

There were so many new rules to this life that she was preparing to live. She had already learned to measure liquids by tucking one finger inside the rim of the cup or glass to keep from over-pouring, and to avoid cutting herself while slicing by tightly crooking her left forefinger so that the fingertip was pointed back into the palm of her hand and then using the straight, smooth surface formed between the first and second knuckles as a guide for the flat of the knife. She had learned to put her shoes in the same spot whenever she removed them, and to sign her name on a check by using the edge of a credit card as a physical manifestation of the dotted line on which to sign. She had seen her new signature. It looked eerily like the one she had produced in second grade.

The heat had become almost intolerable, especially with the blackout shades in place. She felt as though she were back in the restaurant, standing at the open oven door. Just walking to the bathroom raised a film of sweat on her cheeks and brow. Stooping, she felt around the inside of the tub, making certain the shower curtain was completely pulled inside, and then adjusted the water to tepid before stepping in. It felt icy against her overheated skin. Forcing herself to shower in the darkness took an effort of will, even more than most situations. There was something especially ominous and vulnerable about standing on the hard, slick porcelain, naked and wet, the rush of the water blurring sound from outside the room. Would she know if someone had quietly sneaked in and stood there watching her, only a few feet away? She felt the fragility of her safety, the *in here* versus *out there* sensation of being in her skin, but unable to see beyond herself. It had been easier to learn to bone a fish with her eyes closed than it was to acquiesce to darkness for the entire length of a shower. Now she was almost, if not entirely, used to it.

A thudding bass beat rattled the window frame. Outside, the nightly party was beginning to crank up as the sun went down. From her windows, which faced the alley, Danielle couldn't see the street, but dozens of cars cruising by lent the thrum of their engines to the mixed rhythms of salsa, rock, R&B, and over it all, in sharp relief to the indecipherable whole, came the calls of the boys and the shrieking laughter of the girls on the block. The mix of ethnic groups resulted in what sounded to Danielle like music wars: The white chicks in the apartment below – City College girls from Long Island – played Fleetwood Mac's *Rumours* over and over until Danielle wanted to grind their album into a fine powder and sprinkle it on their scrambled eggs like pepper. The Latinas blasted Ray Baretto and Ruben Blades; the black girls favored Teddy Pendergrass. Everyone agreed on Bob Marley. No one but Danielle played Talking Heads or Elvis Costello. One woman, in an apartment on the floor below, played mainly classical music on the radio and occasionally sang in a language that struck Danielle as faintly Russian, faintly German. The tunes were like vintage wine, orchid and smoky topaz.

When Danielle first moved into the building, it had been winter and silent as a tomb out on the street. But the first warm days of spring in this neighborhood had nothing to do with daffodils and everything to do with the mating rituals of Latinos. Cars cruised by with their windows down, music blaring, serenading the *chicas* and warning off rivals from other neighborhoods. Cases of pale Corona appeared on the stoops where men hung on every radio-announced play from Shea and Yankee Stadium. Children called up to their mamas for money for the *helado* man in his truck tinkling its inane and circular theme song, chairs and tables dragged from basements were set up along the sidewalks under the streetlights, and endless games of dominoes occupied the old men until dawn. One advantage to the closed and shaded windows was that it turned down the volume on the street cacophony. She barely even noticed it much of the time.

Stepping from the shower, Danielle wrapped a towel sarong-style around herself and walked six steps into the living room, turned forty-five degrees to the left, bent slightly and turned up the volume on "Psycho Killer," her favorite cut on the new Talking Heads album, which was already on the turntable. She noticed, not for the first time, that the turntable was starting to go – the notes shimmered slightly, like the air over a highway. How would she tell her albums apart when she could no longer see the covers? Danielle did not look forward to trying to learn Braille in order to label them. The few times she had experimentally run her fingers over the tiny dots, she had been completely unable to discern any pattern. Dr. Schein said people who lost their vision as adults often couldn't learn Braille. She didn't like to think how much more than albums she would lose if she were one of these people. Cookbooks, for instance. She forced the thought from her head. She had already signed up for a course in Braille in the fall. Now, she picked her way carefully back to the bedroom. She unwound the towel and hung it neatly on the back of the desk chair. Danielle swept one arm over the surface of her bed until she found the bra and panties she had previously laid out. Then she ran her fingers across the tops of the hangers in the closet until she came to something smooth and cool. She pulled a cotton sundress over her head, smoothed it across her hips and belly, stepped into a pair of pull-on Keds, and went back to the kitchen, all in the pitch black dark.

Simultaneously hungry and too buzzed from the drinks to concentrate on cooking, Danielle reached into the pantry cabinet for a box of Saltines. Her hand came up empty and she remembered finishing the box yesterday, along with the last of the sharp Cheddar.

She felt around the counter until she found a small tape recorder and flicked it on.

"Memo," she intoned. "Pick up crackers, cheese, peanut butter."

She snapped the recorder off and replaced it gently, edges neatly parallel to those of the countertop, and a hand's span back from the edge. The tape recorder had been another adaptive idea she had come up with. Danielle used it more and more lately, for memos, directions and grocery lists, although she had occasionally noticed some funny looks from fellow shoppers in the Met Food. Reaching back into the cabinet, she brought out a box of corn flakes, poured some into a bowl and sliced a banana against the palm of her hand with a butter knife.

As she opened the refrigerator door, she dutifully shut her eyes against the light and chose the container on the right. Reflexively, she sniffed its contents. Her mouth hated a surprise. Once, her first year at Camp Housatonic, her bunkmate Aileen came out of the concession and offered her a cold can of orange soda. Grateful, she tilted her head back and took a swig. But what met her tongue couldn't have been more wrong. She gagged on the sour dairy of buttermilk, its texture like mucilage on her tongue, and she spit a mouthful of curdled liquid all over her sneakers. It turned out to be a secret initiation rite. She was now one of the Housatonic Hooligans – a camp tradition of pranksters – and she wore the skull and crossbones patch they gave her proudly. It still resided in a wooden cigar box in her closet along with the stainless steel I.D. bracelet given to her by Pete Winokur in sixth grade. But she no longer drank anything from a container that she didn't sniff first. And she never went near buttermilk again.

Careful to keep one finger inside the edge of the bowl to judge fullness, she poured the milk. Just as she finished, the Talking Heads seemed to morph into a chorus of Papa Bears, slowing and deepening to a throaty halt. Danielle placed the bowl carefully on the counter, well back from the edge. She navigated easily to the stereo in her bedroom where she removed the turntable arm from the surface of the record and fiddled with the stereo controls, none of which had any effect. The arm dropped from her sweaty fingers and bounced on the record's surface.

"Shit."

Surely the vinyl would be scratched. She had only bought the record a week ago and the purchase was outside of her ordinary budget. In frustration, Danielle reached up and flicked the light on, determined to save the record from further damage. The dark remained unabated. She blinked once and then again, staring hard into the gloom. Her stomach lurched. She could see nothing more than she had before she turned the light on. Only faint dark outlines on a darker ground. Danielle moved unsteadily into the kitchen where she reached above the sink to remove the blackout shade from the kitchen window. Even her neighbors' windows, which she knew would be brightly lit by this time, appeared as nothing more than the haziest of gray-black rectangles. She turned away quickly, close to panic.

Danielle forced herself into the living room and peeled back the Velcro-ed sheets from the window and tugged at the shade, which retracted into its roller with a sharp bang, but the bared window illuminated almost nothing beyond a murky darkness. She moved as swiftly as she could with safety to the lamp by the side of the couch and turned the switch once, twice, a third time. Nothing. Around her huddled a faint landscape of dark and dreadful forms, nothing more. Danielle's heart beat so hard and fast that she had to slump herself over the arm of the couch to keep from falling. So, it had finally happened. The dying of the light. Not death, in her case, but blindness. How could it have come this suddenly? Why didn't Dr. Schein warn her that this could happen? Or had she refused to hear? The blood rushed like a vortex through her head. She thought: *Book*. And in her mind's eye an image instantaneously arose. *Spoon*, she said to herself, and a long handled wooden utensil appeared inside her head. *Mother. Father. Horse. French horn. Celery.* Then *Purple. Green. Dragonfly.* How long would memory supply these pictures, she wondered. She struggled to keep from puking onto the couch cushions, to which she clung like an infant as vertigo washed over her.

A deep keening moan rose through her throat and loosed itself into the darkness. She lowered herself to the floor and lay prone on her belly, pounding the floor with one fist in furious grief. Wave after wave of cries broke from inside her, flooding the small room until she felt herself drowning in her own grief.

She didn't know how long she had lain like this, but now she noticed a pounding noise that came from outside herself. Someone was at the door. *Go away, go away, go away*, Danielle's blood thrummed in her ears. She thought of her great Aunt Agnes, who had faced this same dark demon long before Danielle was born. A fall from this height, five stories up, would only take a few seconds and might bring an ending more swift and sudden than the perception of pain. The pounding on the door continued. Danielle's fingers gripped the shag carpeting as if keeping herself from sliding off the planet.

Pound, pound, pound. *Pound, pound, pound, pound.*

"Hey! Anyone home? Are you in there?" The voice came to Danielle as if from down a long, winding corridor. The same one into which her vision had disappeared? She couldn't say. The hammering stopped. Someone was listening for a reply.

"Ouch! Shit!"

Whoever was out there fell against the doorframe heavily, then scraped against the wood, sinking down the length of the door to the carpeted floor. "Damn it."

Danielle sat up. She crawled toward the door. It was as if she had never done this before, this moving through darkness. Gone were the months of careful practice. She was as lost as a rat at sea. She stayed low to the floor and waved one arm clumsily ahead of her like a flesh-and-blood antenna, until she found the door.

"Who's there?" she called hoarsely.

"Danielle? Jesus, it's about time. Let me in, for fuck's sake. It's *dark* out here."

Geoffrey? What did he know about dark? Reluctantly, she rose and unfastened the lock. Was it really Geoffrey out there?

Could someone have followed them and used this ruse to break into her apartment? This is what it will be like forever, she thought. Blind trust. It could be the Son of Sam, for all she knew. Or, if not the Son of Sam, some other psycho killer. *Que'st que c'est?* A coarse and bitter joke. She opened the door the few inches the chain would allow. But she could see nothing.

"Danielle, it's me. Geoffrey. I thought I'd never find your apartment. I ran into your neighbor – I mean literally *ran into him* – on the stairs and he told me where you live. Let me in, okay?"

She slipped the chain and let him enter. How long would it take before he noticed the change in her?

"The whole city – it's dark everywhere," he continued in a rush. "A total blackout. Thank God I wasn't in the subway. Do you have a flashlight? Candles? A transistor radio?" He paused. "Are you okay?" She heard him place two heavy packages down to one side of the door. Heard the dry rub of paper as he slipped his hands from the handles. Shopping bags.

"Blackout?" she repeated, stupidly. That was when she first noticed the hollowness in the air. It was as if a hood had been thrown over her head. The bubble of hum that she took for granted had burst. No air conditioners, no muttered TV and radio blather from the apartments around her, no distant fans from the restaurants that vented into the alley. There was no "I Don't Love You Anymore," no "Jammin'," no "Dreams," no clanging salsa beat. Nothing but stillness as thick as fleece. Silence. For a moment that stretched toward eternity, Danielle was aware of nothing but the knocking of her own heart beating with the strength of piston against her chest. And then, one car horn after another began to blare. Someone was shouting something incomprehensible. Someone shouted back. The city had met its own blindness and was feeling its way through.

Blackout. Slowly the word drilled through the cold steel of her fear and made its meaning felt. Danielle had to clutch something to remain upright. What she clutched was Geoffrey. The solid heft of him, which felt to her at that moment like a raft sent to save her from drowning in the sea. It was a reprieve; she should feel grateful. Instead she felt a growing rage arriving in waves of ice and fire, that somewhere down the road, some time soon, she would have to live through this moment all over again. She held her breath to keep from screaming. Then she succumbed to the only thing that trumped rage for her at this moment – desire. If Geoffrey was surprised, he gave no sign. Their bodies met the scratchy fabric of the couch as one.

ᘒ☉ᘓ

Judith stood breathless in the dark room, staring off into the black emptiness that only seconds before had been a brightly lit city.

Just minutes ago, she had been bent over deeply from the waist, letting her long hair spill almost to the floor as she ran the hairdryer from roots to ends. Perhaps it was irrational – or worse, vain – but in the moments after she had hung up the phone with Michael, Judith had developed an overwhelming urge to shower and wash her hair. She pulled a pair of stockings off the shower door where they had been drying and stepped into the needling spray.

It had felt so good, the warm water streaming across her scalp and down her neck, her shoulders, the sensitive skin of her torso; the flowery suds and brisk motion of her fingertips rubbing away a day's tension and dirt. She hummed with pleasure. Judith lathered oatmeal and honey soap over her shoulders, her legs and under her arms, sweeping the sweat and grime from her skin and leaving a silky clean in their place. Her nipples rose pink and firm from the delicate skin of her breasts. Judith blushed to see them like that. Was it the hot water that made them so sensitive or the anticipation of Michael on his way uptown to see her? She forced the thought from her head. It was foolishness. Wanton foolishness. She finished the shower with a rinse of cool water and wrapped a thick towel turban-like around her hair as she stepped out from the shower and into a terry robe that had been a Chanukah present from her mother. Drops of water traced winding paths from her scalp down her forehead and cheeks, not unpleasantly.

The air in her apartment seemed charged in some new way. There was an unusual skipping sensation in her chest and she felt flushed and feverish. Objects in the room had taken on a new clarity, their borders knife-edged. She felt as if on the cusp of some greater *da-at*, some inner knowledge. This, of course, was heresy, Judith told herself. In her community, the miracle of *da'at* was pretty much limited to men. Boys became Bar Mitzvah at age thirteen because they had grown to embrace this sort of awakening, a state of consciousness, the realization that *I exist*. And along with that, had grown to contemplate and question the purpose of existence.

"Only in the knowledge of our own selves and the choice to become whatever we desire to become – in this we stand even beyond the angels. And that is the pinnacle to which we climb on the day we become bar mitzvah," the rabbi said when her cousin Dovid recently became Bar Mitzvah. But no one said this when she brought forth the hard truth that she believed her future lay in becoming a doctor.

"We'll find you a good match, a nice boy," her mother pleaded that night at the table. "You'll get over this *mishugas* and be happy when you look on your firstborn's face."

The phone rang again, startling her. Could it be Michael saying he'd changed his mind? Judith answered with trepidation.

"*Shalom*, Jehudit, *libling*! *Vos makhstu?*" Her concern shifted to discomfort. It was her aunt calling to check on her health.

"I'm fine, Tante. Much better. *A sheynam dank*. Thank you for asking." Judith wrapped the belt of her robe tightly and sat down at the edge of the bed.

"Good, good. Your uncle and I, we were worried. You looked so pale."

"No Tante, I'm fine. It must have been the heat. And you? Are you home?" She traced the flowered pattern of her pillowcase with her free hand nervously. *Nukhamol*, again a lie. She hoped this wouldn't be a long conversation.

"We're at your Tante Suri's house for dinner. But I wanted to tell you. A boy called this afternoon at the shop. He asked for Judith. He said he was from school and had some books for you. I gave him your telephone. This was alright?"

Judith smiled with relief. She could hear the trepidation in her aunt's voice.

"Yes, certainly, Tante. Thank you so much. It was all right." Better than all right, she thought.

"Your uncle thought I shouldn't have done this, but he sounded like a nice boy…"

"It's fine, Tante. Really. But I have to get off the phone." Judith took a deep breath. "I have something on the stove." Lie begat lie. "I have to go now.

"But Jehudit, you are sure that you should be accepting things from this boy?"

"Yes, Tante. I am sure. It is only schoolwork. I will see you in the morning." She had to extricate herself from what she knew could become a debate of Talmudic proportions. "Please send Tante Suri my love. *A gute nacht.*" That ended the conversation.

Her love. She had so much love for them all. And they for her. Although she knew they were at once angry and fearful for her, she was blessed to have a family to love.

Judith drank a full glass of ice water and yet excitement still burned inside her chest. She didn't feel ill, but she touched her forehead with the back of her hand. With the turban still wrapped snug, she changed out of the robe into a clean skirt and blouse. She skipped the stockings and stepped barefoot into a pair of clogs. The feel of air against her bare thighs under the skirt felt new, almost sinful. Then she returned to the bathroom to dry her hair. It would never do for Michael to find her with her hair wet and wild.

If she were still living at home, she would be going through this same ritual to walk out with the boy chosen by her mother and the *shadchan*, or matchmaker. This matchmaking had officially begun when she was eighteen. The boy would be a scholar, sometimes a distant cousin or brother of one of the school friends, and because her family was more 'modern' than some, she might have spied on him herself to see if he pleased her before letting negotiations get too far. On their first date, they might go to a restaurant or some other public place. If they seemed mutually compatible, they might go out a second time. But there wouldn't be so much as the briefest physical contact between them – right up until their wedding night. When Michael grabbed her hands this afternoon, it was the first such touch she had ever felt. She could still sense its imprint on her skin. Judith was sure that Michael would laugh if he knew this. In fact, she had never had more than a second date before she determined that the boy the *shadchan* had sent was not meant for her.

"How do you know you're not rejecting your *bashert*?" her girl-friends asked her.

"I can't reject my *bashert*," she replied breezily. "He's my *bash-ert*." Of course, that was true. Hashem did not match up people by interest or looks or dollars and cents. Somewhere, Judith believed, her *bashert* was ready and waiting – brought forth by the Primal Mind of the same One who brought forth heaven and earth. He would arrive, inevitably.

I am my beloved's, and my beloved is mine, who grazes among the roses. So read the Song of Solomon, she thought.

With a brush in one hand, the dryer in the other, she coaxed the rhythmic curls of her hair into a smooth overall wave. She had her mother's hair – a turbulent black gypsy tangle that required diligent taming. She had learned to brush it into submission early on. The key was not to stop until it was quite dry. It was almost there now; just a few more long strokes and she could flip rightside up again and go downstairs to wait for Michael. That's what she had decided. She would wait outside. She could thank him, take her package back and make her excuses to return to her apartment alone. Or, if he wanted to stay a while, she could suggest that they sit on the steps outside the building. She felt pleased with this solution. It allowed her to spend time with Michael, and yet not occupy the intimate space of her apartment with this male stranger.

It was not at all uncommon to see people sitting out on the stoop on these humid evenings. There would be nothing strange about it. Indeed, she felt she was finally learning to find her way through this new world. Judith paused in drying her hair and stood up to stretch. She rolled back the sleeves of her blouse to expose her wrists. They were slender and graceful. How did they compare to others that Michael had seen, she wondered. For a moment Judith recalled the sight of herself in the wrap dress in the Saks dressing room mirror: the sensual curves of arms and calves and silky bare skin, the crisp V at the front that drew her eyes down, down, down, between her breasts. She blushed deeply to think of it and at the same time, wondered what it would be like to share that view of herself with someone. Her *bashert*.

> *A bundle of myrrh is my beloved to me;*
> *between my breasts he shall lie.*

Judith patted cold water on her cheeks and shifted her attention to wiping the sink clean of a few long black hairs. She glanced at the alarm clock by her bed. It was, already, 9:30. He would be here any minute. Her heart sped up again at the thought. She wanted him to see her at her best, especially after her humiliating exit from lunch. Once more, she tasted the bitter smoke and bile, then gulped to rid her mouth of the sensation. Sweat broke out on her upper lip and she swiped at it with her shoulder. Perhaps she should pat on a little powder, she thought, to keep the shine off her nose. Maybe some lipstick. She laughed out loud at herself. She was preening exactly as if she were stepping out with her intended. Judith turned the hair dryer up to high and suffered the screaming desert hot wind in an effort to hasten the drying. Could Michael, of all people, be her *bashert*? For a moment she imagined circling him at the *chupah*, their first kiss after the glass had been broken, the intimate touch of his fingers on her skin. She pushed the thought away. It was unseemly. Unholy. Unholy thoughts were the mothers of demons, *Bubbe* Esther used to say. Suddenly, the hair dryer slowed to an angry buzz and stopped, dead. At the same moment, the light over the sink blinked off, as did the light outside the bathroom door, leaving her in darkness.

What have I done? Judith thought, as she stood and quickly flipped her hair back. Could she have blown a fuse with the dryer? And how does one fix such a thing in an apartment building? As she stood, she faced the window, open to catch a breeze. What she saw brought an icy finger tracing its way down her spine.

The lights of the city were flickering out, block by block -- twinkling like those last bits of sacred Light in the first days of creation, as the holy pots in which Hashem stored his divine Spirit shattered into infinite shards and were scattered over the entire realm of the Earth. The darkness that was left was like the beginning of time. Or the end.

∽⊚∼

It was completely still in the train. No vibration at all, neither from the fan nor the engine. In the absolute darkness, Pia heard a dozen people breathe in, hold their breath for a moment, then exhale. In the absence of air movement, the moist earthy smell of an electric storm rose around her. And, behind that, the ghost smells of the countless commuters who had shared the car that day. She wiggled her foot impatiently and waited for light and movement to return.

Pia felt a touch of pride that she no longer panicked every time a train ground to a halt, or the lights cut out. She was becoming a New Yorker, inured to these periodic disruptions. Still, she really hoped it would be brief – she was utterly exhausted and ready for this day to end. In the moment before the lights went out, Pia had been reading over the shoulder of the person to her left. Well, not reading, exactly, but doing the Jumble. Now, she moved the letters around in her mind, trying to solve the ones she could remember. TONJI. NOTJI. JONTI. *JOINT.* URPPE. PERUP. UPREP...

"Do you have any gum?" The woman next to Pia asked in

slow, thickly accented English.

"Sorry. I don't," Pia told her.

"Do you know how far is Sutter Avenue?"

"Sorry, no" she repeated.

The seat had been sticky with the sweat of strangers when Pia boarded, but she was grateful for the opportunity to sink down and slide her blistering feet out of the shoes that seemed to have shrunk to the size of teacups as she stood waiting on the platform. She thought of the year in school – fifth grade? – when she had doggedly read all of the Pearl S. Buck she could get her hands on, lying under the covers at night with her flashlight, cringing at the torturous scenes of foot binding in the girls who grew to womanhood in those books. The sick and wild feeling in her stomach as she imagined the pulsating pain of their bones and blood vessels straining against the intransigent bindings, all in the effort to raise their value in the marriage marketplace.

Restless, Pia felt for her portfolio, which remained undisturbed on the empty seat to her left, and repositioned the plastic bag of art supplies on the floor between her feet. She could swear there was heat coming out of the ducts beneath the seat, and the air in the train was stifling. Someone had wrenched open the narrow windows above the bench directly across from her, but what blew in was more dust than air. The window itself had been opaque with spray paint. Pia imagined the furtive broad strokes applied by the artist and his crew as they crept into the yard at night and plied their craft on the involuntary public canvas. Under cover of darkness now herself, she raised her own right hand index finger cocked against the imaginary nozzle of the spray can.

Pia thought of her friends at school – the ones who left her behind, asleep, as they tagged the railroad overpass. With their picked-out Afros and their all-night consciousness-raising-sessions, they thought they were so much hipper and angrier – and blacker – than she. Now James was studying optometry, Willa was teaching junior high art in Vermont and Pete, last she had heard, was driving an eighteen-wheeler in his daddy's long-distance hauling company.

So much for their revolutionary fervor, Pia thought. Meanwhile, here she was in the belly of the beast, surrounded by guerilla art and the huddled masses her friends had spent so much time ranting about. Of course, at least they had jobs. She only had about $800 left in her bank account. And $200 of that was promised to her aunt on August 1 for rent. Reluctantly, she considered that maybe she should actually invest in a typing class and hope that might in fact buy her a foot in the door somewhere. As ignominious as that felt. What she needed was a sign from the art gods about what she was meant to do.

Pia placed the notebook she was holding into the bag at her feet. Waiting for the train, she had been thumbing through some designs for her own tag. She liked the one with the boxy *P*, the purple pupil of the dot over the *I,* the *A* piercing the space above it, especially where the lightning bolt ripped a jagged fault line through the letters so that their bottoms raced just ahead of their tops. *PIA 177* – her aunt's house number – she thought that was her handle of choice, although she was increasingly fond of the name that Rosie had suggested over drinks tonight. Pia had waited in the Irish pub on 41st Street for half an hour before Rosie arrived, lugging her suitcase. They drank tepid beer and ate greasy burgers until Rosie had to leave for Port Authority to catch her bus back upstate. *R-TGRRL*, Rosie had written in loopy letters on the damp cocktail napkin that she unwound from her drink. In the moment after she wrote it, the ink spread through the cheap paper until it resembled the gas-propelled pigments favored by the subway crews. Shortly after that, it became an unreadable blur.

"Rat Girl? You think I should call myself Rat Girl?" she asked Rosie, incredulous.

"Not *Rat*, idiot – *ART*. You should call yourself Art Girl. *R-TGRRL*," and Rosie shoved Pia's shoulder, hard.

On the ride downtown, Pia had amused herself coming up with designs for *R-TGRRL*. Uppercase and lower, with and without the hyphen, alone and with the house number – sometimes the letters floated like dinghies behind a stylized boat, sometimes they bobbed like buoys in a sea of fluorescent whitecaps.

She was getting restless. It was so dark in the car that Pia's eyes could no longer discern her fellow passengers. Black, black, white, black, Hispanic, Hispanic, Hispanic: she had counted on the seats across from her, when she first boarded. Now they were all shadows in the dark.

At Wall Street, only minutes before the train stopped, half a dozen tired-looking suits came through the door carrying briefcases and carefully folded copies of the *Times*. One of them had his tie neatly draped over his arm, his top buttons open and shirt pulled well away from his neck. They were gathered around a pole in the center of the car and had been reading with the practiced grace of those for whom the *New York Times* subway fold was as natural as turning down the bedcovers. Pia could never get the fold to go right, so she stuck to the *Post* and the *News*.

"You hear the score?" one of the men asked another.

"Cubs were leading, two to one, last I heard," the man answered.

"Fuckin' Mets," the first man grunted and returned to his paper.

Pia guessed that they were now somewhere under the East River. It was the longest interval between stations. The woman beside her had fallen asleep and her head lolled back and snapped forward every now and then. Pia was pretty drowsy herself. Her mother had warned her never, *ever* to let herself fall asleep on the subway. She read this, she said, in a magazine. Her mother was justifiably concerned about Pia's safety, but had obviously never experienced firsthand the soporific inevitability of subway heat, noise, and a full day of pounding the Manhattan pavements. She was fairly certain that none of the other passengers were going to snatch her purse or stab her while her eyes were closed. For one thing, they all seemed too exhausted and overheated to make the effort.

Pia thought about what her father might have made of this train with its motley collection of exhausted passengers. She imagined him suddenly, not at the prow of a boat, but on the roof of the train, out there as it sailed through the excavated blackness. The stone and cement walls rushed past, fetid wind ruffling his hair like the breeze off Cayuga Lake as he balanced against the sudden lurches and shifts.

She missed her father. She reached up and fingered the tiny glass ball hanging from a chain around her neck, his last birthday present to her. It was filled with viscous liquid and a bunch of tiny crystals that swam in it, glinting with the refracted colors of light. An Aurorea Borealis, he called it. Not *the* Aurora Borealis, which he had woken her late one night to see – a vibrating curtain of shifting colors that rang out against the pitch black hills – but a reminder. Of a phenomenon. Of him. Of home.

How many words a minute do you type? That's really all anyone wanted to know about her. R-TGRRL might defenestrate those bastards, but as Pia, she didn't even call their bluff. Give me a sign, she cried out silently to a deaf universe. Give me a job or a sign that it's time to give up.

The train had been stopped for several minutes now and people were beginning to shuffle with discomfort. Someone lit a match. "Put that out, fucker," someone yelled. The men at the pole began grumbling about the mayor.

"Beame's a bum. He's always been a bum, he'll always be a bum." No one bothered to disagree.

The woman on Pia's right shifted a little further away and the spot where her thigh had been touching Pia's now felt cool, as if a little breeze had blown in. But there was no breeze – even the ceiling fans had ceased their imitation breeze noise. Pia lifted one leg and then the other slightly off the seat, mildly disgusted by the way her thighs peeled stickily away from the plastic.

The pride of place she had felt just ten minutes ago had ebbed considerably. Now a note of anxiety was indeed creeping in. She could barely breathe this humid, stinking air. Pia felt virtually alone in this city. Aside from her aged aunt, who would even set out to look for her if she were to disappear? She had no friends in the neighborhood. There wouldn't even be a mural painted in her memory. She gripped her portfolio and swallowed hard. She summoned up that part of her that really was R-TGRRL and pantomimed a decisive spray-painted P in the air before her face. If there were ever to be a mural with her name, Pia thought, she would have to paint it herself.

❧

The door slammed shut behind Althea and she found herself on the pavement, enveloped in blackness. Random headlights, glaring at odd angles from the broad avenue, illuminated nothing familiar, only made things more bewildering, and for a moment Althea wove dizzily, feeling as though she might tip over. The last thing she had done before pushing through the heavy industrial gate was to throw Oscar's flashlight behind her into the building. She didn't dare look back. She knew from the crash that he had, indeed, tripped and fallen down the final steps as she ran from him. He screamed for her to stop. Shouted that he thought he had broken his leg. She never slowed her flight, but she did throw him the flashlight at the last second. Now, she was out on the street in darkness.

Althea paused a moment in confusion. She had been expecting the usual flood of amber streetlight and instead it was almost as dark out here as it was in Oscar's building where the power was out. Although she wasn't surprised to be the only person on this street, where the businesses were shuttered each night, she had expected to see the usual girls at the corner bar at the end of the block. Instead, she could see almost nothing.

Something shattered in the distance. Blocks away, sirens blared. Is it war then? Are we under attack, Althea thought, in a moment of terror that raised cold gooseflesh on her sweating arms. She had never lived through war, but her parents had often told her the stories of the horrors it had inflicted on their country. As a child she had known people on her island who had lost an arm, an eye, or other body part – the legacy of war. They talked of the years of starvation and humiliation inflicted by the Germans. She crossed herself and sent out a silent prayer for protection. Not for herself, but for her daughter. She had to get to Celia. She had broken another promise to her child, she was a terrible mother, but now all that mattered was Celia's safety. She could make amends later.

A man's face appeared suddenly, so close to Althea that she smelled the stale sweat through his clothes.

"What is happening?" she called, but he had already hurried past. Althea moved heavily, as in a dream, up the block. When she reached the avenue, another man, walking a large dog, came by and although she had no fear of animals ordinarily, this one looked dangerous with unease. She gave them wide berth and pushed on. She had to get to Celia. A couple, hand in hand stopped near her, both of them looking up and craning their necks toward the missing skyline. Althea approached them cautiously.

"Please, can you tell me what happened?"

They turned toward her with looks of disbelief further shadowing their faces.

"It's a blackout," the girl said, spilling over with laughter. "The whole city is dark. There's no electricity anywhere. Look!" They pointed to the west, where a soft glow in the sky announced New Jersey. "Isn't this amazing?" They swiveled around again, as if to assure themselves that the phenomenon persisted.

"What is this – this blackout?" Althea asked them.

"The storm knocked out the power lines to the entire city," the girl's boyfriend explained. "It was on the radio. Transistor." They held up a little leather-covered radio by means of explanation. "The police are out with bullhorns, telling people, listen." She cocked her head. But the words were indistinct and far away. "We're going to a blackout party," he continued. "Wanna come?"

Althea shook her head *no*, mutely, invisibly. So it wasn't a war, after all. But still, there was no time to waste.

She wondered about the subways – did they take their power from the same source as the rest of the city? The absence of the

familiar rumble from underground told her that no trains were moving down there. And the lack of traffic lights made Althea doubt
that buses were running. She had to make her way uptown. She
calculated quickly: there were approximately ninety blocks between
here and her mother's housing project. She had heard that there
were twenty blocks to the mile, which would make it four-and-a-half
miles – about seven kilometers – which she had to walk to get there.
Seven kilometers. It would take her over an hour to reach Celia, even
if she walked quickly. Althea's heart was pounding although she had
taken barely ten steps.

Her eyes had now adjusted to the point where she could make
out familiar landmarks – the plate glass windows of Barneys, the
menswear store, like blind eyes without their lights, the thick candy-
striped pole, still for once, outside the seedy barbershop on the corner
of 18th Street. Althea worked her way up the block in the opposite direction from the trickle of confused traffic on Seventh Avenue.
Giving up the flashlight was, perhaps, not the smartest thing she had
ever done, Althea thought. But, she realized with a grimace, it was
hardly the most foolish.

The argument with Oscar had built quickly from ice to fire. He
sat on the huge leather sofa listening to her accusations without the
slightest trace of shame. She loomed over him, refusing his suggestion that she sit down, calm down. Not once did he deny what he had
done – how could he with the evidence of the phone message. But
he did, at first, try to convince her that it was for her own good that
he had her fired. Some rubbish about an audit and how she would
have come under suspicion, maybe been charged with fraud for what
she'd done. *What she'd done?* But this way, he tried to persuade her,
she could apply for unemployment – he would make sure her claim
went unchallenged.

"And how would you make sure?" she screamed at him, dry-
eyed with rage. "By fucking some other stupid woman in Human
Resources? Gail, maybe? Or Theresa? She's just off the boat. A real
greenie. I'm sure she could use some of your 'help.'"

He looked wounded. And then angry. He stood so quickly and so close against her that she toppled backward. The chair she tumbled into slid on the bare wood floors, hitting the wall with a thud. She screamed -- and then everything went dark. First thought: it was something he had done to her. But she felt nothing except the next scream scraping her throat.

"Shut up!" he spat. "The chair must have knocked something loose in the wall. The power is out."

Althea lay sprawled, unmoving. She hated him even more in her blindness. She heard Oscar bump his way across the room to the desk. He reached into a drawer and brought out the flashlight. When he turned it on, it transformed his face into the mask of the devil she now knew him to be. Gripping the light, he strode back across the floor to where she remained, frozen in the chair.

"You need to understand one thing," he was saying through clenched teeth, the light bobbing closer with each syllable. That's when she leapt at him, snatching the flashlight from his hands and racing to the loft door. She didn't pause to hear what it was he wanted her to understand. For a moment there was no sound of movement behind her. She flung the door open and began running down the metal stairs, the beam of light leaping just ahead of her feet. Thank God she had both her shoes on, she remembered thinking. Suddenly, there was the sound of heavy footsteps behind her. Steadying herself with one hand on the banister, she leaped down the last several steps of that flight, spun around the landing and continued down the next set of stairs. Oscar had to slow as the light faded from him, but even so, he had almost caught up to her by the time she reached the final bank of stairs. She imagined him grabbing her long hair as it flew out behind her, and she raced faster until she reached the ground floor. That's when she heard a sickening crash followed by his screams. She threw the flashlight backward as hard as she could, hoping it would strike its mark. In another moment, the heavy steel slammed between them and she was free.

Now, as Althea picked her way up the avenue, pale faces appeared before her, bobbing over dark and shapeless forms.   She pushed on, staring hard into the gloom, stumbling repeatedly over the uneven sidewalk. She was not afraid of the dark, she reminded herself. Many were the summer nights she had spent outdoors on the wild Skiathos beaches with only the stars for light. Her feet swelled and rubbed against her shoes, but she forced herself to keep moving forward. Again she regretted having given up that light. Oscar could rot in the darkness for all she cared. But he wouldn't, she knew. Someone would come along, find him there on the landing, and help him upstairs or to a hospital. His injuries would be attended to; he would find soft berth somewhere. Men like Oscar always did.

When she got to 35th Street, a line of people blocked her path up the sidewalk. The line snaked its way to a pair of public telephones. Of course! She could call her mother's house and tell Celia she was on her way. She would be there as soon as she could. Althea stood with the others on the line, shifting from foot to foot. Sirens echoed. An ambulance shot past and bathed all their faces with flashes of red. She hadn't called Celia at all today; a phone call that might have set her mind at ease. How could she have failed to do such a simple thing? The line inched forward almost imperceptibly as each person found relief in depositing a few coins and saying a few words. But it felt to Althea that the longer she waited, the farther the phone inched away. She thought of Sisyphus, whom the gods tormented unto eternity by being made to roll a huge boulder up a steep hill. Before he could reach the top, however, the massive stone would always roll back down, forcing him to begin again. He had angered them with his deceitfulness, and she by failing to safeguard the precious jewel to which she had been entrusted. She shook her head to clear such backward thoughts. This was America in 1977 – the Gods on Mount Olympus had been rendered impotent by the gods of Mammon. The man behind Althea coughed, pointedly.

"You're next," he said.

Althea stepped up to the phone, lifted the receiver still warm from the palm of the person ahead of her, deposited change in the slots and dialed, praying for the sound of Celia's voice on the line. Everything would be all right. The sound through the receiver was like the rush of a wave, and then, nothing. She hung up the phone. Three nickels clinked into the receptacle at the bottom and she tried all over again. This time, she was met with a busy signal: Who could they be talking to? Once more, then. Or as many times as it took.

The people behind her were muttering. Let them. She needed to hear Celia's voice. Instead, the rush of waves again. And this time, no money returned. This was just wasting her time. She had to keep walking. She slammed the received into its cradle and spun from the booth into the arms of a man in a uniform that reeked of garbage.

"Take it easy, lady," he said, steadying her. "The phones lines are burning up from too many calls." She pushed off his burly chest and continued on her way.

Althea had only walked a couple of blocks further before a sharp twinge in her ankle made her stop and lean against the nearest useless lamppost. Although she hadn't felt any pain in the adrenaline rush of fleeing Oscar's apartment, she must have twisted it on the stairs. Now it was throbbing. Inside her right shoe, her foot felt hot and thick. Broken? Althea thought not, but she wasn't sure she could walk many blocks further. Nor could she stop, she knew.

But surely she could rest a moment. Nothing bad would happen to Celia. Celia, she assured herself, was in the safest place possible, at home with her yiayia who had most likely tucked her into bed and told her not to open her eyes until the sun kissed them in the morning.

೧◉౷

The meds were kicking in. Johanna had found the three red and white capsules stuck to the inside of a balled up sock. Staccato images were beginning to bleed into coherent dream, cream, scream, something mean. She plunged her arm into the plastic garbage bag right up to her shoulder and still didn't touch bottom. She grasped and released any number of things – torn pantyhose, crumpled tinfoil, a rubberband ball she had assembled over weeks of urine-scented boredom on the psych ward at Roosevelt Hospital, a half-empty bottle of toilet water she shook up and down before letting it go and, finally, a shoe – a black pump minus its heel – which she removed triumphantly and held aloft in the light of the single bulb that shone just outside the excavated cove in which she had settled for the night.

The subway tunnels were full of these coves, small incroppings where equipment might be stored or into which a lineman might slip for safety. This was her favorite hidey-hole, like a mole, a toe, ahold, cold, overload…She had left a bag of her stuff and a piece of carpeting here to claim it. She looked up and down the track, marked by lights sharp as ice picks. A thought was trundling down the track, pumping itself through her, heavily.

"My grandmother liked to say," she blurted loudly into the gaping tunnel, the shoe still raised before her. "My grandmother liked to say that Adolf Hitler had very, very diminutive feet." She paused to see if there was any disagreement. Hearing none, she continued. "It was something he didn't want generally known," here she paused in her lecture to giggle, "but she had it on good authority that before the war there were regular deliveries of large unmarked cartons that contained shoes – Women's size 8 brown oxfords – delivered to him from Sears, Roebuck and Company in Minneapolis, Minnesota." She lifted the shoe higher turning it this way and that, offering up a panorama of views. "After the war began, of course, he was forced to wear ordinary German shoes, size 12. He filled in the toes with kapok." Johanna lowered the shoe and peered into the thick gloom beyond it to see if there would be any questions.

In the intervening silence – sometimes it took a while for her audience to formulate their queries – Johanna took a long swig from the Boy Scout canteen she had found this afternoon at the Wall Street station. It had been propped up on the top of a cable box on the station wall and she had waited several trains to see if anyone would return to claim it. She rinsed and filled it with scalding water from an open utility closet where she sometimes went to bathe. The utility closets were supposed to be kept locked, but the locks were often nothing more than a joke. The water in the canteen was warm and she tried to imagine the taste of coffee.

The tracks clicked once or twice. Another train in the distance. Johanna pulled her bags closer around her into the safety of the cove. The rocks at her back sweated in the heat. She heard some grumbling and tried to follow the sound with her eyes. In the gloom she could only see a few dusky feet. But there, at the very edge of her vision, was some movement. A rounded lump pressed hard against the jagged stone. Gnawing vehemently at what might be a snake or no, just a length of thick, black cable that hung from the wall. Her nemesis, here to heckle: Rat.

"You. Rat," she screamed. "Beat it."

The filthy creature ran in circles, mocking her.

Fuckyou old crazybitch. Fuckyfuckyou fuckyou.

Phnfff... Phnnff...Mud eater. Glasseater. Taleteller.

Glass strewn. Gas prone. Phnnfff...phnnff...phnnff.

She closed her ears against its derision. The rodent stood up on its hind legs and boxed its puny arms in her direction. It chattered and turned its back to her. She heard its teeth resume grinding against the cable. She pictured the orange teeth, the black rubber hose, the implacable metal wires inside.

In a fury, Johanna raised the shoe and threw it. It flew well beyond its intended target, was swallowed up in the blackness and finally made a soft splash as it landed. The rat froze, then turned and ambled back into the empty tunnel, following the sound. Johanna grabbed a rock, which had previously been a sharp pain in her side, and threw it hard. A spark flew from the gnawed cable as the stone bounced off it and onto the track. Then another and another and another – a fountain of sparks. A torrent of electric shards. Fear sliced through her gut, releasing her bowels in a sinking rush. Then they were all plunged into utter darkness. Sucked into a vacuum that swallowed up all light, all sound. The stillness was suffocating. Johanna felt as if she had been abruptly erased and with her had gone the entire known world. If she'd known it was that easy, she would have done it long ago.

ᘒ◉ᘖ

Black, black, black, orange. Black, black, black, black, orange.

Flames and sparks licking upward from metal garbage cans up and down the block made everything around them even darker. Watery beams of flashlights brought feet moving out of the dark toward Celia. Like ghosts, they disappeared as soon as the beams passed by. No one looked at her – each person glued by the light to a tiny patch of illuminated sidewalk. Celia slipped from the doorway of Yiayia's building and snapped on her own little flashlight to find her way.

She wasn't afraid of the dark. She wasn't afraid of anything. Almost.

Something small and quick dashed across the lighted patch just ahead of her feet. A rat! – she saw the tip of its tail coil through the beam – the flashlight dropped from her hands and bounced off her big toe. Celia screamed, just a quick squeal, and a woman moving past turned to her.

"Are you all right? Are you out here alone? Lost?" the woman asked, bending down to bring her face close to Celia's. She smelled something like Yiayia's bottle of Listerine.

What should she say? *Don't talk to strangers,* Yiayia had said. Everyone was strange out here in the darkness.

"*Habla ingles?*"

"I saw a rat."

The woman grimaced, her face a witch's face with dancing shadows.

"Ugh. I hate rats." She turned in a circle looking down at her feet, swaying unsteadily. "Which way did it go?"

Celia shrugged. Did the lady think she knew? Celia thought quickly. "I'd better go now, I think I hear my Mami calling," she said, pointing into the dark nowhere all around them. "There she is."

"Well, you go straight to her and be careful," the woman said, her face lifting away, her eyes darting this way and that. "It's not safe for a little girl to be out alone on these streets." Celia could tell the woman was distracted. Probably trying to stay clear of rats, she figured. The woman wobbled off into the darkness.

Celia kneeled and rubbed her toe where the flashlight had bumped it. She wished she'd worn sneakers instead of the pink plastic sandals she'd picked out that morning when there had been no thoughts about rats or darkness, only of the blue, blue sky and a day at the pool. It was such a long time ago; she was practically just a baby back then. Celia brushed her hands lightly around the pavement in widening circles. Her fingers knocked against the flashlight, found the switch, turned it on. She could walk all the way home if she had to. She knew she could. Mami had shown her just this morning on the subway map that hung above their seat on the train.

"Here's our house, and here's Yiayia's house," Mami had said, tracing the long road upward from one end of the island of Manhattan toward the other as they rocked and bumped along the tracks. *Broadway.* It didn't look all that long. She would walk the length of the island, the same way her Mami did back on her island of Skiathos, to go to school. And she would find Mami. Just like little Tragos.

Celia stood and trained the beam of the light just ahead of her feet as she walked.

What a clever girl I am, she thought, and she skipped a little, even though it hurt her foot. That's not what her Yiayia had called her, though, only a little while ago.

By the time they had gotten back from the playground, Celia's shoulders had turned an angry red. When Yiayia tried to rub them with Noxzema, they burned so bad she had screamed and Yiayia tugged her hair, which made Celia scream more.

"You're a naughty little girl!" Yiayia had said to her. "You've made my head ache. I'm going inside to lie down and you can take care of yourself." Yiayia stomped off to her bedroom and left Celia standing half in and half out of her shirt.

Celia wriggled both her arms back into the tee shirt. She wanted, with all her might, for her mother to come through the door right this second and take her home. She was hungry — she had refused to eat the lunch Yiayia packed for them, the chicken was salty and the bread was stale. She had asked for ice cream from the Mister Softee man, but Yiayia said no ice cream for little girls who didn't eat their lunch. That was okay. Mami would be here soon to take her out for pizza. She had promised. In the meantime, Celia opened Yiayia's refrigerator and ate some cold leftovers. Then she turned on the TV, with the sound off, and watched cartoons until she started to fall asleep. Celia didn't want to be asleep when Mami got there, or they might not go out for pizza. She walked to the window and squinted down into the street to see if her mother was coming up the walk. She watched the sky turn purple and orange.

Celia had bounced on the couch for a while, then went into the kitchen and picked at the leftover *pastitsio* she found in a covered dish in the refrigerator. Finally, she got up and walked down the hallway to Yiayia's room, stopping just inside the doorway. She waited a few minutes and then began flicking the light switch on and off. She was just playing. She started out doing it slow and then got faster and faster. Yiayia told her to stop but it was so neat, the way the room looked in the flickering light. Faster and faster, and she waved her left hand in front of her face to watch its cartoon progress in the flashes of light produced by her right.

"Stop it right now, or I promise I will spank you!" Yiayia said, through gritted teeth. Celia did not stop. But the light stopped flashing anyhow.

Click-click-click-click-click.

Still, it was dark. Yiayia sat up in bed.

"See? Now look at the trouble you've made, you bad little girl."

The block between Yiayia's house and Broadway was thick with people clustered hip to hip, talking excitedly and fanning themselves with rolled up newspapers. Celia slipped quietly between little knots of them, hoping that no one would notice her and ask where she was going. She thought she heard the gravelly voice of Yiayia's friend, Maria, who always insisted on giving Celia a big hug and a kiss that smelled like ashtrays and breath mints. Staring hard at the pavement, Celia pulled into herself and made herself small in her own mind, no bigger than a pigeon, no brighter than a mouse, almost invisible. She scurried quickly past the last houses on the block. Daylight was completely gone now and darkness rose from the sidewalks like thick fog. Pale faces hung suspended along the street like party balloons. White teeth flashed from between dark lips.

When she reached Broadway, Celia turned left. The intersection was tangled with cars and trucks at funny angles, like a train set dumped out on the floor. A group of boys raced through the snaggle of vehicles, whooping and giving the finger to the helpless drivers. The street looked like a giant's playground. Then a car jumped the curb trying to get ahead and collided with a trashcan with a sound like a whole building coming down. After that, Celia clung the inside edge of the sidewalk nearest the shops. Some grownups moved into the intersection and began shouting and trying to direct the traffic.

Celia hesitated. Yiayia would be furious when she realized that she had lied about Mami being downstairs. But it had been so simple to fool her. After Yiayia came in from the hallway to announce that her neighbors told her the whole city had lost electricity, she went back to bed with a damp cloth covering her eyes.

"It's almost 10:00 and past your bedtime," she had told Celia. "Just go to sleep. In the morning it will be light again and Mami will be here."

Yiayia didn't understand. Where was Mami in the dark? Yiayia said Mami must have gone straight home from work – it was closer than coming uptown. But Celia knew something was terribly wrong. It felt like a nightmare she had dreamed only last week, in fact. Mami was missing. Celia was alone. She awoke drowning in sorrow. That was all she could remember – the bitter feeling of being left alone. She must have been crying in her sleep, because her pillowcase was wet in the morning.

Your mommy has a boyfriend. That's what stupid Marissa said, but what did she know? Celia had watched the teenage girls with their boyfriends, all kissy-faced and cow-eyed. Her mother would never leave her for some stupid boyfriend. But what if this boyfriend tried to keep her for himself? There was a movie she had seen on television late one night while Mami was asleep. The man had hidden a girl in a locked room to keep her from running away. To keep her for himself. He collected butterflies, too. Celia's skin prickled, she felt close to tears. She wasn't letting Mami disappear again. She would go after her. She had a plan.

On the last day of school, when all the other mothers were gathered around the gates of the schoolyard – all but Mami – Celia had told the yard teacher, Miss Ortiz, that her mother was waiting for Celia in the back of the crowd. Distracted, happy to be rid of screaming children for the summer, Miss Ortiz let her through the gate and Celia walked four blocks toward her house before she actually ran into Mami, sweating and rushing toward her. Instead of yelling at her for sneaking out, as Celia expected, Mami grabbed her up in a big hug and took her out for ice cream. While they sat at the table waiting for their sundaes, Mami made her draw a map of the path from school to home on the paper placemat to prove she knew where she was going.

"You turn left at the barber shop, and right at the bodega and keep going straight until you reach the pink brick buildings. Then you cross the street – at the green light – and that's our block," Mami said, using a black crayon to walk the path. "But don't you ever sneak out and do that again, *kukla*."

Celia followed Yiayia into the dark bedroom and felt her way to the window. "Mami's calling from downstairs," she told Yiayia excitedly. "She wants us to bring her a flashlight so she can come up," Celia had insisted.

"Where? *Where?*" Yiayia had said, pushing Celia aside and

straining out the half-opened window to see through the gloom.

"Right there: by the benches – didn't you hear her?"

In the end, Yiayia had turned over the flashlight to Celia's waiting hands and told her to be careful not to drop it and not to talk to strangers.

Now, there were strangers everywhere. It wasn't too late. She could go back and say that she'd been mistaken. Someone else, some-one who sounded a lot like Mami, must have been calling up for her little girl. Not Celia, but Delia. She giggled in spite of herself. She had never realized how easily grown-ups could be tricked. But she was so hot and thirsty. And already the blister that had risen on her big toe on their way home from the pool had rubbed raw on her foot. If she went back now, Yiayia would pour her a tall glass of lemonade and pull a couple of leaves off the mint plant from the pot that Papi had wired to the windowsill. And Yiayia might rub her feet until she fell asleep in their big soft bed. Celia had slowed to a stop and was about to turn back when a crash and a loud shriek came from a store just ahead. *Fang and Claw*, the sign said. As she watched, the store window cascaded down like a million tiny ice cubes and a huge bird, brighter than anything she'd ever seen flying in the New York City sky, flashed through the air just in front of her. Even in the dark, Celia could see the brilliant blue and yellow wings so close she had to jump out of their way. Instead of making for the sky, the bird, flap-ping wildly, sank toward the concrete, shrieking.

A man rushed from the store and swooped toward the bird, grabbing him up in one hand. He stood and settled the struggling creature into the crook of his elbow like a football. Under his other arm, he held an enormous lizard, its tail thrashing furiously. The man turned in Celia's direction, then pivoted and sped away down the av-enue, carrying the beasts. Celia stared after him, her heart racing. People passed her, pushing toward the shattered window and then backed away, staring at something in front of them. Celia squeezed in closer to see, shuffling through the million glass jewels at her feet until she reached the storefront. Inside, a platform was covered in sand and rocks to look like a little desert. A miniature mountain with a cave had been built into the rocks. Celia inched closer to see inside. There was nothing but more sand. She was about to grab a handful, just for the heck of it, when something in the corner moved. Then something else. The entire platform appeared to shimmer with subtle movement. Half a dozen tan and black snakes, awakened from sleep, began to slither toward the open window. Celia leaped backward with a muffled shriek and bounced off someone's big belly. Snakes. Rats. Strangers. Mami must need her right now, more than ever. Celia took off down Broadway. There was no turning back. She had made her decision. She had to find Mami. She had to find the way home.

Chapter Nine

No need to panic. Pia heard this from the gruff voice behind the flashlight, as the door at the rear of the subway car slammed shut. She had been sitting in the blackness only a few minutes, she calculated, but already her eyes were blinded by the sudden beam of light. Behind it, she imagined a hulking presence. Pia hadn't actually considered panic until he told her not to. Where a moment ago she was sweltering, now she felt plunged into ice. Her heart took a sudden lurch upward, making her cough, and the beam of light swung around the car as if trying to locate the sound. *Don't look at me, don't look at me, don't look at me,* she thought desperately, pressing herself back into the unforgiving plastic of the seat. Who was this man? Was the train being hijacked? Could you actually hijack a subway train? Of course you could. There was that movie, *The Taking of Pelham One, Two, Three.* Pia was bathed in sour sweat. The man behind the light cleared his throat with a growl. Pia imagined him spitting on the already filthy floor and waited for the splat of the impact, but it didn't come.

"Ladies and gentleman," he intoned, and then paused until a hush indicated general attention, "there is no need to panic." Just what hijackers always said in movies, Pia thought. All around her, dark forms seemed to draw in a breath and hold it. She realized that she was blinking rapidly, as if that might clear her vision. "Everyone will be all right if you follow my directions." Pia was rocked by vertiginous waves, whether from the heat or fear, she couldn't bother to decipher. The air was wet and thick. A soggy rag held to a fevered forehead.

With his next breath, the voice introduced itself as the train's motorman, an official MTA employee, and gave his name and badge number, both of which Pia had already forgotten by the time the last number was called out. She wanted desperately to believe him. In a communal exhale, the car erupted in questions. What? Why? How long? The woman beside her groaned and said she needed to use a bathroom. The motorman told her she'd have to wait.

"I don't think I can," she complained.

"Then piss in your drawers, you dumb bitch," a man called out from the darkness. "Just don't tell us about it."

Pia bristled at the meanness of the remark. Even after a month in the city, she still hadn't gotten over her shock at the abuse these people hurled at each other on a regular basis. With the boys on her block, it was *niggah* this, and *niggah* that. The girls, too. Each time, it landed on her ears like an assault. She actually felt her shoulders twitch up around her neck as though blocking a blow. If anyone had ever called her father that, she was sure blood would have been shed. What would people call her? The other day she overheard one of her aunt's neighbors wonder who "the white girl" was who had moved into the apartment. She couldn't make out the hushed reply. But in the Jewish shops on the south side of Eastern Parkway, the sales help all looked at her suspiciously as if to ask, what is this black woman – this *schvartze* – doing in the store? On this train, in the darkness, she was without color completely. She thought of Miss Netter, her eighth grade art teacher, who taught her that in the absence of light, color ceased to exist.

The woman next to her wiggled and bumped Pia's hip. Pia

edged a little further away with distaste, then felt embarrassed and moved back.

"You'll be okay," Pia said in what she hoped was a comforting voice, although she had no idea whether this was true. She could sympathize. She had wet her own pants at the circus with her first grade class, when a clown came running toward them with an out-sized black bomb that burst into a bouquet of paper flowers. One of the boys called her Puddles the Clown for the rest of the year. The humiliation of it still made her cheeks sting.

"There's been an electrical outage," the motorman continued. "Probably caused by everybody running their air conditioners. Nothing to worry about. I've been instructed to get you off the train safely and out the nearest emergency exit." A dozen separate conversations broke out between strangers.

"I'm from Des Moines," Pia heard one woman say. "They'll never believe this back home."

"Do you have kids?" a woman asked. "I've got three and they're home with a baby sitter. I hope she got them to bed," her voice breaking just a little.

The Wall Street men rattled their newspapers and cleared their throats.

"Oh my god. Oh my god," someone at the far end of the car began repeating.

"Ba-DUM, Ba-DUM, Ba-DUM," a deep voice intoned, aping the soundtrack from *Jaws,* in the moments before the shark struck.

"Par-tee!" someone else whooped, followed by snorts of laughter from around him.

"Behave yourself!" a prim voice rebuked, drawing more guffaws.

The woman next to Pia whimpered just a little.

"Ladies and gentlemen, please!"

But the pitch of conversation continued to rise until a shrill whistle slashed through it like a serrated knife slicing canvas. In the shocked and immediate silence the whistle seemed to go on forever, ricocheting off the metal walls in the blackness. Pia felt, suddenly, as though she had lost all sense of spatial relationships. The car seemed to expand and contract around her. Maybe I'm dreaming, she thought. She pressed her fingernails into the back of one hand and knew otherwise.

"Folks, listen up," the motorman began again. "We are only a short distance from the station. With your cooperation, I can have you all out in ten, maybe fifteen, minutes. Now please, form a line here in the aisle and take each other's hands. Hey, who knows," he chuckled, "maybe you'll make some new friends." The motorman excused himself to visit the other cars, and promised to return. He left a spare flashlight with one of the men.

Reluctantly, people rose from their seats and shuffled toward the middle of the car, trying to avoid bodily contact as much as possible. Pia strained to see and failed. The best she could do was feel other people – the heat of their bodies. Poles and benches, though, were unpredictable, and the silence was broken repeatedly by muttered curses as people smacked into them. With the exception of the dancing beam of the motorman's flashlight, the total darkness rendered vision useless.

Pia found blindness dizzying. Not only had shape and color disappeared, but her sense of self, as well. The acuity of her vision and her ability to organize and reproduce form and substance on the page had brought her to New York City. And abandoned her here in the darkness. Even the sounds around her were now bleeding into one undifferentiated buzz. With a jolt, Pia realized that she was lapsing toward unconsciousness. The crack of her shin against a bench brought her back, and she let herself turn to fall gratefully into the seat. She breathed slowly and evenly until she felt, once again, whole, if not wholly well. Then she stood, slowly, and worked her way toward the group.

"Ouch!" someone yelped.

"Touch my ass one more time, shithead, and you'll leave this train without your balls."

Pia smiled in the dark. People were apparently recovering from their initial alarm.

Slowly, and with some grumbling, hands were linked. For

people who rarely made eye contact, palm-against-palm must seem an insufferable intimacy. Pia, though, eagerly accepted the physical assurance of another being. She slung the strap of her portfolio over her shoulder and pushed the handle of the plastic shopping bag up her forearm. The motorman returned – this time Pia distinguished him by way he cleared his throat.

"If you're all together now, then let's start moving along. We will exit the train from the first car, and walk carefully along the track bed to the exit at Clark Street."

Clark Street. Pia recognized the name from her daily commute. She envisioned the unusual tube-shaped station, the rounded walls unlike those of any other station she'd seen. But she had no idea what the streets above it might be like, or how she would find her way home. Clark Street was the last stop in Brooklyn on her way to work. That meant that they were not only underground now, but most likely under the river as well. Pia fought off a dizzying breathlessness, her skin slick with sweat.

"Excuse me," someone called out. "Why can't we just wait for the power to come back and ride to the next station?" The other passengers began to weigh in on this possibility – the volume rising as they spoke over one another – until the motorman gave another toot on his whistle. On this planet of the blind, the loudest man was obviously king.

There was a moment's silence.

"It may be some time until that happens," the motorman admitted. "Seems the whole city has gone dark. A blackout. The conductor just got word on his radio."

Pia expected a cacophony of voices. Instead, everyone was stunned as silent as she. Led by the motorman, they stepped clumsily from car to car until they reached the front of the train. From there, the conductor and a transit policeman who had been on board helped them out of the front door and onto a catwalk, and finally down onto the tracks.

Pia held tight to the damp hand that had been thrust at her.

She imagined a carload of commuters linked into a chain – like elephants on parade, she thought, recalling the stinking and lumbering beasts that traveled from the train station to the giant tents set up at the edge of town each year – and inching forward through the thick and unrelenting gloom. Pia was the last beast in the line.

The person just ahead of her was the woman who had to pee. Pia wondered how she was faring, but didn't ask. They had now been standing in one spot for what felt like a long, long time, waiting for an opportunity to move forward. Behind them, the train itself was like another giant animal alive with the electric smell of frying cables and seared brake pads. The tunnel reeked of urine and sweat and something musty and organic Pia couldn't name, but it made the back of her neck prickle. The ground felt dusty and pebbly, but up ahead she heard an occasional splash of water. She tried not to think about her feet, naked in their sandals, and what might run or slither across them.

Somewhere further on, the line seemed to be moving ahead slowly, making frequent stops that elicited muffled apologies as people ran into one another or stepped on preceding heels. A baby was crying in the distance. Someone a little closer laughed and the sound echoed harshly. Pia steadied her portfolio on her shoulder with her free hand and then felt around. Almost immediately, her knuckles brushed raw, damp stone. Bedrock, she thought. The naked bones of New York City. She touched it gingerly, pressing the cleaved angles with her fingertips, and hoped she'd remember it, like the features of a face she would someday try to paint from touch memory. If I make it out alive, she thought... and then, how ridiculous, of course I'm going to make it out alive. This is just a blackout, like the one in 1965. She distracted herself with the memory.

In 1965 Pia had just turned thirteen and was living with her mother in their tiny house outside Ithaca. She was at home with her mother when it happened, writing a paper on the invention of the sewing machine, for which she eventually got an A-plus, and watching *The Mike Douglas Show*. Who were Mike's guests, she wondered now as she walked through the tunnel. Petula Clark? Moe, from

The Three Stooges? She hated The Three Stooges. There had been soup cooking on the stove. Chicken soup? Vegetable soup? Chicken soup with noodles. And it *was* Petula Clark – singing *Downtown*, and wearing those white go-go boots. By the next day there were stories of strange lights –aliens! – landing in nearby Newfield and sucking up all the power.

Pia's breathing eased as she focused on her memory. The line moved forward a few dusty steps, then stopped again. The motorman came by and handed a small flashlight to the woman in front of Pia.

"Looks like we're going to be here a while," he confided in a low voice. "Maybe you'd like to use this." Then he walked back on down the line.

In 1965, Pia had a pen pal in New York City – the result of a project in fifth grade where they adopted a sister school, P.S. 201, in Queens. The blackout had hit New York City, too. Karen, her fifth grade "sister," sent Pia articles from the *Long Island Press* and the *New York Post* about the event. For a current events project, Pia pasted the articles into a binder. *Housewives in high-rise buildings, who had never known their neighbors, found themselves knocking on apartment doors offering candles and snacks*, she remembered reading in the news accounts. *A spirit of mutual cooperation and kindness proved all the stories of the meanness of New York City to be lies.* Pia squeezed the hand of the woman ahead of her in what she hoped was an encouraging fashion. They would all pull together. And she would have a great story to tell. Already, she imagined regaling Rosie with it: *He said there was no need to panic...so you know me: I took that as my cue to panic.* She hoped Rosie's bus had made it out of town before the power went out.

A series of clangs and pings began emanating from the train behind her as the huge expanse of metal cooled and contracted.

"Excuse me," a small voice ahead of her was saying. Pia leaned forward to better hear the woman, who was almost as small as a child.

"I hate to ask you this, but could you help me? If you could hold the flashlight and block me with your packages, maybe we could go back a little way and I could... I could..."

"Of course," Pia said.

The two of them broke off from the rest of the line. They retreated just far enough into the musty darkness to become invisible. But as they broke away from the group, it felt to Pia as if in the depths of the sea she had agreed to share her oxygen tank. She tried to will a calm she hardly felt. Hand in hand, haltingly, the two women took five or six steps, and then another five or six.

"I think this is far enough," the woman finally said, to Pia's great relief. She slipped her hand from Pia's and handed over the small metal flashlight, hot from her grip. Pia placed one edge of her portfolio in a patch of dirt between the two of them, and held it upright – an ad hoc wall of privacy. She turned away toward the motionless train only inches away and began to hum a little under her breath. Pia could hear the woman's clothes rustling slightly and she let the beam of the flashlight play on the wall of metal that rose in front of her to try and help her see.

"This is so embarrassing," the woman whispered. "I'm so tense I can barely go."

"No problem," Pia mumbled. "Take your time." She ran the beam of light back and forth over the hulking steel, not much more than an arm's length away. The wheels glinted where they were polished smooth by thousands of miles of friction along the tracks. Between the wheels themselves, complicated machinery was crusted with dust and soot. Up close, the train smelled something like the welding barn at the shipyard where her father had worked. Pia played the light up the siding of the car. A large patch of blue and white, and then some green. And then red. And green again. She realized that the entire side of the train was covered in colors. As she slid the beam of light along the flank of the train, she began to make out thickly outlined letters and wild, soaring shapes. Of course: the train was covered in graffiti. Pia ran the light back and forth as if reading lines of type in a book. It was a complete car "throw up" – a consolidated piece of art that made use of every inch of the siding. Impossible to decipher with the tiny beam lighting one small spot at a time, however, and at such close range.

So this was what it was like to be up against the train cars in the yards at night. Pia felt dwarfed by their grandeur. Huge steel canvases, hot and still. Before she had time to finish examining the car, a hand tapped her gently on the elbow. She jumped so that the portfolio fell from her grip.

"Oh, I'm so sorry. I didn't mean to startle you. I'm ready now. I can't thank you enough." The woman winced as Pia swung the light into her eyes. She was a small, Asian woman, Pia realized with surprise as the beam swept over her. Race had been obliterated in the darkness, her counting game made obsolete.

Pia stooped to retrieve the portfolio. The plastic bag from Sam Flax bumped onto the track bed. Up ahead, the line had begun snaking forward again, but Pia was less eager to escape now. She clutched the bag of marking pens closely and with new purpose. Cerulean, crimson, chrome yellow – colors bloomed in her imagination and her fingers itched with intent. One chance: she had only one, she figured. TAKI 183, Julio 204, StayHigh 149, Barbara 62, Stitch1, FabFiveFreddie, HiP, the mental recitation of their tags kept her from losing her courage.

"We'd better hurry and catch up," the woman told her.

Pia pointed the beam down the path to the others.

"You go ahead,' she told her. "I'll light your way and catch up in a minute. I, I need to do something, too." Pia's heart was now thumping so loudly, she half expected to hear it echo off the stone walls.

"No, no. I'll hold your bag for you. You go," the woman offered.

"No, really. I'll be fine."

The woman looked dubious. "Oh, I couldn't leave you. You were so kind."

"Go," Pia practically hissed. The woman took a startled step backward and stumbled, catching herself with one hand against the side of the train. Then she turned and began her slow retreat down the tracks, leaving Pia, suddenly brave and completely alone with her tiny beam in the dark.

Once the woman had rejoined the group, Pia swung the narrow belt of light slowly along the side of the car, taking in as much of the rogue art as she could. It would be criminal, she thought, to mar or cover up a single square inch of it. She walked alongside the hot metal until she came to one end of the car, then she popped the butt of the flashlight into her mouth freeing both hands to hoist herself up between the cars and let herself back inside.

Judith fumbled through the apartment, tripping over shoes she had failed to put away and chair legs that stuck out aggressively, until she arrived at the kitchen where she kept the Shabbat candles and candlesticks. There were only two candles left, which she lit gratefully and carried to the living room. There she rummaged through a drawer until she found a pair of flashlights – housewarming gifts from Tante, who prayed that Judith would never be lost in the dark. She blew out the candles, and set them on a coffee table by the couch. Armed with a flashlight in her hand and the other – for Michael – in a string shopping bag looped over her arm, she left the apartment and descended the four flights of stairs to the front of the building.

Milling about on the broad limestone stoop were many of the other tenants, all wielding flashlights, fanning themselves with sections of newspaper and talking over each other in a frenzy to relate what they had been doing, what they thought, who they felt was to blame, when the lights went out. Judith stood near the edge of the crowd – feeling herself an eager observer, not quite a native of this place.

"*Martians*, that really is the first thing that I thought: It's the Martians," said a man's voice from behind her.

"Martians? You are a moron, you know that?"

These people – most of them around her own age, some even

older – seemed like children to her, with their eagerness and lack of gravity. Still, she enjoyed being in the presence of their effortless banter. Ordinarily, they hardly spoke to one another. She had seen them pass each other going in and out of the building with barely a nod. None of them had ever spoken to her. So different from Crown Heights, where a blister on Chana's toe brought a bandage from Chayke's medicine cabinet. The *yentas* on her block made certain her mother knew every time she or her sisters shouted or laughed inappropriately loudly or ran down the block, their skirts whipping up around their stockinged legs. Judith found this infuriating, but her mother would pat her arm and remind her that they acted from love and concern – and that it might not hurt to try and be a little more ladylike.

But in tonight's crisis, these people – as unlike one another as she was unlike them – had united in fellowship. Judith listened with envy and considered how she might join in.

"I thought it was the Son of Sam about to come through my window. I screamed," said a woman nearby, carrying a huge rucksack. Judith wondered if she was planning on spending the night elsewhere. She tried to formulate the question, but couldn't quite get the words from her lips before the conversation moved on.

"I heard you all the way from the sixth floor," another woman said. "I thought maybe you fell out the window or something. I was about to call the police." Judith hadn't heard the scream, but then, the women might live in one of the front apartments. In the back, where she lived, the street noise was muffled.

"Yeah, well." The first woman slung the backpack over one bare shoulder. "I'm sleeping at my brother's tonight anyway. You can't be too careful, in this crazy city."

Judith took a deep breath. "Do you have bars on your windows?" she began, in a small voice. Too late; the women had already turned and were laughing about something she couldn't see. She felt mildly embarrassed by the way her voice hung limp in the air, like an outstretched hand that remained unshaken.

"I figured it was me," said a man just beside her in a white undershirt with the sleeves rolled up revealing a heart-shaped tattoo. Judith tried not to stare. In her world, a tattoo was far from a decoration. "I had just slammed the phone down on my girlfriend."

"Your mother, you mean!"

"Asshole." The two men laughed and punched each other like brothers.

Judith felt herself redden and step back a little so their arms would not brush. She hoped no one would notice, and then was disappointed when no one did.

"Maybe there was a bomb and they're not telling us. It's a conspiracy."

"You and your conspiracies. You think it's a conspiracy when the toilet don't flush right."

"Did you notice you can still flush, though? Even without electricity?" Judith put in, quickly. A few people turned and looked up but no one took up the thread. What a stupid thing to say, she castigated herself, and slid back into the shadows.

Beers and bags of chips were being passed around as if at a giant *simche*. Someone reeled up to Judith and offered to share the bounty, but she managed to wave off their *treyf* as she maneuvered herself to the front of the group to keep anxious watch for Michael. He was the reason she was out here, after all. What would these people have said if she told them she had thought that *she* brought on the darkness with her impure thoughts? They would think she was a *mishugener*, a crazy person. Malke would understand, though. Or Rachel. Or her sisters. Thinking of them, only a handful of miles away – but in this blackout the kind of miles that separated Lyubvichi from Smolensk in the old days – Judith felt plunged into another kind of darkness. She wished for another soul with whom to share her thoughts. She hoped Michael would arrive soon. The glow-in-the-dark dial of her watch said 10:07. It had already been almost two hours since he called. Surely he would be here soon, even if he were walking.

The inky velvet air beyond the stoop was perforated by tiny

pinpricks of light from burning cigarettes and the more substantial beams of flashlight as a thin but steady stream of people passed Judith on their way down the block. Each time a ray of light caught her full in the face, she suffered several moments of blindness in its aftermath, the instant of enlightenment followed by a seeming eternity of futility. For a while, she stood and shifted from foot to foot, torn between wanting someone to come and break into her solitude, and dreading it. Finally, she succumbed to fatigue and sat down on the stoop, resting her back against the coarse concrete.

"They're giving away free ice cream at the bodega on 75th Street!" someone ran by shouting, and the entire gathering rushed down the steps and past Judith, in their eagerness to get something for nothing. No one stopped to ask her to come along; she didn't exist at all for them, she realized, just as, some day, she might no longer exist for her family and her community. Was her family thinking of her now?

Judith was now the only person left in front of the building. She arranged her legs demurely, crossed at the ankles and tilted to one side, as if she were sitting at a picnic in the country instead of on a hot, scratchy New York City stoop. When Michael arrived, she hoped she would appear cool and tranquil. He needn't have any knowledge of the sweat forming along her thighs and calves. She turned off her flashlight to conserve the batteries and let her eyes become accustomed to the scant ambient light.

From an apartment above her, a cat meowed pitifully. She imagined it locked in a stifling room, its owner out here in the dark somewhere – chasing down free ice cream, perhaps – while the pathetic creature cried out for its dinner. She could relate. She was, in her own way, starving in the midst of plenty. Forbidden to partake of the apparent pleasures of the ordinary world and estranged from the riches of the world from which she came. Like that pathetic mewling creature in the window above, she needed someone to unlock the bounty and make it accessible to her.

In the distance, sirens wailed. Ambulances, fire engines, police cars – it sounded as if the city were one giant, throbbing emergency. She kept her eyes averted from the passing flashlights now. She could just make out the white shoelaces on her dark Adidas sneakers sticking out from the hem of her skirt, like pale creatures in the deepest realms of the ocean.

A pair of young people – they sounded about Rivka's age, maybe fourteen or fifteen – came by singing, their voices coming from inches apart. *Dancing queen, feel the beat from the tambourine.* A couple of children skipped past, their mother calling out from right behind them to slow down and walk carefully. Judith pictured her mother and sister at home, sitting out on the front porch with Tante, who would have come from around the block to keep them company. Her father, she guessed, was at 770 with the rest of the men and boys, learning by candlelight, probably. The studying never stopped. Soon he too would be negotiating the dark streets in the company of her cousins and their neighbors. Once again, Judith found herself humming the *nigun* from Rachel's wedding.

The melody was so poignant, each part of the tune repeated twice, each a gateway to a higher consciousness: the first time tracing a contour, the second time carving it deep into the soul. The fact that there were no words was no deterrent to the emotion it provoked in her. The great rabbis had been clear about this: while words might carry light downwards from the Primal Consciousness to the mind, melody carries the soul upwards to be absorbed within the Infinite Light. Words limited and defined, but the *nigun* shredded the soul beyond all bounds. In the dark, tears trickled down Judith's cheeks. With a *nigun*, her mother told her, what is held imprisoned in the soul is freed to fly up into the mind and from the mind to the heart.

Eventually, the tears passed, leaving her feeling comforted. She envisioned Michael coming to Brooklyn to meet her family. It was absurd, of course – impossible – but in the new world she was forging for herself, anything might happen. She imagined her mother noting Michael's wise expression and her sisters admiring his handsome face. She couldn't imagine what her father would notice, though, aside from Michael's shocking lack of *Yiddishkeit*. Would Michael, or someone like him, someday want to learn with her father? And it stood to reason that if a man from this secular world could come and find a place in her community, she should be able to remain and find a place in his. Here in this secular world, where Judith was free to follow the dictates of her heart.

She heard voices drawing near and looked up. Several people were climbing toward her on the stairs, probably her neighbors returning. She hoped they might stop and talk. Instead, they walked by her blindly, until one woman tripped over Judith's foot.

"Ouch!" they both cried out as one voice.

The woman stumbled forward, one hand touching down near Judith's hip, her face hanging inches away from Judith's own. It was the woman from the sixth floor who had heard her neighbor's scream. Judith smelled the milky remains of vanilla ice cream on her breath.

"Excuse me," Judith exclaimed involuntarily, as if the upset were her fault. Without acknowledging her apology, the woman regained her balance and nimbly bounded up the rest of the steps to catch up with her friends who were laughing at her apparent clumsiness. Without a word, they skipped on and the front door closed with a loud click.

It was as if she didn't even see me, Judith thought, in amazement, or feel me under her hand. As if I were nobody.

Beyond her, the sidewalk was now almost empty of pedestrians, although the occasional car passed by tossing light wildly from side to side. And still no sign of Michael. Or maybe he had come and gone without noticing her sitting there. Just as that woman had not noticed her. Judith had the awful feeling that she had been, well, *erased* was the only word that came to mind. As if she had ceased to exist in any corporeal sense, but was only alive in her own head. The feeling was claustrophobic. It made her want to cry out, but she knew no one would hear. She gathered herself up quickly and stood.

Once, she had been a whole person. Once, other people had cared for her and loved and nurtured her. But those people were far away. She had left them behind for the world of strangers. And this – this wrenching loneliness – was what came of such a choice.

"If you try and live with a foot in each world, you will quickly sink into the void between them," her father had warned her the day she left home. He didn't wish this on her, he said, but he feared it for her. She had had no room in her heart for his words or his fears.

Her watch read 10:57. Michael would not be coming. Not tonight; probably not ever. Judith had been naïve. She could see that now. And if she had misled herself about Michael and his interest in her, how much more might she have been deluding herself about? She could see now that she was a *naar*, a fool, in so many ways.

There are no accidents. Everything – *everything* – happens for a reason. Everything.

Everything,

    Everything,

        Everything.

Those words rang out at her with each step as Judith trudged up the stairs to her apartment. Michael's failure to arrive, the rant of the woman on the train, her inability to connect with her neighbors, even the blackout itself: She had been quick to absolve herself from blame when she heard the mundane facts, but there are reasons and reasons for things, she rebuked herself now.

By the time she reached her door she was panting from more than the effort of the climb. She felt utterly and entirely solitary; cut off from the birthright of family, friends and, most terrifying of all, God. Absence – she felt it like the raw and gaping hole that opened up between her teeth when she lost her first molars. As a child, that emptiness had haunted her, although she had no words to explain why. Alone in her bed, she moved her tongue over the tender bloodied gap nightly with both fascination and terror until a new tooth poked its ragged mountainous head up to fill the allotted space. Now, she better understood the dreadfulness of that gap. Emptiness, nothingness, the missing world – it was the dark, airless chaos of the time before Hashem brought light into being.

The flashlight in her hand dimmed to little more than an amber glow and went out. And, she realized with dismay, she had left the string bag with the second flashlight outside on the steps. She had, quite literally, abandoned the light.

Judith reached up, reflexively, to touch the *mezuzah* on the doorframe and her knuckles struck the icon clumsily, sending it clattering to the hallway floor. In horror at such a holy object touching the ground, she dropped to her knees and began searching for it blindly on the filthy linoleum. Her fingers trailed in the dust and debris of the street tracked there daily. When she found the relic, she pressed it to her lips, as she might the holy *Siddur* prayer book, trying to restore its purity.

I opened for my beloved, but my beloved had hidden and was gone; my soul went out when he spoke; I sought him, but found him not; I called him, but he did not answer me.

Judith clutched the soiled mezuzah to her chest like an infant and struggled to her feet. She had rejected the rituals of obedience and faith, now these same rituals were rejecting her. Letting herself into the apartment, she went straight to the wall where the Rebbe's portrait hung – but the darkness rendered his face invisible to her.

It wasn't the darkness that was her punishment – it was the isolation. This is the world you have created for yourself, Hashem was telling her – a world of *one*. Judith clutched at the placket of her blouse with such frenzy that a button tore away. She heard the rip of fabric and it brought her back to those torn garments she had worn to sit *shiva* when her sister died. In a spasm of anguish, she now yanked all the buttons free and stood with her chest bared in grief.

She thought of her mother – a paradigm of holiness and love – and thought about her sisters, who would surely suffer because of Judith's own willfulness and evil. Who would want their sons allied with the family of such a one? Unless, unless...

Judith stared as hard as she could through the gloom. She thought she could just make out the shape of the face on the wall, although its countenance certainly did not shine upon her. What would happen if she admitted her foolishness? If she prostrated herself before her community and the Rebbe and begged for their forgiveness and permission to return to her place beside them? Of course, they would let her come back. They would welcome her back. She was certain of that.

In the morning – there would be a morning, she was almost certain there would be – she would call her mother and tell her she was coming home. Judith didn't fool herself into thinking that all would be as it had been – no one would forget that she was a rebel; that she had flown in the face of the blessed Rebbe's authority. There would be no *shidachs* any time soon – what mother would have her for a daughter-in-law? But she would accept that – she deserved to suffer whatever consequences came her way – and she would be grateful for the chance to atone. And, of course, in another couple of months, she could join her mother and sisters and throw her sins into the water on rafts of stale bread – Tashliken on Rosh Hashoneh would let her wipe her slate clean, and Yom Kippur services would let her fast and atone. Hashem would hear her prayers. He would know her contrition was genuine.

The path back to righteousness would begin at sunrise.

Celia pulled the bill of the baseball cap down firmly on her forehead. It was a dark blue hat with a single white "C" on its front. She had nearly tripped over it a few steps back and was about to kick it to the curb when she saw the big letter C by the beam of her flashlight. For Celia, she thought, so she picked it up and took it along. For company.

She felt as if she'd been walking for days. At first she counted the blocks, certain that she would be home before she reached one hundred. But she kept losing count and now it seemed like she must have walked about a thousand or more. And still, she wasn't any place she remembered ever being. The street was lined with windowed storefronts, but who knew what was in them. The buildings stretched up into the blackness of the night sky. Celia tried to read the street signs, but it was too dark. Sometimes she was alone. Sometimes, crowds of people swarmed around her like buzzing flies and then moved on. When she was alone, she was scared. When she was in the middle of dozens of tall strangers, she wished she were alone. The grownups seemed uneasy too – some of them. The rest seemed mean or drunk, slurring angry words and occasionally knocking into her. They muttered curses her mother would have smacked her for. Mainly, though, these grownups ignored her, to Celia's great relief. She thought again about going back to Yiayia's – even though she knew she'd be in trouble – but the way back was, by now, as big a mystery as the way home.

Some day it will be tomorrow, Celia thought, and then... But she didn't have any words for what the "and then" might bring. Her tongue felt thick in her mouth. Her stomach was growling so loud. Her feet hurt everywhere – tops and bottoms, and all ten toes. Celia leaned up against a building. It felt good to stand still. It would feel even better to sit down, and she let herself slide to the pavement and into a little ball. The brick was warm against her back. She folded her arms across her knees and propped her mouth against her forearm. Her skin tasted salty and good. She sucked on it for a while. When she stopped, there was a puffy spot left behind. Celia thought about staying right there until morning. It would have to be morning eventually, wouldn't it? Yiayia had said so.

But she had to keep going. Mami was probably home by now and calling Yiayia. Celia struggled back to her feet and turned in a circle, deciding which way to go. Suddenly, a couple of boys came flying around the corner on bicycles, almost slamming right into her.

"Hey!" she shouted, then wished she hadn't. Two more boys rounded the bend and they all stopped and stared at her.

"What the fuck...?" one of them called out.

Celia looked all around, hoping that some grownup – a policeman would be best, but any old grownup would do – would come by. But the street was empty now except for her and the boys, who came closer until she couldn't see anything but them. She thought about jumping up and running. She thought about making herself invisible. Both seemed about equally possible. One of the boys took another step toward her until his big, sneakered feet were almost touching her own. He was so much larger than she was. He must be twelve at least. Maybe thirteen. Celia was sure he could hear her heart thumping away. She stared down at the giant feet.

She felt the cap being lifted off her head.

"Hey TJ, look, she's a Cubs fan," one of them said. The rest laughed.

"You a little Cubbies fan?" the tall one at her feet asked.

Celia continued staring at the ground. The boys were shuffling around as they spoke. The circle around her grew tighter.

"Cat got your tongue?" the boy asked. "Forgot how to speak?"

"Maybe she doesn't speak English," another boy offered.

Celia's face began burning. Her eyes were filling with tears.

"Mira, chica – hablas español?"

Digame, como te llamas? Donde esta tu madre?

"Maybe she's an idiot."

They laughed and jostled each other.

Celia's throat itched with a scream that wouldn't come. The boy with the cap tossed it to his friend. Then he bent down and turned her face up until it was staring straight into his. His nose and cheeks were dotted with angry red bumps. His breath smelled like cinnamon. It made Celia nauseated and hungry at the same time.

"Hey, *mira*, I think she's going to cry."

She took a big, shuddering breath.

From above her, a couple of rough hands came down and lifted her up. As the ground flew out from under her, she tried to resist, but found she couldn't move at all. She gasped in and in and in until her lungs felt about to burst. Then, all at once, she found her voice and her strength. *Na pas sto diaolo!* she screamed. "Go to hell!" She kicked straight out and landed one foot against the chest of the pimple-faced boy.

Puta! he grunted, gasping for air and falling back.

She struggled from the arms of the other boy and fell hard against the sidewalk. Pimple-face was on her in a flash. He pinned her arms and legs to the ground.

"Mami!" she shrieked. "Help!" She shut her eyes and braced herself against what she felt sure was going to be a punch. But instead, she felt a hand wipe the hair from her sweaty forehead.

"Calm down, little one," the one named TJ said. "No one's gonna hurt you. You lost, or what?"

She struggled some more.

"If I let you go, promise you won't kick me in the balls?"

She nodded, her face inches from his.

"What difference would that make," his friend scoffed. "You have no balls." The rest laughed.

"Promise?" he insisted, pushing down harder on her wrists.

She nodded solemnly, and slowly he let her go and helped her to her feet.

"Where do you live?" he asked.

"228 Baxter Street," she sniffled.

"Where's that? Any of you know Baxter Street?" The rest of the boys looked blank, except for one who looked up suddenly from scratching his ankle.

"Chinatown. My *tia* Rosa lives on that street."

"Whoa! That true?" TJ whooped. "What the hell you doing up on 98th Street?"

She wasn't supposed to talk to strangers. Especially strange men. Mami said so almost every day. Celia clammed up. Yet another boy came shooting out of the dark on his bike and skidded to a stop next to TJ and Celia.

"Yo, TJ, that your girlfriend?"

"Shut up, jerk. She's lost."

"She's not lost, her grandma lives in the projects. Same building as *mi abuela.*" Celia looked hard, but didn't recognize him.

"Your grandma?" said TJ to Celia. "You want us to walk you home to your grandma's house?" He leaned in close. She smelled Wrigley's on his breath.

Celia shook her head no. Maybe the boy looked a little familiar.

"Come on. We don't have time for this. We got work to do." The boy walked over to Celia and grabbed the hand holding the flashlight, turning on the light just below his chin. He looked like Dracula. Now Celia thought maybe she did recognize him after all. She grabbed her hand out of his and spit on the ground.

"Well, come on, then, Cubbie." TJ popped the cap back on her head. "You can't walk around here alone. Get yourself in big trouble. They's some badass people out tonight. We'll get you home. Eventually." He hoisted her to her feet. Celia felt a trickle of blood inch its way from her knee down her shin, but she couldn't take her eyes off the boy. Angel. That was his name. His grandma was the skinny one with the mole on her chin. The mole had hairs like a spider. Yes, that was him. He, at least, wasn't a stranger.

"Jesus, TJ," one of the boys said. "You can't be serious. Taking a little girl with us? You *loco*?"

"Shut the fuck up, *puta*. Don't you got a little sister? What if she was lost, you'd want somebody to find her, right? She'll be fine, won't you, Cubbie?" He turned back to the gang. "Anyway, we need someone to keep an eye on the bikes while we're shopping." If they disagreed, no one said so.

"So, Cubbie, you coming?"

Celia nodded and grinned. She would watch their bikes and they would help her get home. She aimed the beam of light down at her leg and, sure enough, there was a sticky trail of blood. TJ noticed it, too. He unwound a bandanna from his neck, spit on it two or three times and crouched to the ground. He rubbed hard and Celia tried not to wince. He spit again into the filthy rag and swiped it, more gently now, over the raw bruise of her knee. This time she gasped.

"You gotta be tough, *chica*, if you want to ride with the Mad Dogs."

Celia nodded, solemnly, and TJ stuffed the bloody rag into the pocket of his cutoffs.

"Well, let's go then."

TJ straddled the bike, with its big banana seat, and Celia struggled to climb on. She could ride a two-wheeler well enough, but she had a girl's bike and her legs could barely reach over this one. Finally, he yanked her by the elbow and hoisted her up behind him. She made a quick grab for his tee shirt to keep from flying over the other side. Laughing, he unlatched her fingers and placed them around his middle.

"Hang on, Cubbie. Don't wiggle around or you'll knock us over, *comprende*?

He didn't wait for Celia to answer but kicked off and began peddling madly, the other boys following behind, whooping as they rode. They were flying through the gloomy streets, dodging potholes and occasional pedestrians as though guided by radar. They were now heading in the opposite direction from where Celia had been going when she met them. They rode until her head began to nod with sleep, even as she continued to hang on for dear life. She bit her lips to stay awake. Then suddenly, they stopped.

"Where are we?" she whispered into TJ's back.

"Twenty-eighth Street," he told her. "My cousin's coming with a truck. We're going shopping. If you're good, I'll bring you a present."

Shopping? The block was one long line of dark windows.

"You stay here," TJ said, pushing Celia off the curb and down between the sharp fins of an aging Cadillac Eldorado and a peeling snub nosed Volkswagen. "Don't move. Watch the bikes for us."

Celia crouched between the parked cars and peered through the tangle of bicycles into the darkness where she could just make out the boys as they hoisted the newspaper-stuffed trashcan into a shopping cart, lit the paper at the bottom through the metal mesh, and ran with it, shrieking wildly, straight at the huge glass storefront. Sparks and bits of flaming paper flew into the air around their heads like lightning bugs until, with a communal grunt, they gave a final tremendous push and sent the wagon on its way, alone. TJ was the last to let go and when he did, he fell forward onto his hands and knees. The others began to laugh as he picked himself up and brushed dirt and blood from his palms, but in an instant, all of their attention was wrenched back to the flaming cart. It slammed through the window and rolled on into the store leaving the glass to fall in its wake. After the crash, silence and more darkness. Somewhere deep inside the store a few sparks continued to appear at intervals. Otherwise, nothing much happened. The boys moped and grumbled with disappointment and huddled, deciding what to do next.

A couple of men, already carrying stacks of shoeboxes came up to the boys.

"You do that?" one asked, jerking his head admiringly toward the window. He turned on a bright beam. Without waiting for an answer, he and his companion stepped through the breach and dumped their boxes on an upholstered chair, which they quickly hoisted and carried from the store.

"We're going in," TJ yelled in Celia's direction. "Get you something for your mama!" Laughing, they surged forward and began picking their way across what looked to Celia like a lake of diamonds. The four boys disappeared into darkness. In a matter of moments, a small crowd of people, mainly men and boys, had converged on the storefront. Some were climbing into the building, others were already on their way out, their arms filled with cushions and stools and lamps. Two balanced a huge couch between them, stepping gingerly over what remained of the window. They trundled slowly down the block. A small boy on the sidewalk was handed a stack of plates that fell from his arms, shattering. The older boy with him cuffed him across the head and jumped back inside for more. Celia waited for TJ and his friends to come back and get her.

Then, a muffled whoosh, and blackness was replaced by hot orange light. Objects suddenly appeared, silhouetted in the glow.

Rocking chairs, La-Z-Boys, couches, end tables, pole lamps, magazine racks, all were fodder for the flames, which edged forward   rapidly. The wall of heat and light surged until Celia could no longer make out the familiar stuff. A pair of men who emerged gagged and spit noisily onto the pavement before scurrying away with their loot.

Behind them the four boys tumbled back out the gaping window, coughing and spitting as well, only yards ahead of the brilliance. Celia was too terrified to move. TJ and the boys were holding their sides, doubled over with laughter. They began to circle and whoop like cartoon Indians in the flickering light until they dissolved to the sidewalk, still shrieking.

The heat stung her face. Her eyes burned and she squeezed them shut, forcing tears onto her lashes. The play of flickering light on her closed eyelids reminded her of making a birthday wish. "I wish, I wish, I wish," she whispered to herself. When she opened her eyes, she saw that the flames had begun licking the facade of the building. A window on the floor above blew out from the heat and tongues of flame climbed the pitted brick wall. She closed her eyes again against the acrid smoke. The pulsing heat from the fire pressed against her eyelids. She thought she might fall asleep; it was so warm and dreamy. It would be good to sleep.

From far away, Celia heard shouts and sirens and people running. Hoofbeats. Horses stamping and rearing. Her mother on the back of a huge gray horse with little goat horns riding straight at her across pink sand, one hand extended as though to snatch Celia up for a ride. *"I wish,"* she whispered again, and felt her body fly upward. Just as she was about to settle into place on the saddle, behind her mother, someone shoved her hard. She tumbled back down and cried out. It was TJ.

"Shhhh. Don't make a sound, Cubbie. It's me," TJ hissed into her ear. "We gotta get outta here. Cops." He yanked her up by one arm, she felt something inside her shoulder twist and she yelped in pain and pulled away.

"Look out! There's a cop car turning the corner!"

TJ was already running alongside his bike. With one jump, he threw his leg over the bar and began peddling. Celia tried to   follow him but he was too deep into the darkness for her to see.

Where was her mother now? Not on a great gray horse or there beside her in the burning streets. Celia rubbed her sore shoulder and ducked down again, close to the ground. The sirens grew louder and higher in pitch as they approached the block, then whined lower again as their path veered away toward another block, another blaze. The flames, too, died down, at least as far as Celia could see. Now only smoke was billowing out the window.

Celia's legs ached from crouching. But before she stood, she reached down and pulled her shorts and panties to one side and peed gratefully into the gutter, her feet splayed wide and raised onto tippy toes to avoid the puddle. Relieved, she struggled to stand and wobbling slightly, quietly walked off in the direction of TJ and his crew. But they were gone, without her. And more police cars were rushing by.

I want to go home, Mami, Celia thought. She stepped into the street, toward the cars with their red lights flashing. She would tell a policeman she was lost. He would help her. That's what they told you to do at school. She took one more tottering step. A car swerved around the corner, red lights setting all the buildings ablaze. It bore down on Celia who waved her flashlight back at it to make it stop. But the car didn't stop. It sped by so fast and so close that the mirror grazed Celia's outstretched arm and snatched the flashlight from her hand. The light flew in a high arc and smashed somewhere behind her. The car, too, disappeared into the dark, Celia staring after it, the skin of her arm stinging like a whole hive of bees.

The feeling that hit her was like the numb and sickening jolt she had felt when she was eight and had leapt from the swings only to land flat on her back. And her response was the same, as well. Celia leaned over deeply and puked what little there was in her stomach into the steaming gutter. She was all alone now. Even the last meal she had eaten with family – the leftover lamb *pastitsio* from Yiayia's fridge – was gone.

Chapter Ten

Rousing in the damp tangle of sheets, Danielle lightly skimmed the hairs on Geoffrey's chest with the back of her hand. She wondered whether it was morning yet. With the shades drawn it was impossible to know. She felt as if she might have been sleeping for hours, or only moments. Time was as elastic as cheap mozzarella on a hot pizza. Danielle closed her eyes and inhaled the scent of Geoffrey's skin, a comforting fuchsia mix of their combined sweat and hormones. How long had it been since she had woken up against another body? And how long since she had felt released and emptied of nervous energy in the way that only good sex can bring?

It wasn't just the usual post-coital stillness either, as exquisite as that was. The muscles of her shoulders, neck, arms, actually felt relieved of a physical burden, as though she had set down a huge stone that she had been hauling uphill for miles. What had Geoffrey made of her revelation? She still wasn't sure. He mentioned that he had noticed she'd been uncharacteristically clumsy at work lately, then plumbed her thoughts, setting his aside. He didn't jump in with advice as she spilled her guts. In this, he was unique. Although Paul had been, in many respects, a capable and caring guy, he was, at heart, a *guy*, and suffered from the common allergy of guys: feelings. *How are you?* was about as deep as he probed. And even then, she could feel his discomfort if her answer turned out to be more problematic than complaints of a minor headache or a spat with a co-worker. Before the words were out her mouth, Paul was offering a quick fix for the problem.

Geoffrey, however, seemed unable to get enough of who she was and how she came to be herself. He hadn't avoided the subject of her impending blindness; he tried to discover everything that made her the person she was – the person who was trying so hard to befriend the darkness, as he put it. Between bouts of kissing he asked question after question. By the time they actually made love he had probably learned more about her – her mother's periodic credit card binges, her father's perilous emotional outbursts and obsession with efficiency, the imaginary friends that populated her childhood, and of course, the emotional roller coaster that she'd been riding since learning about the retinitis – than any other single person in this city. Amazingly, he remained silent throughout her answers, holding her close when she moved in toward him and even tighter when she tried to push away. Far from resenting it, she felt comforted by his consistent – and insistent – embrace. She felt as swaddled as a *filet en croûte*.

Now Geoffrey's shoulder twitched and he muttered something that sounded like *moth*. One of her legs was trapped between the two of his and she longed to move it, to separate her skin from his in the sticky heat. But if she moved, he would surely wake up, and she wasn't ready yet to face him in this changed state of affairs.

"You were right," he said, startling her. "You can do anything in the dark."

She laughed and swung her legs over the edge of the bed.

"Are you leaving me?" he asked.

"Just getting some water." Suddenly self-conscious, although she knew he could barely see her, she tossed a shirt over her shoulders on her way to the kitchen. She poured two glasses of water still cold from the fridge and carefully returned to the bedroom without spilling a drop. Danielle felt a little stab of pride. All her practicing had paid off, at least for this night.

"It's almost 2:30," he told her when she got back. "Glow-in-the-dark watch hands. I peeked."

Settling back into the pillows, they sipped the ice water and smoked a bit of the bulging, misshapen joint that Geoffrey had rolled earlier. While they did, he peppered her with more questions – this time mainly factual ones about her impending blindness. His interest seemed neither forced nor prurient.

"You can tell me to shut up, it's none of my business," he said. "Believe me, I've been told that before. If I hadn't become a chef, I'd probably have been a news reporter – some job where I could ask all the questions I wanted and get paid for it."

"Do you have any idea how hard it's been to have absolutely nobody I could talk to about this? Well, nobody I wasn't *paying* to listen me. Just promise you'll stop me before you start feeling like my personal wailing wall."

"What I really want to know is how you feel," he insisted. "I hear all the facts and figures. I get all the ways in which you're steeling yourself against the inevitable. But what I don't hear is how you *feel*, deep down inside about this." He adjusted his position so he could put one arm around her shoulders. Danielle eased back into this arrangement, which felt at once vulnerable and comfortingly familiar.

Danielle was silent. Feelings streaked through her inebriated brain like a shower of meteors across the night sky. The excess made it impossible to grasp one long enough to put it into words.

"I don't want to go home," she said at last, surprising herself. There, that was the crux of it all. That was what made all the cut fingers, stubbed toes, bruised shins and humiliation worth the price of admittance. Would he get it? Or would he recite the usual list of homilies: there is no shame in accepting help. Home is the place where they have to take you in, no matter what. All that happy horseshit.

"But you are home. You've built this home. You've earned it."

That did it. She sobbed. Tears streamed over her cheeks and dripped from her chin to his chest. Snot hung from her nose. With her arms pinned under his elbows she couldn't even reach up and wipe it away. So it, too, dripped. The crying didn't seem to throw him at all. He let her blub on and on and just stroked her head and neck. Didn't once try and shush her or exhort her not to cry. She wondered if he had sisters. This idea made her laugh out loud.

"What?" he said, in some consternation. At least something surprised him.

"I was wondering where you got so comfortable with crying women. Did you grow up with a houseful of sisters?"

"Bingo. I not only learned to listen, I was taught – painfully, I might add – not to offer advice."

But now that Danielle had begun talking, she couldn't hold herself back. The words poured faster than the tears had.

"I don't want to go back to my parents' home," she explained. "I don't want to be dependent on them. Or anyone. I want my life back. I want my life here, as a miserable, struggling, disrespected and underpaid cook in New York City. I worked my ass off for this. And I swear I'll have it, too."

She explained everything to him – the hours of cooking, dressing, living in the dark – that she had been doing to prepare.

"Maybe" was all he said when she finished.

"Maybe what?" she demanded. Was he stoned, or did he always talk in riddles, she wondered. Or was he doubting her plan, after all? She felt a warning stab of regret and pulled away faster than he could pull her back.

"Maybe you could make us something to eat then, since you've got all this blind cooking practice under your belt. I've got a terrible case of the munchies."

Danielle was astounded. Unless he was an even better actor than he was a chef, he seemed honestly to consider her plan not only possible, but practical. He wanted her to blindly cook him dinner.

Danielle slipped into her shoes and swept gentle circles around the floor until she found Geoffrey's. "You'd better put these on," she warned him. "The dark is not kind to toes." She led him through the apartment. In the kitchen, she carefully removed the fish and an assortment of other ingredients from the fridge and the cabinets. It was a whole fish, she noted appreciatively through the wrapping, head and tail still attached.

"Stand back and prepare to be dazzled," she told him, rinsing her hands in the sink. "I know it's hot, but since the gas should still work, how about whole roast snapper with aioli?"

Geoffrey responded with an admiring whistle.

Danielle took a large measuring cup from the cabinet and filled it half-way with olive oil. She smashed three cloves of garlic with the side of a knife and tossed these in along with some salt and pepper and a big squeeze from a half lemon she had on the refrigerator shelf.

"You're in luck," she told him. "I just happen to have a couple of egg yolks from yesterday that I'd saved. I haven't quite mastered separating eggs blind yet." She threw the egg yolks in the cup, as well, and began beating vigorously. In a few minutes the resistance of the sauce told her it was adequately thickened, and she placed the cup into the freezer to chill, opening and closing the door quickly to avoid losing any of the cold air. She turned her attention to the preparation for the fish. Geoffrey leaned against the kitchen wall and gave her space.

Danielle poured more olive oil, lemon juice, salt, pepper, and a pinch of some za'atar spice mix into another bowl.

"Here." She thrust a balloon whip into his hands and guided him to the large cupful of ingredients. "Beat these into some-thing tasty."

"Your whip is my command," he told her. Cheesy, she thought once more, but sweet.

Meanwhile, she greased a roasting pan and sliced the tomatoes he had brought, then arranged them so that they covered the bottom. She laid the fish on its side on a cutting board and, holding a sharp paring knife at shallow angle to the fish, cut three vertical slits through its skin and partially into the flesh, equidistant down the length of the body.

"Ouch!" she yelped suddenly.

"What? What? Did you cut yourself? Here let me see." He rushed to her side with concern. A flare of annoyance shot up in Danielle.

"I caught my palm on a damned fin. Relax, okay?"

She flipped the fish over and did the same to the other side. After patting the fish dry, she rubbed it with the olive oil and seasoning mixture, tucking some into the slits. She laid the prepared fish on the tomatoes and sprinkled a little thyme and rosemary around generously, crushing the herbs. Their aroma perfumed the steamy air of the small room.

"Okay," she told Geoffrey as she opened the oven door and stood back for a moment from the hellish blast. "All we have to do is wait." She put the pan on the middle rack, set a wind-up timer for fifteen minutes (a quarter turn of the dial) then chopped a little more garlic, which she pushed to one side for later.

"What other vegetables did you buy?" she asked him.

"Baby artichokes," he told her. "I was thinking of rolling them in some egg and breadcrumbs and deep frying them, but given the situation, maybe we can just drizzle them with oil and salt and roast them with the fish."

Danielle took hold of the knife and worked slowly and carefully to trim the ends and the woodier leaves from the artichokes.

"Who in the ancient world do you imagine was clever enough to figure out that spiny artichokes could be eaten by tender human mouths?" she asked, enjoying the rhythm of the knife working against the wooden board. "I always picture some starving Italian gnawing away painfully on one."

"Actually," Geoffrey said knowingly, "even before the Italians turned it into their own personal veggie-du-jour, artichokes were native to the Middle East. Its Arabic name, *al-khurshuf*, which means thistle, became *carciofo* in Italian, so it was probably first turned into supper by some wandering Jew about 3,000 years ago."

"So how did Italy get into the picture, Chef Know-it-All?" she asked.

"Marco Polo, maybe," he conjectured. "It just didn't quite take off internationally until Catherine de Medici got a yen for the taste of home while she was living with old Henry, in France."

Danielle was amused and impressed. She wished she could see his face as he recounted these arcane bits of knowledge. His voice didn't betray arrogance, but it might have been nice to see his eyes. She would have to remember to commit that face to memory, she thought.

Although the heat was intense, neither of them made a move immediately to leave the kitchen. A skittish silence had developed between them.

Half an hour later, they were sitting at a well-set table, with a pair of lit candles between them – Danielle's acquiescence to what she called Geoffrey's *special needs*. Unsurprisingly, the fish was delicious, made all the more so by their sex-and-drugs-driven hunger.

"I can't believe you've been coming home every night and voluntarily locking yourself up in the dark." Geoffrey asked, unable to keep the admiration – or was that disbelief? – out of his voice. He had asked some form of this question at least four times already, and Danielle was starting to find it a little less amusing, and complimentary, than it seemed the first three times.

"As you can see, I'm pretty much the Queen of the Night," she told him. "If I can keep even some of my vision, or at least keep it long enough to get really proficient, I've got to believe I can keep working and keep my life. I assume, given the portion you have just wolfed down, that you agree." She had spent sleepless hours on many nights planning how she would approach her boss about her situation and her future. Now she had found herself a powerful ally. Danielle stabbed a piece of artichoke and popped it into her mouth, chewing appreciatively. It was tender yet chewy – like Geoffrey.

"Hmm... Keep your life, definitely. Please. It's a very valuable life, you know," Geoffrey said, reaching out to cover her hand with his own warm palm. She couldn't see any better in the candlelight than she could in the darkness, but she could tell from his inflection that he was smiling fondly. Still, there was something in his words that rankled.

"But?" she asked.

"But what?"

Danielle drew her hand back and reached for another slice of bread to sop up the sauce that puddled around the succulent flesh of the fish.

"I may be going blind, but I'm not going deaf. I know a *but* when I hear one."

"Well, you know as well as I do – a restaurant kitchen is hardly the safest room in the world. Look at my arms," he shoved one in front of Danielle's face, oblivious to the fact that in this low light her condition rendered her pretty much blind. He went on. "I've got burn scars, cut scars, even nerve damage in two fingers from the time I bumped another cook on the line and he dropped a cast iron skillet on my hand. If nothing else, you need to be able to get out of the way pretty quick."

"So what are you saying? That in your esteemed professional opinion a blind person can't manage in the workplace? Are you one of those people who think all handicapped people need to be kept cloistered in sheltered workshops?"

She laid her fork and knife down beside her dish. Things didn't taste so good suddenly. "Do you, or do you not, think that a blind person – no, *this particular* blind person – might be able to work side by side with a sighted someone like you?"

Goeffrey was quiet a beat too long.

"I didn't mean to start an argument," he finally said. "I admire you. You must realize that by now. I've wanted to find a way to get to know you better for a long, long time. You may have noticed, I don't know. Tonight has been amazing for me. I thought for you, too." He forked up fish from the serving dish.

"Is that the answer to my question?" The smell of the food before her was making her ill. Here was the gaping maw around which she had tiptoed for over a year. If even Geoffrey, who had seen her cook in the dark with his own eyes, (how galling it was, the number of expressions of *truth* that rested on those gelatinous orbs) did not believe in her plan, then maybe she was, indeed, setting herself up for failure. What, for pity's sake, might it take to prove herself to someone with whom she hadn't just gotten out of bed? Danielle stood abruptly and her chair tipped to the floor. Taking no notice of the crash, she stormed into the kitchen and dumped the rest of her dinner into the trash.

✕◉◞

Pia climbed out the open door at the front of the first car and down the short ladder to the tracks. The beam of light that she aimed ahead of her footsteps quivered, and she stopped and steadied her hands, shaking with heat and exhaustion. She couldn't afford to drop the flashlight again. That had happened once while she was inside the train car and she had almost lost her mind in the minutes it took to creep around the filthy floors, feeling for it. Her skin crawled, anticipating the stuff – living and otherwise – she might touch as she scuttled around in the dark. Now, Pia's nose itched. She gritted her teeth and prayed for it to stop. First thing she would do when she reached safety was to wash her hands.

It was as quiet on the tracks as it was dark. Everyone was gone now. She was alone. Or at least she prayed she was. Anyone else crazy enough to be standing in this pitch black hell was someone she didn't want to meet. Silence – thick and steaming – crowded her on all sides; again she had that stomach-churning sense of nonexistence. Pia tried breathing to a slow count of four to calm herself. She shot the beam of light around her to take her bearings, and began to walk away from the train that now held – in brilliant colors – gleefully illicit evidence of her existence in this city. If she never made it out of here, that car would house her magnum opus. A little jab of terror broke through her triumph and sent her heart skittering. Of course you're going to make it, she told herself sternly. Don't be dramatic. Stay calm; move carefully.

R-TGRRL, her tag had read, splashed again and again on the walls and seats in the vivid emerald, crimson and cobalt of the Prismacolor set, each letter as plump and air-filled as a Stay-Puft marshmallow. Each letter as large as her hand, which, just for good measure, she traced in black at the very end. Then, she turned the hand print into an exclamation point filled with tiny R-TGRRLS. Something completely original, she thought. She would have to thank Rosie if she got out of this hot and dusty hole. *When* she got out, she reminded herself. She had considered adding, I DO NOT F***ING TYPE FOR ANY MAN! across the seats, but feared she wouldn't survive the stifling heat for the amount of time that would take. Several times, as she hungrily tagged a dozen seatbacks, she had had to rest with her head between her knees until a wave of dizziness passed. Again and again, she wiped away the stinging sweat that blurred her vision.

Still, she had done the thing she feared she might never do. She had left her mark on this colossal city and when the power came back on, millions of people would see her work. Her brain spoke in news headlines: *Subway Riders Stunned: Who is R-TGRRL?* She had joined the ranks of her writing heroes. The joy was sublime. Or maybe the heat was making her punchy.

Dust from the track bed rose up and coated her legs like flannel as she shuffled along. It rose higher and made her sneeze, the jagged sound bouncing off stone walls and down the tunnel in both directions. Something skittered ahead of Pia, giving her chills. She started to hum the few bars of the song that had been playing in her head all day *"ah, ah, ah, ah, stayin' alive, stayin' alive..."*, but the silence overwhelmed her, shattering her resolve, and she crept forward soundlessly.

As she got farther from the train, Pia heard the sound of water nearby. More than a trickle, closer to a splash. She looked down, pointing the light into cracks in the walls and the gullies between the rails. A rivulet of water had formed on one side of the tracks, next to the wall. It was building quickly, carrying small bits of trash like miniature boats on tiny waves. She tried to imagine where the water was coming from. Tried *not* to imagine it rising much further. Was she under the river? Could the tunnel have sprung a leak? Her heart was beating so savagely she could feel her pulse against the loose neckband of her shirt. She took a deep breath – air as hot as a cup of tea – and held it. The conductor had said they were only a few hundred feet from the station. They were *not* directly under the river, in that case.

One step, another, another still. The station couldn't be too much further, could it? The water was actually lapping at the rocks now and Pia swiveled the light to assess its progress. As the beam played over the stonework, she saw its source. Water spurted from between a combination of brick, rock and cement. Maybe a water main had burst. Maybe it was merely an open fire hydrant raining water down below. The kids in her aunt's neighborhood did that, wrenching open the hydrants on steamy days, creating their own water park in the 'hood.

The neighborhood. Pia wondered how she would find it even after she made her way out of these urban intestines and back to the planet's surface. Especially with the lights out. She wasn't at all sure how to walk from Clark Street station to her aunt's house, even in broad daylight. Would there be people on the street? Was it safe to be out? Suddenly she thought about Son of Sam and wished to hell she hadn't. Fear hit her in the belly this time, a cramp in the gut. She fought it back and forced herself to think of something else. Music. She hummed a few more bars under her breath and finally succeeded in pushing the thought, if not out of her head, at least to one side.

Pia sent the beam of light – by now weakening – out ahead of her and imagined that she could see the cavern widening into a station. Like Jonah in the whale, she scanned the darkness for the open maw and thought that maybe there was a light off in the distance.

Pia was about to continue forward when a quick movement on the edge of the light caught her attention. She shot the beam in that direction just in time to see a long gray tail slip between some rocks. The hackles on Pia's neck rose and she felt lightheaded. She wanted to run, but her feet wouldn't obey her command. Instead, she stood, rooted to the spot as the mottled gray and brown creature returned, carrying something in its mouth, poking first its nose and then its entire self through the merest crack in the rock, just above the place where the water poured out. The object in its mouth was a miniature version of the rat itself. Was the large rat going to eat the small one right before her eyes? Pia's skin prickled with disgust. Sensing another presence, the animal stopped as still as a shadow. It started to turn back, but then raced a short way up the wall, hanging tight to its booty, which it deposited in an outcropping about three feet away from where Pia stood. The rodent turned and faced her without fear.

Pia kept the light trained on the spot, but the large rodent darted past the edge of illumination, leaving the smaller one behind. Where could it have gone? Was it about to bury its famously yellow teeth into one of her naked toes? Pia swung the beam along the jagged bedrock, down to her feet, out into the tunnel, searching for her would-be attacker. But it was nowhere. Then she turned back to the rock.

It was like watching an instant replay. The rat emerged, its fur clumped and sticky with mud, from the same spot in the rocks (at least Pia thought it was the same spot) and once again, it had a smaller rodent hanging from its mouth. The animal picked its way down the side of the wall and deposited its quarry next to the first one, then turned and dashed back up to the hole.

Pia understood. These weren't food – they were her *babies*. And the mother was racing the clock to rescue them, one by one, from a nest behind the rock, which was quickly filling with water. Pia was equal parts repulsed and fascinated. How many could there be?

It occurred to Pia that she could do the world a service and eliminate an entire generation of the vermin with one blow. She looked around for a loose stone. Meanwhile, the mother rat appeared again, struggling up the rockface with another…, another…, *another what?* What would you call a baby rat, Pia wondered. A ratlet? Ratling? Ratette?

She shone the light into their new temporary shelter. The pale gray rodents, each hairless and no larger than Pia's thumb, were curled together now, one of them opening its miniscule mouth in a toothless pink yawn. The third rat baby joined its siblings, squeaking loudly. It shouldered its way between them. Their mother had already disappeared. A stone fell from the wall, startling Pia who almost tripped over the tracks as she jumped back.

Pia wished she could draw what she saw next. And tomorrow, she surely would. Once more the mother rat emerged from between the rocks, this time carrying not one, but two babies in her mouth. No sooner had she appeared, than a cascade of water began pouring out from the space where the nest had been. The mother rat was losing ground in her effort to climb the rock wall to safety. She made it up six inches or so and fell backward, bumping against another outcropping. One of the small ones slipped from her mouth. She turned to get it, then stopped and turned the other way. Back and forth, back and forth, the wet and muddy rat wavered, the tiny one on the rocks below now squeaking pitifully. Almost against her will, Pia found herself rooting for the mother to succeed.

As if coming to some resolve, the mother rat headed down the rock wall. But at that same moment a loose stone dropped from the waterfall and landed squarely – silencing the small rat. The mother rat circled it once, twice, then dashed up the wall with her remaining baby. She tucked the survivor in with its siblings and covered them with her body. Pia played the beam of light onto the new nest. Ten beady eyes glared out at her defiantly. Then, the flashlight flickered and went out. Gasping, Pia shook it and, *thank God!* it went on once again. It was definitely time to go.

Her calves ached; her shoulder was sore where her portfolio

strapped rubbed. Sleep was overtaking her, even as she walked. To keep herself awake, she anticipated the stories with which she would regale her parents and Rosie once this was all over.

"It was like painting a mural on the walls of Hell," she imagined telling them. "I thought the pens would melt in my hands. And the *smell!*" She envisioned the look of horror on her mother's face, the look of admiration on Rosie's. She would bring them to New York and they would ride the trains, all day and all night if necessary, for the pleasure beyond words of having the doors swing open to find her very own tags. And tomorrow, she would draw the rat and her babies. Five beady-eyed, pink-gray bodies, their patchy new hair slick with water, their miniscule noses rooting through the warm belly fur of their mother, looking for *home*.

The bottoms of Althea's feet were on fire by the time she reached the housing complex where her mother lived. Blisters had formed, broken, formed again. She lurched from step to step, each one an angry reprimand. She was sure she was bleeding, but dared not stop to check. Her blouse was as wet and sticky as if she'd been splashed by a wave, and it clung like a second skin. Heat radiated off the buildings and pavement. The smell of her own sweat rose from between her breasts in hot clouds like gas from a fissure in the earth.

With each block further uptown the world had become increasingly chaotic and threatening. Like locusts, people swarmed up from the side streets and dispersed along Broadway, and more than once Althea ducked into the shadows to avoid notice as rowdy gangs whooped past. Window after window gaped, ragged, raw and empty, the store within trashed and plundered beyond recognition. At first Althea thought she might be dreaming. Had sleep overtaken her as she walked? But the acrid smell and the shrieking sirens made it clear that this nightmare was far from imaginary.

It was no longer pitch dark, strictly speaking. Flames leapt from the upper stories of a building about a block away. Above, the sky flickered with heat lightning and a malevolent orange glow in the north that allowed Althea to see a short distance ahead. On Skiathos, her uncle Demetrios had a coal furnace he used for turning bars and sheets of iron into pots and utensils. This sky was not unlike the terrifying light of his workshop, where Althea was warned never to linger. Hints of smoke wafted through the air, tangling in her clothes. She could not remember what Demetrios' face looked like, but she had a clear memory of his arms, hugely muscled and pocked with scars, smelling of singed hair.

At 98th street she was passing in front of a Met Food market when its mammoth pane of glass shattered only a couple of feet away from her. Her scream went unheard in the pandemonium that followed. Like maddened cattle, people stampeded inside and returned under immense loads of groceries. Some pushed baby carriages so full they left a trail of stolen merchandise in their wake. Others, following behind, scooped it up. The faces that flashed by her were mad-eyed with greed. She pressed ahead despite her pain and her fear.

Men and women trundled by with trains of shopping carts lashed together and heaped with stolen goods. Many were piled high with cases of beer and meats. Some came away without food or drink but loaded down with cartons of disposable diapers and cleaning supplies. Children, some younger than her daughter, raced through the streets scavenging items that had fallen from the arms and carts of looters. The world had gone mad. It looked, she thought, like Christmas in the underworld.

In the angry, sweat-streaked faces of the men she saw Oscar's face. The fury and loathing in his eyes, where once she saw desire. She had been a fool, and now she would pay the price. Althea had gambled her pride and lost. She had lost it all – her job, her lover, her self-respect. Only Celia remained. She raced ahead to safeguard and take solace in her only treasure. She would make everything up to her. The late nights, the broken promises.

Althea stumbled over something on the ground. Reaching down, she found a dented can of beans. She was about to toss it aside and then thought better of it. She had seen mothers and their offspring, sometimes not more than a few months old, wrapped in rags, homeless, begging. They were the hungry ones, the angry ones, the ones who had no stake in the ordinary commerce of the city. And now, in the course of one day, she had become one of them. She tucked the can into her purse.

A car swerved around the corner, the sound of its horn the bleating cry of a wounded animal. Althea narrowly jumped out of its path. Her pulse drummed in her ears, her eyes clouded with sweat and tears. She tried to pick up her pace. It was like running through soup, and she almost fell to her knees with the effort. Finally, there was only one long block to go. Althea slowed to a limping walk, reassuring herself that Celia was surely fast asleep by now and wouldn't see her until the morning, anyway. As she turned the final corner into the entrance of the housing project, she found herself stopped by a line of wooden barriers and half a dozen police cars, their headlights ablaze.

She edged her way around one of the barriers but was blocked by a fat policemen in full riot gear.

"Sorry, miss. No one goes through here. Crime scene."

She stared at him in mute disbelief for a moment, until she found her voice.

"You have to let me through," she insisted, pointing. "My daughter is in that building."

The cop looked at her and laughed. "Lady, no one gets by here. Not even Hizzoner da Mayor's own sainted mother. That's my orders. You'll have to move along until we've finished our investigation." Crime scene? Investigation? The entire world had turned into one gaping wound of a crime scene. She wondered if she could slip between the barricades and outrun this fat, greasy man in his heavy Gestapo uniform. Then she thought about what might happen if he caught her. If they took her away to jail, would they find out about what she had done at work? Oscar, she feared, would be only too happy to speak out against her. She slinked back into the shadows and stood, trembling in the heat.

A volley of gunfire ripped her thoughts to shreds. Althea flung herself face down onto the ground and waited while her heart pounded as if it would drive a stake into the concrete beneath her chest. She pivoted her head to see what was happening, one cheek still pressed to the sidewalk. The policemen – including the fat one, Althea noticed – ran toward a building in the center of the compound. This might be her only chance. Not daring to rise to her feet, Althea crawled the last yards to her mother's door. She dragged herself upright and pushed, but the door was locked. The buzzer, of course, useless without electricity.

"Mama!" Althea screamed up to the skies. Her mother's window looked out on the front of the building, but she knew her attempts were useless. No one could possibly hear her from seven stories above the street. Still, the cry burst from her several more times anyway, until she was too hoarse to continue. A teenaged boy ambled by, pushing a shopping cart of boxes.

"Pampers? I sell them to you cheap," he said to Althea. "Five dollars only."

"No," Althea could only whisper. "I don't need Pampers. I, uh, I lost my key and my child is upstairs alone. Can you help me?"

The young man looked at her pityingly, then laughed.

"You don't need a key to get into *these* buildings," he crowed. He pulled a plastic card from his back pocket and thrust it between the door and the jamb. Then he hip-checked the door open. Althea started to step inside.

"You wanna pay for that?" he asked, leaning in close and winking. "Five bucks for the Pampers, five more for the doorman service."

Ten dollars? A fortune to her now. But Althea reached into her purse, handed the boy a couple of bills and slipped through the opening like a wraith. She climbed the seven flights of steps to her mother's apartment and stood, with her head swimming, before the green metal door with its Cyclopean eye. Out of habit, she rang the bell, and then realized that it would make no sound. She knocked, lightly at first, then heavier until she was pounding. The locks clicked and the door opened on the chain. One side of her mother's face, its eye red and swollen, skin mottled, peered out at her.

A wail escaped the older woman as the door swung fully open and Althea entered. Her eyes were almost purple with grief.

"Where is Celia?" Althea demanded.

"She isn't with you?"

Althea stared as though the woman had gone insane.

"Of course not. What do you mean?" Althea heard the pitch of her voice rise with each question. She grabbed her mother by the sleeve of her robe.

"I don't know. She's not here. *Den einai edo*," her mother whispered, pulling away as though she were afraid that Althea would strike her. "*Efige*."

Efige? Gone? Althea stared and saw nothing, grasped again for her mother's arm and felt nothing. The sea pounded in Althea's ears. She lowered herself into a chair, then doubled over into darkness.

Chapter Eleven

Crying hadn't done any good. After she smeared the last hot tears off her cheeks, Celia still had no choice but to keep going. She was too far from Yiayia's house ever to walk back. At first she got turned around and found herself back up at 31st Street before she realized that she was heading in the wrong direction. And she only realized her mistake because the headlights of a car lit up the street sign just as she was about to cross.

After her close scrape with the police car, the few vehicles that sped by terrified her and she shrank from the small knots of people she saw wheeling drunkenly down the street. Instead, she clung to the shadows like a rat and swallowed the fear that lumped like sour milk in her throat.

Celia walked until she limped, and limped until she slumped on the sidewalk against a building for a short rest. Her head lolled onto her chest and she jolted awake in panic, a dream of flames flickering behind her eyelids. Aching with exhaustion, she dragged herself to her feet and began to walk again. Surely she must be getting closer to home.

She was walking down First Avenue now, not Broadway anymore, which was too bad, since Broadway was the street her mother had shown her on the map, but she knew that she lived at the bottom of the island, and if the numbers got smaller, she was getting closer. Celia figured she would recognize something when she got really close. Maybe the big Chinese grocery store where bought candied ginger and fish and tea, or even the long block of kitchen supply stores that she passed on the way to school. She'd recognize something. She knew she would.

Hoping to make the blocks go by faster, she played the counting game Yiayia had taught her when she was little.

Ade milo sti milia,
Ke heretam ti griya;
Posa hronia the na ziso?
Ena, dio, tria, tesera...

As she whispered the words in Greek, she pictured the scene they described: Apples hanging heavy on a tree. Herself below, saluting their abundance.

"How many years will I live?" the rhyme continued. "One, two, three, four..."

She kept up this rhyming and counting with her eyes focused mainly on her toes, the better to avoid the attention of anyone she passed in the street. *Posa hronia the na ziso?* Seven, eight, nine, ten. After a while, she got bored with counting and moved on to a different game. *I went on a picnic and here's what I brought: an apple. I went on a picnic and here's what I brought: an apple and a banana.* But by the letter N, she was dizzy and confused, unable to remember the items she had already named and tired of playing stupid games that didn't bring her any closer to home. Also, the thought of all that food was making her feel even hungrier. *I went on a picnic and here's what I brought: Nothing.* Her stomach rumbled.

She wished Mami were here now, walking beside her, telling

her a story. No one knew more stories than Mami, except maybe Yiayia, who knew the history of all the gods and goddesses on Mount Olympus and the heroes that roamed ancient Greece. Poseidon, Apollo and Zeus, mean old Hera and beautiful Aphrodite. The Minotaur. The giant wooden horse filled with soldiers that fooled the Trojans who had stolen beautiful Helen away from Greece. Odysseus and his sad adventures. Like Celia, Odysseus just wanted to go home. Mami knew those stories, too, but Celia liked Mami's special ones – like the one about Tragos the goat – even better. Mami said Yiayia's stories were myths – not true stories. Hers were true, she said.

In school this past year, Celia's class had studied mythology. The first day, her teacher read them the story of Pandora's Box.

"Long, long ago when the world was young and the gods and goddesses ruled over the lives of the earthly peasants, a rebel god, Prometheus, took pity on the weak humans and gave them fire, which he had stolen from Zeus, king of the immortals." The teacher looked around to make sure no one was whispering or sending notes under the desk before she went on.

"Zeus was so angry that he decided to punish both Prometheus and the mortals he helped. He sent a beautiful woman, Pandora, to marry Prometheus' brother, and gave them, as a wedding present, a little box with a big lock. He told them never, ever, to open the box. But Pandora, curious to know what treasures were inside, smashed the lock with a stone one day and lifted the cover of the box. Out flew all the evils that Zeus had hidden inside: Sickness, Worry, Crime, Hate, War, Envy." The teacher wrote each of these on the board.

"In a panic, Pandora tried to catch the hideous evils and stuff them back into the box, but it was too late. The evils flew from that place to everywhere in the world, where they still live today, plaguing mankind. All because of her curiosity." The teacher looked deep into the eyes of the students, driving the point home. "The last thing to leave the box, however, was Hope, which Zeus had included to give people comfort and help them go on when things got bad."

Hope, Celia thought to herself now. She still had Hope.

Celia had been thrilled that the stories from her country that Yiayia had told her since she was a baby were stories that people all over the world knew. But when she showed Yiayia the mythology book her teacher lent her, the older woman got furious.

"These are not the stories of our gods, our land. These are only bedtime stories for little children," she shouted. "There was no box – Pandora herself was the cursed thing. It was she who brought evil to our land. And as for Prometheus, Zeus had him chained to a rock where an eagle ate out his liver each day and he was left shivering in the cold each night." The idea of such a punishment made Celia's stomach turn over uncomfortably. The only thing that Yiayia admitted was correct as the teacher told it, was the part about Hope.

The next day, when her teacher pointed out to the class that Celia was from Greece and probably knew these stories, she stood and faced the class with defiance.

"You've got the story all wrong," she declared. "My Yiayia says you don't know anything about the ways of the gods."

Her teacher looked shocked and made Celia sit down and stay after class instead of going outside for gym. In frustration, Celia ran from the classroom, crying. Mami had to come in and talk to Miss Carlin, to explain. Of course, that was when Mami was Mami, and not this mysterious, disappearing person.

What was her mother doing now, Celia wondered. Was she alone in the apartment, or was her *boyfriend* there with her? Was there really a boyfriend? With kissing and all that? Celia didn't believe it. Her mother was too grown up, and too *good* – hadn't Yiayia said that only bad girls did those things? Marissa was a liar; Marissa's yiayia was probably a liar, too. Maybe this was all a myth. Still. If her mother did have a boyfriend, that would be better than if she was sick, or just sick of spending so much time with Celia – wouldn't it? Celia had watched people kissing. Sex kissing, not kissing their kids or fake kissing like when they met friends on the street. She and her friend Cora had once hid behind the bushes in the park to watch the big kids smoking and kissing after school. Then Cora's mother started shouting for her and they had to pretend they had lost some money in the dirt. Celia and Cora had tried kissing like that later. It wasn't so great. Instead, they decided to make the My-T-Fine chocolate pudding her mother had bought for them at the supermarket.

Celia wondered what time it was. It seemed like it had been dark for way too long. Where was the sun? She thought she saw it beginning to lighten the sky behind her, but that was a long time ago. The coppery glow never got any brighter, but only flickered now and then ominously. *Once upon a time, there was a planet where the sun forgot to shine…*

Reaching a corner, Celia looked up. She waited for the beam from a passing car – there were fewer and fewer as the night wore on. She was at 22nd Street. She cocked her head to one side. In the quiet that followed the vanishing engine noise, she could swear she heard the distinct sound of splashing water and laughter. Was she dreaming again? More than once tonight she had thought she heard Mami's voice talking in her ear, but so low that she couldn't make out the words. She saw their front door, too, with its familiar purple, red and green graffiti – the exact words as impossible to read as the ones on an Egyptian sarcophagus she had seen on a school trip. Each time that happened, she realized she had stopped walking and her eyelids had fallen shut. The images she saw on them were nothing but dreams. Now, she pinched the skin on the inside of her forearm and it hurt – she blinked – and so she was awake. But the splashing sounds persisted and Celia began to walk in their direction. She had almost reached the street that ran under the elevated highway when she realized that the wall she was following ended in a gate that was exactly same as the one she had entered with Yiayia earlier today. Was that really only this morning? Celia felt as if a week's worth of nights might have come and gone.

The gate to this pool had been yanked part way open. Celia had no trouble slipping through. Beyond the entryway was a darkness thicker than any she'd been through so far, but the smell of chlorine and the clear splashing sounds lured her. Taking a deep breath to press the fear down into her belly, Celia crept through the blackness as if she were leaving this world behind and hurtling into the great unknown.

She had to move more slowly than she would have liked, careful not to trip or run into anything. After a short, narrow hallway, the space seemed to open up around her like a cave might, although she had never actually been in a cave. The sound of her breath echoed back through the stillness. It smelled damp as a cave, too, but also familiar. Her nose prickled. Disinfectant. The room smelled exactly like the one in which she and Yiayia changed into their swimsuits this morning. She stopped for a moment and reached down to touch the floor. Tiles, clammy and cool, just like ones at her pool. If this *were* like the changing room at the pool uptown, the shower stalls were on her right and the toilets on her left. And the door to the pool itself was straight ahead.

She kept moving forward, more confident now, reaching out with her arms to find the expected wall. Once she touched it, she followed it until she reached the doorway, and found herself back in open air.

After the complete darkness of the locker room, the night seemed lighter. What she saw made her gasp. At first, the dark shapes outlined against the sky looked like mythical beasts forming and changing shape as they moved between air and water. She flattened herself against the doorframe to watch. A moment later she recognized them as dozens of grownups, jumping in and climbing out of a large swimming pool, laughing like lunatics. A few grabbed at each other and then spun away, splashing back into the water. Celia stepped into the shadows in alarm. She knew she should run back through the darkness to the street and continue on her way home, but every pore in her skin, her lips, tongue, eyes, ached to be bathed in that cold water, if only for a minute.

How could a short rest hurt? She had been walking for so long in the heat. She hadn't had anything to drink since the warm can of orange Crush she'd almost slid on, stepping off a curb into the gutter.

The sugary liquid was a tease. The instant she swallowed it, her thirst returned like the mosquitoes that whined in her ears.

A noise from behind made Celia spin around. A teenaged couple emerged from the dark building, holding hands and kissing. They walked right by without seeing her at all. They had a lit flashlight, but it dangled uselessly from the boy's belt, the pale beam bouncing along the ground, as they clung to each other. She followed in their wake, as though she were Marissa, an annoying kid they were forced to baby-sit. She ambled along just far enough behind them that they didn't sense her presence, but close enough not to draw any unwanted notice from anyone else in the pool. When she felt she had gotten far enough away from the crowd, she broke off and fell back, taking a seat on the bleachers. She took off her shoes. Strap marks, etched into her skin from hours of wear, burned as the plastic pulled away from her flesh.

Celia got to her feet shakily and headed for the water, praying for continued invisibility. The warm, rough pavement felt solid and good after the sweaty plastic sandals. She reached the perimeter of the pool and sat down gingerly, dangling her feet over the edge. Celia stretched out with one pointed toe and then another, but the water remained tantalizing inches away. She was at the deep end. She could make out the number nine painted in white on the ground next to her and the ladder to the diving board was just ahead. Once, on a dare, she had started to climb those stairs at the pool near Yiayia's house, but the lifeguard stopped her before she got halfway up.

"Hey, you – girlie," he had shouted. "No one under twelve goes up there. Get your skinny little butt down here before I climb up after you!"

Celia had been relieved to be caught. She had no idea what she'd do if she made it to the top. Jumping off was unimaginable, and coming down might not be possible, if anyone were climbing up behind her. Once on the ground, she slinked away quickly. Now Celia thought about Marissa and her fear of the slide with shame. She should have been nicer. And she would have been, if Marissa hadn't said all that about her mother.

Sitting on the edge of the pool, Celia stretched a little more, but the water remained out of reach. She pressed her palms into the pavement and lowered her body a little over the edge. One foot touched water and the chill of it sent thrilling waves of dizziness through her head. More, she needed more, and she lowered herself a little further until both feet were submerged and the muscles in her arms trembled from holding up her own weight. The surface of the water tickled her ankles. She felt a quick burn as the chlorine bathed the blistered skin and then all the pain in her feet disappeared as if touched by magic. Then, without thought, without fear, with nothing but insatiable desire for the cool, the liquid, the relief of water, Celia let her arms go limp. Her head spun as she slipped quickly into the icy cold and she blew out through her nose forcefully as her head bobbed momentarily beneath the surface. She pushed off the side of the pool with one foot as she had seen swimmers do, and with a sense of surprise that couldn't have been stronger if she had suddenly grown flippers and fins, she began to cut through the water, arm over arm, her legs kicking out behind her – a swimmer, at last.

Like flying, like dreaming, like being tossed about by angels, the feeling of water slipping past her skin thrilled her as she took stroke after stroke. Celia wished again that her mother were there to see her in her moment of triumph, or that her friends from up-town were around with their *Marcos* and their *Polos*. Long tethered to the land, she had now – finally – been embraced by Poseidon. She was one of the Nereides, sisters who dwelt in their silvery cavern at the bottom of the briny Aegean. In her charge, all the ocean's trea-sures. In her care, the shipwrecked sailors and fishermen who cried out to them in distress. She would show those kids the next time they played. She'd turn and flip and race away faster than a dolphin. No one could touch her. No nasty, grabbing little boys, no laughing, teasing girls. She was a swimmer now, a creature of two worlds, and even the memory of fear had disappeared as she cut through her new watery atmosphere.

Celia swam counting her strokes – seven, eight, nine – triumphant, until her arms ached from their unaccustomed new exercise. Her legs kicked more slowly now and failed to break the surface. She was getting tired. But where was the edge to grasp onto? In the dark, the water stretched out from around her in all directions. Far at the other end of the pool, people were still leaping and shouting with pleasure. The tee shirt she was wearing bunched up around her neck. Heavy with water, it dragged at her. She struggled to push it down and away from her mouth. All at once, something slammed into the water less than a foot from her head. Terrified, Celia realized that she must be under the diving board. Another body slapped down, a little farther away.

Celia twisted and turned and flailed her arms clumsily. Her legs felt heavy as stone, her breath came in choppy gasps. She snorted and coughed as water splashed her face. Her head slid beneath the surface once, and then again. Celia's attempts to scream for help only filled her mouth with water, her throat with terror. Her eyes stared wide as she slid underwater over and over, sputtering each time she managed to pull herself up for one more gasp of the beautiful, beautiful, oh-more-beautiful-than-anything air.

Reflexively, she held her nose with one hand, as she had this morning, before she had fooled herself into believing she could join the world of the water nymphs. She squeezed her eyes shut as she slipped deeper into the water. She wrapped one arm around herself and then, letting go of her nose, the other. From far away she heard the beat of drums, or no, horses hooves. *Hippokampi*, she thought, those fishtailed horses come to save her, but it was too dark to see their approach. Where were her fifty sisters – Thetis, mother of Achilles, Amphetrite, her hair streaming long and black as a nest of eels? Now, yes, now she saw them racing toward her, their eyes sad, shedding salty tears that became silver and gold fish swimming in their wake. And behind them all, her own mother, carried on the back of a dolphin, racing to find her at last.

Mami! Mami! Celia called, breathless with wonder.

Chapter Twelve

Judith opened her eyes into a world of continuing darkness. She was not in her bed; that much was obvious. Her cheek itched where it pressed against rough fabric and her legs were numb, bent against a space too short to stretch out flat. One hand trailed onto the shag carpeting, still gripping the mezuzah that she had rescued from the hallway floor. She blinked away the crust of dried tears and realized that she had fallen asleep on the sofa. What time was it? There was no way to know. Not yet dawn, that much was certain.

She had been dreaming. In the dream, she crouched in one corner of a large room. She was alone in the room but at the same time, the darkness with which she shared the space was so profound that it threatened to crush her. She strained against its formidable weight to keep open enough space to breathe. Meanwhile, something nearby rocked back and forth, knocking rhythmically against the wooden floorboards. She struggled to turn her head and see.

Just beyond her reach a tiny light flickered on and off peeking out from beneath the rocking object. If she could grasp it, the light would open up space for her in darkness. But her arms were useless, crushed beneath her. The darkness was insistent; she was dissolving into it. Her eyelids were so heavy. All that was left was the rhythmic sound.

Her eyes were open now, but the knocking continued. Judith lay as still as stony death and waited. Was she still dreaming? She tightened her grip on the mezuzah and felt the pain of its edges cutting into her palm. Awake then. Was there something in the room with her? A mouse? A rat? The *Shekhinah* herself? Rebecca said that the *Shekhinah* had taken away the fear of death as it enfolded her in its wings. But Judith wasn't dying, was she? She squeezed her eyes tight shut and forced her breath to slow and deepen. In her bedtime *Kriat Sh'ma al ha-Mitah* prayers, she nightly invoked the angels Michael, Gabriel, Uriel and Raphael for protection through the hours of darkness. But tonight she had fallen asleep without completing this ritual. And here was the result.

The knocking came once more, this time tentative as a familiar question. Now she understood. The door. There was someone at the door. She swung stiff legs to the ground and struggled to stand. Awake, the darkness in the room was less crushing, but more dizzying.

"Yes? Who is it?" she called, trying to sound awake and in charge. Had she locked the door when she came in? Even in her distraught state, she thought she would have remembered to do that. "Who's there?" she called again, louder and more assertive now.

"Judith? Is that you?"

Judith froze with more dread than she had felt confronting the darkness in her dream. What should she do? Unconsciously, she smoothed her hair, brushed the wrinkles from her skirt.

"Hello? Are you there? I'm looking for Judith Fein," the voice called again through the door. "Is this the right apartment?"

Judith's mouth opened and closed but no sound issued from

it. She needed time to think. Once again, she squeezed the ritual object in her grip and forced sound from her throat.

"This is Judith. Who is this?" she asked, although she knew only too well.

"It's me. Michael. I'm so glad I found you. I'm sorry it's so late. Can you let me in?"

Judith peered through the peephole in the door. The face that appeared, lit by flashlight from below, was as chilling as a *dybbuk*, but it was definitely Michael's. She began, clumsily, to unlock the door and open it a crack, but did not at first ask him to come in.

"What are you doing here?" she demanded, peering out through the narrow space.

"I told you I would come and I am a man of my word. I have your bag." He lifted the shopping bag in one hand and pointed the light at it. "I had a little trouble getting here, though," he laughed. "I'll tell you the whole story. Can I come in?"

Yes, that is the question, Judith thought. In light of her earlier promises to return to piety and obedience, this was no small request.

"This is a little awkward," she said. "Jewish law forbids a man and woman who are not married to each other to be alone together in a private place. But I think, under the circumstances..." She sent up a silent appeal for guidance and unlatched the chain that she had, in fact, remembered to fasten. She opened the door wider. A hot breeze from the open window in the room behind her rattled the venetian blinds against the window frame. The sound startled her. It also brought an answer to her plea.

Michael stepped tentatively across the threshold.

He said, "I probably shouldn't have even come up at this hour, but I was passing right by your block and I did promise to bring this to you." He held out the Saks bag, and Judith took it and placed it on the couch. As she did, Michael's flashlight flickered. Judith relit the Shabbat candles on the table. By their light she found her remaining flashlight on the floor near the couch.

"I should probably leave. You don't happen to have any extra batteries?" He held up the now dead flashlight.

"Sorry, no, but I do have an idea if you want to stay a while. It's a bit unusual, but if you're feeling adventurous," she said.

"Adventurous? You have no clue. I had the adventure of a lifetime just getting here. It was like a TV movie of the week. What have you got in mind?"

By candlelight, Judith led him through the apartment, offering him a stop at the bathroom where she handed him the flashlight, and then through the bedroom where she opened the window as far as it would go and pointed.

"Would you care to join me on the balcony?" she asked, laughing. A sooty wind rose from alleyway and blew out the twin flames, leaving Judith unable to see the expression on Michael's face as he contemplated the fire escape with its peeling paint and dust rimed slats.

"With pleasure," Michael replied, scanning with the flashlight to find the best way out. He finally sat on the windowsill and swung his legs round to the floor of the fire escape. Grabbing hold of the bars, he hoisted himself outside and waited for her to follow.

"If you move over just a little, I'll bring out some pillows," Judith said.

"Or maybe the whole mattress," Michael said.

Judith was glad it was too dark out there on the fire escape for him to see her blush. She stripped the pillows and blanket off her bed and handed them through the window to Michael. Michael folded the blanket and laid it on the slats as a rug and then arranged the pillows on two of the steps leading up to the next floor.

Judith climbed out the window, careful to hold the long skirt around her legs for modesty as she pivoted across the sill. They both stood in the sultry air that smelled of rust and sweet smoke drifting up from somewhere below and then worked their way to sit. Judith shifted slightly to find a more comfortable position in the narrow confines of the space. Michael, only inches away, rustled around in the less-than-hospitable environment. He eased back against the pillows on the stairs and they settled into silence. Outside of their little nest, the air swirled with sirens and shouts, with strains of thumping music and what Judith thought were muffled sobs from somewhere close by.

Now that he was here and they were installed in this space, Judith found herself at a loss for words. In her experience, polite conversation between young people walking out together on a first date was more like a job interview: *Can you describe your goals for yourself and your family?* And it took place in a restaurant or on the sidewalks of Eastern Parkway, not holed up on a fire escape in the dark. A simple *nice night, isn't it?* was completely out of the question.

"So, you mentioned you had an adventure?" Judith finally asked.

"I was stuck in the elevator in my office building," Michael told her. "With a guy from the office and a pregnant woman from another floor. We had no idea what was going on in the great wide world, but in our little tiny world all hell was breaking lose."

Again, Judith realized with relief that the darkness kept Michael from noticing that just hearing the word *pregnant* issue from his lips made her blush. In her world, men kept themselves strictly blind to the condition, except, of course, in relation to their own nuclear families. Even then, it was the custom to conceal pregnancies until at least the fifth month.

"Is she, is she....all right, *b'Hashem*?" Judith finally found it in herself to say.

"She thought she was going into labor. She started hyperventilating and screaming. I tried doing magic tricks to distract her," he laughed, "but it was too dark to see. It was terrifying. The other guy I was with had kids, thank God. Oh, sorry. But at least he had been through the process. That was reassuring. He started timing the contractions by the glowing dial of his Timex. The only birth I'd ever witnessed was a cow at the county fair New Hampshire when I was twelve."

"Did she actually give birth in the elevator?" Judith asked, amazed and horrified. She couldn't imagine what it would be like for the woman to have to give birth attended by two strange men. Judith's aunts had attended her mother at all five births, along with a woman doctor at the last two. Judith, ten years old when Rivka was born, had begged in vain to be allowed into the delivery room. She wished she could have been the one in the elevator instead of Michael tonight.

"False labor," Michael said. "The contractions stopped. No more screaming. Meanwhile, I was pounding on the door of the elevator and calling out for help. We were between floors. Closer to the floor below, though. Someone heard us and yelled in what was going on. Finally he managed to get one of the building's maintenance men to wrench the doors open and get us out."

"And the woman?"

"The maintenance man and another guy carried her down the stairs. They took her to New York Hospital, I think. I spent close to an hour trying to get a call through to her husband at home. He just about had a coronary when I told him." He laughed. "So how was your evening?"

The telephone, Judith thought: It works? She hadn't even considered that this might be the case. She thought about calling her family. But it was probably three or four in the morning already, and a ringing telephone would only frighten them. Still, why hadn't they called her?

Michael whispered, "Judith, do you hear someone crying?"

Indeed, the sound came from the floor directly above them.

"Do you know the woman who lives up there?" Michael asked.

Judith shook her head *no*, then realized that Michael couldn't see that in the gloom.

"Not really. I've shared the elevator with her, though. She has the oddest habit of closing her eyes and counting the buttons with her fingers." Judith straightened the folds of her skirt beneath her. "I've heard her crying before. I will pray for her and *B'Hashem*, things will get better for her."

They settled into silence. Judith wondered whether she should go upstairs and see if there was anything she might do.

"Do your people always think that God will make everything better?" Michael asked.

"My people?"

"Well, I don't know anything about your brand of Judaism. It seems to rule every part of your life. I mean, mine was pretty much the revolving door variety."

Judith stared at him, silent with confusion. "You said that at lunch," she finally said. "What does it mean?"

"You know, in for the High Holy Days, out the rest of the time. Eight nights of Chanukah presents as a kid, and a bar mitzvah that pretty much put an end to all future religious obligations. I guess that would make me, in your book, a bad Jew."

She laughed at the idea. "I don't think I would be qualified to pass that kind of judgment," she said. "But if you're asking whether you could be a more observant Jew, bring your soul closer in line with Hashem's laws, I'd have to say yes, you probably could."

"But you've got to know that here in America, in 1977, you people are kind of viewed as, well, *extremist*, even by your fellow Jews. Kind of like the Amish with their horses and buggies and refusal to use zippers in their flies. Sorry, I don't mean to be insulting. I'm just curious. What do you get out of living the way you do?"

Judith was quiet. She tried not to feel offended, but she did feel defensive. What he was asking would take a lifetime to explain. If she were even qualified to begin to explain it. And it wasn't as if she didn't suffer from doubt. Look where she was right this moment. It didn't escape her awareness that only a few hours earlier she had sworn renewed faithfulness and repentance. But still, he was asking. And it would be a *mitzvah* to answer. She took a deep breath.

"According to the Talmud, the soul of a Jew descends into a body for a purpose – in order to fulfill a specific spiritual mission in this world. I grew up believing this absolutely. There was a purpose to every aspect of our lives. Every moment of every day was spent fulfilling Hashem's commandments and bringing us another day closer to His joyous return. I was happy knowing this, living this way. It was a good life." Judith blinked back unwilling tears.

"But if it's so wonderful, why did you leave?" Michael asked.

"It *was* wonderful," she said defiantly. "The world I lived in was very small, like a village, and everywhere I looked were people who lived – and believed – as we did. The rest of the city was almost invisible to me."

Michael shifted position on the iron steps. She imagined his perplexed expression.

Judith warmed to the challenge of enlightening him. "The most important thing is knowing that every single one of our actions plays a crucial role in unfolding the future. It is the responsibility of each of us to live the best possible life in order to make the future a joyous one."

"Where is free will? Where is experimentation and playfulness? Where is there room for personal fulfillment and creativity? You've really never watched TV? These are the questions that baffle me."

"See, that's the difference between us. I am not in the least troubled by those particular questions." Even as the words came from her lips, Judith wondered at their truthfulness.

"I don't believe you," Michael said quickly re-crossing his legs.

"The *Tanya*," she began again, "a holy book, teaches that Hashem infused the universe with his most sacred Light, which fuels every aspect of the world, from the creatures and plants that cover the earth, to the desires, virtues and dreams of our deepest hearts. But the Light was too pure for the world to bear, so he concealed it in mystical urns that shielded his creatures from the brightness."

In the dark, Judith couldn't read Michael's face for clues to how he was receiving this.

"Even these were too fragile to bear His radiance," she continued. "They shattered, and countless sparks of divine illumination scattered throughout the world, hidden beneath the shards. With his Light dispersed and hidden, human beings became free to disobey God's will. But Hashem makes no mistakes. The same catastrophe that obscured his Light also gave people the free will to perform acts of righteousness. It is these acts that directly uncover the Light and gather it back together, spark by spark."

Judith smiled wryly.

"So you see, I am as responsible as any Jew to act in a way that unearths the sparks – that brings us a step closer to reuniting with Hashem. Truly, any one thing that I or any of us does could possibly save the entire world."

"Is that why you want to become a doctor? To save the world?"

"Now that *is* a confusing question." She told him about her sister and about the Rebbe's response.

"He refused to let you continue your education?" He sounded incredulous.

"To tell you the truth, I've already gone further than most of my schoolmates. I graduated secondary school – Bais Rivka, all girls, of course – and was granted permission to attend two years of seminary. I have about enough college credits for an associate degree. But in order to take pre-med classes, I applied to Hunter. And the rest you know." Except for her decision to abandon her plans.

"But what about love? What about dating and meeting people until you find the person you want to spend your life with?"

At that she smiled.

"Oh," she said, "On this we completely agree. According to the *Tanya*, each and every one of us has our soulmate, our *bashert*, the intended one, waiting somewhere out there to complete us. It is a great joy when you find him, or her."

"How do you know when you've met him if you don't get to know any men?"

Now she laughed out loud.

"I think Hashem takes care of that part without us needing to sample for ourselves. Hashem and the *shadchans* – the matchmakers!" She laughed and pulled a face at the idea.

"So only someone from your own community could be your *bashert*? God would never match you up with, say, someone like me from the outside world?"

Judith was caught off guard. Her skin flushed with excitement that yes, it might be possible, he might be the one, while her mind insisted that, no, Michael could never be her *bashert*. In a duel between the desires of the heart and the holy knowledge attained through years of contemplation and study, she knew that Hashem's laws would surely prove the stronger. Still, she could envision the once unimaginable – that Michael could be a friend – a friend close as her own heart, who was neither a woman nor a brother. That alone was revolutionary. She knew her cheeks were glowing. She was grateful for the cover of darkness.

But when she looked down at her hands, she was suddenly struck by how much lighter the world around them had become. Somehow, dawn had slipped in unnoticed.

"Michael?"

"Um-hmm?"

"It's morning." She indicated the sky, unnecessarily.

"So I see."

She folded her hands into her lap. "I need to say *shacharit* – morning prayers."

"Do you want me to leave?"

"Not at all. You can say them with me, if you like."

"I wouldn't have a clue."

"Well, it's not hard. This was one of the first prayers I learned as a child. It thanks Hashem for bringing me through the long dark night and allowing my eyes to once again see the light of day. But more than that, it thanks Him for his promise to resurrect us to eternal Light."

Judith stood and faced east toward the lightening sky and Michael did the same. Her eyelids were heavy with lack of sleep. Glancing at Michael's face, only a foot or so away from her own, she took note of the skepticism in his eyes, but believed she could also see there an openness that he had yet to realize. His hands grasped the dirty iron railing and his face was soot streaked where he had rubbed sweat from his forehead and nose. Her face must be similarly marked. But she felt beautiful in the dawn light – made fresh and whole once more by the new day.

It could only be by Hashem's will that she was here, that she had embarked on this terrifying journey, this extraordinary new life. This meant that it was His will also that brought Michael to her side on this strange morning. She was no longer alone, imprisoned in isolation. This would have to be enough to go forth on for now. As for later, she would have to see. Once she had achieved her goal – *im yirtse Hashem* – perhaps there would be room for her to reunite with her community, to become one with her *bashert*, to know the joys of family again. All that would be revealed in the fullness of time. In this moment, however, her duty was only to give herself over to prayer – and to thanks.

Sweatsoaked and headspinning, Johanna awoke to a swirling fog, and worked to gather her flapping thoughts as they floated down into reach. She divided those she could capture into piles and placed large stones over each to keep them pinned down. "This is a dream," she said, smoothing one onto the top of a short stack of similar thoughts. "Dream, dream, dream," she repeated, placing several more onto the pile. "Reality!" she screamed, grasping at one that floated up just beyond her fingertips. She jumped at it and it flew further above her head, as if blown upward by the force of her desire, while a different one fluttered down closer to her grasp. "Delusion," she spat, as she grabbed it and stuffed it under a rock with lots of others, all similarly crumpled and torn. From the corner of her eye, she saw reality settle into a corner and she flung herself at it with all her ferocious might. Trapped beneath her, reality gasped and gave itself up, and Johanna rested, still and heavy against the tissue-thin prize.

The air continued to shimmer with the trembling thoughts. But the heat. The heat and her thirst had become unbearable. Johanna raised her head listlessly and tried to shout for a nurse. All that came out was a dry croak ending in a fit of painful coughing that

shook her eyelids open. Darkness was everything. A thick imperme-
able fleece that bonded with the heat and left her blind, bathed in her
own sweat. Not the hospital, then, where darkness was strictly forbidden, driven off by ranks of fluorescent sentinels. The hospital was
never dark. Home? Hell? She sniffed the air for the stink of sulfur
and fell back into another paroxysm of coughing.

Johanna stared into darkness that did not easily offer up
its secrets.

She pushed herself into a sitting position. Her palms came
away gritty with cinders. Now she knew where she was. Pressing
herself further back into the alcove, she listened for the familiar metallic ticking that preceded the rush of wind and the howling trains.
Minute after minute, all she heard was the drip, drip, drip of water
taunting her. She knew better than to fall for its seduction. Only
a crazy person would walk further down the tracks where the walls
closed in and the approaching eyes of the next train would be the
last things she'd see. But where was the train? Johanna reached out
for the walls of stone. Grabbing an outcropping, she hauled herself
thickly to her feet, but was immediately tossed back to the ground. It
was as if the ground had rolled out from under her. Each time she
turned her head, roiling waves of dizziness batted at her. Infection.
Infraction. Infarction. Her inner ear, filling with the saltedy salt salt
sea. She lay still, naming her parts and gathering them into a memory
of herself, whole. Monstrous. Did she really have that many eyes?
Arms? She giggled and grunted and lopped off the extras, which
dropped from sight. She had to get out of here. She had to get to the
surface, to quench her thirst, to bring her temperature down before it
stopped her heart for good.

Unable to stand upright, Johanna began to crawl through the
cinders, reaching out over and over to skin her knuckles against the
edges of the tracks that she prayed would finally lead her home. If
a train came through now, she would be flattened, probably no more
than a gentle jolt to the conductor and passengers. Jolt. Johanna
remembered the third rail. The power source that could fry a body in

seconds. An omelet. An ending. The hairs rose on her neck. She was on the opposite side of the tracks from it, though.

Johanna tried to raise her head to look for the lights of the station. She was certain they were just around the bend. She hadn't ventured far onto the tracks. She remembered that much. But darkness stretched in all directions and waves of nausea assailed her each time she turned her head. She crawled forward, mere inches at a time, her hands and knees beginning to ooze blood, caking the cinders into mittens.

They will know me by these signs, she thought: the blood, the steel, the filth. Still, the lights remained out of sight.

As she pushed forward, she heard something crunching toward her, chewing up the intervening blackness. Johanna found herself completely unable to move for terror. A beam of light, like a sword, pierced the darkness, bouncing crazily in all directions and a rush of human voices echoed off the stone walls.

"There's someone down here!" a voice exclaimed. Here! Here! Shouted the rocks around Johanna, as if calling out to them for her.

Heavy footsteps splashed and thudded in her direction. If she could have run, she would have, but Johanna felt as bound and paralyzed as if she were wrapped in canvas and Velcro. She could neither hasten their coming, nor prevent it. She could only wait in her own pooling sweat. In a moment, thick boots appeared at her head and rubber gloved hands reached down and pulled her up. The light hit her like a club. She twisted away. Again, the world spun and she fell forward heavily, into a pair of arms, thick and hairy. She felt her legs leave the ground, and she had no strength to fight as she was hoisted onto a broad back and carried like a sack.

Bounced along as the men negotiated the track bed and a series of stair cases, Johanna felt herself drift in and out of awareness. She caught only random words from the two men around her. *Stinks. Coors. Sack of potatoes. Disinfect. Retire.* When they got to the street, they propped her sitting upright against the side of a building. Heat from the concrete penetrated her damp clothes. One of the men pulled a walkie-talkie from his belt and began to mutter into it. He turned his back on her and she couldn't understand what he was saying. The other man bent over her. He had a bandanna wrapped around his head and another around his face like the Lone Ranger. Sweat dripped from his chin onto the pavement next to her hand. Johanna wanted to scream, but she had no voice. She waited for the attack she knew was coming.

"Are you hurt?" the man said. "Do you need a doctor?"

"I am a doctor," Johanna tried to explain, but the man wrinkled his brow and shook his head at her, without understanding.

"Do you have someone to contact? Do you have someplace to go?" he tried again.

"Where am I now?" Johanna managed to enunciate, slowly and clearly, for the man was obviously an idiot.

The man looked around. His partner was still talking on the radio. He scratched his head through the damp cloth, with what Johanna took to be complete lack of comprehension.

"You're at the corner of Fulton and Park Place," he told her, gesturing into the darkness. "This here's the Fulton Street subway stop."

"Yes," she nodded. "Exactly. Here. And there." She had answered his questions, but still he looked unsatisfied. Mental defective, she noted. She laughed, but the sound was nothing more than the scrape of spoon against cup.

The man looked confused. His partner holstered the radio and turned to him.

"I called an ambulance. They said it'll take a while. If she's conscious and not bleeding, we can't stay here to wait for it. Sergeant says to move on and check the next stop on the line." His friend looked dubiously at Johanna.

"There are people coming to help you," he said. "Will you be okay until they get here?"

Johanna said nothing, just shut her burning eyes. In the distance, she heard the sound of smashing glass. So, it has begun, she thought, wearily. Just as I warned them. Glass swirled like stars

through smoldering space. Fuckers didn't listen. She opened her eyes
and smiled a dismissive benediction at the men. From this moment,
they were on their own.

The one with the radio reached into his pocket and handed
her a small flashlight and an oozing Snickers bar. "You stay here and
wait for help," he told her. "When you see an ambulance, wave the
flashlight in a circle. Tell them you need help. Do you understand?"
Then, without waiting for her answer, they both turned and walked
away into the dark.

Johanna pushed the flashlight into the neck of her shirt. She
sucked the molten chocolate from the paper, swallowing over and
over to force it down her swollen throat. In a little while, she realized that she could, indeed, move. She stood shakily, clinging to the
hot bricks until the ground stopped its rolling, and then made for the
subway entrance that was barely a whisper in the dark. Grasping the
banister with both hands, she let herself down the steps, slowly, painfully. She took the light from out of her shirt and used it to find her
way under the turnstiles. There it was, her bench, her bed, her bower.
She dropped down onto it and turned heavily to one side to get comfortable. Her hips sank into the familiar form. She was as *home* as
she was ever going to be, cocooned in the soft darkness. The sound
of the glass was farther away here, almost musical, the shards dancing
across a blind-dark sea.

A muffled crash and a growled *Damn!* issued from the bathroom but, from behind the closed bedroom door, Danielle refused to
acknowledge the disturbance. Let Geoffrey figure it out for himself,
she thought. Him and his skepticism and his fear of the dark. She
had been alone in the bedroom for at least a couple of hours now,
pretending to be asleep while writhingly conscious. Surely it must
be getting close to dawn. The darkest hour, if some old proverb and

a song by The Mamas and the Papas were to be believed. But what did any of them know about dark? The bathroom door opened and she heard the tentative sounds of Geoffrey trying to navigate his way back to the living room sofa without crashing into anything else. She felt trapped in her own room.

I should have thrown him out, she thought. In fact she had tried, but he protested, calling it "absurd and mean spirited" to think that he could find his way home in the midst of the chaos. Through the half-opened windows they could hear the constant shriek of sirens. The smell of smoke drifted in alarmingly. It felt as if the entire world were coming to a dark and brutal end.

"Be reasonable," he argued. "I'm only trying to be honest with you, and maybe even helpful."

"You want to to be helpful? Then just stay the hell out of my way!" she finally said, stomping off to her room, and snatching up the candles as she went. Let him sit in the dark.

Sit in the dark. What horrible thing had she ever done to deserve a lifetime of sitting in the dark? Aside from painting, all she had ever wanted was to cook.

Now, when she imagined returning to her parents' home, she foresaw her life as an unbroken series of lonely, monochromatic meals. Her mother no longer cooked; a housekeeper took care of that, turning out bland dinners of pork chops and steamed broccoli. This kind of thinking would get her nowhere. She could cook in the dark, couldn't she? She could cook for herself. She could – she *knew* she could – cook in a professional kitchen – one that was open-minded enough to give her a shot. Which most likely is *not* the one I'm working at, she realized. Danielle's face flushed again with anger. Geoffrey knew her secret. He would probably tell Chef first thing – he couldn't risk losing his own position by having it come out in some other way.

She sank into herself like a mishandled soufflé. Geoffrey was right, and she knew it. Who was going to agree to take on the liability of a blind chef? Who would put their restaurant's precious bottom line – already under siege by competition, rising costs, taxes and insurance – at risk by taking on a *handicapped* person in such a role? Her carefully shaped plans were going to amount to nothing. With crystal clarity, she knew that now. Danielle lay as still as a corpse. How could she have been so, so fucking...*blind*? She was a fool for letting herself be taken in by this man. She was a bigger fool for putting faith in what had been a delusional pipedream. She could see it all now (again, that ironic verb).

"Do you ever have thoughts of suicide?" Karen had asked her, not long ago.

"Never," she had lied. Or no, not really lied, because by then she had begun practicing. The future loomed. Death receded. Now the spectre had returned, stronger than ever. It was only a matter of method. How much time did she have to make a decision before this and so many other decisions would be taken from her?

The whole idea of *practicing* was intended as a distraction from thoughts of suicide. There was no longer any point in that. The future was untenable. She didn't want to be anyone's ward, anyone's burden. But there was, as always, the question of *how*? Knives? Painful and messy. Jump from her fifth floor apartment and she ran the risk of agonizing survival. Poison was out of the question. She did not want her final moments to, well, taste bad. An overdose required the right drugs in the right quantities. But what could be simpler than merely stepping off the curb into traffic? An unfortunate accident. A speeding ambulance or fire engine on a dark night – *tonight?* – would be completely effective, almost foolproof.

Danielle could no longer stand to be contained in her bed, or her room. She needed movement, direction. She extricated herself from the sheets and swung her legs over the side of the bed and into the sneakers she had left there, and felt around for her clothes. The smell of leftover food wafting in from the kitchen disgusted her.

All was quiet in the living room. When she opened the bedroom door she heard Geoffrey's breath, soft and regular. So he had managed to fall asleep, she thought, bitterly. Quietly, she slipped into the kitchen and began to clean up. The smell of fish weighed heavy in the air. Finding the sink still full of dishes, she thought with some resentment that Geoffrey might at least have done these. Actually, it was better that he hadn't. Without her finely, if uselessly, honed abilities, he probably would have broken half the dishes. She turned to the garbage in which, sadly, half of her supper sat. She heard a fly buzz and then go silent as it landed on it. Again, her stomach churned. She gathered the top of the garbage bag, knotted it and carried it to the door. On her way out she squelched an evil impulse to slam the door just to startle Geoffrey awake. But she didn't want him awake.

Danielle walked down the hall toward the garbage chute. With her hands full, she guided herself down the length of the corridor by sliding her right elbow along the wall. The sultry darkness was as thick and brown as molasses – one of the few foods that tasted the same color it looked, she noted. Under the weight of the garbage bag, Danielle felt as though she were swimming rather than walking through her native element of air. Each step was an effort of will. My Last Will. And Testament. The words appeared as headlines in the air and floated up like party balloons in the swirling heat. Her thoughts jumbled. Came in shorter and shorter bursts. Then, from somewhere ahead of her, a scraping noise yanked her attention back like a tether.

Was she alone in the hall? Danielle heard one painfully thudding heartbeat – her own – but were there two distinct sharp breaths?

"Is anyone there?" she whispered hoarsely.

No reply. Had she imagined it then? It's easy to be deceived in the dark, she told herself, ruefully. She tried to banish thoughts of lurking serial killers from her mind.

Still putting her full attention into listening, Danielle continued to move down the corridor more quickly now, clutching the plastic garbage bag close to her chest like a shield. Suddenly her foot caught against something and pitched forward. The bag flew from her hands. In slow motion, as if she were tumbling through viscous water or a dark cloud, Danielle felt balance desert her and gravity take its place. The fall through space was as protracted as a dream. Where was the floor, why wasn't she on it already? When she finally stopped moving there was a moment of stunned stillness, and then the answer came to her with a sickening lurch.

While part of her body lay on the filthy hallway floor, both her arms and her much of her torso – almost from her waist up – continued to dangle free in space. The elevator: Danielle realized she had fallen through the open elevator doors; she must now be suspended, somehow, over the shaft. With the slightest shift in balance, she might fall five flights, no six, to the very bedrock of the cellar. As if watching a movie, she could see her own crumpled, pulpy body as it appeared through a long lens. The sight was dizzying. An acrid sweat spread over her skin and for several seconds she couldn't catch a breath. This could be it, she thought. It would only take the slightest shift in momentum. It would be over in seconds. Then Danielle gasped and felt a sharp pain in her ribs.

Don't move, her brain screamed at her.

She froze as still as alabaster, obedient to the command. But a piercing howl she hadn't even known was coming ripped from her throat. Once the shriek began, it was unstoppable. It uncoiled from her gaping mouth, unfurled like a banner and echoed down and back through the cavernous pit below her. It was, she realized, something she'd wanted to do for a long, long time. It wrapped would around her like a sheet, swaddling, binding, wrapping her like a corpse even as she waited, terrified, to pitch headlong toward death.

Heavy arms pulled Danielle backward into the hallway. Her skin burned where it was rubbed along the carpet. The pain was as welcome as a kiss. Arms – Geoffrey's arms – half-dragged, half-carried her back down the hall and through a doorway. She heard the locks open in her neighbor's door and the beam of a flashlight lit a feeble path for them. Danielle tried to stand, but her legs wouldn't hold her.

She tumbled to the floor. Her floor. The apartment door slammed shut. Geoffrey gathered her up clumsily and settled her on the couch.

"Are you all right? Do you think anything is broken?" He began to press methodically up and down her arm and legs. Miraculous, she thought, unable to speak a word. Miraculous arms. Incredible legs. She nodded, mutely. Apparently satisfied that she was whole, Geoffrey stood. "I'll get you something to drink." He began fumbling his way to the kitchen.

I was almost killed, she thought. And I screamed. For help.

I screamed. She heard the water begin to pour from the tap and a glass rap sharply against the faucet.

Because she didn't want to die.

Danielle's limbs were as weak as overcooked bucatini as she made her way to her bed. In a moment – how had he managed to move so quickly? – Geoffrey was standing there beside her with a cool glass of water.

Because she didn't want to die.

He smoothed strands of hair from her sweaty face. "I'll leave if you want me to," he said, sitting on the very edge of the bed and placing a glass on the nightstand. "But don't want me to, okay?" For a long time they sat like that, waiting for their adrenaline-charged muscles to stop trembling.

Finally, as if in answer to his question, Danielle moved to make room for Geoffrey on the mattress. She reached up and loosed the blackout shades. Above, in a narrow sliver between the rooftops, the sky-blue-pink of dawn and a weak but fresh breeze stole in through the hands-width of open window. They lay back on the pillows without talking, enjoying the dawn light. From somewhere outside and above them, the fire escape, Danielle assumed, came soft voices; a man and woman, and a musical cadence of words she didn't understand, but could only intuit as prayer.

"Modah ani l'faneykha, melech chai vekaiyam, shehechezarta bi nishmati bechemlah, rabbah emunatekha."

❧

Phnff....phnff....babybabybabybaby mine.

A greasy pre-dawn light filtered into the room as Althea stared through swollen eyes at the small body in the bed, so slim and still that it barely disturbed the coverings. A generator that had been grinding away somewhere nearby cycled off and in its absence, the rhythmic sigh of the ventilator was as shattering as a siren.

There was no telling how long she'd been in this room. Althea's arms and legs were numb. Her fingers, which were wrapped around the tiny hand sticking out of the sheet, were frozen in place. Althea had long since stopped crying. Her voice dead in her parched throat.

She had been brought to this place – Bellevue Hospital, the policemen informed her as they hurtled through the lampless streets, siren blaring – after the cop who she had found standing outside the door of her mother's apartment picked up a call on his radio. Through the static he made out the description of the girl who had been dragged, not breathing, from the bottom of the Asser Levy pool.

Althea hadn't understood a word that issued through the radio's tinny speaker. She and her mother were alternately shouting at each other and holding each other in tears as they explained about the missing girl.

Her first impulse, when she recovered from the shock of being told that her daughter was gone, had been to hang out the window, screaming Celia's name into the dark. It was like shrieking into a pile of hot felt.

"Why did you let her go?" she kept demanding, as her mother wept and begged her forgiveness.

"She said you were down there in the street, calling us to let you in. *Orchistece.* She swore." After that, her mother seemed to have lost all ability to communicate in English, and resorted to helpless wails of Greek.

Althea grabbed the keys to the house and raced down the stairs and back out into the night. She half ran, half walked for random blocks, calling her daughter's name as angry hordes of people spewed from battered storefronts and hawked stolen wares on corners. Sirens blared. Even if Celia had been nearby, she could hardly have heard her mother over the uproar. Nearly hysterical and stumbling with exhaustion, Althea returned alone to her mother's building. When she arrived for the second time at the apartment door, breathless and hoarse, it was blocked by the boxy body of a policeman. At first, Althea felt a swooning wash of relief – he must have brought the wayward girl home. But when she pushed past him into the small dining room, she realized he had arrived alone.

"Are you the missing girl's mother?" he asked. It seemed to Althea that he asked it accusingly. The beam from his flashlight blinded her as it played over her face. What had her mother been telling him?

"Yes. Yes. I walked all the way uptown from 16th Street to get to my daughter. My mother was supposed to be caring for her today while I was at work."

"Your mother tells me that the girl says she heard you calling to her from the street. Is this possible?"

Althea suddenly wondered how he had gotten here. How had her mother managed to get a cop to come up all those stairs on a night like this? As if in answer to that unspoken question, her mother let loose a long explanation in Greek. All that Althea caught was word: *pyrovolismos* – shooting – and her knees gave way beneath her. She leaned heavily on the wooden dining table for support. Then she realized that her mother was telling her that she had called and reported a *shooting* to get their attention. She turned to the older woman in amazement.

That was when the radio began its crackling message. The officer turned away from both of them to better hear what was being broadcast. When he turned back he had a strange look on his face.

"Can you describe your daughter? What was she wearing?"

Althea thought about their trip uptown this morning. She could picture Celia clearly – every detail of her clothing, her hair, her shoes. At the end of her description the officer looked down at his feet.

"What did they say?" Althea demanded.

"I'd like you to come with me," he finally said.

"Are you taking us to jail?" Althea's mother asked in panicky

Greek. Althea glared at her. Her mother belonged in jail, she thought, merciless in her fear, and then she was immediately repentant.

"A girl with your daughter's description was brought into the hospital. She was rescued from a public pool. My partner is downstairs in the car." He stood aside to let her out the door.

Rescued, Althea heard. Rescued means alive.

"Mama, the policeman is going to take me to Celia. I want you to stay here. I promise to call you." She squeezed her mother's hands between both her own. For a moment it looked as though her mother would insist, but then the fight drained from her eyes and she nodded mutely and let Althea follow the man back out the door.

The trip downtown, during which the officer described the events that brought the child into the hospital, was like a ride through the many levels of hell.

At the emergency room parking area, the policemen led Althea through a maze of gurneys and doctors practicing medicine by headlight, candlelight and almost no light at all. Inside, a nurse with a flashlight navigated the dark hallways and flights of stairs alongside them. She warned Althea to prepare herself – that the child had been put on a ventilator. There was no knowing exactly how long she hadn't been breathing. No way to determine how much damage oxygen deprivation had done to her brain. The prognosis was still unclear. As they entered the room, she explained – with obvious discomfort – that the equipment they were using was rudimentary and came from the ambulance, because it could be run with minimal power. She also warned Althea about the catheter and the gastric tube that had been inserted through her daughter's nose.

Even so, Althea was unprepared for the sight of her daughter, pale and still as death. A rubber bag hooked up to a tank of oxygen sucked in and out like a child's toy. The tube that snaked from Celia's nose gurgled as warm water replaced the icy water that had been in the child's stomach. Everything was run off a car battery that sat next to the bed. Althea's first impulse was to bundle the girl into her arms and rush her away from this awful place. But as she pushed forward, the sheer amount of equipment sticking out from the girl's tiny body sent her spinning crazily back until she half-fell into the nurse's arms. The woman settled her into a chair by the side of the bed and helped to slide Celia's hand – the one not tethered to an IV drip – into Althea's own. She murmured a few words of encouragement, and then she left them. A battery-powered lamp in the corner gave off a greenish light, and Althea's eyes adjusted to the gloom. Behind her, she heard the squeak of the cop's shoes as he turned and left the room, muttering into his radio.

Althea had a sudden flash of her daughter spinning across the subway platform only that morning, magically alive to the world around her, oblivious to danger. It was Althea's job to protect the child. The weight of her failure to do that one thing pushed her deeper into the sagging chair.

Lypamai, she whispered. I'm so, so sorry, my little *kukla*. Her throat constricted painfully, making any further speech impossible.

Althea reached out her free hand to stroke Celia's forehead. The girl's smooth skin was cool and damp. Instead of rushing to Celia's side today, Althea had chosen – as on too many days before – to rush into Oscar's bed. Shame spread across her cheeks like a slap. Oscar. His silken sheets, his silken lying tongue. She could still see his face, contorted with rage, as he lunged toward her. She thought she had escaped his anger, but her own indiscretion, like a malicious spider, had already spun an ironbound web around her life. Oscar had betrayed her and she had betrayed Celia.

Althea rose from the suffocating depths of the chair, replaced her daughter's limp hand on the scratchy sheet, and crossed to the other side of the bed. Glancing at the doorway to make sure she was unwatched, she crept with the utmost delicacy onto the mattress beside the sleeping child and wrapped her body around the tiny form, terrified lest she disturb the medical equipment that tethered the girl to life. When Althea had finished arranging Celia's limbs, the child lay tucked and protected inside the curve of her body.

"Oh gods of my fathers," she groaned softly. "Oh healing

Apollo, do not turn away from me now. Send your beloved grand-daughter Panakeia, to press her sacred lips to those of my baby lying here on this bed. Return her breath to her, mighty ones. Take mine instead. Take mine instead."

Althea's voice cracked and her breath came as ragged as if she had been pulled from the depths of that pool herself. She lay silent and spent, grateful for the warmth of Celia against her belly. She tried to will the venerable goddesses into the room – imagining their pale, draped forms passing cool hands over her daughter's cheeks, their sublime faces dipping to breathe life back into Celia. But the air around them remained dank and empty. Althea's eyelids were as heavy as two stones, but she forced herself to stay awake.

The light through the dirty window was almost pink, now. Celia's favorite color. The color of her sandals. All this time, the little body hadn't stirred at all except when the ventilator forced the tiny chest up and down. Worried that one of the nurses might return and banish her for violating the sanctity of the hospital bed, Althea rose as carefully as she had lain down, after placing one more kiss on the nape of Celia's neck. She stood at the bedside, once more cradling Celia's hand in her own.

A man came up behind her and coughed politely. Althea turned. He was wearing a green surgical gown, but his face was un-masked. A two-day growth of beard stippled his cheeks.

"Are you her mother?"

Althea nodded. "Yes, doctor," she managed to mumble.

"No. No. I'm not a doctor." He sounded confused. "Oh, the outfit." Now Althea was confused. "No, sorry, I'm the guy who found her in the pool. Guillermo." He stuck out his hand, but Althea did reach for it. "My name is Guillermo," he continued, speaking more slowly now, as though he thought maybe she didn't speak English all that well.

"My clothes were soaked. The hospital gave me these." He pointed to himself.

Althea didn't know what to say. There were no words, only

feelings that sped through her too quickly to be deciphered by the meager abilities of brain or tongue. She twisted the fabric of her skirt in her free hand in an agony of silence.

"I dove into the pool, to the bottom, and I felt her foot," the man continued. "At first I thought it was my girlfriend, goofing on me. I pulled her up. That's when I realized." He stopped suddenly. Althea winced as she felt his hand on her shoulder. "My girlfriend, Janine, works in a nursing home. She took CPR in school. We tried giving her mouth-to-mouth, but..."

Althea wanted him to leave. She didn't want to hear this. She felt as if her flesh had turned to glass. The mere act of moving her lips might cause her to shatter. A woman, the girlfriend, Althea assumed, had come into the room quietly and now stood by his side.

"Someone managed to flag down a cop car and we brought her here," she said in little more than a whisper. "Guillermo and I followed on foot. Is she going to be all right?"

Althea had no answer. Why, in heaven's name, had Celia left the safety of her grandmother's house in the middle of a night such as this? Althea was afraid that she already knew the answer.

Yet another woman, also dressed in hospital garb, walked into the room. She pulled a curtain around the three people surrounding the little girl on the bed.

"I'm going to have to ask all of you to step out for a moment," she said, looking directly in Althea's eyes. "I'm going to remove the breathing tube." Althea's eyes grew huge with protest. Her mouth opened and closed silently. The nurse saws her panic.

"Your little girl is strong, a fighter," she assured Althea. "We need to see if she is going to breathe on her own."

Instead of leaving the room, the couple moved a little closer to Althea, as if closing ranks on a battle field.

"It's okay," Althea whispered, turning slightly toward them without letting her daughter escape from the periphery of her view. "We have to let the nurse do her work." And then to the nurse she said, "I am her mother. I will stay here."

The other two people left the curtained area, the squelch of their sneakered feet on the linoleum receding down the hallway.

"I'm actually not the nurse," the woman explained to Althea once they had left. "I'm the resident – the doctor on call. I got here just as your daughter was brought in."

The doctor adjusted the equipment that forced life into Celia. Althea's head spun with confusion. The world had tilted off its axis; she scrambled and slid helplessly toward the edge.

"She was lucky to be rescued by someone who knew CPR," the woman continued. "And lucky, too, that the water in the pool was as cold as it was. That may have slowed her system down enough to allow her to survive. I'm sure the nurses explained everything to you, but do you have any questions for me?" The doctor bent to listen to the girl's chest through a stethoscope.

The nurses had explained nothing. Althea had a million questions that added up to only one. The one she couldn't ask out loud for fear of having to hear the answer.

"She hasn't moved in all the time I've been here," Althea finally managed.

"We had to sedate her pretty heavily to make sure she didn't regain consciousness and try to rip out the tubes," the doctor replied. "I'm sorry they didn't tell you that. Her heartbeat is strong though," she added with a smile.

Althea nodded, mutely.

As the doctor leaned over Celia, blocking her view of the girl, Althea stared through the window where a blade-thin sliver of sun was crowning the buildings to their east. A scrim of clouds had gathered into a soaring column aflame with its rosy phosphorescence. Blown by high and sultry winds, the clouds now split in two and took on the shape of wings, shimmering with the iridescence of a heavenly bird – or an angel. Althea stared, rapt. The wings spread wide over the seething urban landscape, offering protection, she thought, or maybe compassion to a city that contained so little of its own.

Athena, Queen of the gods, by whatever name thou lovest best, give ear to my plea, she found herself reciting silently. She had learned the words when she was only Celia's age, as Mr. Papoutsis stood and recited the writings of Cicero to a class of children nodding sleepily in the noonday heat. But Althea had no worthy sacrifice to offer the gods in exchange for the life of her daughter. She sank into despair. I have neither white sheep nor ram to send smoking skyward, she thought, but please, restore my daughter, my heart, to me. And, she thought, restore the heart of this city. The rosy form of the angel continued to hover above the stark roofscape and Althea took comfort from the sight.

The doctor stepped back from Celia's bedside and a sudden sucking noise drew Althea's eyes sharply back to her daughter's face. Celia's lips were cracked, her cheeks pale. Her eyelids were blue and twitched slightly. The doctor stood, holding the flexible tubing with one hand and stroking the girl's damp forehead with the other. She looked up and met Althea's eyes for only a second. Althea could not read what was written in that look. The wing-like clouds blazed in the window beyond the doctor's head then began to dissolve in the heat of another day.

Breathe, Althea prayed. Take one breath. Then another. She prayed for the girl and she prayed for the city.

A small cry, not more than the birth call of a tiny animal, came from the bed. Althea's eyes leaped back to the face of her child, now contorted in distress. Celia's eyelids shuddered and then opened. The girl darted uncomprehending looks at the doctor, her mother, the walls and window of this strange room. Her eyes fell closed once again. The doctor touched Althea's arm.

"Call her," she said softly. "Call her name."

ACKNOWLEDGMENTS

For years I have been waiting to thank you people, and at last I can!

First of all, limitless gratitude to my writing posse: Natalie Danford, Moira Trachtenberg-Thielking, Allison Lynn and Ruth Gallogly, whose insight, love and unstinting scrutiny helped make this the best work it could be. Also, to Maria Feldman and Natasha Hirschhorn, for their generous linguistic and cultural guidance. Thanks too, to the abundantly gifted Jamie Greenfield and Tony Robinson, for artwork that speaks volumes, and to Alex Martin, a multi-talented young man, for his cover and book designs.

I am grateful to the Virginia Center for the Creative Arts (VCCA), which provided space, time and wonderful company in which to work, and to Anthony Piggott, who has always known what I was all about, and kept me gainfully employed in spite of it. Heartfelt thanks also go to Jezra Kaye and 3RingPress for support and companionship on this publishing adventure. And belly rubs to Lily and Ruby for the same, if furrier.

Above all, my deepest love (and then some) to Mark Dallara – builder of studios and Inukshuks, buyer of candlesticks, dearest of all curmudgeons – and to Jake Dallara, the perfect Boy for me. And, while I'm at it, thanks to the City of New York and everyone who ever offered me a seat on the subway.

A graduate of the MFA writing program at New York University and the graduate program of journalism at Syracuse University's Newhouse School of Public Communications, Ellen Greenfield is a poet and novelist living in Brooklyn and Jefferson, NY. Her debut novel, *Come From Nowhere*, was a finalist in the Pirate's Alley Faulkner Society's competition for Novel-in-Progress.

The author is available for reading and book club appearances, in person and online. A Discussion Guide is available online. Your comments are welcome.

ComeFromNowhere.com

Made in the USA
Lexington, KY
21 April 2012